10/6/17

book is also about hope and survival'
CHRISTOPHER ONDAATJE, *Spectator*

'[A] lovely, vividly described novel . . . [set] against a background of lush scenery and looming civil war'   *The Times*

'*Mosquito* lyrically captures a country drenched in both incomparable beauty and the stink of hatred'   *Guardian*

'*Mosquito* is a beautifully moving, suspense-filled story about unlikely lovers that's gripping from start to finish. Set in Sri Lanka, it tells of a bittersweet romance between a young artist and a writer, a relationship that slowly becomes entangled in the mess of the local civil war. Tearne's ethereal descriptions of the Sri Lankan coastline and the powerful accounts of a country ripped apart by violence make for an emotional and exceptional novel'   *Easy Living* magazine

'Beautiful and evocative . . . The true horror and unreason of terrorism as depicted here speak to our own worst fears and remind us that terrorism has been with us in many guises and many places for a much longer time that we tend to remember . . . Gripping and original'
Sydney Morning Herald (Australia)

'*Mosquito* shimmers with evocative prose but it also resonates with the darkness of men's cruelty. This is not a thriller, but the tension is palpable. Don't be surprised if the film rights are snapped up quickly'   *Courier Mail* (Australia)

'*Mosquito* is full of sensuous imagery'   *Sunday Tasmanian*

'A tense, delicate and very personal rendering of a tragic political situation'   *Big Issue*, London

'An enchanting story. The beautiful paradise of the tiny teardrop shaped country is described with the aid of artistic visuals and set to a bittersweet love story that is a thought-provoking must read'   *Asian Woman*

For Barrie, who understood,
and for Oliver and Alistair and Mollie

. . . they are places that don't belong to geography but to time.

SAUL STEINBERG, *Reflections and Shadows*

1

THE CATAMARAN, ITS BLUE-PATCHED SAILS no longer flapping, its nets full of glistening catch, came in after the night's fishing. The breeze had died down, the air had cooled, and the fishermen's sarongs slapped wet against their legs as they swung the boat above the water, to and fro, and up and along the empty beach, scoring a dark, deep ridge in the sand. Often, before the monsoon broke, the sea was like a mirror. The sky appeared joined to it with barely a seam, there was a faint vibration of thunder and along the shoreline the air hung in hazy folds, suspended between land, and sea, and sky. In a few hours the heat would spread insidiously, hovering with the mosquitoes and the spiders that waited motionless and lethargic, trapped by their own clammy inertia. But still there was no storm. Every year it was like this, before the monsoon, for three or four days, sometimes even longer. Every year, around the third week in June, a yellowing stickiness, a blistering oppression clung everywhere, so that even the bougainvillea lost its radiance.

Theo Samarajeeva walked back from the beach with fresh fish for lunch. It was still early. The manservant, Sugi, had brought breakfast out on to the veranda. A black-and-gold lacquered tray with a white cloth was placed on the cane table. There was a silver teapot, a jug of boiled milk, one cup and a saucer. There was some freshly cut pineapple and some curd and roti.

'You had better get the lime juice ready, Sugi,' said Theo Samarajeeva wryly, hearing the gate click shut. The manservant grinned and went inside.

'You see, by a process of elimination I knew you would be coming here,' Theo said, turning towards the gate by way of greeting.

'How?' asked Nulani Mendis, appearing, sitting down opposite him, and helping herself to the glass the manservant held out to her. Theo Samarajeeva watched as she drank. He watched her gasp as the cool, sharp liquid caught in her throat. He noticed that her fingernails had small slivers of paint under them. She wore a green skirt wrapped tightly around her waist, and a soft faded white blouse of some thin opaque fabric. The skirt was old, and almost exactly the colour of the lime juice.

'How did you know I would come today?' she demanded again when she had finished drinking.

'Well,' said Theo, 'I saw you walking on the beach earlier, and as I hadn't seen you for at least twenty-four hours I told Sugi: Ah! Miss Nulani will be here later so don't forget her lime.'

Nulani smiled guiltily, remembering she was meant to go straight home.

'So, poor Mrs Mendis still waits for her daughter, no?' he guessed.

Inside, in the dark interior of the house, music was playing on the radiogram. It floated out through the open windows, tripping effortlessly down the steps from the veranda before dispersing into the trees.

'I've been drawing,' said Nulani, taking out a small notebook from her satchel. 'Look!'

She moved her chair closer to his, giving him the book. Images rose out of it, they fell hither and thither, marvellously, on to his knees. A man sat under a tamarind tree, another squatted in the narrow spit of shade afforded by a house. A woman stretched out on a makeshift bed staring at the rough edges of a palm roof through the bars of the window. Someone, a middle-aged man, lean legs stretched in front of him, was writing, head bent at a table. He had a cigarette in his left hand and behind him was the blur of tropical trees.

'This is me, no? When did you do this one?'

'Yesterday,' said Nulani, laughing. 'I was hiding over there, you didn't see me.'

'You little pest! Why didn't you make yourself known? Sugi had made a fine red mullet curry. You could have eaten with me.'

'You are not angry?'

'I feel the bushes have eyes,' he teased her. 'I shall have to watch everything from now on. No talking to myself any more! But seriously, these are good. Are you going to use them in a painting?'

'I don't know,' said Nulani, frowning. 'Do you really like them?' And boldly, 'I want to paint you. But . . .'

Theo considered her. For a moment he felt lost for words. Nulani Mendis had been visiting him for nearly three months now. It had begun when he had first moved to this part of the island. The convent school had invited him to give a talk on his latest book. He had not long been back from the UK, some perversity making him give up the modest success he enjoyed there. People thought him mad. The Liberation Tigers had been demanding a separate Tamil state for years with no success. Civil unrest grew daily. Then, after Singhala was made the national language, discrimination against the Tamils became commonplace. A potential guerrilla war was simmering. Why did he want to go back to that hell? they asked. Was he off his head? An established writer, with a comfortable life in London, his own flat, his work, what could he want with Colombo? Was it not enough writing books on the impending violence, did he want to *live* it too? But, he had no ties. Perhaps it was sentimentality in early middle age? Perhaps the terrible events from the past had finally got to him, they said.

Theo could not explain. He himself barely understood this sudden compulsion, this urgency to go home. It was a time when everyone who could was escaping. Perhaps simply because he no longer had anything to escape from, going back was not a problem. So he told his agent he would work better if he had some sun and, putting his flat on the market, he left. The agent said nothing, thinking privately that what Theo really needed was some distraction, danger even. Do him good, thought the agent; add richness to this next book. Other men might have given up writing altogether after what he had been through, but Theo had carried on. He probably needed a complete change of scene, needed to put the past finally behind him. So, with this in mind, the agent encouraged him to go back, for a time at least.

It was 1996. While he had been away Sri Lanka had changed. The change confused Theo. He found himself remembering the liberal atmosphere of his youth. Where was it? In England, whatever corruption there was, was kept discreetly out of sight. Or maybe he was less critical because the British were not his own people. It was a different matter in Colombo where every small injustice, every appalling act of violence seemed a personal affront. The civil unrest he had predicted in his books, the beginnings of rage seemed to have been nurtured in his absence, and spread, like a newly germinated paddy field. He left Colombo, moved to a backwater, and began writing his fourth novel. His second book was being made into a film and an article about him appeared in one of the papers. The local schools, having noticed it and having registered his arrival in the town, asked him to speak to the pupils. At first he had hesitated, worrying. But what was there worth worrying about in these troubled times? People had been garrotted for less outspoken views, so why did he care? His life would go on for as long as it would, or it simply would cease. Why worry? He was no longer a Buddhist, but Buddhism had worked on him like milk and honey nonetheless. He agreed to give two talks, one at the boys' school and the other at the convent. Nulani Mendis had been one of the students. She had held her hand up and asked him several questions.

'The girl hardly speaks,' the teacher had told him afterwards. 'Since her father was murdered she has become silent. The mother has given up trying to make her talk. All she does is draw, draw, draw.'

But on that day she had spoken to Theo and later, on one of his early-evening walks along the narrow strip of beach behind the house, he saw her again. He had smiled slightly, registering her good looks, and remembering the story of her father, he waved. But she seemed to vanish into the darkness. After that he kept seeing her and he guessed she lived nearby. Then Sugi caught her in the garden. She was drawing his stone lions. Sugi began complaining loudly.

'Sir, sir, these local children are pests. They've started coming into the garden again. We need to get rid of them or they will multiply!'

Surprised, Theo came out and, recognising her, asked her name. Then he invited her, in spite of Sugi's protest, to come over at any time and draw. This had been nearly three months ago. She never called him anything except Mr Samarajeeva. He supposed, wryly, that this was out of a sense of respect for his age. But she came back, again and again, and, if she did not appear for a few days, he became inclined to drift into bad temper.

'Can I go now?' she asked, breaking into his reverie. 'I want to draw the house from over there.'

She had been with him since breakfast.

'Won't you be late for school?' he asked. 'Does your mother know you are here?'

'No,' she said, disappearing around the side of the house. Her voice reached him from another part of the garden, vague and indistinct. 'No, she's out. And I've finished the jobs she gave me so I can go straight to school from here.'

Theo shook his head, amused in spite of himself. The man-servant gave him a look that said clearly, 'I told you, these local children are pests.' But she's different, thought Theo.

At first she came only once a week, barely speaking, staying further back in the garden. But as she grew bolder she seemed to be there all the time. Then, one day, out of the blue, she showed him her notebook for the first time. The sketches were all of him, delicate, and with a clear unwavering likeness. Startled, he took down his book of Picasso drawings and talked to her about the artist. After that she began to talk to him.

'I will be seventeen in three months,' she said.

On another afternoon she told him about her brother Jim. He was only eighteen months younger. She told him, they were not close.

'It is our karma,' she said solemnly. 'We have brought it into this life.'

Their father, she said, had known most of this long before the astrologer came to visit. He told their mother, soon after the birth of Jim, he had seen it in a dream; the children would never be close. He could see it written on their faces, he had said, the girl child, and his infant son. Their mother, hearing this pronouncement, had begun wailing. After all her labours was this the future? But their father told his wife sternly to stop her noise. Be thankful, he said, for the fact that both children were healthy. After puberty, he suspected, after they came of age, they would cross a great expanse of water, leave Sri Lanka. Go to mainland India even. It would be a good thing, he had said, for peace in this country was always uncertain. Thus had her father predicted, long before the astrologer came to plot their horoscopes, walking up the steps of the house. With his saffron robes and his sandals dusty with beach sand, and his black umbrella faded with the heat. Their father, not foreseeing his own death in the riots of the following June, felt the future of his children grow large in his own mind.

How long was it before she realised the strange masculine world inhabited by her brother was not for her, wondered Theo. Was it when she was still small? Did her understanding come, as all unshakeable beliefs do, not at any given moment but slowly, like seawater seeping into a hole dug on a beach? Lucky Jim could pace his domain freely, marking his undisputed territory, certain of his own image of the future. But what of Nulani?

Sometimes while her brother slept, before the father's unpredicted death, when they were younger, Nulani told Theo, she would bend over Jim and smell the sugar-sweet baby scent of greenness on his skin, run her finger across an old scar that straddled the rounded grubbiness of his brown leg. Later when she was older, she told Theo, she stole a box of Venus B pencils (Made in Great Britain) from the house of their English neighbour, to draw her sleeping brother. But the neighbour found out and demanded she be punished for stealing. She returned the pencils; two of them were used and broken.

'All right, Mrs Mendis,' the neighbour, the Englishman, told her mother angrily, 'I know it must be hard for you, with your husband dead. But "render unto Caesar" and all that!'

He had laughed, without rhythm. Nulani had wondered if

that was how the English laughed. She knew she would not be allowed into the Englishman's house again. She would not be able to play with his daughter Carol any more; she would never be able to touch her shining golden hair.

'Why did you take them?' her brother had demanded. 'Render unto Caesar,' he had said, sounding like the Englishman.

Nulani's uncle came. Because her father was no longer alive, it was his duty to beat her with an *ekel* stick.

'Render unto Caesar,' he had said. They were ashamed of her. The whole family avoided the neighbours now, eyes cast down whenever the jeep drove them about, into the city, to the beach, shopping.

'See what you've done to us.'

Nulani could see. She stopped drawing her brother when he slept. She just looked at him. Her little brother. She was his *loku akka*, his big sister. Her father had said they would not be close. But no one, she told Mr Samarajeeva, not even the astrologer, had said she would not love him.

And now she came here to draw. Arriving early, leaving late. Always talking. Transformed.

'Child,' Theo said suddenly now, drifting back from his thoughts and realising the time, 'you'll be late for school.'

When there was no answer he went to look for her at the back of the garden, but then he heard the gate click again.

'I'm late,' she called, grinning at him, hurrying off. 'But I'm coming back!'

And she disappeared up the hill with a wave of her hand.

They swarmed so thickly that they might easily have been mistaken for smoke. Rising swiftly from the water-filled holes dug by the gem miners in their search for sapphire, the mosquitoes seemed suspended in reflected light. For a moment the holes appeared as

mirrored surfaces, blue as the sky. Further out towards the coast
the rainwater filled the upturned coconut shells, as they lay scat-
tered across the groves. Here the beautiful female anopheles
mosquitoes, graceful wings glinting in the sun, landed lightly and
prepared to create a canoe of death for their cargo of eggs. The
Ministry of Health sprayed the coconut groves with DDT to prevent
outbreaks of malaria. The metallic smell drifted and mixed heavily
with the scent of frangipani and hibiscus. There had been no
epidemic for nearly five years.

Theo liked to spend the morning writing, but lately it had been
difficult to concentrate with the girl present. She sat against a
wall, almost in the bushes, drawing him. He had tried to make
her come inside but she was stubborn and stayed where she
was, far back along the veranda, crouching beside the lilies and
the ferns.

'How can you draw like this? You can't see me,' he had
protested. 'Why do you want to crouch so low?'

She had refused his invitation and in the end he had just
shrugged, leaving her alone, going back to his typewriter in the
cool of his study. It was hot. For some reason the fans had all
stopped working. Perhaps the generator had broken down again.
He would have to get Sugi to look at it. Every now and then
as he worked he would look up and catch a glimpse of her
faded lime-green skirt translucent against the extraordinary
light of the untamed garden. She folded and rearranged herself
until from where he sat she was a smudge of green and white
and black. He could not see her face; it was hidden by her dark
hair. He found her presence disturbing. How was he supposed
to work? Surely it must be lunchtime? He half hoped she would
stay to eat with him. Sometimes she did; at other times, although
she hesitated, an inner tempo seemed to call her, guilt perhaps,

a sudden memory of an uncompleted errand for her long-suffering mother. Every time Theo asked her to stay for lunch. He waited, unaware that his breath was bated, for her reply, knowing only his irrational disappointment if she went home.

He had decided then, the best thing to do was to commission her to paint him. It was clear that, once voiced, she would not give up the idea, so one evening he strolled over to Mrs Mendis with the suggestion. Mrs Mendis welcomed him with some *aluva* and coffee. He told her he wanted to commission Nulani to paint his portrait. He would like to pay her if Mrs Mendis did not mind. Mrs Mendis did not mind. Mr Samarajeeva was extremely kind. She just hoped Nulani would do a proper job.

'The girl is a dreamer,' said Mrs Mendis. 'She does not talk much and she is stubborn. If you can get her to do anything it will be a miracle. Most of the time, if there is any work to be done, she disappears. She won't help in the house or with any of my sewing. How am I to make a living, with no one to help me?'

Having started her complaints, Mrs Mendis found it curiously difficult to stop. Her thin, high voice rose like the smoke from a mosquito coil.

'I am a widow,' she said. 'Has Nulani told you? Has she told you my husband was set fire to during the rioting in the seventies? They threw a petrol bomb at him. Aiyo, we watched as he went screaming down the Old Tissa Road. Fear kept all the people hidden behind closed doors.' Mrs Mendis waved her hands about in distress. 'Everyone watched through the shutters of their houses,' she said. 'But no one came to help.'

Harsh sunlight had pressed itself on the edges of the house and then Mrs Mendis had run screaming into the street, chasing hopelessly after her husband, but it was too late. He lay blackened and burnt; clear liquid oozing out from his staring eyes, his body charred, the stench of flesh filling her open-mouthed screams.

'The neighbours came out of the houses then and pulled me away,' she said.

They had been fearful she might throw herself on to the flames. By the time the ambulance came he was beyond help.

'Luckily,' said Mrs Mendis, lowering her voice, 'my son Jim was somewhere else and did not see his father's life as it left this world.'

Lucky Jim. 'He had been so close to his father,' she said. 'The shock is still with him.'

Only the girl had been at home. Mrs Mendis wasn't sure how much she had seen. Always quiet, she became mute after that.

'She's difficult,' said Mrs Mendis, 'obstinate and odd.'

Theo Samarajeeva, who had not meant to stay for long, looked around for escape. There was no sign of Nulani, but something about the stillness of the air made him certain she was listening.

Walking home he turned several times, convinced he was being followed. But the road was empty. The air was choked with the heavy scent of frangipani. As he entered his house he noticed Sugi had lit some oil lamps. Theo could see him fixing a few cheap Chinese lanterns to the trees. He poured himself a whisky, and was still listening to the ice crackling in the glass when he saw her. Standing in his doorway holding out a branch of blossom, the rich scent filling the room, her smile wide, her eyes as bright as the new moon.

She came almost daily after that, before school, after her evening meal, at odd unexpected hours, nearly every weekend. A notebook was filling up with small studies of him. Sometimes she showed him what she had done. She seemed to be trying to record every slight movement of his face, he thought, amused. Such was the minute detail of the drawings. He was astonished by her perception. Thin pencils, stubs of charcoal, delicate brushstrokes,

whatever she used, all had the same fluid quality, the same effortless logic as they moved across the page. Each time she showed
him what she had done, he was astonished all over again.

'Nulani,' he asked once, after looking at these drawings for
a long time. 'Why me? Why draw me? Why not someone
younger, your brother's friends perhaps?'

He was genuinely puzzled. But she had only laughed.

'Wait till you see the painting!' she promised.

Now he watched her as she drew him from the corner of
the veranda.

'Why don't you sit somewhere better, child?' he asked again.
'You can't possibly see me clearly from where you are!'

'I don't want to see you, Mr Samarajeeva. I'm learning to
draw you from memory.'

'Will you please stop calling me Mr Samarajeeva.'

'OK, Mr Samarajeeva.'

He never knew if she was teasing him. He had a feeling she
could read his mind, that she liked to make him feel older than
he felt already, because it amused her, because in fact his age
made no difference whatsoever to her.

'I want to be able to draw you from memory, with my eyes
closed,' she said, 'so I will never forget you.'

Startled, he stood up. Sugi came in to announce lunch was
ready. Lunch was some fresh *thora-malu*, seer fish, from today's
catch.

'When will you start painting?' he asked while they ate. A
small beam of sunlight fell on her face. Her skin glowed with
a sheen of youthfulness. Through the curtain of thick hair her
eyes were as bright as a pair of black cherries. He thought of
all the years of living that lay between them, as heavy and as
sweet as a piece of sugared coconut jaggery, irreplaceable, un-
exchangeable, for ever between them.

'I have already started the painting, but I must draw more. Can I come here and paint?'

Theo laughed. 'At this rate you will always be here. What will your mother say? She won't be happy with that idea. She must want to see her daughter *sometimes*.'

'I want to be here all the time,' she said.

Theo looked at her. The beam of sunlight had moved and rested on the top of her head. Her hair was a sleek smoky black; it reminded him of the blue-black cat he and Anna had once had, in that other life. But all he said was: 'I have to go to Colombo tomorrow, is there anything you need? Any paints I can try to get you?'

He did not tell her that he had done no work since she had been drawing him; he did not tell her that her presence in his house, like a beautiful injured bird, was distraction enough without the drawing. London seemed far away.

'Has your mother seen the painting?'

'No. Amma, my mother, worries too much all the time. She doesn't have time to look.' She seemed to hesitate. 'Her worry is because she hopes.'

'She hopes?'

'She hopes things will not get worse than they already are. She hopes my brother does not leave, go to England. But she also hopes he *does* go because he will have a better life there. She hopes she will never see the things she saw once. So she does not look.'

It was the first time she had made reference to her father's murder.

'We are not like you,' she said.

'But you paint,' said Theo, '*you* still look.' And he thought how it was, that this beautiful place, with its idyllic landscape of sea and sky and glorious weather, had lost its way. Both through the lack of human intervention and, also, because of it. How many generations did it take before all the wondrous things of the island could be described again? Twenty years? Fifty years? Would a whole generation have to grow and be replaced before that could happen?

'You must never stop looking,' he said firmly. 'Never. Even when it becomes hard you must never stop. Also, you are a woman. It is important for women to do something about what they see. Only then will there be change. My wife was like that, she would have loved your drawings.'

'Your wife? Where is she?'

'She's dead,' said Theo.

He kept his voice steady; surprisingly he did not feel the usual sharp stab of bitterness. The beam of sunlight had moved and now shone against the edge of the huge mirror that stood above the Dutch sideboard, reflecting the fine golden sea dust that foxed its surface. Sugi came in with some mangoes. The afternoon heat, dazzling and yellow, was at its worst. It stood in abeyance outside the open door.

'What was her name?' asked Nulani, after Sugi had gone.

'She was called Anna.'

He noticed they had both slipped into their native Singhalese. Was pain easier to deal with in one's mother tongue? Nulani was thinking too.

'My brother has a long scar on his leg,' she said.

When he cut it he had cried. She could remember how his leg had bled, she told Theo. The blood had poured out like rain.

'There was no blood when Father died. After the ambulance took him away to the mortuary I went back to look at the road. I wanted to see the black dust. It was his dust, his body dust. That was all there was of him.'

She had rubbed the palm of her hand in it, she told Theo, until someone, some neighbour, had pulled her away. She still knew the exact spot where it was. There was a traffic island there now. It was her father's headstone. It was her scar.

'You have a scar, no?' she said. 'While I have been drawing you I have felt it. It is all over you, no?' She traced the shape of his spine in the air. 'It is under your skin, between the back-bones,' she said.

'It was a long time ago now.'

'Is that why you came back?'

'No, yes . . . partly.'

'It will get better here,' said Nulani softly.

She was too young to give him firm comfort but her certainty, though fragile, comforted him anyway. He was twenty-eight years older than her. Mango juice ran down her arm as she ate. Her lips were moist. Anna would have loved a child, he thought. Her generosity would have rushed in like waves, enveloping Nulani. Why had they never come here when Anna was still with him? Fleetingly, he thought of his old home in London, with its books and rugs and old French mirrors that filled the apartment with the light that was always in short supply. How different it was now, where they shuttered out the light instead.

The sun had moved away from the glass as they finished their meal and Theo lit a cigar. Nulani was fidgeting, wanting to get on. She remembered she had to go home. Her uncle, her mother's brother, was coming to see how his niece and nephew were. He was all they had for a father these days.

'Sugi will clear the space at the back for you to paint,' said Theo finally. 'You can come any time you like, but I shall be in Colombo tomorrow.'

He waved, watching her walk away, the dust from the garden washing brown against her open-toed sandals.

*   *   *

After he had cleared the room Sugi polished the floor with coconut scrapings. He rubbed as hard as he could, using first his left and then his right foot until the house smelt of it and the floor shone like marble. Then he went outside into the backyard and chopped open a *thambili*, an orange king coconut, and drank from it. After that he went back to work. There were several jobs he hoped to finish before Mr Samarajeeva returned from Colombo. He liked to surprise him with some small task or other well done. Last time it had been the fixing of the stone lions to the garden wall. The time before that he had painted the shutters.

Mr Samarajeeva was always weary when he returned from Colombo. He looked as he did when Sugi had first seen him, on the day he came to live here, walking from the station with his bags, a piece of paper in his hand, the address of the beach house on it. He had asked for directions and Sugi had brought him to the house, and stayed ever since. At the time he thought Mr Samarajeeva was a foreigner, in his fine tropical suit, with his leather suitcases and his hat. But then Theo had spoken to him in their mother tongue with such fluency that Sugi had grinned.

'I have been away a long time,' said Mr Samarajeeva. 'But my Singhala isn't bad, is it?'

He had wanted Sugi to work with him, help him set up his life here in the house. He would need some cooking, some domestic chores and some house maintenance. Could Sugi manage all that? Sugi could. As there was no one else to talk to, Mr Samarajeeva talked to Sugi. When his things arrived from London he unpacked them with Sugi and talked about his life there. He unpacked several framed photographs. They were of the same woman, blonde, curly-haired, smiling at the camera.

'My wife Anna,' he told Sugi.

Then he unpacked his books. There seemed to be hundreds

of books. There were other things from his old life. Later Sugi found out more about his wife. He tried to imagine the type of woman who had collected all these things. The mirrors, the plates, the cutlery. She must have been a fine woman, thought Sugi. When he found out Mr Samarajeeva was famous, the books he had written, and soon the film, he felt it his duty to warn him. These were troubled times. Envy and poverty went hand in hand with the ravaged land, he said. Even though he was a Singhalese, Mr Samarajeeva should be careful. His sympathy for the Tamil children was too well known. The house should be made more secure. Locks were needed for the shutters and the doors. The garden wall needed to be repaired in order to keep intruders out. Sugi made a list. Theo smiled lazily. He did not stop Sugi but he did not care much either.

'Sir,' said Sugi genuinely puzzled, 'you don't understand. There can be sudden outbreaks of trouble here. When you least expect it. You must be careful. People know who you are and they talk too much in these parts. It's not as you remember, no?'

All this was before the Mendis girl started visiting. Sugi knew the family.

'The boy is the only son, Sir,' he said. 'He is arrogant, and clever. There is talk of him getting a British Council scholarship in spite of what happened to the father. The father was warned several times, you know. Before they killed him, they warned him. But he was a fearless man who spoke out against the injustice done to the Tamils long ago. So, even though he was warned, he ignored the warnings.'

He paused, remembering.

'He was an educated man, too. He wasn't a fool. But in the end it did him no good. He was very handsome, and he had strong principles. Always campaigning for the Tamil underdog. What they did to him was a terrible thing. But you know, Sir, he should have been more careful. Someone should have advised him. That silly wife of his, someone.'

'And the girl?' asked Theo.

'Oh, the girl looks just like him,' said Sugi, misunderstanding. 'But you know the whole family is being watched now. They were never popular. And the boy is very selfish. He is only interested in himself.'

It was clear Mr Samarajeeva was not interested in the boy, thought Sugi, disapproving of the girl's visits.

'She comes here too often, Sir, now,' he warned. 'There are certain people in this town who are very interested in that family.'

She was friendly enough, thought Sugi, but still, she might bring trouble with her. Someone had once told him she had stopped talking after her father died, but from what he could hear she never stopped when she was with Theo. Her drawings, he reluctantly admitted, were another matter. They were good. Sir had them scattered all over the house and now, in this latest development, the girl was going to work on Mr Samarajeeva's portrait in the house. Sugi shook his head. He could not understand how the mother could care so little that she let her daughter wander around in this way. How could a respectable Singhalese woman be so negligent? Rumour was that Mrs Mendis had become unhinged since the tragedy. But then, thought Sugi, going off on another track, everyone is strange nowadays. The things that had happened in this place were turning people mad. It was not possible to have normal lives any longer. It was not possible to walk without looking over your shoulder at all times. Without wondering who was a friend and who a new enemy. Fear and suspicion was the thing they lived off, it was the only diet they had had for years. Almost every family he knew was touched in some way by the troubles, living with the things they were too frightened to talk about. There was no point, no point to anything. One just waited, hoping. Dodging the curfew. Hoping not to put a foot wrong, thought Sugi, hoping not to tread the rusty barbed wire hidden in the sea sand.

A few nights previously Sugi had cautioned Theo again. Not that it was any use, but he had tried.

'You must not walk on the beach when there is a curfew. The army is watching. Or if they are not, then there are thugs who will watch for them. Believe me, Sir. And another thing, you shouldn't have given your talk about your book at the schools. They won't like that.'

'It is no way to live,' said Theo Samarajeeva frowning. 'No one owns the beach. Sugi, there are many countries all over the world that have trouble like this. We must not give in to the bullies.'

'Ours is a very small country,' Sugi said, shaking his head. 'No one cares about us. Why should they? Only we care about the differences between the Singhalese and the Tamils. No one understands what this fight is about. We hardly understand ourselves any more.'

Theo nodded. He brought out his pipe and began tapping it.

'When the British brought the Tamils here from India, some people thought they brought trouble to this island,' Sugi said.

Theo was trying to light his pipe but the breeze kept whipping the flame so that he had to turn away. Sugi continued to stare into space. When he spoke at last he sounded agitated.

'What is wrong with us that we behave in this way?' He watched as Theo struggled to relight his pipe. 'Isn't it possible for us to solve this thing peacefully?'

'It will take longer than we think,' Theo said, He put his match into the ashtray Sugi handed him. 'Why should the world care, Sugi?' he asked gently. 'We aren't important enough for the British any more. And unlike the Middle East, we have no oil. So we can kill each other and no one will notice. That's why things will take longer than we think.'

He knew from his life in England, people thought Sri Lanka was a place spiralling into madness; and yes, he thought, it was true, no one cared.

They had taken to having these conversations in the evening when the curfew was on. The girl never came after the curfew. Sugi was thankful that at least her mother had the sense to keep her in at night. So Theo had only Sugi to talk to. Sugi was always careful to keep a respectful distance from Mr Samarajeeva during these discussions. Occasionally he accepted a cigarette or a beer but never anything else. He stood a little away from the chairs; he would never accept a seat. Sometimes he squatted on the step, the end of his cigarette glowing in the dark.

'I would like to see England,' he said one night. 'I think the people there are not like us.'

'No, they're not. But they have their own problems, Sugi, their own battles. Just as pointless in their different ways. And I never really felt I belonged there.'

'Even after all that time, Sir?'

'No,' said Theo with certainty. 'These are my people. *This* is where I belong.'

But Sugi was doubtful.

'Don't mistake our friendliness, Sir. We are Buddhists but these days we have forgotten this,' said Sugi. 'We are quite capable of killing. It isn't like before. When you were last here. Things are complicated now. These days we don't know who we are.'

Theo nodded in agreement. 'They should have known it wouldn't end simply,' he murmured.

'Who? The Tamils?'

'No, Sugi,' Theo said. He sounded sad. 'I mean those who

conquered us. I mean the British. Their presence casts its shadow on this island. Still.

'Cause and effect, Sir. Just as the Buddha said.'

But Theo was following his own thoughts.

'Why are we surprised by this war, Sugi? Has there ever been a country that, once colonised, avoided civil war? Africa? India? Burma?'

Night flowers appeared everywhere in the garden, blooming in ghostly clusters, their branches pouring scent into the air. Frogs croaked, small bats moved silently in the trees, and here and there, in the dull light of the lamp, silvery insects darted about. On one occasion Sugi shone a torch into the under-growth, convinced a nest of snakes lurked close by. He advanced with his axe but then the moon had gone behind a cloud and he could not find a single one. At other times, on certain nights, suddenly there were no sounds at all. No drums, no radios, no sirens. Nothing moved in the darkness and at such moments Sugi's nervousness would increase. The silence, he complained, was worse than all the noise, the atmosphere created by it, terri-fying in a different way. Suspense hung heavily in the air; at such moments anything could happen. For in Sugi's experience, most murders were committed in the lull before the full moon. Whispers alighted as softly as mosquitoes on unsuspecting flesh; whispers of torture. And the smell of death brought the snakes out. Theo listened to Sugi's fears without speaking. But then, sometimes, on these faceless nights, as they sat talking in the garden, they would catch the unmistakable sigh of the great ocean drifting towards them. They would hear it very clearly, rushing and tugging, to and fro and across, in an endless cycle as it washed and rewashed the bone-white shore. And as always, as they listened, the sound of it comforted them both.

By the time Theo Samarajeeva returned from Colombo the

back room of his house had been cleared, the walls lime-washed, and Nulani Mendis was installed with her canvases, her paints and her cheap thinners. The house smelt of coconuts and linseed oil. He knew she was there even as he approached, even as the bougainvillea cascaded into view over the new garden wall. The light from the mirrors in this hastily devised studio flickered in a dazzling way, casting intermittent reflections on everything in the room. Theo watched through the open window as Nulani crouched on the ground working on the painting. She used rags to mix the paint, and rags to layer it smoothly on to the canvas. All around were her pencil drawings of him. He could not see her face. Slivers of light danced on her hair. He did not know how long he stood watching her. Time stood still.

After a while she moved, placing the painting against the wall beside a chair where the reflections continued to tremble, uninterrupted. There was an old jug made of thin dusty glass nearby on a shelf. Shadows poured endlessly into it where once it must have held liquid. The heat was impossible. Before he could say anything she turned suddenly and saw him. Her instantaneous smile caught them both unawares. It must have been a trick of the light, thought Theo surprised, but the day seemed exceptionally pierced by the sun.

'So you are back,' she said. 'Sugi said you wouldn't be back till later.'

How to tell her that Colombo seemed unbearably hot and crowded? That what he thought he had needed to look up in the university library had in fact been irrelevant? That he knew, if he hurried, he would be able to catch an earlier train and be back before she went home, thereby seeing her a day sooner? How to tell her all this when he was unable to understand these thoughts himself?

'I have brought you a present,' he said instead, handing her a paper bag. Inside were all the colours she wanted but did not have. Cobalt blue, crimson lake, Venetian red. A bottle of pure turpentine, refined linseed oil. The paints were good-quality pigments, made in England, of the sort she had seen long ago in the English neighbour's house when she had stolen the pencils. The tubes were clean and uncrushed by use. She opened them and watched as traces of oil oozed slowly out; the colour was not far behind. They looked good enough to eat. Her bright red dress was new.

'It's my birthday today,' she said delighted, seeing him look at her dress. 'I was hoping you would come back today.'

'I know!' he said. 'Happy seventeenth birthday!'

Again the day seemed suffused by an inexplicable green lightness, of the kind he remembered in other times, in other places. Maybe there will be rain later, thought Theo, confused.

She had begun to paint him against a curtain of foliage. There were creases in his white shirt, purple shadows along one arm. She had given his eyes a reflective quality that hinted at other colours beyond the darkness of the pupils. Was this him, really? Was this what *she* saw? In the painting he paused as he wrote, looking into the distance. Aspects of him emerged from the canvas, making certain things crystal clear.

'You were looking at *me*,' she said laughing, pointing to one of the drawings.

He did not know what to say. Her directness left him helpless. Perhaps it was this simplicity that he needed in his new book. Once he had been able to deal with all kinds of issues swiftly, cut to the heart of the matter. Now for some reason it seemed impossible for him to think in this way. Had fear and hurt and self-pity done all this to him? Or was this the uncertainty of middle age? Suddenly he felt small and ashamed. He stood looking at the painting and at the girl framed by the curtain of green light, aware vaguely that she was still smiling at him.

He stood staring at her until Sugi called out that lunch was ready.

'Tell me about Anna,' she demanded, over lunch. 'I have been looking at all the pictures of her. They are very beautiful.'

So he told her something about Anna.

'I used to see her every morning in a little café where I went for breakfast.'

'In London?'

'No, in Venice. She was Italian. We used to glance at each other without speaking. It was bitterly cold that winter. The apartment I was renting was so cold that I would go to this little dark café for breakfast. And I would drink a grappa,' he said smiling, remembering.

'What happened then?'

'One day she came in with some other people. Two women and a man. The man was clearly interested in her.'

'So what did you do?'

Theo smiled, shaking his head. 'Nothing. What could I do? My Italian was not very good in those days. But then she turned and waved at me. Asked me if I would like to join them. I was astonished, astonished that she should notice me.'

'But you said you used to look at each other every morning.'

'Yes,' said Theo. 'I suppose I mean I was surprised she noticed me enough to want to talk to me.'

He was silent again, thinking of the fluidity of their lives afterwards, the passion that never seemed to diminish as they travelled through Europe. Then he described the high tall house in London with the mirrors and the blousy crimson peonies she loved to buy. He spoke of the books they had both written, so different yet one feeding off the other.

'She was very beautiful,' he said, unaware of the change in his voice. 'Now *she* was someone you should have drawn.'

Nulani was listening intensely. He became aware of her

curious dark eyes fixed on him. He did not know how much she understood. What could Europe mean to her?

'My brother Jim wants to go to Europe,' she said at last. 'He says, when he is in England studying it will be easy to travel.'

'And you? What about you?'

But he knew the answer even before she told him. Who would take her? What would she make of Paris. And Venice?

'I will go one day,' she said as though reading his mind. 'Maybe we will go together.'

He felt his chest tighten unaccountably, and he wondered what her father had been like. What would he have made of this beautiful daughter of his, had he lived? Nulani had told him he had been a poet. She remembered him, she told Theo, but only as a dreamer. Always making her mother angry as she, Nulani, did now. What fragile balance in their family had been upset by his death? The afternoon had moved on but the heat showed no sign of letting up. The sun had moved to another place.

'You should go home,' he said, suddenly anxious, not wishing to keep her out too late. 'I'll get Sugi to walk you home.'

But she would have none of it; standing close to him holding her paints, so close he could smell the faint perfume that was her skin, mixing with the oils.

'Thank you,' she said and she went, a splash of red against the sea-faded blue gate, and then through the trees, and then taking in glimpses of road and bougainvillea before she disappeared from view around the bend of the hot empty road. Taking with her all the myriad, unresolved hues of the day, shimmering into the distance.

2

THEO HAD NOT SEEN THE GIRL for five days. He waited, watching the geckos climbing haltingly across the lime-washed walls. He walked on the beach most evenings, much to Sugi's alarm, ignoring the curfews, hoping she might be doing the same. He sat on the veranda smoking; he wandered into the room strewn with her paints. The smell of turpentine and oil remained as strong as ever. It was the way of smells, he knew. It had been this way when Anna had died. All the smells of beeswax and red peonies, of lavender-washed cotton and typewriter ribbon had gathered together, bringing her back to him in small concentrated fragments. So he knew about smells, the way they tumbled into the air, falling softly again, here and there, like confetti without the bride. The sunlight seemed suddenly to have lost its brilliance. His old anger returned. He had thought he was over it, but bitterness attacked him in waves. Ugliness remembered. Sugi watched him surreptitiously, serving his meals, bringing a tray of morning tea, cooking a redfish curry in the way he liked it. The fans had stopped working again and the lights often failed at night. Sugi watched him in the light of the coconut-oil lamps.

There did not seem to be much evidence of Sir working. Across the garden Theo felt the silence stretch into eternity. The leaves on the pawpaw tree looked large and malevolent.

'Sir,' said Sugi finally, 'Sir, why are you not writing?'

Beyond the light from the veranda the undergrowth rustled vaguely. Two mosquito coils burned into insubstantial columns. A black-spotted moth circled the lamps, mesmerised. Sugi looked at Theo. This is a fine state of affairs, he thought. It was as well he was here.

'Maybe there is trouble at her house, no?' he ventured tentatively. 'Shall I go and find out?'

'No,' said Theo quickly.

Such an intrusion was unbearable and he could not allow it. Sugi fell silent again. Maybe he should talk about something else instead. Sir was a grown man after all. He had lived all over the world. Given the things he had been through, his innocence was surprising.

'There is a shortage of food in the market this week,' Sugi said. 'I don't know why. I could only get river cress, a coconut and a bunch of shrivelled radishes.'

It was true. The rice was appalling too, and there were no fresh vegetables to be had.

'Of all the places on this island,' he continued, complaining loudly, hoping to distract Theo, 'this should be the place for fresh fish. But the day's catch had vanished by the time I got into the town. There's been some kind of trouble further along the coast; maybe that's got something to do with it. Someone told me the army drove their jeeps on to the sands, chasing a group of men. And then they shot them. They were all young, Sir. Nobody knows what they had done.'

He spread his hands helplessly in front of him.

'The army left the bodies on the beach, and the local people cleared up the mess. There is always someone prepared to clean up after them. Either a Buddhist or a Christian. They will always find someone to do the dirty work.'

Theo shifted uneasily in his chair. Sugi's anxiety was different from his.

On the fifth evening of Nulani's absence, in spite of Sugi's entreaties, Theo decided to walk along the beach again.

'Look,' he said, 'nothing can happen to me. It's not people like me that interest them. I'm too well known. I'm safe.'

And he went out. A full moon spilled a continuous stream of silver on to the water. An express train hooted its way along the coast, rushing towards Colombo. But there was no sign of the girl on the empty beach. What *is* the matter with me, he thought, exasperated. Am I going mad? She's probably busy, helping her mother, sewing, being seventeen. And she never said when she would be back, he reasoned silently. He was puzzled by this disturbance to his equilibrium. Time was passing, in a few months it would be winter in England. His agent would not wait for ever. He had not written much. As he watched, the moon spread its phosphorescent glow into the sea.

'Look,' Sugi said when he returned.

He held out a piece of paper. Thick heady blossoms glowed white under the lamplight while Theo unfolded it quickly. It was from the girl. She had drawn a picture of a man. The man was sitting on one of the cane chairs on her veranda. There was a cup of tea on the table beside him; it was placed on a heavily embroidered cloth. The man's face was in profile, but still, it was possible to see the fine lines of dissatisfaction and anger and suppressed cruelty. It was possible to see all this on the small piece of paper, clearly marked by the stub of a pencil.

'It's her uncle, Sir,' said Sugi when Theo showed him. 'I know this man. He is a bad man. The talk is he betrayed Mr Mendis.

That it was because of him, the thugs came. He never liked his sister's choice of husband. There are seven brothers in that family, you know, and they like their women to do as they are told.'

Theo felt anger tighten its belt around him. His anxiety for the girl intensified.

'I think I'll take a walk over to Mrs Mendis's house,' he said.

But Sugi was alarmed. He would not let Theo be so foolish.

'Are you crazy, Sir? Leave that family alone, for God's sake. I'm telling you, you don't understand the people here. You must not meddle with things in this place. Please, Mr Samarajeeva, this isn't England. The girl will be OK. It's *her* family, and she is no fool. She will come here, tomorrow or the next day, you'll see.'

He sounded like a parent, quietening a restless child. In spite of his anger another part of Theo saw this and felt glad. He was amazed at the easy affection between them. They had slipped into a friendship, Sugi and he, in spite of the rising tide of anxiety around them, perhaps because of it.

'Sugi,' he said softly into the darkness, feeling a sudden sharp sense of belonging. 'You are my good friend, you know. I feel as if I have known you for ever.'

He hesitated. He would have liked to say something more. Moved by their growing affection for each other, he would have liked to speak of it. But he could not think of the right way to express himself. Sugi, too, seemed to hesitate, as though he understood. So Theo said nothing and instead poured them both a beer. But the warmth between them would not go away, settling down quietly, curling up like a contented animal. He looked at the note again. Underneath the drawing Nulani had captioned it with two exclamation marks. What did *that* mean?

'I told you, Sir, the girl understands her family better than you. She is probably laughing at her uncle right now. You must not worry so much. She'll be able to take care of herself. And tomorrow she will be back, you'll see,' he added, cheerfully, for he could see that Theo was less worried now. 'I'll squeeze some limes and make a redfish curry. Tomorrow.'

'I would have liked children, Sugi,' Theo said later on, calmer now than he had been for days.

Sugi nodded, serious. 'Children are a blessing, Sir, but they are endless trouble as well. In this country we seem to have children only to carry on our suffering. In this country it's only one endless cycle of pain for us. Some terrible curse has fallen on us since we became greedy.'

Startled, Theo looked sharply at him. He had forgotten the slow and inevitable philosophy of his countrymen. But before he could speak, Sugi put his hand out to silence him. The moon had retreated behind a cloud and a slight breeze moved the leaves. It reminded Theo of other balmy nights long ago with Anna, spent in the fishing ports along the South of France. Something rustled in the undergrowth; Sugi disappeared silently along the side of the house. Thinking he heard the gate creak Theo stood up. A moment later there was a muffled grunt, the sound of a scuffle and Sugi reappeared, emerging through the bushes, pushing a boy of about fourteen in front of him. He had twisted the boy's arm behind his back and was gripping him hard. In the light of the returning moon a knife glinted in his hand.

'He was trying to break in, Sir, from the back. With this,' he added grimly.

And he held up the knife. He pushed the boy roughly towards Theo, speaking to him in Singhalese.

'He says he was only doing what he was told.'

'What were you trying to steal?' Theo asked him, also in Singhalese.

But the boy would not reply. In another moment, with a swift jerk of his elbow he broke free and vaulted over the garden wall, vanishing into the night. And although they ran out into the darkened road there was no sign of him anywhere. Sugi began bolting the windows and checking the side of the house, shining a torch on the dense mass of vegetation.

'Tomorrow,' he said, shaking his head, looking worried, 'I will cut some of it back.'

Tomorrow he would rig up a garden light to surprise any further intruders. The boy was probably just a petty thief, stealing things to sell in order to buy drugs. But still, one could not be too careful. Tomorrow he would make some enquiries in the town. Meanwhile, Sir should go to bed.

After he had lit another mosquito coil and closed the net around himself, just at the point of sleep, Theo realised he had forgotten to ask Sugi who had delivered the drawing from the girl. And he thought with certainty, Sugi was probably right; the girl would reappear in the morning.

She was waiting for him the next morning in her usual spot on the veranda, drawing his lounge-backed cane chair.

'So,' he said sitting down, filling her view, smiling, 'so, welcome back!'

And he seemed to hear the faintest flutter of wings. Small banana-green parrots hopped restlessly in the trees, music floated out from the house, and the air was filled with beginnings and murmurings. Last night seemed not to have happened at all. Her uncle had just left, she said. It was Saturday; there was no school so she had escaped from home. She wanted to work on the painting. Too much time had been wasted by her uncle's visit. He had come to discuss Jim's future. The days had been filled with squabbling and the thin raised voice of her mother. Her uncle had not cared about his sister's distress. He merely wanted Jim to join the organisation he ran.

'It's something to do with the military,' Nulani said scornfully. 'I think they spy on people, for the army. My uncle said Jim is old enough and it was time for him to give up his studies. He said there's no time for studying right now, when Sri Lanka needs him.'

'What?' said Theo. 'Are you serious?'

'Yes, but Amma does not want this kind of future for her son. She is frightened, she has lost my father, she does not want to lose a son as well.'

Sooner or later, Nulani's uncle had told them, sooner or later Lucky Jim's luck would run out. Then what would he do? Better to start now, show which side of the fence he was on. Before questions were asked.

'So he was threatening your brother?' Theo asked.

'Yes, but Amma will not allow it. So they were fighting.'

Sugi brought out a dish of pawpaw. He had been preparing the table for breakfast. He covered it with an indigo cloth. Then he brought out some freshly made egg hoppers and some seeni sambol. And a small jug of boiled milk with the tea. A band of sunlight had escaped from the roof and bent across the table, stretching across the floor. Theo went inside to turn the record over.

'And you? What did your uncle have to say to you,' he asked, coming back.

Nulani pulled a face, laughing up at him. 'I dropped two dishes yesterday,' she said. 'I was in a hurry. I thought if I cleared up quickly I might be able to come here. But then I dropped the dishes and Amma shouted at me. So I couldn't escape.'

'What happened then? Were you punished or something?' It all sounded ludicrous.

Nulani shrugged. 'No. Amma just said, "What's wrong with the girl?" and that started my uncle off again, only this time he began to shout at *me*. He said I hadn't been trained properly and I needed a husband!'

'What?' asked Theo in alarm.

'Oh, he's full of talk,' Nulani said dismissively. 'He can't do anything. And I just ignore him anyway. He told Amma he would find someone suitable for me to marry, but Amma was too angry about what he had said to Jim to worry about me.'

The sky seemed cloudless and suddenly overbright.

'I don't have to do what he tells me,' said Nulani. 'My father hated him.'

But her father could no longer help her, Theo thought uneasily. Thinking also, in spite of this new threat from the uncle, how glad he was she was here now, and how empty the days had been while she had stayed away, wondering too, what he might do that would be of any help to her. Wondering if the chasm of age and life and experience left room for giving her anything on his part.

'I haven't seen you for five days,' she said, suddenly, and in that moment, it seemed to Theo, the sky had changed and was now the timeless blue of the tea-country lakes.

'But I have been drawing you from memory. Look, they're nearly perfect,' she told him, moving her chair closer and handing him her book. Once again images rose from the pages, tossed carelessly out, those aspects of himself that he barely intuited. There he was smiling, pensive, staring owlishly into the distance, cleaning his glasses. Oh Christ, he thought, Christ! What was this? He looked at the drawings helplessly, feeling his heart contract painfully. Lighting his pipe he drank his tea in silence. Then he stood up and held the door of her new studio open, smiling down at her.

'Work,' he said firmly, wanting for some aching, unaccountable reason to touch her long dark hair.

What remained of the morning was spent in this way. Nulani worked on the two canvases that would eventually be the portraits of Theo. The smell of her colours, mixed with the turpentine, filling the house. Outside a monkey screamed and screamed again. The heat draped itself like a heavy leaded curtain across the veranda. They would have to take their lunch indoors. Somewhere in the kitchen Sugi was scraping coconuts. Theo had so far written two sentences towards his new book. The image of the girl wove into his thoughts; it ran with the sound of the piano music from the record, it merged confusingly with the heat outside. Why had he ever imagined he could work in this place? I need the cold, he thought, restlessness stirring in him. He thought of the muffled noise of traffic rising up towards the tops of the plane trees in Kensington. A memory of his wide airy flat returned to him with the mirrors and the pale duck-egg walls, broken by patches of Kandyan red and orange cloth. Once he had been able to work among all that elegance, once he had had another life. Perhaps, thought Theo, perhaps I have no more to say; perhaps this latest book is doomed? Perhaps the sun has sapped my inspiration?

But then he went to get the girl, for the lunch was ready, and he saw the light flickering against the walls of the room where she worked. Her small face was smudged with paint, and it struck him forcefully that no, his book was not doomed at all. For the early-afternoon sun seemed to turn and pivot on a new axis of optimism. Sugi too seemed to have excelled himself with the lunch. All he said was that the market had been good as he set the jug of lime juice down and brought in the curries; *murunga,* bitter-gourd, *brinjal,* fish and boiled rice. He was smiling broadly and his previous disapproval of the girl seemed to have evaporated. Nulani, unaware of any difference, chattered happily with him as he brought in the food. But he would not stay while they ate, shyly asking instead if he might take a look at the painting of Sir.

'Yes, yes,' the girl said delighted. 'But Mr Samarajeeva must not see it yet.'

'Will you stop calling me that!' Theo laughed. 'Come back and tell me what you think.'

But Sugi could not be persuaded. He had work to do, he said. He was going to put barbed wire over the back-garden wall, whether Sir liked it or not.

So that it wasn't until much later, when they were alone and he smoked his cigarette on the veranda with Theo, that he said, 'She is very talented, Sir.'

They sat for a moment in companiable silence.

'And she has become too attached to you,' Sugi said.

All afternoon he had been working on the garden. The heat had eased off slightly, and then the girl, having cleared up her paints, had gone home. Huge tropical stars appeared between the leaves of the plantain trees. The garden was as secure as it was possible to make it, he told Theo. It had not been easy to get barbed wire; in the end, hoping no one had seen him, Sugi had picked up what had been lying around the beach. He was still worried about the boy from the night before, he told Theo.

'You worry too much,' said Theo, smiling at him. His affection felt clumsy. Again he recognised his own inability to speak of the growing bond between them.

He is like a brother to me, he thought with amazement. If I believed in it, I would say we had known one another in a previous life. It occurred to him that he would like to give Sugi something to mark his feelings, some tangible thing, a talisman for the future that was nothing to do with payments or employment. But he did not know how, or even what. And then, once more, he found himself thinking of the girl and her extraordinary quiet ability to make sense of all she saw, with delicate pencil lines overlaying more lines. The evening, and the night ahead, seemed suddenly interminably long until the morning. He hoped she had reached her home safely. He worried that she let neither Sugi nor him walk her back. He worried that her uncle was waiting for her. What on earth is *wrong* with me, he muttered, half exasperated, half amused at himself. I'm acting like her mother. And then he thought, Am I simply being sentimental? Perhaps this is what middle age is about. As he lit the mosquito coil, before he got under the net, he remembered again that he had forgotten to ask Sugi who had delivered Nulani's drawing the night before.

One morning, some weeks later, Theo decided to visit the temple on the hill. The girl had told him it was very beautiful.

'You should go,' she had said. 'We held my father's funeral there.'

He had sensed she wanted him to go for this reason and he thought of the irony of it. Burning the man who had already been burned. Mrs Mendis was leaving the temple as he entered. He heard her calling him and looked around for an escape but there was none.

'I have brought an offering for my son,' she said. 'He sits his scholarship exam this morning. I think his karma is good but I want to be sure he passes. I don't want him to join the army. I don't want him to die like my husband,' she said, talking too loudly.

Theo looked at the woman with dislike. She had not mentioned her daughter once. Inside the temple it was cool and dark, and further back, out of sight, the monks sat in rows, their chants rising and falling in slow, low folds. The air was crowded with sounds, like the hum of hundreds of invisible birds. It reminded him of his childhood, of his mother. He had not been in a temple for many years. He stood in the coolness, thinking of Mr Mendis, wondering what he might have been like. And then he thought of the girl, wishing he had known her as a small child. Thinking how fleeting glimpses of that lost time often emerged in her mischievous laugh. Certain, too, that her father would always remain within her, however long she lived.

That afternoon, Nulani talked about her brother's probable departure.

'I think he will be happier in England,' she told Theo. 'And maybe he will come back to see us when the trouble is over.'

By now she was working on the larger portrait. She wanted it to be a surprise, she said. But she was less happy, he saw. Something was ebbing out of her, some vitality moved away leaving her drawn and hurt. Watching this, Theo felt unaccountably depressed.

'That boy will never come back,' Sugi said quietly, when he heard. 'He only thinks about himself. Once he leaves he will forget about them.'

Sugi watched Theo. Although he said very little he knew all the signs were there. If he is not careful, he worried, Sir will get hurt. Why doesn't he see this? Why, after all he has been through, is he not more careful? He's a clever man, but . . . And Sugi shook his head.

'Maybe,' Theo said, 'things will be easier for her when Jim goes. Maybe the mother will care more.'

'The Mendis woman has only ever cared about the son, I tell you, Sir,' Sugi said. 'I know all about her. After the father was murdered, she used to talk to my friend who works in Sumaner House. And it was always the boy she worried about. Lucky Jim! That's her name for him. She hardly notices her daughter.'

They were sitting on the veranda once again. It was late and the heat had finally moved a little distance away. Most nights now Theo listened to the menace of the garden, the rustlings and unknown creepings that scratched against the trees. He was hardly aware of doing so, but since the intruder, both he and Sugi were watchful.

'And her father?' he asked. 'What was he like?'

'People used to watch them,' Sugi remembered. 'Mr Mendis used to walk with his daughter every evening, up and down the beach. They used to say you could set your clocks watching those two. They always walked at five o'clock, every day, except when the monsoons came. He used to hold her hand. She was devoted to him.' Sugi's eyes moved restlessly across the garden. 'It must have been terrible for her after he died. She must have felt so alone.'

They were both silent. Then Sugi went off for his nightly surveillance of the perimeter walls and gate, testing his barbed wire, wandering silently through the undergrowth. When he was satisfied that everything was in order, he came back and accepted a beer.

'She needs to go from this place,' he continued. 'There is nothing here for her. Her uncle is a very unpleasant man. And, Sir, I know I've said it before, but you should be careful with this family. The girl is good but you are a stranger to these parts. Please don't forget this.'

The night, once again, was quiet. There were no sounds of gunshots or sirens. Nor were there street lights here, for it was too far away from the other houses. The scent of blossom drifted in waves towards them. Occasionally the plaintive, lonely hoot of a train could be heard in the distance, but that was all.

'You can't change anything,' said Sugi. He sounded sad. 'You are right, things will take longer than we expect. Life is just a continuous cycle. Eventually, of course, at the right time there will be change. But however hard we try to alter things ourselves, what must be will be. Who knows how long it will take, Sir. Sri Lanka is an ancient island. It cannot be hurried.'

Theo watched the headlights of a car disappeared from view. The yellow beam stretched through the trees, bending with the road, piercing the darkness, searching the night. Then it was gone. It occurred to him there had been no car along that particular stretch of road for weeks.

Someone had thrown a plucked chicken over the wall into the garden. They had tossed it over, cleverly missing the barbed wire. It was trussed; legs together, smeared with yellowish powder, a thin red thread wound tightly round its neck. Even though death had come swiftly, leaving traces of blood, staring at it Theo imagined the frenzy of anger that had brought it to this state. A whole pageant of slaughter lay here, he thought, in this one small carcass. Mesmerised, he gazed at a half-remembered history, of sacrifice both ancient and bloodied. The turmeric had given the chicken's skin the appearance of a threadbare carpet. He touched the bird with his foot; it was so long since he had seen something like this he had almost forgotten what it was meant for. And as he stood gazing at it, he remembered, in a rush of forgotten irritation, the reasons he had never made this country his home. Impatiently, for the waste of energy angered him, he kicked the chicken across the garden, and in doing so crossed a hidden boundary. For in that moment, it seemed to the horrified Sugi looking on, he did what no man should ever do: he tampered with those laws that could not be argued with.

'Don't touch it, Sir, for God's sake,' implored Sugi, but he was too late. The deed was done.

'Don't touch it, Sir, please. I will see to it. Someone is trying to put a curse on this place.'

Theo grinned. He has been away too long, thought Sugi, distressed. He questioned, instead of accepting. Twenty-odd years living away had made Theo forget. He was trying to single-handedly alter the inner structure of life. And seeing this, Sugi was frightened. His fear clung to the barbed wire that was pressed against the garden wall. Fear had been stalking Sugi daily for years.

'This town is not as it used to be,' he said. 'We used to know everyone who lived here. We knew their fathers and their grandfathers too. We knew all the relatives, Sir. Many people have moved into this area, thinking it is safer here. But the trouble is, this has made it *less* safe. There are thugs in the pay of the authority, and there are thugs working for those who would like to be rid of the authority. Singhalese, Tamils, what does it matter who they are, everyone spies on everyone else.' A nation's hatred has split open, he said, like two halves of a coconut. 'People are angry, Sir. They can barely hide it.'

Theo was silenced. Other people's jealousies spilled out around him, dismembered bodies, here and there they scattered randomly, saffron yellow and cochineal. He could say nothing in the face of Sugi's certainty. He did not want to hurt his feelings. Only the girl, arriving soon afterwards, expressed contempt. The dead chicken did not bother her, she said; she had seen so many before. Her father, she told Theo, had laughed at such nonsense. Her father had been full of peace, she told him. He did not believe violence answered anything, and so Nulani Mendis believed this too. She drank the lime juice Sugi had made for her and it was she who tried to reassure him. She was wearing her faded green skirt wrapped even more tightly around her slender waist and her skin appeared flawless through the thin cotton blouse. Sunlight fell in straight sheets behind her, darkening her hair, shadowing her face, making it difficult to read her expression. For a moment she seemed no longer a child. Had she changed since yesterday? puzzled Theo.

When she finished working on her painting she discarded her overall. There were still some slivers of paint in her finger-nails. Today they were of a different colour. However hard she scrubbed her hands there was still some paint left, thought Theo amused. The day righted itself. The soft smell of colour still clung to her and seemed to Theo sweeter than all the scent of the frangipani blossoms. The picture was nearly finished, she told him, and she wanted to do another one. She needed one more sketch of him. Would Theo be able to sit still, please? He hid his amusement, noticing she had become a little bossy. Her notebook of drawings had grown and she wanted to use them in one more painting. She wanted to paint Theo in his dining room with its foxed mirrors, its beautiful water glasses, its jugs. She wanted to paint him surrounded by mirror-reflected light. Light that moved, she said. This was what interested her, not the trussed chicken. And no, she did not want him to sneak a look at the portrait, she added, laughing at him.

'You can see it soon,' she promised, as though *he* was the child. 'When it's finished.'

For now, she told Theo, he could look at her sketchbook instead. Once again she gave him the fragmented stories she had collected. And again they fell from the pages in a jumble of images.

'Look,' she said laughing, 'my uncle!'

She stood too close, confusing him, making him want to touch her hair. Their conversations were a running stitch across her notebook, holding together all that he could not say.

'There's no one at home,' she volunteered. 'Jim has gone to Colombo with his teacher and Amma is visiting a friend. So I'm all on my own.'

She did not say it, but it was clear she was free to do what she pleased. How can I encourage her to defy her mother in this way? wondered Theo.

'Jim has to get all the documents he needs to leave.' Her brother's departure was never far from her thoughts.

'Doesn't he want to wait?' asked Theo. 'Doesn't he want to be sure he has passed the exam first?'

But, Nulani told him, Jim was certain. His teacher too believed he would pass the examination and be awarded the British Council scholarship. Such certainty, thought Theo, raising an eyebrow. He said nothing, watching as the thought of Jim's certain departure darted and fluttered across her face.

'He wants to leave Sri Lanka by October,' Nulani said. She dared not think what that would mean for her.

For the moment, though, with the absence of her family, something, some unspecified tension seemed to ease up. She would stay late and the mornings were fresh and unhampered by the heat. The days stretched deliciously before them, slipping into an invisible rhythm of its own. By now Theo had become used to her presence, and he worked steadily on his manuscript, distracted only occasionally. Perhaps, he thought, Anna had been right. She had always insisted they needed a child to give purpose to their lives. A child was an anchor. It brought with it the kind of love that settles one, she used to say. When she had died Theo had remembered this, thinking, too, how useless a child would have been when all he wanted had been her. Now he wondered if Anna, wise, lovely Anna, had been right after all.

3

THERE WERE FLEETS OF ENORMOUS ORANGE MOTHS in Sumaner House where Vikram lived. Moths and antique dust that piled up in small hills behind the coloured-glass doors. The beetles had drilled holes in the fretwork of the frames and sawdust had gathered in small mounds on the ground. It was a useless house really, everything was broken or badly mended, everything was covered in fine sea sand, caked in old sweat and unhappiness. Objectively, it might have made a better relic than a house, but relics were plentiful and houses of this size not easily found. The fact was Sumaner House was huge. Once it must have been splendid. Once, rich Dutch people would have lived in it and crossed the Indian Ocean in big sailing ships, carrying spices and ivory and gold back to their home. Once, too, the filigree shutters, and the newly built verandas, and the black-and-white-tiled floors must have looked splendid. The green glass skylight would have filtered the sun down into the dark interior. But what was the use? Time had passed with steady inevitability, washing away the details of all that had gone before, leaving only small traces of glory. Now the furniture was scratched and full of decay. These days only Vikram and his guardian and the servant woman lived here. Most of the time it was only Vikram and the servant woman who were in the house. She stayed in her quarters, cooking or cleaning, and Vikram came and went as he pleased. There was no one to stop him. No one to ask him questions or argue with him, for Mr Gunadeen, his guardian, was hardly ever present. He was in Malaysia. Why he had ever wanted to be Vikram's guardian was a mystery. Perhaps he had wanted to protest against the exploitation of child soldiers. Perhaps, he had hoped, that by adopting a Waterlily House orphan he would build up good karma. No one knew, because after that one act of enigmatic charity, Vikram's guardian went off to work, first in the Middle East and then in Malaysia. Supervising telecommunications systems in other developing countries. Perhaps the war had made him restless, the people in the town said. At least by adopting Vikram he had done something to counteract the work of those murderous Tamil bastards. For, it was said, he was a good Singhala man.

Having picked Vikram more or less randomly from the Waterlily orphanage, Mr Gunadeen put him in the local boys' school.

'He needs a good education,' he told the headmaster privately, without noticing the irony of his words.

The headmaster knew, but chose to forget, that in the wake of independence the Singhalese had slowly denied the Tamils any chance of a decent education. Well, things had changed and these were desperate times. The headmaster knew nothing about child soldiers or their psychological scars. He thought Vikram was an orphan without complications. He knew nothing of his soldiering past.

'I shall be gone for a few months,' Vikram's guardian had said.

'Don't worry,' said the head. 'He'll be fine. You'll notice a change in him when you return, I promise.'

Vikram's guardian paid him handsomely. Next, Mr Gunadeen instructed the servant woman, Thercy.

'You know what to do,' he said. 'The boy's a little restless, but just feed him well and make sure he goes to school. I'll be back in a few months or so.'

And then he went, giving Vikram a contact address and a phone number. He did not think things needed to be any more complicated than that. So Vikram had a home now, a new school and plenty of food. What more could an orphan boy expect? He was far away from the brutal place where they recruited underage children into the military. What more could be done? The people in the town shook their heads in disbelief. What a good man Mr Gunadeen was, they said again, hoping Vikram would be worth the effort put into him. That had been four years ago.

But Vikram seemed not to realise the significance of his good fortune. Right from the very beginning he did not appear to *care* about anything. At first, when he came to live in Sumaner House, he used to kick the walls, treating the house as though it were a person, scuffing the furniture slyly, gouging holes in the doors when no one was looking, and cracking the fine-coloured glass into as many lines as he could, without breaking it completely. Torturing the house. Only the servant woman knew what he was up to. Thercy the servant woman saw every-thing that went on.

Then later, as he grew into adolescence, Vikram quietened down. The servant woman noticed this too. Almost overnight Vikram became monosyllabic and secretive. Whenever Thercy looked at him she noticed how expressionless his face was. In the last four years, since the random killings here in the south, the troubles had worsened. Nothing was certain any more but Thercy had learned to keep silent. Privately, she thought Vikram was disturbed. His disturbance, she was certain, lurked, waiting to pounce.

The only person the servant woman trusted in the whole town was Sugi. She knew Sugi was a good man. Often when they met at the market they would walk a little way together (not so far or so often as to attract attention) and exchange news. Thercy often talked to Sugi about the orphan from Waterlily House.

'He has everything he needs and nothing he wants,' she liked to say. 'It's his karma. To be saved from his fate in the orphanage, and given another sort of fate! But it won't work,' she added gloomily.

Sugi would listen, nodding his head worriedly. He had heard all this before. Vikram hadn't been a child soldier for long but Sugi knew: once a child soldier always a soldier. Why had Vikram's guardian tampered with the unwritten laws of the universe? What had happened to him was unimaginable and because of this he should have been left alone, in Sugi's opinion. Thercy had told Sugi the whole sorry story many times and each time Sugi had been convinced, Vikram should not have been brought here. The army entered Vikram's home in Batticaloa and raped his mother and his sister. They raped them many, many times, Thercy had said, beating the palm of her hand against her forehead as she talked.

'Then they took them away,' she had said. 'The army never thought to look under the bed. Vikram was hiding there. His father was away at the time. Someone went to find the poor man, bring him the news. They told him, his whole family had been wiped out.' Thercy had sliced the air with her hand. 'Just like that,' she had said. 'Gone! What could the man do? His grief must have been a terrible thing. He found some poison and, God forgive him, he swallowed it. It was only afterwards, when it was too late, that the people in the village thought of looking under the bed.'

She shook her head recalling the story. Sugi had heard it many times. Each time he was shocked. So much for our wonderful army, he thought each time.

'So much for our wonderful army,' he said again today, when they talked. 'What d'you expect?'

'We'd better go,' Thercy said, noticing how long they had been standing together and suddenly becoming nervous. 'There he is, over there. I don't want him to see us talking together.'

'Who's that man he's with?' asked Sugi, looking at Vikram, stealthily.

The boy was standing with an older man at the *kade*, the roadside shop. They were both drinking. Sugi had heard other rumours about Vikram. After his parents had died the Tigers were supposed to have got hold of him. But then, as luck would have it, the Singhalese army rounded up some of the Tiger cubs and handed them over to the orphanages a few months later. Vikram was one of them. He was only seven. He had already been carrying equipment for the guerrillas. Sugi could hardly believe that. A boy of seven, being a runner for the Tigers.

'And what would all that have done to him?' asked Sugi, watching Vikram now.

How could his past be changed? How could he be given new thoughts simply by being adopted? Thercy agreed.

'Aiyo!' she said, remembering. 'You should have seen him when he first came here. Mr Gunadeen wasn't around of course. He just went off and left me with the boy. I had to deal with everything all alone. Vikram used to run riot in the house. He's calmed down a lot now. In fact . . .' She paused.

'What?' asked Sugi.

'Well . . .'

Thercy hesitated. The truth was, there was a kind of empti-
ness to the boy. He seemed such a strange, mysterious crea-
ture, silent and friendless. Well, almost. Today she had some
new information for Sugi.

'You know he's made friends with the Mendis girl?'

'What?' cried Sugi in alarm.

Thercy shook her head quickly. She hadn't wanted to alarm
Sugi.

'No, no, I didn't mean to worry you. I know what you're
thinking. He's not likely to visit you. And anyway the girl doesn't
speak to many people either, and I only saw her talking to him
once. I shouldn't have said anything.'

Sugi relaxed slightly, although he still looked distracted.

'It isn't good,' was all he said, not knowing how to express
his disquiet. How much would Nulani Mendis tell Vikram about
her visits? About Theo?

'His Singhalese is faultless, you know,' continued Thercy. 'Not
many people around here realise he's a Tamil. Mr Gunadeen
didn't want that to be common knowledge. For his own safety.'

'That's exactly what I mean,' said Sugi, uneasily. 'He could
be working for the Tigers, couldn't he, for all we know?'

'Who, Vikram?' Thercy laughed. 'Is that what you're worrying
about? No, no, Sugi, he's harmless really, I promise you. In that
way, anyway. He's just a little strange, that's all. I can't explain
it . . .' Again she hesitated. 'And he has a temper. To tell you the
truth, of late I feel *sorry* for him. What chance is there for him
to ever have a normal life?' she said, adding, 'He's so disturbed.'

Vikram had no idea that people were talking about him.
Even had he known he would not have cared much, for Vikram
lived in a world without people. The space inside his head was

so empty that it almost echoed. Long ago, when he was at Waterlily House, he had begun to cultivate indifference. Nobody knew of course, but indifference had become a way of life for him. By the time he was twelve, before his guardian had arrived on the scene, he had learned not to make a fuss. What was the point? He could manage his life with ease without noise or fuss. He did whatever random thing he wanted, took what he liked the look of, unrestrained by anyone, neglected and unloved. By the time he reached the age of sixteen, he had grown enormously, was not bad-looking and was more or less friendless.

Sumaner House stood on the crest of a rise away from the immediate town; there were no other houses nearby. The view of the sea was uninterrupted. Vikram had his own room in the house. For nearly four years he had lived like this. He went to school and worked hard. For four years, while his guardian dipped in and out of his life, he studied. He soaked up knowledge like a sponge. The head was pleased. He wrote to Mr Gunadeen.

'*It's been a success,*' he wrote. '*And, it proves these children can be rehabilitated,*' he added triumphantly.

So Vikram was a success story. He was good at English and his Singhalese was brilliant.

'He writes beautifully too,' his teachers said.

In this way they continued to encourage Vikram. For, as everyone knew, whichever way you looked at it, the boy had had a bad start to life.

Every morning Vikram walked to school. It was the same school that Jim Mendis attended. It was generally expected that Lucky Jim, in spite of having no father, would one day go to the UK because he was so clever. And so, because of his luck, and quite possibly also his loss, the boys all wanted to be Jim

Mendis's friend. All except Vikram, that is. Vikram watched the Mendis boy quietly. Nobody noticed, because he was so quiet, but Vikram watched him idly, wondering if there was a chink in Jim's luck. But it seemed Lucky Jim was luck-tight. Soon after this, Vikram began to notice Jim Mendis's sister. She too walked to school and now Vikram noticed with some surprise that she was sweetly pretty. Something about her puzzled him. Then one day, as they stood at the crossroads, she turned and smiled absent-mindedly at him. Startled, he stared at her, his uneasiness growing. And then, because he couldn't think of anything to say, he looked quickly away. His heart was pounding as though he had been running. The Mendis girl reminded him vaguely of someone else. He could not think who it might be. After that he began to hear little things about her, little bits of gossip.

People said she did not talk. And she had no friends. All she did was draw, draw, draw. Vikram began to watch her secretly and with new interest. One day he saw her go over to the road island on the Old Tissa Road. He saw her touch the ground, rubbing her hand slowly in the dust. And then she looked up and down the road. Vikram hid behind a tree. What on earth was she doing? he wondered curiously. Again the girl reminded him of someone but he could not be sure whom. He felt an unaccountable fear bubble up in him. He did not see her again for a long while after that. He was busy doing other things. Having discovered furtive sex with the daughter of a local shop-keeper, he was often occupied. The shopkeeper's daughter had not wanted his advances, but Vikram had told her calmly, he would kill her if she told anyone. He had only meant it as a joke but she took him at his word. Pleased with his success, he took her to the back of the garages, close by the railway line. After a while she stopped struggling and accepted the inevitable, crying silently and allowing him to do whatever he wanted. Once, he brought her to Sumaner House, but the servant woman had stared meaningfully at him and although he behaved as though he did not care, the woman's look had put him off. He took the girl back to the garages after that.

Then, as Vikram approached his sixteenth birthday, he met Gerard.

Gerard was not his real name, he was really Rajah Buka, but no one knew this. He owned a gem store in the high street, and although there was an intermittent war on, he did good business with the foreigners who occasionally passed through. Gerard had seen Vikram on several occasions, loitering at the junction buying cheap alcohol. He had struck up a conversation with the boy. He appeared interested in everything Vikram had to say. How well he was doing at school, whether he had any friends. He found out that Vikram talked to no one, and so he invited Vikram to his rooms above the shop and he gave him some *vadi*, a special Tamil sweetmeat. Vikram was pleasantly surprised.

'Where did you get this from?' he asked.

Gerard laughed and gave him a Jaffna mango by way of answer. Vikram was amazed.

'How did you get to Jaffna?' he asked. 'Isn't it impossible to cross Elephant Pass because of the army blocks?'

'Nothing is impossible,' said Gerard meaningfully.

He paused and lit a cigarette.

'How do you feel about being adopted by a Singhala?' he asked casually. 'They killed your family, I heard. And they hate the Tamils, don't they?'

Gerard flicked ash on the floor and waited.

'How d'you feel about that?'

Vikram said nothing. He had been told by his guardian never

to mention the fact he was Tamil. So how did Gerard know? Gerard watched the boy's face and he laughed, finding it hugely funny.

'Don't you want to avenge your family, then?' he asked softly, easily.

Still Vikram said nothing. He felt as though a large cloven-hoofed animal had clambered on his back. The feeling sent a small shiver running up and down his spine. He felt as though his back might break under the strain. The palms of his hands became moist. An image of a young girl pounding spices flashed past him. Gerard smoked his cigarette and continued watching the boy with interest. There was the faintest hint of a smile on his face. When he had finished his cigarette, he went over to a desk and took out a key.

'Come,' he said. 'I want to show you something. Don't worry,' he added, seeing Vikram's wary look. 'We're on the same side.'

Gerard knew he had been right all along. He had told them many times at headquarters, the advantage of boys like Vikram were that they were halfway to being recruited already. Lupus, of course, had been sceptical. He was sceptical of everything Gerard proposed. Naturally he saw Gerard as a threat. Naturally anyone with independent thoughts worried Lupus. Which was precisely why Gerard did not want to operate from the north. There were terrorists and terrorists, Gerard knew. Not all of them were bright. Not all of them had had the kind of univer-sity education that Gerard had, or his never-ending passion and capacity for rhetoric. Not everyone had his vision, he decided regretfully. Having declared war on the Singhalese government, Lupus and his guerrilla organisation wanted a separate Tamil state. But they have no plan, thought Gerard, inclined to laugh, no strategy. Except to blow up as many people, and make as many enemies as possible in the international community. No diplomatic skills, sneered Gerard, whose own plans were far more ambitious. His plan was about *unity*. Of course he *wanted* a different government, what Tamil didn't. But the difference was that Gerard wanted the new government to be central, not separate. And he wanted the Singhalese *out*! He wanted a single, powerful Tamil government for the entire island. *He* wanted majority rule for the minority. Actually, what he really wanted was to be Prime Minister! But first things first, thought Gerard. He was a patient man and he was prepared to wait. There was a little groundwork to be completed, a government to be destabilised. It was work that needed a certain amount of brute force. Which was where the likes of Lupus came in, Gerard believed.

Long ago, when he had been on one of his recruiting visits to Waterlily House, Gerard had noticed Vikram. The boy had been small then, traumatised, but bright. On his next visit to the orphanage he had seen Vikram's guardian-to-be. And that was when he had laid his plan. For as he had noticed instantly, most of the spadework had already been done for Gerard on that memorable afternoon when the Palmyra toddy was on the kitchen table and the red dhal was in the clay pot. Later he heard about the day that Vikram had played hide-and-survive while the sunlight mingled with the screams of his mother and his big sister. The day the sky had boiled and the light had fallen, harsh and green and terrible, down through the rattan roof, and Vikram's sister prepared an offering of pawpaw and king coconut washed with saffron water. On the fateful day when his sister had never made it to the temple, what had to happen, happened. So now, guessing correctly, fully understanding, Gerard earmarked Vikram for greater things. He knew he had picked a winner. Backed by Gerard, Vikram would go far.

Gerard unlocked the drawer and watched Vikram's face.

'Well,' he said very gently. 'Don't tell me you're scared? Don't tell me you won't avenge your family, given a chance?'

'Will you teach me to use it?' asked Vikram, startled from his usual reverie, staring at the gun.

'Patience, patience,' Gerard laughed, closing the drawer, amused by Vikram's sudden interest, preferring it to the boy's usual indifference.

'All things come to those who wait. You must learn to clean it first.'

It was the best way to start; it would keep Vikram's interest alive. Cleanliness was next to godliness, he told the boy, and God was the gun. Vikram liked the idea of the power of God. He liked the mantras Gerard was always reciting. For a moment he felt as though he had a purpose in life. Most of the time the empty, shut-down feeling in his head made him lethargic. But now, for the first time in ages, he felt a stirring within him. A new energy. Avenge your family, Gerard had said. Vikram looked at him and thought, Gerard likes me. The notion was oddly pleasing.

One morning soon after all this happened, having decided he had no need for school, Vikram was on his way to Gerard's gem store when he saw the Mendis girl again. He had forgotten all about her. But she stopped and began to speak to him.

'Don't you go to school any more?' she asked.

Vikram was confused. He thought she didn't speak. And how did she know he was not at school? He stared at her.

'I'm Jim's sister, Nulani, remember?' she said, clearly thinking he did not recognise her. 'You live at Sumaner House, don't you?'

Vikram nodded. Nulani Mendis fumbled in her satchel. She took out a small battered notebook.

'Look,' she said, showing him a drawing.

She was laughing. He could see her teeth, white and very even. Vikram took the book reluctantly. Then, in spite of himself, he too grinned. It was a picture of a teacher no one liked. Nulani Mendis had drawn a caricature, catching his likeness perfectly. Suddenly, Vikram felt shy. The girl was standing close to him. He could smell a faint perfume.

'You're good,' he ventured at last, hesitantly.

For some reason she scared him. There was an air of determination, a certainty about her that confused him. He felt as though she might ask him for something he could not give. He saw she was still smiling at him and again he felt an urge to run away. Then he noticed that close up she was even prettier than she had appeared from a distance. Tongue-tied, he continued to stare at her, hardly aware she was still speaking.

'Has your brother gone to the UK?' he asked finally, with some difficulty, not understanding and wanting to distract her.

The girl shook her head. 'Not yet,' she said.

She smiled again, but this time it was she who hesitated. Then she seemed to withdraw slightly. He thought she appeared older than he remembered, and he saw her eyes were very dark and deep and sad. They seemed full of other puzzling and unnamed things. He stared at her for a moment longer and nodded. Then, making up his mind, he loped off.

That afternoon, after he had finished his target practice with the silencer on the gun, Gerard told Vikram he had something important to say.

'First,' he said, 'well done!' He took the gun from Vikram. 'Congratulations! You've worked hard and as a reward I shall take you on a little operation with me at the end of the month. If you do well at that, there will be bigger and more interesting assignments ahead, OK? And then, in a few months' time you will go to the Eastern province for something extremely important.'

'What?' asked Vikram. 'The Eastern province? Isn't that where the Tigers are trained?'

'Vikram,' said Gerard, 'you must learn not to ask too many questions. You'll be told everything. But, all in good time. Don't ask questions. You aren't going to be an ordinary member of the Tigers, believe me. *You* are both intelligent and a good shot. So now you're going to be trained for something top class. Trust me, men.'

'When?' demanded Vikram.

'Patience, patience,' said Gerard, holding up his hands mock-ingly, shaking his head. 'Patience is what's required now. We've both waited a long time to prepare you for this. Don't ruin things. I promise you the time is coming when you *will* avenge your family. I fully understand how you must feel. Just wait a little longer. And for heaven's sake, Vikram,' he added, 'do me a favour. Go back to school for your exams. You don't want to attract any notice at this stage. If the Mendis girl knows you're absent, then others will too.'

Vikram picked up the gun and held it below his crotch. He stroked the tip of the barrel. He laughed, a high-pitched out-of-control scurrilous screech.

'That's enough,' said Gerard sharply. 'Put it down. It's not a toy. You can have all the things you want if you show restraint. You've been earmarked for great things. Now, go back to school.'

Gerard was aware that underneath his silent exterior Vikram was coiled like a spring. He knew whatever simmered in Vikram was dangerously near the surface. And that it was best to keep a tight control over him. Just in case.

A few days after his exams, Vikram saw the Mendis girl once more. She did not see him. She was hurrying in the direction of the beach. Interested, he decided to follow her. He watched her body move darkly beneath the lime-green skirt, in the sunlight. Her hair was tied up and it swung to and fro as she walked. Where is she going? Vikram wondered curiously.

The road went nowhere in particular. In fact, it was not possible to reach the beach this way without scrambling over the giant cacti. Then the road curved, and suddenly it was possible to see the sea. The beach was completely empty and scorched. Just before the road came to an end, there appeared a long, low house, surrounded by a flower-laden wall and flanked by two stone lions. The top of the wall was covered in barbed wire. Vikram remembered now. It was the house where the UK-returned writer lived. He had seen the man once when he had come to the school. The teachers had shaken their heads, saying he was a Singhalese who was pro the wretched Tamils. What kind of a Singhalese was he? they asked. Still, they had said, he was famous. Misguided, but famous. So they had invited him because of that.

A large jackfruit tree overhung Theo Samarajeeva's garden wall. Its leaves were thick and succulent, and the girl, stopping outside the gate, began to draw in her notebook. She had no idea she was being followed. Nor did she seem to notice there was no shade. Nulani Mendis sat on the withered grass verge absorbed in her drawing, as the low hum of mosquitoes and the drowsy buzz of other, more benign, insects slowed to a halt in the baking air. Across the sun-drenched garden Vikram could just make out the writer, in his pale linen trousers and his white shirt, working at a table on the veranda. The veranda had been bleached white by the sun and appeared dusty in the dazzling light. Then the manservant came out to fetch the girl in for lunch, and shut the gate. And that was all Vikram saw of any of them that day.

*   *   *

Nulani had almost finished the portrait. In a week she would be ready to show both Theo and Sugi.

'I will cook *kiribath*, some milk rice, ' Sugi said. 'And buy the best fish.'

'I shall decide where it must be hung!' said Theo.

An air of gaiety descended. Sugi replaced the lanterns in the trees. And Theo declared the day of the unveiling a holiday from his writing. His work was progressing slowly. In October the film of his second book would be out. He would have to go to London for the premiere.

'For how long will you be gone?' asked Nulani, her eyes suddenly anxious. 'Will they let you come back?'

Her hair was coiled against the back of her neck and a frangipani blossom quivered just above her ear. Theo watched it shake as she moved her head, wondering when it would fall. Once, he nearly put his hand out to catch it. How could he explain to her that no one could stop him coming home? When had he started to call this place home again?

His agent had rung him complaining. It was impossible to get a call through to him, did he know that? The lines were always down. How could he live in a place with no access to the outside world, where the lines were always down? The agent hoped he was working. Through the crackle on the line the agent sounded like a peevish nanny. The summer in London, he told Theo, was disappointing. Wet, cold and miserable. The only consolation, he supposed, was that the telephones worked!

Because the curfew was not in operation just now Theo walked openly on the beach. The sand, ivory and unblemished, seemed to stretch for ever, smooth and interrupted only by his footsteps. One evening Nulani went with him. She had told her mother she was working late on the painting. They walked the wide sweep of beach without seeing anyone, with only the slight breeze and the waves for company. It felt as though they had walked this same beach for an eternity. She walked close to him, like a child, her hand brushing against his arm. He felt her skin, warm against him. He had an urge to take her hand and cradle it in his two hands. He knew she was worrying and he wanted to tell her to stop. But he felt helplessly that he had no right to intrude.

'I feel as if I have known you for ever,' the girl said suddenly. 'D'you think we knew each other in our last birth?'

He swallowed. Her eyes were large and clear. They seemed to mirror the sky. Looking at her he could not think of a single thing to say. Twenty-eight years between them and still he was lost for words, he thought, amazed. They walked the length of the beach and he watched the frangipani in her hair, marvelling that it did not fall; half hoping it would, so that he might catch it.

4

'WHEN CAN I SEE WHAT YOU'VE DONE?' asked Theo impatiently. He sat squinting at the sun. His white shirt was crumpled and the light cast purple shadows against the creases of the cloth.

The girl smiled. 'What if you don't like the painting?' she asked, teasingly. 'What if the money you are paying my mother is wasted?'

'I will love it,' he said, certain. 'No question. I can't wait. Don't forget, I saw it when you began. And another thing, while I remember, I want the money to be kept for your work only. Should I tell your mother that?'

She laughed. What did she need the money for? She had wanted only to paint him. It will soon be October, thought Theo. The rains would come then, he knew. When they broke he would be in London. He did not tell her but he no longer wanted to go. The film had no significance for him. It was all part of another life. A life he seemed to have discarded with alarming ease. Living among his own people, here in this amorphous heat, seeing the mysterious and uneasy ways in which one day flowed into another, he felt as though he had never left.

The girl was sitting close to him on the veranda, staring dreamily at the garden. She was so close her arm brushed against his. She had the ways of the very young, he mused. Physical closeness came naturally. He could see the shadows of her breasts, small dark smudges, rising and falling through her thin white blouse. She looked very cool and self-possessed. And she seemed happier. He realised with shock that loneliness had clung to her like fine sea dust when he had first met her. But now she's content, he thought. Now she is happier.

He wanted to think he had given her something, some comfort for the loss of her father. Even if all he did was offer her a space and encouragement to paint, surely that was better than nothing? He felt a growing certainty in his desire to help her. He felt it rise above the anxieties of this place.

'You must work here when I am in London,' he said.

An idea was forming in his mind. He did not know whether to tell her. He wanted to organise an exhibition of her paintings. But she had opened her notebook and was drawing again, her eyes half shut against the glare. Green and red splashed against him, other stories unfolded. He saw she was drawing his outstretched foot.

'You can't keep drawing me!' he said laughing, moving his foot out of sight. 'Now look, I've been thinking, I want to organise an exhibition of your paintings. I can't do that if you only draw me!'

'Where? Colombo?' Her head was bent over her notebook.

'Yes, maybe,' he said, suddenly wanting to take her to London with him in October.

Thinking, what was wrong with him that he could not bear to be parted from her? He knew nothing about art but even he could see the astonishing things that were conjured up by her hands. They were the hands of a magician. Like shadow puppets they illuminated other dimensions of the world, probing the edges of things and those corners where drifts of light revealed all that had been concealed from him until now.

'You must work hard until I get back,' he said instead, trying to look stern.

So that she threw her head back and burst out laughing. And he saw, how in spite of everything she had been through, her youth could not be contained but was mirrored in her laugh. It was low and filled with happiness. October is still a long way off, he reassured himself. I'll feel differently then.

The hot season was coming to an end and the full moon was ten days away. Twenty kilometres from the town was a sacred site where the festivities were beginning. It had been at the time of the festival that her father had been murdered, Nulani told him. Just before the water-cutting ceremony, in the build-up to *poya,* the religious festival on the night of the full moon. All across the town fear mushroomed in polluted clouds, hanging over two thousand years of faith. Fear seemed inseparable from belief. Men with bare feet walked over red-hot coals or swung themselves on metal hooks across the coconut trees. And all the while, interwoven with the sounds of drums and conch shells, the *nada* filled the air.

'You must be careful,' said Sugi. 'Not everyone is a believer. These are troubled times. And even if,' he added, 'even if they are believers, some people still have evil intent.'

Every year Sugi went to the festival. He always met his family there; he had done this for as long as he could remember. But this year he was worried about leaving Theo on his own.

'This is the time when some people try to put curses on their enemies.'

'Sugi, for heaven's sake, what d'you think is going to happen? No one's interested in *me*. I'll be perfectly fine.'

'But the girl won't be here either,' said Sugi worriedly.

Theo laughed. The girl was going with her mother to the festival. They were going to pray for her brother Jim. To be certain he would get the scholarship.

'Well, I thought you'd be pleased about that,' he teased, giving Sugi a sly look.

'Sir!' said Sugi reproachfully.

'Oh, Sugi, I'm only pulling your leg. I'm going to work like mad while you're away. No distractions, no chatting, you know. No stopping for tea. Just work. I shall have most of this next chapter finished by the time you both get back. You'll see.'

In the now skeleton-staffed Department of Tropical Diseases, a conference, planned two years previously, had to be cancelled because of lack of funds and resources. Many eminent scientists from all over the world, having been invited to give papers, were now told the unstable situation on the island made it impossible to guarantee the safety of their stay. It was a disappointment for all those who had worked tirelessly to eradicate the threat of an epidemic. An article appeared in a scientific journal. 'No animal on earth has touched so directly and profoundly the lives of so many human beings. For all of history and all over the globe the mosquito has been a nuisance, a pain and the angel of death.'

Deep within the jungle the festival was in progress. A god with many hands sat inside the dagoba. The monks had placed him there, hoping he would give an audience to the crowds. This happened every year; it was the highlight of the festival. People came from far and wide to pray to him. The hands of this many-handed god were empty apart from his spear. He looked neither right nor left. If he heard the prayers of the tormented he gave no sign. There were peacocks at his side and sunlight shone on his burnished anklets. Young girls brought him armfuls of offerings, walking miles in the boiling heat. Young men came carrying hope. He received each of them without a word. All day long the drumming and the sounds of elephant bells filled the air in a frenzy of noise and movement. Trumpeters and acrobats walked the roadsides while men with tridents chalked on their foreheads paid penance for ancient inexplicable sins. Elsewhere the ground was strewn with red and yellow flowers and the heavy smell of cinnamon was underfoot. There were giant mounds of sherbet-pink powders and uncut limes piled up on silver platters everywhere.

The many-handed god watched them all. He watched the backs of the women bent in devotion. Who knew what they prayed for? Was it for abundance in their wombs? Or was it simply peace for the fruits of these same wombs that they desired? The crowds came with their coins tied in cloth, with their ribbons of desires, their cotton-white grief and their food. As night approached a full moon arose across the neon sky silhouetting the dagoba, white and round, with a single spike pointing at the stars. Hundreds of coconut flames fanned an unrelenting heat.

Midnight approached and the temple drums grew louder, announcing the arrival of the Kathakali Man of Dance. The crowds gasped. With his pleated trousers and beaded breast-plates, the Kathakali Man pointed his fingers skywards. He seemed to be reaching for the stars. With ancient gesture and sandstone smile, he danced for the gaping, amazed gathering. The Kathakali Man had a many-faceted jewel that gleamed in his navel and a peacock's cry deep in his throat. His drum tattooed yet another ancient tale, telling of those things which were allowed and those which were forbidden. His was a dance of warning. History ran through his veins, giving him authority. Everyone heard him in the neon-green night but not everyone was capable of interpreting what he said. Those who ignored him did so at their peril, he warned.

Long ago, in the days before the trouble, people from England used to come to see him. They came simply because they knew they could find native colour and because, in this sacred place, even the statues smiled. They did not understand the real meaning of a sacred site. They came for rest, for healing herbs and pungent oils. And sometimes the many-handed god welcomed them, and sometimes he did not. Now that the troubles were here no one came from England. Nothing but a steady stream of hope walked through the jungle to the dagoba. Nothing but despair showed through the brave colours of the processions.

Sugi stood in the crowds watching the festival. He was waiting for his relatives. While he waited he looked around him to see if there were others he knew. He noticed Mrs Mendis. Ah, observed Sugi, she is here for her son Lucky Jim. Born with the kernel of luck that Mrs Mendis protected with the husk of her own life. No doubt she wanted the kernel to grow. She's a true believer and so she knows, true believers had a better chance. She wants nothing for herself, thought Sugi. But then, he noticed, Mrs Mendis had forgotten about her daughter. Sorrow, like too much sun, has blinded her. Mrs Mendis left her clay curd pots, her crimson flowering pineapple and her *kiribath*, milk rice, at the feet of the god. Without a doubt, thought Sugi, watching silently, the god will grant her wish. For it must surely have been decided in another life that Jim's luck could only grow. Then Sugi glanced at Nulani Mendis. The child was lost in thought. What future will *she* have? he wondered, pity flooding his heart. With a mother like this! Sugi had been watching the girl for months. He was astonished at how she had changed. When she had first come to the beach house she had been silent and unhappy. Then slowly she had begun to blossom. In the beginning, he remembered, her unhappiness had blotted out her light. But gradually she changed. Her eyes shone, she laughed. And she talked all the time. Sometimes she drove Sir mad, Sugi knew. Sometimes they would exchange looks of amusement. And recently, thought Sugi, pensive now, Sir had a different look in his eyes. But Sir himself seemed unaware of this. Only Sugi knew.

A sudden harsh sound in the trees sent a flock of iridescent blue magpies bursting into the sky as though being lifted by a gust of wind. Several people threw themselves to the ground, crying. Was this an ill omen? Sugi looked uneasily around him. There was no wind. Ancient laws were written all over this sacred site. Sugi was a man of simplicity. And he was afraid. He saw the girl ahead of him in the procession look up at the magpies. She was smiling at some secret thought of her own. Yesterday she had let Sugi look at her latest painting. It was nearly finished and was a remarkable painting, of glossy greens and quiet violets. It was full of something else as well, Sugi saw. Something Nulani Mendis had no idea of. Painting was what she had brought into this life, Sugi told himself, watching her now. It was her fate. He knew her talent would never leave her. He watched as she bent her head and prayed. He knew she was praying for her brother. And he knew there were other undiscovered longings in her heart.

The procession had brought all sorts of people out. Some of them were not the kind of people who usually went on pilgrimages.

One of the people in the crowd was Vikram. Gerard had told him about the sacred site.

'Go and see it,' he had said. 'Mingle, learn what goes on there. Watch the Buddhist monks and look out for the army checkpoints. You should always talk to the army. Get them used to your face. Could be useful for the future.'

And he winked at Vikram. Then he put his hand on the boy's shoulders, never noticing how he winced, not realising Vikram did not like being touched.

So Vikram went to the festival. The anniversary of the massacre of his family was approaching. Every year around this time he had nightmares. He would wake up to the sound of grinding teeth and discover they were his own. He would wake with an erection or with his sheet wet. And, always, he would wake with a skullful of anger punctured as though by knives. In the morning he was fine again, back to his usual indifferent self, with all disturbance forgotten. But for a couple of nights, close to the anniversary of the deaths, things were bad. On these occasions, Vikram heard, quite clearly, as if from a distant part of Sumaner House, his mother's muffled screams, his sister's voice crying out in Tamil. Why had they cried so much? What had they hoped to achieve? Mercy, perhaps? Had they not realised they were about to die? That no amount of crying would help them in the long dark place they had reached? From where he crouched, rigid under the bed, all Vikram had seen were their hands waving in a gesture of helplessness. The hands that had held him moments before, and had stroked his head, were now waving their goodbye. From his hiding place he could see fingers threshing and flaying the air, engaged in some ancient struggle, and in his dreams, so many years later, it was this image, of those hands forever beating the air, that he still saw. Gerard had reminded Vikram that his family needed to be avenged. They were waiting for the day, Gerard said, when, like a half-finished jigsaw, they would be made whole again.

So Vikram walked through the jungle, following the sound of the drums like everyone else. Thinking his own thoughts. On the way he passed a Coca-Cola lorry and a black Morris Minor. They were tangled and smashed together in a crash. Curious, he stopped to investigate. Bodies were tossed carelessly across the overgrown path, reddish-brown liquid frothed from under the lorry. Just looking at it made Vikram thirsty. Other people had visited the site of the crash before him. They had plundered the victims, taken their money and their jewellery. There was nothing left to take. Vikram stared. One of the bodies was that of a woman. A long deep ridge exposed the tendons and muscles across one part of her face. Bone jutted out. A fountain of blood flowed from her mouth. Her hands moved feebly like an ant on its back, clawing the air. Vikram looked at her impassively. She was beginning to bloat and her lips reminded him of the blood-swollen bellies of mosquitoes he was forever swiping. But, thought Vikram walking on, she did not look in *so* much pain. How long would it take for her to die? he wondered idly. Would she be dead by the time he had walked two dozen steps, or half a mile? Would she be dead by the time he reached the sacred site? Vikram continued on his way, following the distant noise of drums and the monkeys that swung in front of him from tree to tree. He could hear the bells of the Kathakali dancers somewhere in the distance.

He came to a reservoir. When he had been quite small, his mother had taken him back to the village where she had been born. There had been a reservoir there too. It was so large that Vikram had thought it was the sea. In those days Vikram had not yet seen the sea. There were trees all around the banks of this great stretch of water, frightening jungle vegetation, tangled and ugly. Branches and creepers trailed succulently along the forest floor. Small emerald birds flew harshly about. Vikram was three years old and he had been frightened. His aunt or his sister, he could not remember which, held him up in the water, someone else bathed him. Vikram had cried out. They told him the water was pure and clean. Later, sitting on the steps of a now forgotten house, the same girl, whoever she was, taught him to knit. Knit one, purl one.

'See,' she had said, laughing. 'Look, he has learned to knit. Baby is very clever.'

The sun had beaten down on his head as he sat on the step of the house.

'I'm thirsty,' he had said in Tamil and instantly they had brought him a green plastic cup of king coconut juice and held it while he drank thirstily.

They had called him Baby; it was the only word of English they knew and they were proud they too could speak English, even though they had not been to school. Vikram knew they had loved him. Their excited voices had encircled him, round and round, picking him up and kissing him until he laughed with pleasure. He supposed it was pleasure.

The reservoir near his mother's house was smooth and clean, and aquamarine. A mirror reflecting the sky. The one he was passing now was brown and mostly clogged with weed. There had been no rain here for a long time.

After he had prayed for his sister's family and for his mother's health, Sugi took his leave of them. He needed to get back home. His mother, who was old and frailer since he saw her last, kissed him goodbye. She was glad her son was doing so well, working for Theo Samarajeeva. A decent man, she said, a man for the Sri Lankan people, the kind of man that was desperately needed. They had heard all about his books and now there was to be a film too, about the terrible troubles in this place. It was good, she told her son, the world needed to hear about their suffering.

'But you must be careful, no?' Sugi's brother-in-law asked him privately. 'This man will make enemies too. You must advise him, he will have forgotten how it is here. He has lived in the UK. They are honourable there. And you must be careful. You too will be watched.'

Sugi knew all this. He left his red and silver offerings and his temple blossom for the many-handed god and just as he was about to leave a monk gave him a lighted lamp to carry back in. Perhaps, thought Sugi trustingly, this was a good omen.

Overhead, huge firework flowers and tropical stars filled the heavens as he rode home on his bicycle. Because it was so late, instead of taking the coast road he cut across the outskirts of the jungle. He kept close to the path; in the distance he could see the reservoir gleaming in the moonlight. He passed a largish village on his left. There were green and red lights threaded among the branches of the trees and a small *kade* was still open selling sherbet and plantains. Because of the festivities there was no curfew here, and people strolled along the street. A smell of gram and hot coconut oil drifted towards him. Children shouted, dogs barked, youths loitered. Had it not been for two army tanks and armed soldiers at either end of the village forming a makeshift checkpoint, it would have been impossible to know there was a war on. Soon Sugi was through the village and heading for home.

Night stretched across the road. The sky glowed like polished glass. He would have been back in less than twenty minutes but for the obstruction. The Coca-Cola lorry no longer frothed liquid; the corpses lay naked and silvery, bathed in moonlight.

Everything from the Morris Minor had been stripped bare. Seats, steering wheel, wing mirrors, even the windscreen wipers had gone. All that remained was the skeleton of a car. Suddenly a jeep roared round the bend of the road. Sugi, who had stopped, wheeled his bicycle quickly towards a clump of trees and hid. A soldier leapt down and took out a can. He began to pour petrol over the bodies. Another jeep skidded to a halt and then another. Camouflage soldiers spilled noisily out. Sugi froze. The soldiers poured petrol over the Morris Minor. Someone was shouting orders in Singhala. His face seemed familiar. For a moment Sugi puzzled over this. Then the smell of fuel drifted across the narrow deserted road. It was strong and metallic. In another minute there was an explosion as the Morris Minor blew up. Black smoke choked the edges of the trees. The whole jungle seemed on fire, awash with the sour smells of tamarind and eucalyptus, and something else, something rotten and deep and terrifying. Hiding behind the clump of trees, Sugi recognised the smell. It had never been far from his life since the war had worsened. He waited, knowing there was nothing he could do. He had wanted to see if anyone was, by some miracle, still alive, to raise the alarm if this was so, but he knew now it was an impossibility. The flames would burn for a long time. He felt the heat from where he stood, banking up against him, taut and terrible against his body. Sweat and fear poured down his face and mixed with his despair. There was nothing he could do now. The soldiers stood at a safe distance from the bonfire. For a while they strutted around their vehicles, laughing hollowly, slapping each other on the back. In the moonlight Sugi could see their Kalashnikovs glinting. Then, after what seemed an eternity, they piled into the jeeps and went with a screech of tyres, leaving skid marks on the road, their voices receding swiftly. All that was left were the outstretched arms of the flames, the moon as witness, and an unmarked, communal grave. Far away in the distance he could hear a faint lonely trumpeting. Somewhere, in some impenetrable corner of the jungle, an elephant was preparing to charge. Turning his bicycle towards the road Sugi began to peddle furiously, chasing the moonlight. Carrying his distress with the slapping motion of his sarong, freewheeling down the hill. Silently. Riding his bicycle, accepting his pain. The witness to all that had passed.

The festival was over and the procession had dispersed. The two-toned chanting hung loosely in the air, floating above the white dagoba and away towards the primeval jungle. The monks packed up the many-handed god as though he were a puppet. His anklets made no sound, his paper arms were crushed by the many prayers thrust in them. The monks put away his silver sword. It was time for him to rest. As always after days of observing human nature and all its eternal struggle, the monks were exhausted. Collecting up the prayer papers they packed them into a satinwood box. Then they burned some cinnamon sticks for good luck. The smoke rose thin and beautiful like a mosquito net. Fragments of temple powders and yellow saffron-stained offerings remained on the ground. Somewhere in the forest the devil-bird screeched, but most of the sacred site collapsed like a concertinaed paper lantern, returning to normal. An ordinary village in the jungle; there were so many of them. Overhead, storm clouds walked the telegraph poles, electric blue as magpie wings. As yet nothing happened but the sea currents close by the shore had changed and the fishermen, wisely, did not put out to sea. They were waiting for the storm to arrive.

*   *   *

From his bedroom Theo Samarajeeva had an uninterrupted glimpse of the beach. The wind had begun to die down and although the coconut palms still beat themselves in a frenzy, the sky had changed colour. It was seven o'clock in the morning and a patch of blue had begun to spread across the horizon. While Sugi and the girl had been absent Theo had worked hard on his book. They had seemed to be away for an eternity. Because he had not liked the silence or their absence, he had worked furiously. The book would be finished on time. The girl would come this morning, Theo knew. She would be here soon. Then they would have the great unveiling of the paintings. There were three paintings now. He could hardly wait.

For days after Nulani had left for the festival, the smells of linseed oil and colours had hovered around the house but then it had grown fainter. Theo, remembering once more the loss of other smells, other memories, had buried himself in his work. But then Sugi came back; he had returned late last night. Theo had waited up for him, anxiously, listening out for the squeak of his bicycle brakes and the sound of the gate. He came in and they had shared a beer, although Sugi had seemed exhausted and had not wanted to talk.

'There are many, many more thugs about now,' was all he had said when Theo asked him about the festival. 'Much more than last year. They are all men in the pay of the army. You must not drive out into the jungle.'

'Did you see anyone you knew? Did you see Nulani?'

'Yes,' Sugi had said. He had been unusually silent. 'I think I saw her uncle too.'

'What? With her?' Theo had asked, alarmed. Talk of the uncle always made him uneasy.

'No, no. I saw him on my way back. He was with other people.'

Sugi had looked strained and unhappy in the light from the veranda. There had been something worn and nervous about him, something hopeless.

'Are you all right?' Theo had asked finally, wondering if there was trouble with his family. He had been lonely without him but perhaps Sugi needed some time to himself?

'Yes. I am fine. A little tired. It was a long ride back. And I am tired with how this country has become.'

Theo had become alarmed, then. Sugi had sounded more than tired. He had sounded depressed. They finished their beer to the plaintive sounds of the geckos and the thin whine of swarming mosquitoes that inhabited the humid night. There was no doubt, a storm had been brewing and so, partly because of this and partly because Sugi clearly was not in a mood to talk, Theo had gone to bed.

Towards dawn it had begun to rain. Hot broken lines of water, clear blue shredded ribbons, curtains of rain. The view from the window was fragmented by it, changed and coloured by the water. Smells like newly opened blossoms rose up and lifted into the air. Here and there they flew, rough earth and mildew smells, caterpillar green and plantain savoury. The smells woke Theo, who dressed hurriedly, breathing in the scent of gravel and insects, of hot steam and rainy-morning breakfast. Now, sitting out on the veranda, he lit his pipe and the musty smell of pleasure joined the day. He could hear Sugi moving around making egg hoppers. The noise suggested that Sugi was happier this morning. Whatever had bothered him last night had passed. Relieved, Theo listened to the coconut oil sizzling as it rose in clouds above the blackened pan and it seemed to him as though it had been years and years since he had last seen Nulani Mendis. He knew she would not arrive until the rain had stopped.

5

SHE CAME AS SOON AS SHE COULD. It was later than she had meant it to be but the rain, and the news that her brother had won his scholarship, and her uncle's sharp eyes following her suspiciously, had all contrived to make her late. But she came, with the last of the raindrops trailing the hem of her red dress and her long hair swinging loosely as she hurried. He was out on the veranda, waiting with barely concealed impatience, just as he had told her he would be, smoking his pipe. He watched her as she rushed in through the unlatched gate, caring nothing for the rain drumming the ground or the branches that shook and showered drops of water on her. Her dress was stained with dark patches of water. And she was smiling.

'Well,' he said, coming swiftly towards her, his worries all ironed out by the sight of her. 'Are you going to stand there for ever?'

He made as if to touch her but then, changing his mind, smiled instead. The rain vanished and the previous day's vague anxieties disappeared with it. The leaves shone as though they were studded with thousands of precious stones. And the whole day suddenly seemed extraordinarily iridescent and beautiful.

'Well,' he said again, and he felt, without quite understanding, the light touch of her gladness.

The girl was smiling at him with barely suppressed excitement. Taking his hand she led him back to the veranda, making him sit down, laughing, making him wait. She gave him her latest notebook to look through, while she went to fetch the paintings. But where was Sugi?

'Wait,' said Theo, but then Sugi appeared from nowhere and he too was smiling, for Sir's face had suddenly become transformed.

Sugi came out with the tray on which was a beer for Theo and a jug of Nulani's favourite lime juice. There was a small plate of *boraa*. Theo would not look at the paintings until Sugi had poured himself a beer. Sugi grinned. Sir was impossible of late. Sunlight danced across the canvases as she turned them round.

They were smaller than he expected. In one, Theo sat at his desk in front of a lacquered bowl of bright sea urchins and red coral. The mirror, scratched and marked with age, reflected a different interior. It was of his flat in London. There were peonies in the mirror-interior but none beside the bowl of sea urchins. A small mosquito with spindly legs rested on the edge of the polished wood. Theo sat working at his typewriter. The portrait he had glimpsed months earlier was the largest of them all. It too was finished. The girl had painted herself in one corner of it, as a splash of green and white and black hair. A thin glass jug, cracked and brittle, stood on a corner of the shelf beside Theo. Sunlight poured into it. His face was turned towards the light, looking out at the trees, caught in the moment between thinking and writing. And with an expression in his painted eyes that now confused him. It was the expression of a younger man, he felt; himself perhaps in another life. How had she caught it? How had she even known of it? Oh! Christ, he thought. Oh! Christ. He felt a wave of something, some rush of clumsy tenderness wash over him. It left him suffused with certainty so that when finally he could speak again the day poured its endless light over him too.

'You are a truly beautiful painter,' he said at last, feeling the weightlessness of his words, the mysterious nature of the language as it floated dreamily, tumbling into the thick and languid air. 'Others must see your work,' he said, taking in her shining eyes, thinking, no, there were no words for what he felt. No language, however many civil wars were fought, was fine enough to describe his thoughts. Thinking too, certain also, that her paintings must go to England. It was the thing he could do. Somehow.

The rain was terrible. It filled the upturned coconut shells that littered the ground everywhere. Clear, round mirrors of water reflecting patches of the sky. The Buddhist monks, when they remembered, kicked them over, spilling water. But mostly they did not remember. The curfew was back and there were new things on their minds. Although they knew it was the time when the swarms of mosquitoes appeared, thick as smoke and deadly as flying needles, they were busy with other matters. Language was on their minds, the importance of Singhalese as opposed to Tamil. The army too, who in peacetime might have been employed to spray every house with DDT, now had more important preoccupations. So the rains fell largely unheeded, forming glassy ponds in the shade of the coconut palms, in ditches and in stagnant tanks. Reflecting the sky. It was a mosquito's paradise. They floated their dark canoes on these ponds among the lotus flowers and the water lilies. Waiting for the night. But for humans this was no paradise, and those foolish enough to think this a place to toy with, did so at their peril.

Two British journalists were shot dead. A third man, a photographer, escaped with his life, having lost his left eye. Two Indian students had limbs mutilated. Their stories eventually made news and the international press issued a worldwide warning. Stay away, for the unseen laws that governed this place were not to be tampered with. But the rains, unheeding in the midst of all that was terrible, fell indifferently, and many people thought this was a blessing.

Later, after they had hung the paintings and the girl had gone home, Theo went back to look at them. Paint and linseed oil gathered in the room where they were hung and her presence was everywhere. Again he felt the dull ache of it. He remembered her, in her red dress, with patches of rain falling on it, looking at him, alert as a bird that had evaded a storm. He thought of her silent concentration over the past months as she worked in the studio, and once again he was filled with wonder. At her youth, at her unwavering certainty, and her talent. Staring at the smudges of paint, the light and shade that transformed into the edges and corners of things, he felt privy to her thoughts. He noticed she had placed the framed photograph of Anna in the reflected mirror room. Petals from a vase of peonies fell beside it. She had painted not just a likeness; she had painted some other dimension, some invisible otherness of how he must once have been. And the look on his face, where was that from? Closing his eyes, Theo felt the heat and intimacy of the moment. Sugi, coming in just then, stood looking silently with him. He too saw the face of a much younger man. How had this happened, so quickly?

'I must take her to Colombo,' Theo said, 'to meet a painter friend of mine. I must ask her mother if she will allow it. We could go up on the train.' He nodded, his mind made up.

'Sir,' said Sugi, but then he hesitated.

What could he say? It was too late, what had not meant to be had already happened. He saw it clearly; Sir's eyes were shining like the girl's. Trusting like a child's, full of unspent love. So what was there to say? What was there to stop?

'Be very careful, Sir,' was all he said in the end. 'I told you this girl's family is watched. You do not yet fully understand this ruined place. The uncle does not know you yet but, now that the boy is going to the UK, he is there all the time of late.'

Sugi hesitated again, not knowing how to speak of those things lodged in his heart.

'You do not see how we have changed,' he said eventually. 'We are so confused by this war. Sometimes I hear people arguing that it is the fault of the British. That even though they have gone, we still have an inferior feeling in us. Who can tell?' He shrugged, helplessly. 'Our needs are so many, Sir, and our attitudes have changed because of them.'

A paradise that has been lost, thought Theo, staring out to sea. Before he could speak, Sugi remembered the chicken.

'Who knows where the enemy is, Sir?' he told Theo. 'There are many people who will envy you, who might put the evil eye on you.'

Sugi spoke earnestly, even though he knew his words fell on deaf ears. Sir, he saw, would take no notice. He knew it was not in Theo's nature to be careful. He had been away for too long and too much living in alien places had affected him; it had made him fearless. And he had no time for these dark, point-less evil eyes that could decide what should and could not be. So he watched as Theo went to see Mrs Mendis.

It was as Sugi said: the uncle was there but there was no sign of the girl. The uncle listened without comment. Theo talked quickly, drinking only milk tea, refusing offers of beer, as he tried to impress on them the girl's talent.

'My friend teaches at the British School, he is a well-known painter. He has many contacts in the art world. He is an elderly

Singhalese,' he added, speaking to the uncle directly, knowing the man's politics, his prejudices. The uncle said nothing.

'If she is taken on at the art school she'll be funded by a scholarship,' Theo continued, not knowing if this was really the case.

The uncle swirled his beer. His face was set. What is wrong with me? thought Theo. I am behaving as though he frightens me, when in fact he's harmless, just a provincial man. Sugi's anxiety has rubbed off on me, that's all. The uncle looked at Theo. Then he squashed and tossed the empty can out into the darkening garden. Mrs Mendis began to scold him, calling the servant to pick it up. The uncle stood up, tightening the belt of his khaki trousers. He looked across at Theo; he was smaller than Theo but wider, fatter. His lips were soft mounds of flesh, well defined and full of blood. He laughed a strange high-pitched laugh, ironic and humourless.

'Art!' he said. His voice was falsetto with amusement. 'We are a country at war, trying to survive in spite of the Tamils. What do we need art for, men?' He looked briefly and threateningly towards the house. 'It isn't art she needs. At this rate, she will have a serious problem finding a husband. But it is not up to me, it's up to her mother, no?' And then he went, down the veranda steps, into the threatening rain and out to his waiting jeep, his headlights probing the silent road ahead like yellow sticks of dynamite.

Well, thought Theo, breathing a sigh, that wasn't so bad after all. The man is harmless enough. They would go to Colombo the next morning. Because the paintings were still wet he decided they would go by car. He would pick the girl up early and, with luck, they would be at his friend's studio by mid-morning. And because of the curfew they would be back by dark.

'Tell her to bring her notebooks,' he said to Mrs Mendis.

*   *   *

80

Sugi lit the paper lanterns. They cast a trelliswork of patterns on the walls of the house. Geckos moved between the shadows. He fastened a shutter against the breeze. Then he went into the girl's studio to look at the paintings of Theo. He was alone; Sir was still over at the girl's house. He seemed to have been gone for a long time. Sugi's unease was increasing. He remembered the first time he met Sir, on that afternoon as he walked from the station, carrying his smart leather bags. Sugi had had a good feeling about Mr Samarajeeva. He had thought, ah, here is a real gentleman. He had not known what an important man he was then, of course. But he had seen in him the kind of person that no longer existed. Someone fine and just and clever, thought Sugi, staring at the paintings. Someone who had not been corrupted by the war. It had all been there, quite plainly in Sir's face, even on that very first day. Which was why Sugi had agreed to work for him. When he had found out that Theo was a widower, he began to wonder what had driven him to come back to this place. And later, when he knew more, he had hoped the old home would heal him.

'They are my people here, Sugi,' Theo had told him many times in the following months, as they sat drinking their beer late into the night. 'I have nothing more in Europe.'

'Did your wife have family, Sir?'

'Oh yes, but . . . well, she was not close to them, and after she died they had nothing more to say to me. Anna and I were too bound up in each other, you see. Perhaps it was a bad thing, I thought afterwards it probably was. I don't really know.'

He had fallen silent, straining to remember her voice. Bullfrogs croaked in the undergrowth and in the distance the Colombo express hooted as it rushed past.

'We never seemed to need other people much,' he had continued, lighting his pipe. 'That was part of the trouble. So that even the absence of children did not matter in the end. Only our friends Rohan and Giulia understood.'

Sugi had made no comment. He would not pry. The shadows from the oil lamp had lain in a dark band across Theo's eyes. It had the curious effect of making him look as though he wore a blindfold. His voice had been barely audible, suddenly without energy.

'We had wanted children. But then she died. After that, what was there to want? I was glad we had none.'

He had spread his hands helplessly in front of him as the silence between them lengthened. The air had been soft with unspoken affection.

'You know, Sir, you will meet her again,' Sugi had said finally. 'These things are not lost. Loving someone is never wasted. You will find her again some day, when you least expect. I have heard of such things happening.'

Theo had sighed. He was tired, he'd said. Tired of running.

'I simply had to come back home, Sugi,' he had said again. 'It was the only place I could think of. After she died everything I did, every place I went to reminded me of all I had lost. I was like a man suffering from burns. Even breathing was difficult.'

He had shaken his head, unable to go on. In the distance the sea, too, had sighed. At last he had roused himself.

'In the end, I knew, if I were to survive I would have to come back. I thought I might make sense of events once I was here.'

Sugi had nodded, moved. He understood. Underneath the mess they had created for themselves, the land still had powerful ancient roots. It was still capable of healing. One day it would go back to what it had been before.

'I know. I can wait,' Theo had said as they had sat surveying the garden. 'I'm in no hurry.'

Sir is an idealist, thought Sugi, now, going over the

conversation in his mind, staring at the painting, astonished all over again at the Mendis girl's talent. The child has seen into Sir's heart. She knew. Because she felt it too. Sugi shivered; in spite of the heat, he shivered. They are both such children, he thought. The girl is too young, and he is too innocent. It is left to me to look after them. This is a fine state of affairs. And then Sugi went to fetch a glass of cold beer, thankful that the sound of the gate being opened meant, at least, that Sir had returned from Mrs Mendis's house unscathed.

There had been no problem with Nulani leaving. Contrary to what Sugi had said, the uncle did not return in the morning, and Mrs Mendis had been friendly enough. She asked Theo if Nulani was likely to get another commission. The money was always useful and what with Jim leaving for the UK there were even more expenses. Theo continued to dislike the woman but, folding these thoughts, he slipped them out of sight. He smoothed them down like a sheet on an unmade bed. And then the girl came out with her bouquet of excitement, her dress a scarlet splash across the day, and all his momentary irritation with the mother, and his anxiety over the uncle, all of it vanished and the morning shifted and changed into a different, glorious focus. He turned the car around on the gravel and they left. The edges of her hair were still damp from her early-morning shower.

Theo thought it was best to take the coast road. In spite of the checkpoints and occasional roadblocks, it was quicker and more straightforward. He had wedged two of the paintings in the boot of the car but the third, being so much larger, rested on the back seat. The girl was trying to hide her excitement and failing. It escaped in little green tendrils, curling itself around him, rising like the wisps of mist that were coming in from the sea. It was going to be another scorching day. The girl's excitement was such that Theo was certain she had not slept much.

'You'll be exhausted by lunchtime,' he said looking at her, thinking she looked as though it was Christmas. As though she was about to open her presents. He hid his own excitement at having a whole day with her, talking to her, having her paintings looked at, keeping his delight quiet and cool, even though all he wanted was to hold her small hand. The day lay ahead of them, as clear as the sea emerging from its mist. It felt, for Theo, a snatch-back from his youth. He did not think all this, not in so many words. All he saw was the smoothness of the beach and the shining excited eyes of the girl.

'Why don't you try to take a nap?' he said, pretending to be tired, trying to sound bored. 'It will take an hour to reach Colombo, maybe longer. Why don't you have a little sleep, no?'

And then he burst out laughing, looking at her astonished face and her total incomprehension.

'Well,' he said, smiling, pretending to yawn, teasing her some more, 'It's what you would do if you were *my* age!'

And he thought again how her eyes were like dark cherries.

'Your friend, what is he like?' asked Nulani.

The road wound its way along a picturesque stretch of the coastline. Groups of rocks thrust their way into the sea. Giant cacti clung to the edges of the sand. Coconut palms fringed the beach, sometimes so densely that only glimpses of sea could be seen. At other places whole stretches of white sand, empty and clean, unfolded before them, fringed by the lacy edge of the waves and marked by the empty railway line.

'Rohan? He is a fine painter. He used to live in London, which was where I met him. He was my wife's friend to start with. She knew him long before I did; she used to buy his paintings. Then, after I met Anna, I saw one of them hanging in her apartment and I wanted to meet him too. Because I liked the painting, and because he was my countryman.' Rohan, he thought, how to describe Rohan? How to describe the times they had spent together? Rohan, with his Italian wife Giulia, and Anna, in that other, distant life. The years of holidaying together, in Venice, in the Tuscan hills. The evenings spent arguing and drinking wine, the affection. And afterwards, Rohan and Giulia at the funeral, beside him as he stood blinded by the unnatural brightness of his pain, rejecting all offers of friendship. But they had not minded. Like the true friends they were, they had understood, had waited patiently, year upon year, writing to him, telling him about their lives, their decision to return to Rohan's home in Colombo, in spite of the trouble. So that slowly, given time, Theo began to write back to them. They were his dearest friends. Nulani was watching him intensely.

'You will like them both,' he said, knowing that they would love the girl.

The sun was climbing to its hottest point as they reached the first checkpoint. The currents had subsided and the sea was calm. There were hardly any waves now. The fishing boats had put out to sea again. At the checkpoint a woman soldier examined their passes and searched the car.

'The paintings are wet,' Nulani said, but it was too late, she had already touched them.

'You can't go much further,' the soldier told them flatly. 'The road is blocked. You will have to leave the A2 and go inland through the coconut groves until you get to the ruined city and then you can pick up the Colombo road again after that. There is another checkpoint further up. After that you will have to turn right.'

The detour would add half an hour to their journey.

'There has been an incident,' the woman soldier continued. 'It's over now but it will take some time to clear.'

85

'An accident?' asked Theo.

'No, an incident,' she repeated shortly. And then she smiled, a swift flash of uneven white teeth, from some other long-vanished and different kind of life.

'Look for the ruined city,' she said abruptly. ' It's very beauti-ful. If you are an artist,' she glanced briefly at Nulani, nodding her head, 'you will like it there. You can make a *pujas*, pray for a safe journey.'

And she waved them on.

Further along the road, about a mile away, the land swept into a wide long bend. A whole stretch of beach lay before them. Then the road forked, turning sharply to the right, heading into the coconut grove; suddenly the roadblock the soldier had promised was in front of them. Two army trucks acted as a barrier. A police car was parked to one side, its light flashing pointlessly. On the edge of the cliff, overlooking the sea, there were two limousines piled into one another. It looked at first as though there had been an accident. But there was no ambulance present. Only uniformed men with sub-machine guns paced the road. In the high bright morning light the dead strewn across the side of the road bore the strangest resemblance to piles of scattered dirty laundry, bundled up and ready for washing. All around was the sweet drenching smell of an invisible blossom. There was, too, a curious dry odour, dead and chemical, which Theo knew could only have come from explosives. He stopped the car and a soldier, a man of about twenty-five, came up to the open window. Theo handed over their documents.

'What happened?'

His voice, flanked by the waves and the sound of a train rushing suddenly past, seemed to come from a long way away.

'Open the boot!'

Theo was aware of the girl's anxiety. All the time he was

opening the boot and holding the pictures for the man to see, telling the soldier the paint was not dry and that they were taking them to the university to show Professor Fernando, all that time, while the huge seagulls wheeled overhead, her anxiety drifted towards Theo. When they were finally dismissed, with a sharp movement of a rifle butt, the day itself had acquired a sour hard taste to it. Turning the car into the coconut grove, Theo saw a slender brown arm, fingers curled slightly. It was severed below the rolled-up sleeves of an otherwise clean white shirt. An ordinary white shirt, the sort he owned.

It was another quarter of an hour to the ruined city with its votive dagoba. A woman selling king coconuts stood bare-headed in the burning sun. She knew nothing about the roadblock or the massacre at the crossroads, but the detour meant she had sold nearly all her coconuts even before ten o'clock. They drank the cold coconut water and wandered around the dry earth-caked ruins. Theo watched the girl, a flutter of scarlet cloth against the orange lichen-covered statues. She stood with her head bent, eyes closed, and the sickness and horror and the pity of what he had just seen was touched with the sweetness of her presence, turning slowly within him. They were due at Rohan's place by eleven.

Through the wing mirror Vikram watched them drive off. He was dismantling a Kalashnikov. Gerard had moved the car to a wooded area not far from the ruined city. Now he rubbed the dust from the wing mirror so he could see the Mendis girl more clearly. He swatted a mosquito on his arm and wiped the blood off.

'The mosquitoes are back,' he told Gerard.

Gerard grunted and mopped his brow. They had had a successful morning. Seven dead and the Singhalese army in a quandary. What could be better? Nobody knew there were any Tigers in the locality.

'They didn't see us,' was all he said as the car disappeared round the bend of the road. 'Now you should go back. Walk around the town, talk to people, let them see you. D'you understand? Vikram, are you paying attention?' he added sharply.

Gerard was still a little jumpy. He knew he was happiest when he did not have to do the dirty work. But he had not wanted Vikram to tackle it alone. Not this time anyway. Now all he wanted was to get rid of the boy. He was not interested in his chatter. Vikram's calmness had stunned Gerard. To his astonishment, the boy had hardly batted an eyelid. He's a tough nut, thought Gerard, tougher than even I expected. Handled properly, he could be quite dangerous. Vikram was nodding. He was vaguely aware that Gerard was nervous but by contrast he felt suddenly exhilarated and ready for more action.

'It's important you don't blow your cover. So make sure as many people as possible see you. Pity you don't have more friends. Can't you talk to that Mendis girl?'

'Maybe,' said Vikram, instantly scowling.

'I would take you over to that fellow, you know, Theo Samarajeeva, but the servant is suspicious of me.'

'I'll talk to her,' Vikram said, rather too quickly. He did not want Gerard to get involved with the girl.

'OK, now go,' said Gerard. 'I'll take the gun back to my place. No, Vikram,' he said firmly, before the boy could protest. 'It's for your own safety. You don't want to get caught carrying a weapon. I'll see you back at the shop after dark.' He placed the two dismantled Kalashnikovs in his rucksack. 'It'll take you about an hour on foot,' he said. 'Take the track through the jungle and go straight to the town and have a beer. I'll see you later. And, Vikram,' he added as the boy got out of the car, 'well done!'

Vikram slunk into the trees. He knew this path well, having gone over it many times with Gerard after dark. He would follow the track until he reached the river and then it would be another quarter of a mile until he reached the outskirts of the town. After he had had his beer he would go and find the shopkeeper's daughter, and take her to the back of the garages, he decided. The day had left him with an unexpectedly pleasant feeling. He had not lost his nerve and he knew Gerard had been impressed. It was the first time he had used the gun, the first time he had killed anyone. Gerard had looked at him curiously and not without a certain admiration. Once, long ago, Vikram remembered his father looking at him in this way after he had recited some verse he had learned in school. As he hurried through the trees, lowering his eyes to the ground, watching out for snakes, his mind was momentarily caught in a contented daydream. Then he remembered the Mendis girl. What had she been doing in that car just now, so far from home? Why was she always with that old man? He wanted to see her again, for there was something mysterious about her that eluded him. Gerard was right; he should talk to her, although for some reason, not entirely clear, Vikram did not want *him* to have anything to do with her.

'Nulani,' he said, experimentally.

Perhaps, thought Vikram, perhaps I should talk to her uncle. Yes, that's what I'll do, he decided. I'll make friends with the uncle. Then maybe I'll get invited to the house. Tearing a branch off a tree, clearing a path, he continued on his way.

Rohan was drawing in the garden behind his studio, shaded by a murunga tree.

'Come in, come in. We have been waiting for you fellows. Giulia is preparing a feast. She has engaged the entire service of the black market in your honour!'

He beamed at them and the girl smiled. Rohan was exactly as Theo had described him.

'Now then,' said Theo, watching Nulani, 'don't start drawing the poor man yet!'

In the last part of their drive the day had righted itself somehow. The girl's quiet voice talking lightly about insubstantial things had soothed him. He knew she was talking simply to distract him. He was amazed once again by her intuition and her insight. He knew this quality was also in her work. He hoped Rohan would see it too. Then he caught sight of Giulia hurrying towards them. She was laughing and balancing a tray of soft drinks and ice as she walked. For a second Theo was struck by the returning past. In this way had she come towards him when he had first met her. Again he felt a shift of focus towards all that had gone before, so that the memory of Anna returned to him again. The cuttlefish pasta, the wine, the clove-scented cigarettes. He saw, from the outside looking in, all he had denied himself for so long. And in that instant, the many thoughts he had punished himself with smoothed out and became simple and calm. In this way he remembered it, with a sudden rush, sweetly, and without bitterness. Somewhere nearby were the faint cries of seagulls, and he heard these too, coming back to him hauntingly, as though from another, different, Adriatic sky.

'This is Nulani,' he said, his hand on the girl's cool arm, feeling in that instant a poignant sense of belonging.

The afternoon wove around them. After a lunch of fresh crab curry and mallung, brinjal and *parippu*, of excellent curd and plantain, and beans, after an endlessly long and slow meal filled with banter, Rohan held up his hand.

'Enough!' he said, teasingly. 'This will *not* do. We have serious business. We are here to look at Nulani's paintings, you have all talked rubbish for long enough!'

And he covered his ears at their protestations. Sunlight danced on the walls. The war seemed something they had only heard about.

'I shall clear a space in my studio,' announced Rohan, handing Theo a cigar.

'My God!' said Giulia. 'It isn't often I hear him saying anything about clearing his studio. This is your doing, Nulani!'

'Maybe he has reached a turning point in his career?' suggested Theo. 'Come, Giulia, it's what you've been waiting for. Don't say you're not excited!'

'Yes, yes,' said Giulia earnestly. 'Perhaps meeting Nulani will make him tidy at last!'

'That's quite enough from both of you. Come, Nulani, ignore these philistines. Bring your work in.'

'Well,' sighed Giulia, 'I shall make some milk tea, for Theo and myself. It's clear we're not wanted by these artists!'

'And I shall get the paintings out of the boot,' said Theo. 'It's all I'm capable of doing!'

With a flourish of his hand, he held the door open for the girl and they went outside.

'You're different today,' the girl said, laughing up at him.

They walked along the side of the house keeping out of the sun. The air was hot and still.

'It's good,' she said softly, standing close to him. 'This is the first time you have looked really happy since I met you.'

Theo looked at her. He felt the air, delicate and white, like a gull's egg, charged with unspoken thoughts. Still and unbearable. The heat balanced precariously on the edge of an unknown precipice, so that, hardly conscious of what he did, he reached out and touched her hair. Crossing some invisible boundary, suspending them both in the moment. And Giulia, glancing up through the curtain of creepers growing outside the window, thought, I have seen that look on his face once, long ago, just before Anna died. Looking at Anna, in just this way. Does he know?

Rohan loved the paintings.

'Art school isn't what you need,' he said. 'Art school will only spoil what you already have. You already paint from the inside out. No, what you need is simply to paint. All the time, every *thing* you want to paint, until you have a body of work.'

He paused, staring intensely at the paintings, lost in thought.

'What you need is discussion about your work. You can have that with me. But most of all you must continue working in this way. And we should try to organise an exhibition for you. Here, and also in England, no? What do you think, *putha*? Tell me? Would you like that?'

Theo had left them alone to talk, and after he had looked at Nulani's paintings, Rohan brought out his own work. They were large semi-abstracts in oils. Vast grey canvases. He talked to her of the daily practice of painting.

'Some say art is our highest form of hope,' he said absently. 'Perhaps it's our only hope. Living has always been a desperate business.'

He paused, thinking of Theo, remembering the time when his friend had been lost to him when Anna had died.

'Life is full of pointlessness. Not just now there is a war, but always, before. It's the nature of living. And the wounding of beauty, that's all part of it, no? First you possess it and then you lose it. Art represents that aesthetically. To a certain extent your paintings are already doing this, you know, Nulani. But still, you must push your boundaries even further. On and on, don't stop whatever you do; keep looking, always, for the happy accident, for the things that move you. And don't just paint that bugger Theo, either!'

He smiled at her, for she was so lovely. And so pitifully young. The young, he felt, had little hope in this place. He wanted to give her something to take with her. He knew how hard it would be for her to follow her chosen path. What will she paint in ten years' time? he wondered. Or twenty? What *would* her life be like, in this backwater, married off, worn down by poverty and children? If the war doesn't get to her first, of course. He felt only shame and bitterness for his country. Already he could see she had captured the fragility in Theo, the threads of what he had lost. Already she had achieved something soft and fluid and painterly. If colour *does* express something of our deepest emotions, then these painstakingly beautiful paintings have begun to touch that mysterious thing, he thought. What other things will age and experience bring to her work?

'He is a good man,' he said, suddenly, of his friend. 'And he has suffered.'

He wondered how much she intuited. Probably she knew, possibly she understood more than Theo himself. Women were quicker, thought Rohan. Especially in this country, they were quicker.

'So, now you have lifted that greyness from his life. That is all really, and still it's also everything,' he said, as though she had replied.

They were silent, preoccupied, while the afternoon moved the light slowly around the huge white room. The smell of thick paint and bitumen was everywhere. Rohan's studio was cluttered with objects. Many of the things he chose to paint were those from his daily life. An empty carafe that had once held Tuscan wine, a cast-iron bird bath from their small Venetian garden, three shades of grey Fortuny silk, colours from a museum city. A blackened crucifix resting against the whitewashed wall.

'I myself,' said Rohan, seeing her look at his props, 'I myself, love grey. You may say this is a little ridiculous of me. To come all this way back home to paint with grey? But, grey has no agenda. And that's what really interests me. Its neutrality. Grey has the ability, that no other colour has, to make the invisible

visible. So I paint with grey. I need some spirituality to keep going in this place. For, you see, my heart is saddened by what's happening to our beautiful country.'

He paused, appearing to forget she was in the room. He was thinking he understood what Theo had meant. The girl sat without moving, silently. She had the calmness of an injured bird, he saw. As if some instinct told her, there was no point in struggling. And then Rohan saw that no one had talked to her in this way about painting.

'They are killing each other,' he said softly. 'Day after day. Over which language is more important. Can you credit these stupid bastards!'

Bitterness crossed his face like an ugly scar. The light was fading.

'Where it gets interesting for us, as painters, is in the absence of language,' he said a bit later on, getting excited again. 'You are a good painter. But you know all that, I hardly need to tell you.'

Then he remembered something else.

'Your notebooks,' he warned. 'They should never stop. No matter whatever happens in your life. Remember that. Always, *always*, no?'

The sun had almost gone, unnoticed by them. Deep shadows fell in through the window. In another part of the garden, Theo sat talking to Giulia. They had been drinking milk tea. Giulia had trained the plants to form a shady covering. She had placed some cane chairs and a small table underneath it. Orange blossom and jasmine tangled together overhead. A hosepipe trailed across the small immaculate lawn and somehow the garden had acquired an Italianate feel to it. Theo paused, looking at the terracotta pots of lilies, the cacti and the pink and white oleanders. It reminded him of the walled garden in Venice, where he and Anna had been such frequent visitors. How had

Giulia managed to bring her home here, into the untamed tropics? He began talking about the girl. Words poured out; he could not stop. It was as if a dam had burst in him.

'She is very young and with such extraordinary talent. I wish I knew what the future held for her,' he said.

I have seen this face in so many moods, thought Giulia, marvelling at the flexibility of the human heart. Marvelling that at last the torrent of grief over Anna seemed to have passed. Did he know? Had he any idea at all, of how he had changed?

'So, my friend,' Rohan said quietly, some time later, after they had put the paintings back in the car. 'You look a little better than the last time I saw you. Thank God, no?' And he placed his arm around Theo's shoulder, for he had hated the unhappiness and the anger that he had seen for so many years.

It was time for them to leave. Darkness was descending and soon the heat would lessen. Rohan and Giulia leaned against the gate. They stood arm in arm, smiling at Theo, kissing the girl goodbye.

'Bring her back to us very soon,' said Rohan. 'And, Nulani, remember what I said. I want to see some new paintings. But not just paintings of this fellow, you understand!'

They drove along the coast following the perfect disc of the moon. There were no remains from the day's bloodshed, nothing stirred under the steady beam of the headlights of the car. Theo drove with all thoughts suspended, cocooned within a glow of contentment. Their talk was languid and desultory. In this short intermission between twilight and darkness, a mysterious transformation had occurred. An unusual cast of light made the girl seem both real and yet unbelievable. As they passed along the lonely stretch of road, the sea appeared to drift towards them, so that Theo could not easily distinguish the sound of the water from their voices. A gentle connection seemed to exist between them, invisible until now, yet somehow already present. How this was he could not tell. He heard the girl's voice rise and fall to the sound of the waves; he heard the rustle of the coconut palms and the rush of cool air as they passed. In that moment of neither night nor day it was as though all of it, the girl, the moon and Theo himself, moved together in some mysterious harmony of their own.

By the time they got to the lane that led to her house they were late. She wanted him to stop the car before they reached it. Pockets of fragrance exploded everywhere, jasmine opened into the night, carried on the breeze. The fifth sense, thought Theo, is a forgotten one. Yet for most of us, memory comes with smell.

'My uncle will be at the house,' the girl was saying. 'I want to thank you here, for taking me to meet your friends, without my uncle listening. He does not like to hear talk about my painting. He is a fool.'

It was the first time he had heard this tone in her voice. He thought how far she had come since he had first met her and how much older she seemed in so short a time. How happy she sounds, he thought, filled with gladness. Helplessly, he looked at her and as she smiled, he saw that her eyes reflected the moonlight. Slowly, with unhurried tenderness, hardly aware of what he did, he bent down and kissed her. He felt her tremble as he touched her, and he felt, too, his own sweet shock of surprise. He had never thought to feel this way again. He had been running for so long and now it was as though at last his heart had stilled. Something invincible seemed to settle within him. And then he was driving on, towards the bright lights of the house, and her brother Jim's *baila* music, and her uncle's snaking dislike. And all around, the Milky Way appeared to unfold in an endless canopy above them, scattering its stars far and wide, like fireflies rising in the dark tropical sky.

6

IT RAINED IN THE NIGHT BUT towards dawn the mist began
rolling in from the sea. When it finally cleared, the day would
be hot and dry as an elephant's hide. The news on the radio
was not good. Two Cabinet ministers and their families,
returning to Colombo after the weekend, had been machine-
gunned down. All that was left of them were limbs, studded
with bullet holes, crushed to the edge of bone, brittle, like coral.
No one knew who might have committed such a crime. This
part of the island had always been considered safe. So it was a
mystery how this could have happened. The army began putting
up roadblocks everywhere in the hope of catching the terrorists. But so far no one had been arrested. Rumours were, the
railway line would be the next target. In the main part of the
town, further along from where the Mendis family lived, small
groups of men gathered to talk of this latest, unaccountable act
of violence. The air of nervousness, even here in this backwater,
was no longer possible to hide. A few fights had broken out in
the streets and Mrs Mendis begged her son to stay away from
the town. He was leaving at the end of August. The priest at

the boys' school had organised his visa. Mrs Mendis did not want anything to ruin his future. She was torn between her desperation for Jim's safety and her agony at the thought of his imminent departure. Fear and anxiety, and also irritation towards Nulani, mixed confusingly within her. There was so much to do for Jim and all the girl had wanted was to go to Colombo to talk about her paintings. Why was she such a selfish child? Why did she care so little for what was left of her family? Here was her mother, working night and day to make ends meet, and all Nulani could do was paint. Mrs Mendis complained loudly about her daughter to the servant. She complained about her to the clients who came with sewing. And she insisted Nulani stay in and help her.

'You've had your day gallivanting with that poor gentleman,' she told Nulani firmly. 'He's a good man to take such interest in you, but today you can finish the jersey for your brother to take to England. And then you can clean the house.'

Jim cycled off to his tutor's house. He had some final preparations. And Nulani Mendis sat alone on the veranda step watching him go.

It was how Vikram saw her, spying through the branches of the mango tree. He had been preoccupied for the last week, busy doing important things, being seen by as many people as possible, taking the shopkeeper's daughter to the back of the garage, drinking. Of late the shopkeeper's daughter had begun to irritate him. She had, he realised, become too fond of him and had stopped fighting and started smiling instead. As a result Vikram was becoming bored. He knew he would have to wait a while before Gerard gave him his next task. Gerard was lying low for a few days, he guessed, waiting until the news had died down, until someone had been caught and hung. So with no other excitement ahead Vikram was at a loose end. On his way back from the *kade*, he passed the Mendis house. Idly he decided to see who was in. Perhaps this was the moment to get to know the uncle.

But it was the girl he saw instead. She was knitting her brother a jersey to take to England. Knit one, purl one went her hands, binding the dark green wool together. They were painter's hands, moving quickly, making work. Vikram paused. He had come to see her uncle and found himself staring at Nulani Mendis instead. He watched her cautiously from this safe distance. Something about her made him careful. As always, whenever he caught sight of her, he felt uneasy without quite knowing why. Perhaps it was the tranquillity of her manner; perhaps it was the mysterious certainty in her face. He knew she might suddenly look up and see him, so he held his breath, hiding behind the *ambarella* tree. Her smile gave him the oddest of feelings. It made him remember things best forgotten, things that were no longer his to remember. But the girl did not look up. She was absorbed in her knitting. Knit one, purl one went her hands. Vikram was shocked to see her knitting. His shock was mixed with confusion, for thus had his sister knitted in that other, abundant life that once belonged to him too. The garden was filled with the sound of small birds. An underripe fruit thudded to the ground but still the girl did not look up. She bent over the dark green wool and for a moment, a mere fraction of a second, it seemed to Vikram as though the day had stopped. Shadows crossed the ground. A child's voice could be heard in the distance, repeating a question over and over again, high and clear. The rich hum of a passing mosquito vibrated in Vikram's ear. There were mosquitoes everywhere since the rains had begun. But the girl did not see them; she did not see Vikram either. She had a soft look on her face, like the nearly ripe mango that had fallen too early. She looked beautiful and dark, and mysterious. When she had finished all she meant to do, Nulani stood up and glanced swiftly across the lane. Then she sighed, and, folding up her knitting as though it were a precious thought, went inside.

Vikram watched her retreating back. He saw that even when she walked there was a peacefulness about her. His curiosity grew. What was it about this girl that drew him to her? He knew nothing more about her than the idle gossip surrounding Mr Mendis's death. From where he was, he could see the cool, dark interior of the house quite clearly. He could see also that it was shabby and withered and, in a way, hopeless too. None of this surprised him. Someone had told him that the family had slowly disintegrated after Mr Mendis had died. He could not remember who had said it. Perhaps it had been a student at the school, knowing of his dislike for Jim Mendis. But anyway he sensed this house had seen better times. Vikram imagined Mr Mendis, before his outspoken poetry had killed him, walking the beach with his daughter, carrying his young son. And the young Mrs Mendis, what had she been like? People said in those days she was always smiling. He imagined the house would have had energy then. Now, from where he crouched, he could see the place was a mess. Cricket bats and shoes, he supposed they belonged to Jim, shed like a gecko's skin, strewn everywhere. Vikram edged a little closer and he saw there were empty cotton reels and bits of thread and cloth lying on the floor. He could hear the sound of the sewing machine rattling on and, further back, through the closed doors, he heard raised voices. He watched as Nulani Mendis, ignoring everything, began to tidy up the room. There was something oddly dreamlike in the way she moved, he thought, puzzled. It was as though the girl was somewhere else entirely. She began folding her brother's clothes. She gathered up his books and picked up his shoes. Vikram watched. She moved his cricket bat and his kneepads. And she knocked the mirror over.

The mirror, shattering the light, crashing against her brother's shoes, his cricket bat, his kneepads. It fell to the ground, breaking into many pieces of silver, fragmenting the room, spewing dust, bringing Mrs Mendis in. Mrs Mendis let out a cry, a thin wail of despair, a long whine of sorrow. Broken-mirror dust was everywhere.

'There is no escape,' cried Mrs Mendis, 'Aiyo! My brother was right.'

Misfortune lay across the room. The girl stood looking at her hands while her mother's fears clogged the air. Vikram could feel her fears, even from where he stood, prickling against his own skin. He felt them, darkly unbending. Only Jim's cricket bat remained unharmed. Only Jim, out at the time doing whatever came easiest to him, did not witness the broken glass. Lucky Jim.

Theo had not slept. Happiness stopped him from sleeping. It was no longer possible to hide from his thoughts. The truth washed bare, rising to the surface, clear and clean like the beach. Had it only been a matter of hours? he wondered in amazement. He felt as though he had been travelling for aeons. Sugi had been waiting for him when he finally got back. The lights in the veranda shone, the beginnings of rain dampened the air, and the sound of the waves seemed louder. Sugi had gone for his beer as soon as he heard the gate and Theo insisted he join him. So they had sat and smoked in companionable silence for a while.

'I will set the table, Sir,' said Sugi. 'You must be hungry.'

But he had not wanted food. And Sugi seeing this, waited patiently.

'Have I changed, Sugi?' he asked. 'Since I first arrived here, do you think I am different?'

'Of course, Sir,' said Sugi. 'You have been changing for months now.'

'How?' asked Theo, wonderingly, smiling, wanting to be told.

'You are happier, Sir, you know; really, so much happier. You were very sad when you arrived, but . . .'

'What? Tell me.'

'I . . . Sir . . . you must be careful. I understand and I'm glad to see you this way.'

He did not ask how the day had gone. He knew it had gone well. So he nodded gently instead. For Sir was being blessed by the gods in some way. What was there for him to say?

'I'm no longer . . . a young man, you know, Sugi,' Theo said hesitantly. 'You know that . . . it isn't . . . I'm worried about this. I will grow old long before her . . .' He laughed.

Again Sugi hesitated. The effort of denial had been great, he knew. Now that barrier had been removed. Sir's face was radiant. It made Sugi both sad and happy.

'Some time has been lost, Sir, that's true,' he said at last. 'You had to wait for her to be born, to grow. But she is here now. In your life. I think, for ever,' he added.

'Ah, Sugi,' said Theo, looking up at the star-spangled sky.

He felt overcome, he felt happiness detach itself from him and float towards the trees. Filled with a sudden burst of energy, he wondered if perhaps he should do some work. And then, he thought, perhaps he would simply go to bed. Sugi smoked his cigarette. He was silent. Sir's happiness was such that it should not be disturbed. The darkness enfolded them both.

'Sugi!' said Theo at last, looking at him. 'If only you knew . . . how lucky I was that day to meet you! What would I have done had I not? It was as if you were waiting for the train I was on, waiting for the last passenger to walk up the hill.'

He shook his head, smiling broadly, wanting to say more, unable to express all he felt, his optimism for the future, and his affection for Sugi. But there was no need.

'Perhaps I was,' said Sugi. 'Without realising!' In the light his face looked tired.

'You mustn't worry about me, Sugi,' said Theo, gently. Tonight, he felt his heart was overflowing with almost unbearable gladness. 'Things are simpler than you think. You know I have to go back to England briefly, don't you? For the film?'

Sugi nodded.

'But I'll be back as soon as I can.'

'Everything will be fine here. Don't worry, Sir. I will look after things here,' he said, meaningfully.

There is no finer friend to be wished for, thought Theo. I hardly need to say anything, he knows already. And he smiled in the darkness.

'I think I might go for a walk on the beach. I'm not sleepy. And the day was a success, you know. Rohan loved her. And her paintings!'

'Be careful, Sir,' said Sugi, out of habit. But he spoke softly, as though afraid of breaking some spell.

Twenty-eight years, thought Theo walking across the smooth sand, listening to the screams of the wide-mouthed gulls. All the madness and hell of this country seemed nothing beside the astonishment of what he felt. The last love of my life, he murmured, that's what you are. There, he thought, I've faced it; that's what you are. Beyond reason, beyond practicality, that is what you are. And then he remembered her hands and the ways in which they made sense of the material world. Where has this talent come from? Will you love in the same effortless way that you draw? How *will* you love? Dare I even ask the question? I am forty-five, an old man by your standards. And in spite of the implausibility of our two ages, even as I hear the warning bell, I know it is too late, I will never let you go. He saw that he had arrived at a point of no return and that the girl had left her imprint on his imagination in ways he could never have foreseen. Throwing his head back, breathing in the fresh salty air, laughing out loud, he understood with the utmost certainty there were no more journeys for him to travel. Gazing up at the stars, dizzy with happiness, he cried: 'This is where I shall stay, until I die. Here in this place, with you.'

And as he watched, the ships on the horizon seemed sharply defined, glittering like diamonds against the night sky. Yes, he loved her. And yet, he thought, wistful now, you who are only just beginning to close the gate on your childhood, how could you understand the wonder of loving so late?

Looking out across the water, into the distance, he imagined her father speaking to her. She had told him that her father used to say: 'There's nothing except Antarctica from here. Nothing, no land, nothing.' Staring into the darkness, Theo tried to imagine her six-year-old incomprehension. And then his thoughts turned slowly towards Anna, seeing her with fresh understanding. Remembering too how once, many years ago, he had walked across another, wilder stretch of beach with her. They had been newly married. He had not known that after she died time would stop. But now, at last, he began to understand the indestructibility of things. Overnight almost, the memory of her had shifted and changed and miraculously, no longer cluttered by pain, become a peaceful thing. And it felt, in that moment, that Anna and their time together threaded like the strong ribbon on a kite, running through all he had just discovered, anchoring him. In this way, thought Theo, the dead return to bless us. In this way, through the new, will I remember the old.

He stayed out almost until dawn. And went back to sleep. When he woke Sugi had set the tea things outside on the table and he told Theo that the talk in the town was all about the murder of the two ministers and their families.

'We saw it,' Theo said quietly.

Not wanting to talk about it, not wanting the day to be spoiled, he told Sugi about Colombo and the lunch with his friends, and the girl. The day was hot. Sugi bought some fish. He cooked lunch and squeezed lime juice for the girl. But she did not appear.

'I expect her mother has got some jobs for her,' said Sugi, noticing Sir was not working. Noticing he had walked to the gate and was looking up the deserted dirt track for the fourth time.

The afternoon dragged on. The sounds of the cicadas filled the air and the mosquitoes too were back with a vengeance. But there was still no sign of the girl. They both began to listen out for the click of the gate. Theo had found a place to hang the paintings, away from the light, and Sugi took a hammer and put them up. But still, there was no sign of her. What had happened to her? wondered Theo uneasily.

'Don't worry, Sir,' said Sugi soothingly. 'My friend said Mrs Mendis is very upset the boy is leaving. She's probably given her some work to do.' The afternoon was nearly over.

'Perhaps I should go over there,' said Theo.

'Sir,' said Sugi, and he shook his head. 'It will do no good and it might even do harm. She will come. As soon as she can, she will come, I am certain.'

Towards evening, just before it became dark, Theo slipped out to the beach. Sugi watched him go.

'Don't be too long, sir,' he said. 'There's talk of a curfew. If you see the searchlights, come back immediately. These army types won't stop to look. They simply shoot, you know.'

As always at this time the beach was deserted. Theo was trying to light his pipe, bending away from the wind, when he saw her. Hurrying across to him in headlong flight, running heedlessly along the empty stretch of sand. Carrying her mother's wails of superstitions, chased by unseen demons, straight into his arms. And for the first time, as he held her like a child, relieving her of her fear, he saw how much she had begun to depend on him. And he saw also from her eyes that she was beginning to understand, too sharply and too finely perhaps, the many things that had not worried her until now. At last she saw what there was to be afraid of in this war. And he felt his own feelings for her break open and flower in some unbearable and inexplicable way.

Mirror dust fell everywhere, sparkling between them. Looking at her face he thought, once again with amazement, how it was that in so short a time, she seemed both older and yet so young. And then he knew, without a shadow of doubt, that he could never live in England again. So he laughed at her, teasing her about her mirror-fears, holding her as though she was a child woken from a nightmare, telling her it was all nonsense.

'Will you come back?' she asked anxiously, reading his mind a little. 'No one will stop you from coming back, will they?' Thinking with dread of his trip to London, for the premiere of his film. 'You *will* be allowed back in, no?'

They were sitting side by side on a broken catamaran. Half of it had sunk in the sand, brown-whiskered coconut husks filled its broken base, weather-beaten planks were all that were left of its seats. Her bare legs were close to his. One worn straw sandal had burrowed into the sand and come undone. He bent and fastened the strap, his hands fumbling and unfamiliar in their new task, brushing the traces of fine grains that clung to her leg. He felt her tremble and he knew she was thinking that he had never touched her in this way before. And all the things he had held in check, all the happiness of the past few days, gathered with great sweetness in that touch, of his hand on her skin.

'I will always come back,' he said fiercely, placing his hand against her face. 'You must never doubt that. If anything happens, if my visa is delayed, or the trouble worsens here, or the flights are cancelled, you must *not* worry. You must remember that I have told you I *will* come back. No matter how long it will take I *will* come back. I can't live away from you now. You must take no notice of the news,' he added, with the new urgency he had begun to feel. 'And promise me you will paint while I am away.' And he had kissed her again, for he could not bear the look on her face.

She had gone back then, to listen to her mother's complaints, with the caress of his hand on her legs, her red dress fluttering like a flag in the breeze, trailing the mist coming in from the sea, leaving the night to descend. Leaving the beach to him.

Walking back, Theo heard the sound of police sirens in the distance, rising and falling in time to the rhythmic gnawing of the sea.

On the edge of Aida Grove, on a slight incline not far from Sumaner House was an area where coconut trees would not grow. The earth was bare and wasted, without grass, without bushes, without life. There was nothing there except a lone straggling tamarind tree. Once this patch of land had been part of a larger grove of coconuts. It had belonged to the owners of Sumaner House, but with time, neglect and some erosion it had become common land, useless and uncultivated. Superstition abounded. Local legend had it that long ago a servant girl was ravished by a wandering shaman, here in this spot, and then left for dead. Eventually, according to the story, after many days of searching, the girl's distraught father found her body. His grief was so terrible that the gods, pitying the girl, turned this once fertile grove into barren land. Later on the place was used for human sacrifice. One evil deed precipitated others, and this became a spot avoided by most people. Cattle would not graze, children would not fly their kites and no one walked here after dark. Occasionally, in the hope of changing the atmosphere, the locals would offer *pujas*, prayers to the gods. But to no avail, Aida Grove would never become popular. In recent times the army had tried to make it their own, parking their trucks and using it as a lookout post, staring at the ships through their binoculars, but Aida Grove defeated even them, and after a while they too stopped coming. Only Vikram frequented the place, idly observing the votive offerings, the stray soldiers, the local carrion. Sometimes he would go to Aida Grove in the hottest hours of the afternoon simply to sit under the tamarind tree and watch the dappled light as it flickered on the ground. He was drawn to the place without knowing why. At seventeen he was the size of a fully-grown man. In spite of everything that had happened to him, he thrived. Such was the virulence of youth; such was the ability of unhappiness to grow. These days he kept busy in unexplained ways. He was still waiting for Gerard to give him his next task. But although he had returned to the town, and although someone else was helping the army with their murder inquiries, Gerard told him things were held up for the moment.

'Patience, patience,' Gerard had said. 'I'll let you know in a few weeks' time. When the Chief sends his orders. Now stop pestering me and circulate around the town, will you.'

One evening, as he walked home full of arrack, Vikram heard the usual sound of temple chants filling the air. The sounds floated across Aida Grove and the sky, he noticed, was filled with hundreds of small insects. There was hardly a breeze, the heat lay heavy and close to the ground. In some parts of the island, as Vikram was aware, in places where there was no curfew, Deepavali, the festival of light, was being celebrated once more. When they had been alive Vikram's family had always celebrated Deepavali. Vikram staggered on. Huge, blue magpies chattered a warning in the tamarind tree. The darkness grew stronger. Inside Sumaner House the servant woman Thercy had switched off the naked electric bulb in the kitchen. There had been no news from Vikram's guardian for months now. Thercy had given up wondering if he would ever return. He still paid her wages and he still sent money to Vikram. Everyone was content with the arrangement, so what did she care? All evening police sirens had been screaming. Fighting had broken out further up the coast. Tomorrow, thought Thercy, she would go into the town and meet her friend Sugi. He would know the latest news. Vikram was nowhere in sight. She imagined he was somewhere in the town getting drunk as usual. Thercy had no control over him. It was late, so, turning off the lights, all but the one on the veranda, she retired to bed.

Meanwhile, Vikram paused at the edge of Aida Grove. Something was different about it tonight. At first he couldn't think what it was. The light from the veranda shone faintly on the tamarind tree. Something was swinging from its highest branch. The movement caught Vikram's eye. He looked across the length of the tree trunk and saw the thing hung awkwardly, like a broken doll, swinging in the slight breeze. Slowly, making no sound, Vikram walked towards the tree. What appeared to be a giant pendulum moved backwards and forwards, swinging to an invisible beat. In the darkness, rocking gently, it appeared like an image from a painting.

In the dead of night, before the carrion came, when the air had cooled slightly and the dawn was still some way off, someone took the body down. It was dead-weighted and black-booted, hooded and bound. There were electrodes fixed to the palms of its hands. The hands were still young. A palmist might have identified the dark lines that crossed and recrossed it. A palmist would have seen the history in its fingers. The life and love that had lodged there once. But no such palmist was present. There was no one to display a single gesture of pity. And in the morning, when the light returned to the tamarind tree, the body had gone. Resurrected perhaps, moved to another place maybe. Blood had been spilt, thought Sugi when he heard, and the earth was soaked with it. Behind the tamarind tree and far away through the coconut grove were broken glimpses of the sea. It was blue like the sky, and the horizon was dotted with ships.

Nothing changed. The sea still scrolled restlessly up the beach. The catamarans remained half buried under the sand. When they could, after the curfew was lifted again, Theo and the girl walked on the beach. For Nulani there were two departures ahead.

'My brother goes to England in three weeks,' she told Theo.

He saw she could hardly bear what lay ahead. When would she see her brother again? Theo at least would be back. He tried to comfort himself with this thought, saddened by all that lay ahead for her. Remnants of her superstition had worked on him by some process of osmosis, he now realised. Am I going mad? he wondered uneasily. All this nonsense about broken mirrors; it's crazy. But he could see very clearly how her life rested on shifting sand. Why had he not seen this before?

Sugi watched his struggle. Sugi was his rock.

'Don't worry, Sir,' he said again, and again as they smoked together.

The generator had broken down again. Bullfrogs croaked but otherwise all was quiet.

'I will look after her for you. Always.'

They shared the silence.

'Do you remember when you first walked up the road, Sir, looking for this house?'

He still calls me Sir. That will not change either, thought Theo, his affection lengthening like the shadows.

'She will be fine, Sir. I will make sure of that, not to worry.'

There was money and a forged passport for the girl, hidden in a secret place.

'If there is any trouble, with the uncle, with anything, take her to Rohan,' said Theo in an agony of worry.

Time was passing relentlessly.

'Sir,' said Sugi, 'you must trust me. I will take care of her with my life. She will be fine. You and she are precious to me.'

Theo looked at him; Sugi had never expressed his feelings in quite this way before. His trip was still a month away.

Because of her brother's imminent departure the girl had stopped painting for the moment. These days she was often needed at home, sewing on buttons, and packing, or labelling the jars of lime pickles. How many jars of pickle could the boy take in his suitcase? wondered Sugi. But he refrained from comment. Since the trip to Colombo, Mrs Mendis kept her daughter occupied most of the time, adding to the girl's distress. When she could Nulani would escape to walk with Theo along the beach, and Sugi as always watching with his anxious eyes could see: they were getting closer daily. Sugi looked out across the horizon. The sea is full of fish, he thought. And the fruit is ripening in the trees, but still that isn't enough. Still we fight.

'Will they have egg hoppers for breakfast in England?' the girl asked Theo.

'You *will* see him again,' Theo told her, understanding in a new and mysterious way what she was thinking.

He had begun to feel the leave-taking of her brother almost

as keenly as she did. Her pain had become a terrible thing for him to watch.

'Will you take me to England then?' she asked, and her eyes were very large and dark and full of light in the way children's eyes are. However much she aged in years to come, he thought, she still would remain beautiful because of them. They were the eyes of someone from another age, deep and wise and very lovely. Oh Christ, how he wanted to take her to England, and to Paris and to Venice. He could not bear to leave. When I return, he decided, determined, I will never leave her again. And one day, I will even take her to see that wretched brother of hers and, when the war is over, I will bring her back home again. For I know her heart will always remain here, in this place, her home. So thought Theo as he watched her tenderly, as she drank the lime juice Sugi still served in the tall glass. So thought Theo watching her anxiously and waiting for the rains to come, marvelling at how only last year she had turned seventeen – so young, yet already it felt as though he had known her for a lifetime.

By Christmas there was to be a general election. From all he could glean, in the brief talks with his agent in London, this war no longer interested the foreign newspapers. Sri Lanka was no longer news these days. It was a shipwrecked land. A forgotten place. Lately, Theo noticed, since the curfew had been lifted, a car headlight crossed the top of the sea road each night. It happened always at nine o'clock, every night, sweeping its beam across the road. But it never came any further and their peace, such as it was, remained for the moment undisturbed.

7

'How long will it take,' she asked him, 'to get to London?'

Her brother had gone a few weeks earlier, leaving for the airport in the schoolteacher's car, with his unwavering belief in the new life ahead.

'Gone to the UK,' her mother had told everyone proudly, through her tears.

The house had shrunk. And now, another departure hung over Nulani.

'About a day. From door to door,' said Theo. 'Tomorrow, by this time, I will be in the hotel.'

'And you would have travelled halfway around the world,' she said in a small voice, picking up his passport and reading the names stamped in it.

'Frankfurt, Vienna, Amsterdam, Paris, Venice. You have been everywhere,' she said. 'And I have only been to Colombo, once!'

Theo, who had been gathering his notes for his tour, his money and his documents, stopped and looked at her. He took her hands in his. They were cold. He had been trying to keep busy but he saw now that it was useless.

'I'm so much older than you,' he said finally. 'It's hardly surprising. And you will go to all of these places one day, I promise you. *I* will take you, you'll see.'

She was silent, not looking at him, staring at the patch of sea through the open window. Impassively, accepting. He felt a moment of sickness at the thought of abandoning her. Seagulls circled the sky outside. He thought of how her father left her, not meaning to, but doing so anyway. Then, because he could not bear it, he looked at his watch. In less than an hour he would be gone, sitting on the fast train to Colombo. And he needed to talk to her. He could hear Sugi moving in the kitchen.

'Let's go to the catamarans,' he said quickly.

It was still so early that mist lay in thin patches on the beach. There would be no one about. First her father, then her brother Jim, he thought, and now me. But I shall come back, he reminded himself firmly.

'Listen to me,' he said, his hands gentle on her face. 'You must not worry. I'm coming back. I've promised you. I *will* keep my word. Just look after yourself, for me. Will you? And when I get back . . .'

He hesitated, not knowing how to go on. Her face looked drawn in the faint dawn light. She looked terrified.

'Look at me,' he said. 'Nulani, listen. You know I don't want to go but . . . You must not be afraid. The six weeks will go quickly, I promise you.'

Again he hesitated.

'When I get back . . . I want to talk to you about something. I want to ask you . . .'

He didn't have much time. He couldn't miss his train. There would not be another one today. But he needed to ask her something.

'Please, Nulani,' he said, 'look at me. Are you listening? I

114

want us to get married. Would you like that too? Will you be prepared to do this crazy thing? With me?'

He went on smiling at her, hiding his desperation, holding on to her, knowing she was nearly crying, knowing too he could not bear to let her. For he knew that if she did, he would not be able to leave.

When she spoke at last, her voice was carried by the wind and caught up in the roar of a train rushing past. The sun was moving slowly through the mist; a few fishermen were coming in from the night. The air smelt sweetly of sea and sand and old fishing nets and tobacco as he kissed her.

'Yes,' she said, faintly. 'I want it too.'

Sugi squeezed some limes. Then he strained the juice into the tall glass jug and took it out onto the veranda where Nulani was drawing. Almost four days had gone since Theo had left and his absence was like a chasm between them. They had had a brief talk to him on the telephone but the line was bad and most of the time they only heard an echo of their own voices.

'Don't worry if you haven't heard from me,' Theo had said. 'Sometimes it's hard to get a connection.'

They had told him that everything was fine, that there was no trouble.

'Miss Nulani is here all the time, Sir,' Sugi had grinned. 'She's looking after me in exchange for lime juice! So don't worry. Just look after yourself.'

'And come back soon,' the girl had said. 'I have been drawing you from memory. Please come back.'

Afterwards she had been very upset. Sugi had not known what to do. He could see the signs of strain stretch taut against her. She was becoming silent, as she had once been. He told her she should do what she had always done. Each morning, until Theo returned, she should go into her studio and paint. In this way she could surprise Sir when he returned. Six weeks was not too long, looked at in this way, said Sugi firmly, talking to her as though she was a child.

Thus began a routine. Every morning as soon as she had helped her mother, she went over to the beach house and worked. Her mother no longer complained about her absence. Mrs Mendis too had grown quiet. Life had defeated her. She did not know when she would have word from her son. They did not have a telephone and although Nulani had written a letter there had been no reply as yet. Jim Mendis had vanished, swallowed up by the sky, as far as she could see. There was no longer any purpose to her life. The future held no interest for Mrs Mendis. By now Nulani had stopped going to the convent school. Most of the girls of her age were preparing for marriage, or leaving the country if they could. Those who were serious about their studies had moved to Colombo to a larger school. There was nothing to do except paint. The days crawled on. Soon a whole week had passed and there were only five weeks left.

One afternoon she arrived at the beach house later than usual. Her mother had gone to visit someone in a neighbouring village so she had found she was free. But she was restless. The light was wrong, she said, it was not possible to paint. Sea-damp had curled her notebook, she told Sugi, showing him the pages. Her drawings were ruined, she said sadly. Perhaps she could not paint after all. Sugi looked at her. She looked as though she had been crying and there were dark circles around her eyes. He brought out a plate of sweetmeats and some curd and jaggery. Then he sat down on the step and, in order to distract her, he told her a story.

Once long ago, when he was a young man, Sugi told her, he

had wanted to go to America. The idea of a neon life, Pepsi cola and cars seduced him. Once.

'When I was young I worked for a while in the Mount Lavinia Hotel in Colombo, carrying the bags that had just arrived off the passenger boats. America seemed glamorous in those days, and the women were tall and confident. So healthy-looking,' he said. 'Their teeth were large and white, their smiles spelt happiness.'

He had fallen in love with such a one, a woman called Sandy. He thought she might have been older than him. She had had a fiancé in Germany. Sandy had stayed in the hotel for nearly three months waiting for a passage to Europe.

'During that time we had only four conversations,' said Sugi. And he smiled at the memory.

'The first time was when I took her bags to her room. I read the labels on her bag and saw that her name was Miss Sandy Fleming, from Buffalo. I tried to imagine such a place,' he said. 'She saw me reading the label and smiled at me.'

He saw that her smile was even-toothed and confident. Such confidence frightened him a little. But it also fascinated him. Then the woman had thanked him and given him a tip. The second time she spoke was a few days later. She was poring over a map but, catching sight of him, she asked him for directions instead, saying that maps were too confusing. She smiled at him again and it was then that he had noticed her eyes.

'They were like green marbles,' said Sugi.

He could remember them still. Startled, caught unawares, Sugi had smiled back and Sandy Fleming had touched his arm lightly saying he ought to be coming with her on her trip. He had held the door open and, as she passed through into the blinding sun outside, he smelt the perfume on her skin. Again she touched him, lightly on the cheek.

'After that I was unable to stop thinking of her,' Sugi said. 'I didn't see her again for ages; my shift changed and I was needed to work in the kitchens.'

Often after he finished work he would loiter in the corridor near to Sandy's room in the hope of catching sight of her, but she was never around.

'Then about six weeks later,' Sugi said, 'the manager found he was short-staffed. He asked me to serve in the dining room.'

It was late afternoon; most of the guests had retired to their rooms to lie under their ceiling fans until the worst of the heat had passed. Outside, the sea was an unbelievable swimming-pool blue and the sand was bleached white. The breeze masked the blistering heat. Only fools would have ventured out but Sandy was on the terrace, her yellow straw hat providing her with a slight filigreed shade.

'I went to ask if she would like a drink,' said Sugi. 'A Lanka lime, a gin and tonic? You see, I knew how the Americans loved to drink.'

But in reality he had wanted only to talk to her. So he went out with his silver tray, his clothes a white flag in the sun, and he saw that she was crying. He had been about to move away quickly, eyes downcast so as not to intrude, when she turned and, seeing him, began a conversation as though she had left off a moment before.

'She told me that her fiancé had called off their engagement. She told me he had fallen in love with a German. Imagine that, she said. I didn't know what to say, so I was silent.'

He had seen that her eyes were smudged and greener than the cat's-eye gemstones mined in Ratnapura.

'He prefers Germans!' she had laughed with heavy sarcasm.

She asked Sugi if he had a girl. She was sure he did for he was such a handsome boy, she told him. And if by any chance he did not have a girlfriend, she had said, then he should tell her, because she would not like to think of him being wasted. Sugi saw that she was drunk.

Later, in his room in the servant quarters he thought about her, wishing he had not been so tongue-tied.

'I never asked myself what a woman like her would want with a boy like me,' he told Nulani.

He did not see her the next day, or the day after that, even though he looked for her everywhere. He asked the chambermaid if the American lady had checked out and found that she was still there but her bed had not been slept in for two nights. The chambermaid wondered why he wanted to know this.

'I pretended I had found a brooch of hers but the chambermaid was no fool, she told me to hand it in at the office and not have anything to do with the American.'

'She is a loose woman,' the chambermaid had said, showing her betel-stained teeth, fanning Sugi's interest further.

Then late one evening, after he had descended into a state of despair, when he was working on the reception desk, she had come in with a British Army officer in tow. They were laughing noisily, and Sandy was swaying slightly. She asked for her key, looking past Sugi. Much later she called up for a bottle of champagne and when he took it up himself she tipped him, complaining to the manager afterwards that he had looked at her in a manner that was too familiar.

'Some weeks after,' said Sugi, 'I left Colombo. I felt everyone was judging me. I didn't know if they thought I was a thief or a fool. Or both. So I left and went into domestic service in the south.'

He stopped speaking. In the distance a train thundered by. It was the afternoon express from Colombo. The sun had moved away from the house as he had talked and a cool breeze had sprung up. All of it had happened so long ago, in the days when the war had been something they had hoped would be avoided. He had been young then and his mother and sisters had constantly tried to find a woman for him. But the planets had been fixed in such a way when he was born that his horoscope revealed them to be in discordant houses, so that it had proved impossible.

'I seemed to be attracted only to unsuitable women,' he said wryly. The war and time had eroded his desire, he told Nulani, so that before he realised it, he was too old care any more.

Sugi fell silent. All this had happened long ago. Now his interest lay elsewhere. How many lives does a man have to live before he can finally be at peace? he thought, thinking too of Mr Samarajeeva. These days he wanted only to help Sir. There was something very fine and very noble about Theo Samarajeeva, something that had not been seen in this country for a long time. We are a Buddhist country, thought Sugi, turning things over in his mind. But what has happened to us? Where has our compassion gone? He would do anything for Sir, he knew. Help him in any way. Before he had left Theo had told Sugi he wanted to marry Miss Nulani.

'Do you think it's wrong of me, Sugi?' he had asked.

Sugi had been amazed. Why was Sir asking him?

'You are a wise man, Sugi,' Sir had said warmly. 'So tell me, *am* I doing the right thing?'

'It is the best thing you can do, Sir,' Sugi had said. 'Nothing else will do, for either of you, now. It is meant to be. You were meant to meet, your ages do not matter. At first I was worried, but now, I am certain of it.'

Sir had smiled at that, his anxieties momentarily smoothed out. And then, because he could not say all he felt, he had tried to joke.

'I take it I have your blessing, Sugi,' he had said.

'A thousand blessings, Sir.'

And they had sat in this way, in the darkness, sipping their beers, wrapped lightly in all that was left unsaid. Later, Sugi again said, 'I'll look after her. She'll be safe until your return.'

'I know,' Theo had replied, with calm certainty. 'I know you will, Sugi, you are my friend.' And then early the next morning he had gone.

'Sir is different,' Sugi told the girl, now. 'Sir is a wonderful man. And soon,' he said gently, smiling encouragingly at her, 'when he returns, I hear you'll become his wife. So be patient, have faith. It will be a blessing for you both, you'll see.'

His words settled between them, like the flock of white birds that sat in circles on the empty beach.

While he had been talking, the girl had been drawing him. She had never drawn him before. She did not know why this was, she said. But she had drawn him now. She showed him the sketch. Then she tore it out of her notebook and gave it to him. Tomorrow, she told him, she would start a small painting. It would be of Sugi and it would be finished by the time Theo returned home. It would be her welcome-home present for him, she said, smiling at last.

Vikram was finally preparing to leave for the east coast. He told the servant woman Thercy that he was going away for a time. He told her to pass the message on to his guardian should he contact her. Thercy nodded without questioning him. It was none of her business and Vikram was old enough to please himself. She was glad to have the house to herself for a while. Once he goes, she thought, I will give the place a good clean.

Vikram packed a rucksack. He shouted to Thercy to give him some ironed shirts. Then he went into the town. There had been no trouble for weeks, no curfew, no murders. The army seemed to have gone to ground. It was as good a time as any for Vikram to disappear. Gerard told him the Chief should not be kept waiting. So Vikram went over to the gem shop. As soon as Gerard saw him, he closed the door and shuttered up the shop. Then they both went upstairs.

'Can I have some arrack?' asked Vikram.

Gerard hesitated for a fraction of a second. Since the business at the crossroads, he noticed, Vikram was less polite, more confident and full of demands. But he got two glasses and poured some arrack for them both. He handed Vikram his travel documents. The papers stated that Vikram was a Singhalese man of twenty.

'You shouldn't have a problem with that,' Gerard said easily. 'Your Singhala is perfect, you even look Singhalese. In fact, if I didn't know better I would say you were one of these bastards!'

Vikram grinned. Gerard noticed he downed his arrack in one gulp.

'You know what to do, huh? Take the train to Colombo. Then go to this address and ask for Rajah. Say Singh sent you. Give him this packet of tea. Be careful how you hold it. There's no tea inside it, remember!' He laughed heartily, amused at his own joke. 'Rajah will take you to Batticaloa. You'll have to travel by night because of the daytime roadblocks. But that shouldn't be a problem as there's no curfew at the moment. When you get to Batticaloa you will be given over to a man called Lakshman. You can speak Tamil with him, safely. Lakshman will take you to the Chief. He'll blindfold you for security reasons, OK? Now, any questions?'

Vikram said nothing, looking meaningfully at the arrack bottle.

'No,' said Gerard shortly. 'Not in the middle of the day. I

can't afford to have you drunk in broad daylight. Now, listen carefully. You'll be at the training camp for a couple of weeks, maybe a bit longer. I'll see you only after that. By that time you'll have been briefed for your next assignment. Then there'll be nothing you won't be able to do for the Tamil people. You'll get your chance to avenge your family at last. OK?' He paused. 'Again, any questions?'

'Can I have my gun back?' asked Vikram.

Gerard sighed. The truth was he was getting a little bored with the boy and his monosyllabic ways. After the initial eagerness at the crossroads shootout, Vikram had sunk back into his usual morose silence. Well, anyway, thought Gerard, this latest little job will put some life back into him. Brute force was fine for a foot soldier but Gerard hoped for better things from Vikram. He knew the work ahead would be punishing and rigorous, the assignment the most ambitious the Tigers had undertaken yet. It remained to be seen if the boy was up to the task. Vikram was looking at him expectantly. Oh yes, thought Gerard wearily, the gun. I almost forgot.

'Vikram,' he said patiently, 'you can't take it with you. You will have your own gun once you get to the camp, men. A more up-to-date model. You can't travel with a thing like that across enemy territory. Why can't you understand?'

For a moment he thought the boy would argue. But then Vikram picked up his pass and his papers and left. Silently, as he had come.

Outside, the afternoon was gelatinous with the heat. It was the mosquito season once more. Everywhere the drains were clogged with rotten fruit that had burst open. The sun, dust-laden and harsh, lay with bright indifference over the shuttered town. An occasional bicyclist passed by. Vikram crossed the main road and turned through the coconut grove heading towards Sumaner House and the last of his things. Bony cattle grazed on the common land, chewing a frothy cud, gazing into the distance. A stray dog barked at the breeze. Otherwise the town rested from the heat. Vikram passed by a water pump, stopping to quench his thirst. A few overripe mangoes lay squashed on the ground among a scattering of cigarette stubs and smashed beer bottles. The stench of garbage was everywhere. Since the war had advanced to this corner of the island, even the refuse was not collected. The market stalls had sold out long ago and moved on but the stray cats remained, skimming the ground for a phantom lick of fish, staring sleepily at the flies that swarmed on their sores. Vikram passed the road island and cut across through the temple grounds. Ahead of him was Nulani Mendis. He could see her talking to the local doctor. The doctor was writing something on a piece of paper. Then he nodded and went towards the temple. Seeing Vikram the girl raised her arm in greeting and waited. She was wearing a white dress and she had tied her hair in a coil at the back of her head. She looked cool and very pale. She waited and as he came closer fell into step with him. Vikram was startled. He saw that today she did not smile.

'My mother is not very well,' she said as though she was picking up a previous conversation. She pointed in the direction in which the doctor had gone. 'And I can't get this prescription until four o'clock.' She looked around as though she expected to find what she needed.

'What's the matter with her?' asked Vikram.

'I don't know. I think she misses my brother. It is a terrible thing to lose a son.'

Vikram said nothing, remembering the story of Lucky Jim's departure. Mrs Mendis had thrown a party and most of the school had gone to it.

'I looked for you at my brother's party,' the girl was saying. 'But you didn't come. Have you left school?' she asked, adding, before he could say anything, 'I have. There seems no point. I'm no good at anything.'

She sounded lost. Vikram looked at her curiously. Something, some desperation, uncoiled itself from her and moved towards him. Did she mind that much about her useless brother? He could not think whom she reminded him of.

'You can draw,' he said and the girl smiled so suddenly that Vikram stopped walking, startled.

'Yes,' she nodded. 'I can draw.'

But she spoke flatly, reminding him of the rumours that had once circulated about her silences. He had the strangest of urges to tell her not to mind so much, but the heat and her proximity confused him. Her apparent ease, as though it was an established fact that they were friends, unnerved him too. They walked a little way saying nothing. The girl seemed lost in thoughts of her own.

'What's it like in Sumaner House?' she asked at length. 'Do you get lonely in such a big place?'

She was looking at him. Her eyes were huge and unhappy. He saw that they were very clear, like the eyes of a small child.

'My father was killed too,' she said softly, unexpectedly. 'I expect you've heard. Everyone gossips about it. We never found out who poured petrol over him. The police came, but they never caught anyone. I was in the house when it happened. I saw everything.'

They had come to the top of the lane where her house was. Vikram did not know what to say.

'Don't let gossip worry you,' she continued.

He had the oddest feeling they were talking of something else entirely, that they had spoken in this way before. It seemed to him they were picking up threads from another conversation.

'Everyone does it,' she went on. 'It doesn't mean anything. It's just the way things are.'

'You're friends with the old man at the beach house,' he blurted out unthinkingly.

He knew she would leave in a moment, but he wanted to keep her here, wanted to keep her talking to him. Suddenly he could not bear the thought of her going home. The girl stood for a moment longer, looking at him. Vikram saw that in fact she was exhausted, that possibly she had been crying. Small beads of perspiration had gathered on her brow and there were dark rings under her eyes. And although her hair was coiled up she wore no flower in it as he had often seen her do.

'He has gone away,' she said flatly.

She stared out at the sea. He thought she might say something else but she seemed to change her mind and smiled instead. The smile didn't quite reach her eyes and he wished he hadn't mentioned the old man. Confused, he scuffed the ground with his feet. She put out her hand and touched his arm.

'Don't do that,' she said absent-mindedly. 'You'll ruin your shoes.'

Vikram could think of nothing to say.

'I must go,' she was saying. 'I must make my mother some coriander tea. See you.'

And the next moment she was gone.

Time crawled slowly like the geckos that came out of the cracks in the walls. Every day Nulani returned to the beach house and painted under the watchful eyes of Sugi. He tried to make her eat a little, knowing that when she was at home all her energies were directed towards caring for her mother. Theo had been away for three weeks.

'Halfway there, already,' said Sugi encouragingly.

But it was no use, Sugi could see that her unhappiness was growing and her energy fading like the colour in her green skirt.

'How is your mother today?' he asked. He knew from his friend Thercy that Mrs Mendis was very unwell.

'Must be her broken heart,' Thercy had said. 'Even though her daughter looks after her so lovingly, it's the boy she wants. It was always the boy as far as she was concerned.'

Jim Mendis wrote one letter home. The day the letter arrived the girl came rushing down the hill to Sugi, wanting to tell him the news.

'He shares a house with an English boy,' she said. 'They have become good friends. And he plays cricket,' she said delighted for him.

Sugi listened. Jim Mendis had not asked a single question about his mother or sister.

Theo wrote. Without any hope that the post would reach her, still he wrote. '*I'm longing to come home,*' he said.

Every night, he told her, he put a tick in his diary. He hoped she was missing him as much as he missed her. And, he said, smiling as he wrote, everywhere he looked he saw only her face. Distance had focused his thoughts, stripped him of diffidence. Slowly he wrote his first words of love and, having started, found he could not stop.

The party for the film premiere was very grand, very important, I suppose, but, without you, I didn't have the slightest interest in it. All I could think of was how much I miss you and wonder what you would make of so many strange people, all dressed in their finery. How you would have wanted to draw them all! Everywhere I go I seem to see things with your eyes. You see what you've done to me? And incidentally, have I told you how lovely your eyes are? Or, when you used to sit at the back of the veranda in your lime-green skirt, how impossible it was for me to work? All I wanted to do was to keep you talking so I could stare at you! And now you are so far away. Last night I woke in a panic worrying about whether you were all right. I had to force myself to remember you had Sugi looking after you. I trust Sugi with my life, you know, and so can you. I calmed down when I remembered that. I have told him we are going to get married when I return. I know you won't mind. Sugi only wants us to be happy.

I've been telling my agent a little about you too. Well, he was questioning me. He knew Anna, you see. And he saw how I was after she died. In fact, he was very good to me at the time. Now of course he could see I was different and he was curious to know the reason for this. Transformed, was what he said. Who has done this to you? he asked me. So I told him a little. Not too much, you understand. I'm not ready to share you with too many people yet! But I told him I feel as though a light has been switched on in my life. The light that is you! Three weeks, less, if you don't count the last weekend, and I will be home.

'I can't hear his voice any more,' the girl said to Sugi, panic-stricken. 'He's been away for so long I'm frightened.'

'Draw him, *putha*,' said Sugi soothingly, comforting her as though she was his own child. 'Have faith. He'll be back very soon. You must not be afraid.'

And by some miracle, when she calmed down, she saw that indeed she could draw him from memory. Perfectly.

'See,' said Sugi, triumphantly, 'all those months of practising have been worth it. His likeness is perfect!'

And then, suddenly, her mother's illness was not just simply a broken heart. She had malaria. The doctor was reluctant to admit her to hospital. Conditions were not good there. It would be better, and safer, he told Nulani, if they could nurse her here at home. So Nulani and the servant changed the sweat-sodden sheets and tried as best they could to deal with the deadly sickness as Mrs Mendis's body twisted and turned in agony.

'Soon, very soon, Sir will be back,' said Sugi, who had begun to shop and cook for them.

By the time the first case of malaria occurred Vikram was already in the eastern province at the special camp. The camp was near an underground cave, deep in the jungle. Close by was a river that overflowed in the rainy season. Once this had been a place of pilgrimage but now the ground was full of newly dug graves. The leader of the camp, who was not much older than Vikram, told him the dead were mostly women and children.

'First they were raped,' he told Vikram, 'then we were brought in to shoot them.'

'Who were they?' asked Vikram.

'Muslims.'

The boy told Vikram that the dead amounted to 270. They were people who should not have been living there, it was not their land, it was Tamil land. And their husbands and sons were all in the Singhalese army. The Tigers had turned their submachine guns on them, sending bullets buzzing like bees. And then afterwards the rains had washed the bodies into the river.

Later, the boy told Vikram, the bodies had surfaced, bloated and stinking like cattle, with stiffened limbs. Some soldiers still thought the place was haunted with the souls of the dead, others, that Muslims had no souls to speak of. But that was some weeks ago, the boy told Vikram. Now the whole place had been cleaned up for their camp.

'Were you at Waterlily House?' asked the boy.

'How did you know?'

'I was there with you,' the boy said, grinning. 'You don't remember me, no?'

Vikram shook his head. But he was interested in spite of himself.

'Somebody from your village brought you there after the army killed your family.'

'I don't remember,' Vikram said slowly. 'I've been living in the south.'

The boy nodded. 'My name is Siva Thruban,' he said. 'But everyone calls me Gopal.'

Gopal told Vikram he had been in the camp a long time, perhaps four years.

'After you left, I got moved from Waterlily House. We were on our way by truck to another orphanage when we were ambushed by the Tigers and I was taken to a camp. I was trained there for four months. We did many things,' he added proudly. 'We blew up army jeeps, we carried messages for the Chief, we stole motorcycles and we threw hand grenades.'

He told Vikram the worst fighting was in the north but he had only been on one trip up there.

'What happened to your family?' asked Vikram.

Gopal had no idea. 'The Tigers came in the night to my village,' he said. 'They asked my father where my older brother was. My family had sent my brother away because they knew the Tigers were coming. But the man told my father if they couldn't have my brother then I would have to go with them. I was asleep. They woke me up. My mother was crying, my father was crying too.'

They had taken him away, he said. He had never seen his parents again. He did not know where his brother had gone either. At some point he had been told his family did not want him back. To start with this had angered him.

'It wasn't like your family. *Your family* died. Mine didn't want me.'

But now he no longer cared. Vikram made no comment. He took a can of Coca-Cola from his rucksack and drank it.

'It's not so bad here,' Gopal said after a while. 'It isn't as bad as people think. This is my home now. I wouldn't want to go back to my village. We were forced to pour petrol on the cattle there, and set fire to them. So after that I could never return.'

'You went back to your village?' asked Vikram.

'Oh yes. I had to. It was important that it was my own village. It was my initiation ceremony. Otherwise they told me I would not be able to join the Leopard Brigade. You have to show you don't care about anything! Your family, your village, anything from the past. So, you see, men, I survived all the campaigns,' he said grinning, ticking an imaginary list on his fingers. 'I have been a spy, a courier, a front-line fighter. I have survived all of it.'

They had put him in this special unit because of this ability to court good luck, he said.

'This time we're getting very different kind of training, you know. You've been brought here specially. They told me you are a very good shot, is it true? We're going to be working together on this new campaign.'

Vikram nodded.

'I've been using Type 52 and 58 up to now. But this ambush is different. We'll be told about it tomorrow.'

Gopal took Vikram to his sleeping quarters. They would each have a hammock in a tent on the far side of the camp.

'Have you had suicide training?' he asked Vikram later, when they were alone. 'When I first joined the Tigers I was given a suicide bodysuit with explosives. I wore it when we carried out the attack on Elephant Pass.'

Gopal grinned. He looked for a moment like a small boy. He had been frightened at first, he said, even though he knew they were doing it for the glory of the oppressed. At one point, two of his team stepped on a landmine and were blown up.

'I was very upset at the time,' he continued chattily. 'But, you know, now I've almost forgotten what they looked like. It's the way things are in this business.'

He paused, then made up his mind.

'Look, let me show you something.'

Pulling out a box he showed Vikram his treasures. He had collected razor wire and explosives, wire-cutting tools and a small radio. Then he showed Vikram a pair of designer trainers. They were hardly worn. He had stolen them, he said.

'If my luck runs out,' he said. 'Take them!'

Mrs Mendis was admitted into hospital. Her condition had worsened. All night long Nulani watched as her mother shuddered with the ice-cold chill that shook the bed and sent her body into desperate spasms in its attempt to generate heat. Then, after the terrible cold, came the raging fever. Slowly it became clear that Mrs Mendis was becoming weaker by the hour. Sugi came. He brought food, but Mrs Mendis was beyond eating. So he fetched the doctor instead. The doctor saw the hopelessness of the situation. Where were Mrs Mendis's relatives, her brother? Surely the girl could not make decisions alone? The doctor was not an unsympathetic man but the girl did not seem to understand, the hospital was not necessarily the answer. The wards were overcrowded and understaffed; there was hardly any medicine. Still, something of the girl's distress penetrated some part of the doctor's numbed mind. He found a bed and sent Mrs Mendis there. He could see that Nulani Mendis was at the point of collapse. This was a family well known to him. He had watched as it slowly shrank and dis-integrated. Now, as far as he could see, the daughter had no one left except her thuggish uncle. The doctor had been fond of Mr Mendis; he had seen the children change after his death. The girl had become withdrawn. She has grown very beautiful, he thought, looking at her tiredly. But what use were her looks without her family to protect her? So he admitted Mrs Mendis to hospital in the hope that she would recover. And Nulani, travelling in the ambulance, glad that her mother would get well quickly, thought, in less than a week Theo will be back from the UK.

They were biding their time. In between the training sessions at dawn the Leopards spent endless hours of intolerable boredom. Waiting. Waiting for what? No one would say. They knew the next mission would be dangerous, but that was hardly surprising. Nearly everything they did in this unit was lethal. Only twelve of the original thirty recruits from Waterlily House had survived. The rest were all new and therefore younger.

'Would you swallow the cyanide?' asked Gopal as they began to pack. Finally the orders had come that the operation was to begin. 'If you get caught, I mean.'

'No.'

'What, not even if they tortured you?'

Vikram shook his head. He frowned and continued to reload his gun. This new model was smaller and deadlier. It was lightweight even with the silencer fitted. But he preferred his old one.

'I would,' said Gopal cheerfully. 'What's the point of suffering?'

They had finished their preparation. In a few hours they would move from the camp and head through the jungle for Katunayake Airport. Vikram and Gopal had worked closely together during the past few weeks. As the oldest in the group, they were the leaders. The youngest were only ten. They were the runners and would carry the explosives.

'Your father took cyanide, didn't he? That's what they said at Waterlily House.'

'Yes,' said Vikram shortly.

He clicked the safety catch on. Then he wiped the back of his hand across his face. The humidity had risen to unbearable levels since the morning. The swampy ground was a hotbed of mosquitoes and other insects. Gerard had told him he could go back to the south once this job was done. He glanced at his watch. They were due at the airport by four. It was now midday. Gopal was still talking. He didn't seem to be in any rush.

'Did you have brothers?' he asked.

The appalling heat did not seem to bother Gopal.

'No,' said Vikram. 'Gopal, aren't you ready?'

'Almost,' said Gopal. 'I thought you said you had a brother.'

'I only had a sister.'

Had she lived she would have been twenty-eight now. The thought came to Vikram quite calmly, without effort, as though it was an everyday occurrence for him to think of his sister. There had been a man who visited them, he remembered suddenly. Somehow, even though he had been small, he had known the man only visited because of his sister. He remembered nothing else of the man, except that he was always at their house and his sister was always happy when he was there. She used to smile in a secret, inexplicable way at these times. She laughed when she played with Vikram and she was happy when she helped their mother. But with the man, she had been different. Vikram had not understood the difference, only that it was not how she looked at any of them. He frowned, thinking all this suddenly. Seeing the vivid green of the plantain trees near their house, the walk to the well and the schoolteacher who had taught him his alphabet. H for hollyhocks, the schoolteacher had written on his slate.

'I think I saw my brother when we were at Elephant Pass,' Gopal was saying. 'Just before we blew up the bridge. If it was him he didn't see me, or didn't want to.'

Vikram blinked. For a moment he had forgotten where he was. He looked pointedly at his watch and Gopal laughed good-naturedly.

'OK, OK, men. Have you become our new Chief or something?' He began to collect together the last of his things. He was in charge of the two boys who would carry the explosives. He would see to it they planted them in the correct spot. Unusually, everything had been organised with precision. Vikram would detonate the bombs. For once headquarters wanted to reduce the number of casualties among the Tigers. Gopal opened his box and took out the pair of Adidas trainers. He wiped them with his shirt. Then he put them back in the box. Their belongings were to be loaded into a different truck. The camp was being dismantled for security reasons and would regroup elsewhere. Their possessions would be moved on while they were at the airport.

'What d'you think of Meera?' Gopal asked suddenly, jerking his head in the direction of the girls' camp.

Vikram finished loading his gun and began clearing out his pockets.

'D'you think she's pretty?'

'She's all right,' said Vikram. 'She's a good shot,' he added. 'For a girl.'

Gopal laughed, a high-pitched excited laugh. Vikram looked sharply at him.

'D'you like any of them here, Vikram?'

'No,' said Vikram. 'Not here.'

'Where then?'

'Somewhere else,' Vikram said shortly.

'Really?' Gopal was interested. 'Have you got a photo, men?'

His sharp eyes darted feverishly about and he moved his head from side to side, grinning. He reminded Vikram of a stray mongrel he had once seen. He thought of the temple on the hill, near Sumaner House. The breeze had been clean and fresh, not at all like the heavy, rancid air they breathed in the camp. Through the trees he had glimpsed small cameos of the sea. And the girl's dress had been piercingly white in the sunlight, absorbing the heat, changing it into something sweet and very calm. He heard her voice, over and over in his head. He had seen her twice more before he left. On one occasion, she had been standing in the queue at the dispensary in the lime-green skirt he had often seen her wear. She had not seen him. She stood quietly staring at the ground, patiently waiting her turn in the queue. And her face in profile had such a look of acceptance that it had hit him like a spasm of pain. He had moved away, not wanting her to see him, not understanding why he felt this way. And then there had been the last time on the way to the station when he was leaving. It had been early in the morning and he had been in a hurry. On an impulse he had decided to walk along the sea road and over the hill, as Gerard had advised and in order to avoid being seen. And then he had come across her standing motionless staring at the railway line. She had turned and he saw she was deep in thought and did not recognise him. But then she had come towards him and touched his arm asking him where he was going.

'I like to watch the train from Colombo,' she had volunteered. 'When I can't sleep it's what I like to do. My mother is in the hospital at the moment, and I like to wake early so I can visit her.'

Vikram told her he was going to Colombo. 'To meet a relative,' he lied, and at that she had said she was glad he had someone left from his family. Even in his confusion he had felt the sincerity of her words.

'Hurry or you'll miss the train,' she had said. 'I'll wave to you when it goes.'

She had smiled at him and then, just as he had turned to go, she had reached up and kissed him on the cheek. Gopal was staring at him.

'No,' said Vikram. 'No, I've no photo. And we'd better go.'

They crouched, watching as it came into view. It appeared as a small speck in the sky, glinting in the sun, descending fast, heading for the runway, graceful as a gull. The sun was on its wings and it had travelled seven thousand miles. In spite of the tension Vikram was mesmerised by the sight of the aeroplane. He lay flat on the ground clutching his radio, holding it to his mouth. From where he was he could just make out the outline of the others as they waited for the plane to land. The two boys were already close to the runway, under some airport trucks. Gopal, the most experienced of them all, was not far behind with the silencer fitted on his revolver. He would have to shoot the driver of the fuel tanker and possibly some of the ground staff. The stationary fleet of empty aircraft were dotted around in bays and the two boys placed a small black box close to the base of each fuel tank. So far everything had been straightforward. Someone had provided them with access to the enclosed grounds, and now, Vikram knew, the runners were waiting tensely for the oncoming plane to land. Once the passengers had disembarked the runners would plant the final cache of explosives under it before taking cover. Vikram had had his own private briefing. The Chief had shaken Vikram's hand and told him he had great plans for him. If at the given moment there were still people on the tarmac, he had said, it did not matter. If they did not move quickly enough, Vikram was to trigger the bombs regardless. It was his priority, the Chief had emphasised, somehow making it sound as though he was giving Vikram a warning. Did Vikram understand, the Chief asked? This was a war, not a game of cricket.

'Your responsibilities are to the Tamil people, not to individuals,' he had said.

Then the Chief shook Vikram's hand warmly again.

'We shall grind this country to a halt,' he had said, loudly. 'We have to let the world see that we mean business. Only then, after we've taught them a lesson, will they listen. There will be no aircraft, no runway, no way out! What will they do then, men?'

Having glared at Vikram, he smiled suddenly and reminded him once again of his family, and what had been done to them.

'Don't forget that, Vikram, not even for one single moment. It is your duty to avenge their memory.'

He told Vikram he would be listening to the news all day. And if it was a success, it would be Vikram's doing.

'There will be plenty of rewards,' he promised. 'Plenty, plenty, men.'

Vikram began his countdown, slowly, as the wheels of the aircraft touched the ground. He would wait exactly eight minutes. Eight minutes for it to clear itself of passengers and crew. There would be no time for the baggage trolleys. Anything or anyone still on the tarmac after that had only their karma to blame. The passengers began to disembark. From where he was they were merely a collection of unrecognisable shapes of brightly coloured saris, and the tropical suits of Westerners refusing to believe in warnings. Vikram could not see their faces. He counted silently, staring at his watch, his mind perfectly clear now. He did not look up, he did not see if the small boys had cleared the fence. He could not see Gopal or any of the others. He simply pressed the button.

Turning as he reached the airport doors, hearing the noise, feeling the blast of heat, Theo Samarajeeva saw the plane he had just arrived on become a coffin of flames. There was a shout of warning as another explosion went off. And another, and another. People screamed and begun running towards the building in blind panic. Two more explosions followed. Glass and metal were flying in all directions and smoke poured across the runway. In the chaos no one could tell if it was the airport itself that was burning. The revolving doors became jammed with passengers caught in the rush to escape. As more glass shattered the police appeared and began their stampede on to the tarmac, accompanied by firefighters and ambulance men. The public address system pleaded for calm in English and in Singhalese but there was no calm to be had. A wall of black smoke arose, blotting out the sun, muffling the sounds of the screams of sirens and guns and those who were trapped outside.

He was running through the long grass. Four of them were missing already and Gopal was bleeding. Part of his arm had

139

been ripped off and now hung limply. A piece of metal was embedded in his leg. He was panting and his face was slowly draining of all colour. Vikram was half dragging and half carrying him but he was a deadweight.

'Try to walk,' he said harshly. 'We've got to make it to the trees. Then at least we will be hidden.'

'I can't,' Gopal said faintly. 'You go.' He was fumbling in his shirt pocket.

'It's not much further. Come on. I'm going to put you on my back.' Vikram hoisted Gopal up. 'Put your arm around my neck,' he said with gritted teeth.

But Gopal struggled against him and slid to the ground. There was the sound of something moving in the bushes. Vikram turned swiftly, cocking his gun, looking around him.

'Vikram,' hissed Gerard appearing in front of him on all fours. 'Get to the trees,' he said. 'The army has arrived. They're everywhere. We'll have to go south to avoid the roadblocks. Quickly, now!'

Vikram turned back to Gopal. He was struggling with something in his mouth. Before he could reach him, Gerard whispered sharply, 'Leave him, Vikram! He's finished. Leave him. Come. Now! Before it's too late.'

Through the sour odour of explosives and sweat Vikram caught the unmistakable scent of almonds, and in that instant he realised Gopal had bitten into his cyanide capsule. And he saw too that Gerard was running towards the covering of trees.

By the time the army helicopters were hovering over the airport, Vikram was already heading for the east coast of the island. It had not been an easy journey and they had changed vehicles three times in order to avoid being seen.

'You've got me to thank for saving you,' said Gerard grimly.

'You bloody sentimental fool! A few more minutes and they'd have spotted you.'

Vikram was silent.

'They would have strung you up,' said Gerard. 'You damn idiot! They would have tortured you and made you talk. And then they would have killed you. D'you realise that?'

Vikram was coughing. The smoke had filled his lungs and he was covered in cuts. The bittersweet smell of almonds seemed everywhere, in his clothes, on his hands, in his mouth. The smell came back to him from some place deep within his past. It was now past midnight. He had been without sleep or food for almost a day. Gopal was dead.

'At least he had the sense to take his capsule,' said Gerard pointedly. 'This had better not get back to the Chief. Although,' he added, as Vikram continued to say nothing, 'it was a success in spite of the fact that only you survived. I expect you think you're immortal, no?'

Laughing in a loud and jerky way, his gestures oddly un-coordinated, Gerard turned the radio on. Again Vikram smelt almonds. The news, in Singhalese, was of nothing else except the airport bombing. The runway was unusable. Any refuelling was out of the question; nothing could take off or enter the country. Those foreigners still on the island would be flown from the army airbase to the Maldives where they would wait for any available international flights. Gerard laughed again and switched channels.

'See,' he said proudly. 'My planning and your operation. We're quite a team!'

Vikram was searching the radio stations. He ignored Gerard.

'*In Sri Lanka a series of explosions that set fire to seven aircraft in the international airport of Katunayake has brought the country to a standstill. The Foreign Office has advised against travel within*

*the region. Tamil separatists have claimed responsibility and the
Sri Lankan government has declared a state of emergency.'*

'So the Chief has made a statement,' said Gerard. He spoke
very quietly. His good mood had evaporated and he clenched
his fists. His whole body was tense again. 'He might have told
me,' he muttered darkly. 'Who made the tape? Who delivered
it, huh? Which ignorant Tamil bastard?'

'What happens next?' asked Vikram.

'We go down south,' said Gerard shortly. 'I have a job for
you. Only you can do it. And, Vikram,' Gerard said, 'it won't
involve guns, I'm afraid. Not yet. You'll need to lie low for a
while. Anyway, I've already told the Chief you're working for
me. It's a waste using you as a foot soldier.'

They were reaching the camp.

'Get some sleep,' said Gerard.

'I need to get Gopal's things.'

'What?' asked Gerard. 'Oh, they were probably dumped. Did
you really believe anyone would come out alive from this operation? Count yourself lucky.' He paused. 'You're working for
me from now on,' he said at last. 'Get some sleep. I'll pick you
up in a couple of hours.'

And he stopped the car.

8

SHE WAS WAITING FOR THEO ON the brow of the hill, wearing the red dress that she had first worn on her seventeenth birthday. She looked smaller than he remembered. Her dark hair was loose, and he saw she had been crying. He knew then that she had heard of the bombings on the radio. She had heard it and had not known if he was safe. But he was here now, even though it seemed as though he had been away for years. Suddenly all his tiredness, his anxieties for her safety in his absence, the horror of all he had just seen, and the pity, all of it vanished as he hurried towards her. He could see the house in the distance with the late-afternoon sun, warm and golden on the stone lions, the faded blue gate, the bougainvillea that cascaded over the wall, all exactly as he had left it. The weeks in London, the fuss of the film premiere, the press, none of it was of the slightest significance. The sea swung into view, unchanged and un-utterably beautiful, and the day became fixed in this one moment, with the view and the black eyes of the girl, as he came towards her. Why had they worried?

'I'm home,' he said tenderly, laughing a little, thinking how like this place she was, unchanged and so lovely. 'I told you I would be back, no?' he said taking her in his arms. 'So why are you crying?' he asked. 'And tomorrow,' he continued, smiling at her, delighting in the words, 'tomorrow we will speak to your mother.'

She had begun to cry in earnest then, and he had said nothing. Letting her cry, listening to the sound of the terrible desperation that came of living through a war that had torn apart her family. He said nothing, stroking her hair, thinking of all that she had lost in her short life, and all that she might yet lose, of all the hurt that had come too early, and would now mark her for ever. But she had gone on crying, for how could she tell him, after all the horror he had seen, and her terror that he might have been caught up in it somehow, how could she tell him that her mother had died that morning?

Later, he watched her face, silvery pale in the flight path of the moon. She had not slept properly for weeks, he knew, but now she slept, as trusting as a child. Behind them the sea whispered in the darkness, shimmering like wild silk, and the night returned to him in a series of disconnected moments, with all the rush and touch of unfamiliar love. He could smell the sea as he had kissed the pebble smoothness of her shoulder. So close, they had never been this close. Time had unfolded. The palms of his hands had felt calloused and rough against the hollow of her throat, the lobe of her ear, the corners of her mouth. She kissed him back. She pulled his head down towards her and kissed his mouth. Instinct had kept him still when she touched him; it kept him silent as he watched her shed the last remnants of her childhood. He stroked her back; his hands went on forays of their own, until at last she was naked. They lay on the edge of the moon-white bed and he drew her towards him then, and kissed her breasts and the soft places that had belonged until now only to her young-girl aloneness. He waited, and only when he saw the knot inside her had eased a little did he enter her, moving as though he were a hummingbird, travelling deeper and deeper into the forest. Further and further he travelled until at last, when he could go no further, when all his longings could no longer be contained, when he had touched her deepest, most secret part, he dissolved within her. The lights were out, the darkness was complete and he could hear the sound of the sea rising out of a new distance. The girl had looked up at him with a grave and beautiful smile as they lay on the crumpled sheets and he saw that from now on he would see himself for ever defined by her eyes.

They slept then. And all the sad, terrible events of the day, the bombs at the airport, the hours sitting by her mother's bedside, the agony of waiting, her brother's absence, all these things slept with them. And in this way, serenely and at peace, the night had ebbed away, unnoticed as the sea rocked against the shore. When he woke again Theo knew some rain had fallen. He could smell the fresh green wetness of the garden drifting in through the window. Of such moments was paradise made, he thought, smiling in the darkness. He felt as if he had been travelling for ever, through eternity and through many lives. He thought again of the useless weeks in London, his film, the people he had met, the pointlessness of all of it. He would never leave her again. After her mother's funeral, they would go to Colombo and he would marry her. Sugi had been relieved when he heard. Rohan and Giulia would be delighted. He would ring them again in the morning. Last night had been too fraught, too frantic. Last night he had thought only of her needs. And of his. Tomorrow would be time enough.

The moon had slipped behind a cloud. He had woken and now he was thirsty. The long flight back had dehydrated him.

Something had woken him, some rustle in the garden. He listened, thinking he had heard the gate creak. There were no lights, the moonlight had moved over the sea and the garden. The house was still. But something had woken Theo. Slowly a thread of awareness uncurled itself with the rapidity of a snake. No one could have entered the garden without the light going on, but he decided to check the veranda anyway; and get a glass of water. Outside, the sea breeze moved uneasily with a soft murmur and suddenly he saw a car headlight, thin and sulphurous, on the road. The light was stationary. Sugi too must have seen it for he was up and had moved to the window.

'It's her uncle, Sir,' he whispered.

Sugi was wide awake and holding a crowbar. How long had he been standing there?

'He's been back twice in the night already, while you were asleep. He's looking for her, I think. We must get her out of here quickly. It's a very bad thing that he should be here at all.'

'How long have you been awake?'

'Most of the night. I was worried they would come looking for her. She should have gone home tonight, Sir. Have you hidden the money in the well?'

'Yes, don't worry. I don't think it's money he's after anyway. I'm sorry you were woken, Sugi. Go back to bed. I'll talk to him.'

'No, Sir,' said Sugi sharply, alarmed. 'You don't understand. If the uncle has come here it isn't good. You must not let him see you. With any luck he'll think there's no one in.'

But Theo had lived too long by different rules. It had made him foolish. Nothing of what he had ever witnessed had changed that. He had smudged the boundaries between what he saw and what he wanted to see. He had been an exile for so long that it had altered his judgement, leaving him vulnerable in ways he did not understand. And he had underestimated the nature of things. So he would not listen to Sugi.

'I will go out,' he said, 'I will talk to him. I want to marry Nulani; there is nothing for the man to worry about. I will tell him that. It will make all the difference, you'll see.'

And all Sugi's whispered pleadings were of no use. Theo went out, unarmed and hopefully, towards the uncle.

There were others there, Sugi knew. He could hear their voices, the uncle and Theo and then the voice of another man. They were out of Sugi's field of vision, their voices raised and agitated. Then he heard a sound. In some part of his mind he knew it was the crack of a sharp object as it met bone. He heard a long, hollow scream and a shot, then another shot, and then the sound of a car reversing swiftly up the lane. Standing rooted to the spot, Sugi felt sickness spreading coldly through him, his mind bludgeoned with horror. He heard a voice, whimpering from somewhere nearby, but it was a moment longer before he realised that it was the sound of his own heart, crying.

Sugi bent over the girl. He could see the moonlight on her face as she slept, innocent of what had just occurred. That she was in danger, that she was alone once more. That last night was the last carefree moment of her life; that only minutes before she had held everything she ever wanted. Whoever had brought her the news of her father's death would have known, thought Sugi, how he felt now. Sleep marked her face like a caress as he shook her awake. Three times in her short life, he thought, his whispers fluttering towards her, confused and urgent. In the distance a train hooted, reaching far into the night, a sound of infinite loneliness, hauntingly sad. Sugi could see she was still half asleep. He could see his words shifting in and out of meaning, elusive and insubstantial. He saw that her sleep-filled limbs were still disconnected from her mind, that she could not yet be prepared to feel Theo's absence. Perhaps, he thought, with a feeling of terrible pity, perhaps she never would be prepared. So thought Sugi as he finally shook her awake, seeing also, by the way in which his words fixed in her mind, that she understood in the clearest moment of horror that she would not hear Theo Samarajeeva's voice again.

The moon, like a searchlight, shone relentlessly over the room. It silhouetted the chair, the corner of the wardrobe mirror and Theo's shoes. Staring at them in the second before the girl's despair broke open and he put his hand over her mouth, Sugi remembered also, as though it was an ordinary matter, that her mother had died yesterday. He held the passport Theo had left, and told her swiftly what they must do. They had no time to lose. At any moment the men might return. Sir had wanted her to be taken to Colombo, to safety. He had not wanted her uncle to find her here. It had been Sir's biggest fear, Sugi told her.

'Quickly,' he said, helping her to gather her things, locking up the house, hurrying her out of the back gate and across the moonlit beach. 'There's a train that passes the level crossing by the next cove. It's the mail train to Colombo and it passes in twenty minutes.' Her uncle might be back at any moment. 'I will come with you to Colombo,' Sugi said. 'After I get you to the house of his friends, I will come back with Mr Rohan and find Sir. I promise you,' he said.

Theo had made emergency plans many months ago, Sugi told her. Should there be trouble Sugi was to take her to Rohan and Giulia. She would be safe there. She *must* come, Sugi insisted, desperate now, for the girl refused to move.

'They must not find you here,' he pleaded. 'It will be worse for Sir. I will come back and find him. I *will* find him. You must believe me. Let's not waste any more time, please.'

He would find Theo, he told her again and again, cajoling her across the endless stretch of sand. Dead or alive, he thought grimly, he would find Theo. He saw the moon reflected in her frightened eyes, as she protested.

'I promise, I promise,' Sugi murmured, holding her cold hands in his, knowing only that he should follow Theo's wishes. Knowing only that he could not break his promise.

'Once you are with Sir's friends, I will go back and find him. I promise. I promise. Please, Miss Nulani, Sir did not want your uncle to harm you.'

The beach was cool and smooth, their footsteps clearly visible as they walked in an endless line of steps towards the next bay. They passed the catamarans half sunk into the sand; the places where the coconut palms bent low and local children had rigged a swing once, long ago. The sea and the sky were joined as one tonight as they walked the beach unheeding, looking neither to right or left. Sugi's anxiety propelled them on. The girl carried a small bag with a few things; a comb, her earrings, a change of clothes. It was all she had now. Pity flooded Sugi's heart. He dared not voice his thoughts but he feared Theo was dead.

Memories criss-crossed his mind. Once long ago, when Mr Mendis was alive, before things had become bad, Sugi had seen him take his small daughter out in a fishing boat. They were going out to the reef, he had said. The fishermen had begun to sing a *kavi* and they had waved at Sugi, asking him if he wanted to come with them. The sea was calm, they had said, they could make a fisherman of him yet, they joked. But Sugi had not gone and they had vanished slowly into the night. A few days later he had seen Mr Mendis again. He was walking on the beach with the child. He had stopped to tell Sugi about the trip. He had wanted his daughter to understand the lives of the fishermen who lived here, he had said. Only then, he told Sugi, only when she understands the traditions of her home will she truly love it. Mr Mendis had spoken with a passion that had surprised Sugi. He loved this land, he had said, and he wanted his daughter to love it too. And now, thought Sugi, his daughter was hurrying away, leaving it all behind.

Sugi walked on, his mind darting backwards and forwards in a confusion of thoughts. He desperately wanted to get the girl to safety and return as quickly as he could. He wanted to get help, to find Theo. Dead or alive, he thought, I must find him. But first they must stop the train. If they missed it as it slowed down at the crossing there would not be another one until the morning. Her uncle, or his friends, anyone, might spot them later on.

'I promised him I would get you out,' he said again, in a voice barely above a whisper. 'But I *will* find him.'

As they rounded the corner of the bay they heard the train hooting. The moon had disappeared as they scrambled up and across the dunes to a place where giant cacti grew beside a cluster of coconut trees. They were almost at the crossing now. The coast road, narrow and completely empty, stretched beside the railway line. Sugi was calling hoarsely to her, urging her to hurry for they were in an exposed and vulnerable position. At any moment the train could come thundering towards them, or an army convoy might appear. The moon reappeared, and at the same instant Sugi saw the signal was still green. He needed to get to the signal box beside the level crossing several minutes before the train reached the first bay if he was to stop it. He ran on the last hundred yards shouting to Nulani to keep off the track. His voice whipped across the breeze telling her to be careful. Hardly had he reached the barrier and lowered it, when the tracks began to vibrate. Instantly the lights changed and they heard the train beginning to slow down. In order to scramble on to the truck with the mail bags they needed to run back along the line to a point where they could board the train more easily. They had only a minute to do this. The headlights stretched across the tracks and the train roared into view, hissing and slowing down. It would not stop moving completely, Sugi, shouted again. She must wait until he told her to jump. They were crouching beside the giant cacti as the wheels screeched and the brakes locked. All of a sudden two army jeeps careered across the bend of the road and some figures stepped into the headlights of the train. Two men walked over to the crossing. Two more followed them. Out of the corner of his eye Sugi recognised one of them. He was shining a torch on the track, and under the wheels. The lights had not changed yet.

'Now,' hissed Sugi. 'Jump! Now! Now!'

He pushed a small bag into her hands and in one swift movement she was up and over into the mail truck. The train began to move and as she turned in the darkness of the carriage to see where he was she heard a sharp volley of gunfire. Through the small gap left in the slats she could see Sugi. He had slipped down on to the tracks and had begun to run towards the beach. He zigzagged crazily, shouting at the men, waving his hands, drawing attention to himself. The men turned sharply and began to shoot at him even as the lights changed. The girl stood rooted to the spot, watching with horror, unaware that the train was moving, as they emptied a steady stream of bullets into Sugi, and in that moment she realised that one of the men was her uncle. The train began to gather speed and she saw that Sugi had given her the bag containing her passport and money, moments before he decided to distract her uncle from searching the train. And, as she watched through her blinding tears, as the train rattled noisily along the coast, she saw also that the dawn was beginning to appear faintly from the east, enduring and very beautiful.

At daybreak the seagulls returned with the fishermen trawling their catamarans. The night had been full of fish, silvery-stiff in death, and plentiful. Dragging their nets along the beach, they saw the body. It was completely unrecognisable, blackened and filled with holes, in its stomach, on its legs and what were once arms and face. When the fishermen's gaze reached up to the head, they saw that grey substance had seeped out. In the early-morning light it spread like delicate fronds of coral on the sands. The sea began to edge around, nudging against it, foaming and darkly red. Overhead the seagulls screamed, circling in great wild swoops above the day's catch, while the fishermen watched as Sugi's body rocked gently on its journey out to sea.

9

ONLY AFTERWARDS DID THEY ASK THEMSELVES, why had they not been more prepared? Many days later, when she could think a little, Giulia had remembered, a knock on the door at that hour was never good. Knowing all they did, they should have seen how much there was to lose. Did they think they were exempt from loss? Did they think this war was meant for others than themselves? Somehow, thought Giulia in the small hours of the sleepless nights that followed, we should have been prepared. But they had not seen it, lurking in wait, ready to pounce, sweeping them along in the wave of insanity that characterised this civil war. Theo had rung them briefly earlier the day before. He had told them he had been at the airport but was safe now. He would ring them, he had said, in the morning. And soon he would bring the girl to visit them. There was something, he had told them, laughing excitedly, that he wanted to tell them. They had not heard him sound this way in years. Guessing his news, teasing him, they too had been glad. But Theo, they now realised with horror, had simply come home to die.

The girl stood at their door. She was etched palely against

the moonlight, carved as though in sandstone, surrounded by the sounds of geckos and bullfrogs, and even in her grief her face remained beautiful. Why had this shocked them so much? Here was proof, they whispered, here was evidence of the fragility of life. She had found them by some miracle; she had come, because, she cried, there was nowhere else for her to go. Rohan was the quickest to understand. And he saw in a moment, reading Sugi's hastily scribbled note, that it was all over. Finished.

'Come back with me,' Nulani had begged them. 'Please! Quickly, come and talk to my uncle.'

But, Rohan asked, what about Sugi? Where was he?

And it was only then, with a voice barely above a whisper, that she had cried, 'He's dead.' That was what she had said. 'They *killed* him! I saw him die!'

Wanting to hide their shock, folding it up tightly, they had tried to tuck it out of sight; but it remained, untidily, visible. Forcing them to confront the unthinkable. Rohan, always the quickest, saw the girl still hoped Theo was alive. He saw she was still warm with the touch of him and would not unclasp herself from it. Sugi, it seemed, had known the only way to get her to Colombo was to let her believe this. Giulia sent the servant to fetch the doctor. The doctor had many contacts all over the island, he could make some enquiries in the morning, he promised. For now he sedated Nulani Mendis and together they reread Sugi's note.

'*If I don't contact you in a day, you must send her to safety. You mustn't let them find her. It was what he wanted.*'

Theo, they saw, had taken care of everything. There was a passport for the girl, money for a ticket, instructions in case of an emergency. They were stunned, fearful for her safety. The enormity of their task frightened them.

'But how can we do this, Rohan?!' Giulia said. 'Theo might still be alive. He might be held captive somewhere. We can't just send her away. It's too big a decision for us.'

The sedative had begun to work; at last the girl's eyes began to close. Their whispers were low and vaporous in the darkened room.

'Keep her with you,' the doctor murmured. 'Don't let her out. You don't know what could happen. I'll see what information I can find among my patients. Theo Samarajeeva was well known. But so, unfortunately, were his pro-Tamil views, he should not have come back to live here. It was such a foolish thing to do.'

'This was his home,' Rohan said angrily. 'Where else should he have gone? He wrote the truth, about things we all believed in.'

'Shh!' Giulia said, glancing nervously at the girl.

They watched over her, listening to her breathing, thinking of their friend, knowing that at least while she slept, her pain was held in abeyance.

'He should have lived in Colombo,' the doctor said. 'He might have had better protection here.'

'It's no good talking about what he should have done,' said Rohan. 'We need to find him now.'

The doctor shook his head, sorrowfully. 'I will see what I can do. But I have to say, in my experience . . . once they get into the hands of the army, there's not much hope, you know.'

They fell silent then, their minds numbed as much by the lateness of the hour as the horror of what they were facing.

That had been three days ago. Three unimaginable days of watching Nulani Mendis's descent into hell. On the evening of the third day the doctor returned. It was true, he said, what the girl had said was true. Someone, an unidentified man, had been shot on the beach, beside the level crossing. It must have been the manservant, the doctor supposed. And Theo Samarajeeva had indeed disappeared without trace. Local people had heard the sounds of a shoot-out, but had stayed indoors, not wanting to be mixed up in it. Someone had told him the man who was the girl's uncle terrorised the town.

'Better send her to the UK then,' he said at last, into the silence. 'At least she'll be safe there. Get her out if you can.'

He smiled wearily, waiving his fee. Leaving them with some pills for her before stepping out once more into the night.

'You know she won't go, Rohan,' Giulia murmured. 'Can you see her leaving without him? She'll never leave.'

'She has a brother in England. We'll have to tell her what the doctor said. She'll have to know the truth, if she doesn't already guess it. I think she does, I think in her heart she understands she'll never see him again. So what is there for her to stay for, tell me? What is there for any of us here now?' he asked.

Bitterness formed a crust over his words. Bitterness mixed with betrayal. Until now he had always loved his home.

Later Rohan went out, dodging the curfew, hurrying along the darkened alleyways of the city with the girl's forged passport in his pocket. Somehow, using his contacts, he managed to get a seat on the last remaining flight out. It was on a plane that touched down briefly at the private airport reserved for short local flights. That the girl was Singhalese helped. That she had forged documents stating British citizenship also helped. Theo had thought of everything, it seemed. Everything except his own death. The flight was in the evening of the following day. She would fly to Chennai and change planes there.

But they had reckoned without her. Nulani Mendis did not want to go. Clinging to Giulia, desperate, refusing all sedatives, refusing food, her face swollen with tears, she refused to go. Today her mother was to be cremated, she told them piteously, how could she go? She begged them, and then she argued with them, screaming in a way they would not have believed possible. They began to fear for her sanity. She had come here, she said, believing they would help her. Believing Sugi would find Theo, that he would follow her to Colombo. That was why she came, she said. Didn't they understand? How could they betray her in this way? She was going back, now. No one could stop her. She was going back to find him.

'I don't care what happens to me,' she cried wildly. Anger overtook grief. Why had Sugi lied to her? she demanded. Why had he not told her that Theo was dead?

In the end it was left to Rohan to persuade her.

'Nulani, listen,' he said, stroking her hair, holding her as she struggled. 'Sugi did the best he could. He was frightened. And he had to make a quick decision. He didn't want you to die as well. It had been Theo's last wish, should anything happen, that Sugi would get you out. Sugi was only keeping his promise. Please, Nulani, understand, he loved you both.'

She said nothing.

'Theo always worried something like this might happen. He made emergency plans some months ago, you know. In his heart, I think he knew it wasn't really safe here. If he was forced to leave he wanted to take you with him. Why else would he have got these travel documents for you? It wasn't an easy matter getting a false passport. It took months of negotiation; it was a dangerous business. And he had an instinct, a sixth sense, you know. So that with him, or without him, he needed to be certain you would be safe. So you see, *putha*, you *must* go. For his sake you must. Even more so now your mother has died.'

157

She covered her ears, weeping.

'It's true,' Rohan said. 'While your mother was there you had some protection. Now you have none.'

He paused, shocked by what he was doing but determined nonetheless. She became silent.

'Can't you see, child?' Rohan said more gently, as the storm of weeping showed no sign of abating. He felt the weight of what he had to do grow dark and rotten inside him. He was shocked to the core of his being by it, but still he continued. 'Sugi only did what he believed Theo wanted. He paid a terrible price. But *we* will keep looking. We'll *never* stop looking. And you know that if he is still alive, he'll find you, somehow. *You* know that. So you see, you must go.'

She gave in then, the pointlessness of her struggle leaving her speechless for the second time in her life. And Giulia sitting beside her, holding her, thought, first her father and now this. How will she ever recover from *this*? But Rohan, having seen what he must do, did not waver. He kept talking; about Theo, and what she had meant to him, and the bleakness of his life after Anna had died, before he had met her.

'We, none of us, could give him what you did, Nulani. You were a sort of gift. He told me, I promise you, the last time we spoke. He said it many times; you were the last gift in his life. Hold on to that. Like a coconut palm in the monsoon, you must bend *with* the wind.'

And, he thought, one day, many years from now, please God, you will paint away your grief. One day all this will find its way into your work. An orphan, Giulia thought, giving her the last of the sedatives, waiting with her until she slept the drug-induced sleep of utter exhaustion.

'I can't stay in this place much longer,' Rohan said finally, watching as she slept. He felt utterly desolate and alone, it seemed he had been fighting this war for ever. 'We must go back to Europe. I can't live with this savagery.'

Far away, in another life, were other seagulls sitting on the boat posts, the *briccole*, that marked out the waters of Giulia's home. Now, overcome with longing she wanted to go back to them. She had been away for too long. Lately, even before recent events, the sickness in her husband's country had begun to defeat her. She felt homesickness, never very far away, returning.

'We are all she's got, you know,' Rohan was saying.

I can't take any more, thought Giulia.

'In Europe at least we will be able to keep an eye on her.'

'There's her brother too.'

'Him! Well, I'm not so sure, you heard what . . . she will have no help there.' Suddenly he felt he could no longer bear to say his friend's name out loud.

The girl lay drugged and inert, watched over by them. Twice during that night the telephone rang, slicing into the silence, but when Rohan answered it, no one was there. The drive to the airport skirted the jungle on a road that had been ambushed many times. Their car was old, there were no street lights and they would have to leave well before the curfew. But what if they broke down, on that lonely stretch of road, what if the plane was delayed or her passport did not hold up to scrutiny? What if someone knowing her connection with Theo saw them? Anything was possible.

'This was done because of his books,' Rohan said, at last. They had hardly slept, hardly eaten. Both of them were beyond weeping. 'And the film, of course. That couldn't have helped. They had warned him, you know. He told me this when they visited. He knew they had wanted him for a long time, but he took no notice.'

'I don't understand,' said Giulia. 'He had everything to live for, everything to be careful for. Why did he take so many risks?'

'A man has to survive, Giulia. You cannot expect a man to skulk in fear of everything, especially a man such as Theo.'

Giulia was silent. Truly, she thought, it was time they went back to Europe. Rohan had not been Theo's friend for nothing. He could not skulk either; now less so than ever. And Giulia was afraid.

The cremation of Mrs Mendis, unlike that of her husband, went according to plan. Her brothers, who had shown no interest in her welfare since her marriage, turned up in full force. They sat, all together, with their wives, their children, the neighbours, the schoolteacher, the Buddhist monks and the Catholic priests in the seldom used sitting room. There were so many of them that they spilled out on to the veranda and down the steps into the garden. The servant had so much work that someone had paid for extra help. The woman Thercy, from Sumaner House, helped the servant. Mrs Mendis, in her white sari and the jacket that her daughter had embroidered long ago, was lying in her coffin for all to see. She was surrounded by flowers. There was a wreath from her son with love to his amma. The boy could not get back for his mother's funeral. Everyone understood that. What with the airport closed because of the bastard Tamils and poor Jim's poverty, he was forced to stay away. It was a tragedy. But he had sent flowers, said the aunts and the cousins, he had hardly any money but he had sent flowers. What a loving son. How proud Mrs Mendis had been of him. How lucky she had been with her son Jim. One of the uncles took a photograph of everyone around the open coffin, standing close, as though it was a giant birthday cake, surrounded by flowers and candles. The difference with *this* party was their faces were sad. Another difference was the marked absence of Nulani Mendis.

'What a bitch she is,' said the cousins.

'She was always so stuck-up, too good to speak to any of us. And now she can't even come to her mother's funeral, aiyo!'

'Let's hope she is happy, no?'

'I doubt it. Have you heard the rumour? They were saying in the convent that she's gone off with that man, the one who lives in the beach house! You know, the writer fellow.'

'Twice her age, it's a terrible shame. I'm glad her mother didn't live to feel the disgrace.'

'Well, you know, girlie,' said a distant relative, 'her mother asked for it by marrying that Mendis man in the first place. What do you expect? She left her decent home and went after a pretty face. What d'you expect, huh?'

'Now, now, let's not talk ill of the dead!'

'Aiyo! I'm not talking ill, I'm just *telling* you, men. We all make our own karma, I say.'

Nulani Mendis's uncle listened to the women arguing. He did not put them right. Nulani Mendis was of no interest to him in any case. No doubt she was hiding somewhere, shame keeping her away. What did he care, his sister's family were a dead loss. The monks placed a statue of the many-handed god beside the coffin. The statue watched over the monks as they chanted, their voices rising and falling in sweeping hypnotic drones, backwards and forwards. The air in the room curdled with the stench of over-scented flowers, stagnant water and coconut oil. The monks chanted in low cadences, their saffron robes arranged in bright folds. Their black umbrellas piled outside. Someone brought a silver tray with a jug of water and a silver goblet. A rustle of whispers crossed the room as a priest began to pour the water from the jug to the goblet. He poured the water slowly and the whispers increased. The elderly folk shook their heads in sorrow. The eldest child should have been holding the tray while the water filled and overflowed the goblet. Nulani Mendis should have been there while the waters of her mother's life rose and spilled out on to the tray. What karma was so bad that a woman could not have her own daughter present at her funeral? Nobody deserved such neglect!

Then the brothers closed the lid of the coffin, nailing it down and Mrs Mendis was fully prepared to begin her journey into the afterlife. Mrs Mendis's struggles were over, she had done what she had been meant to do, in so far as she was able. The monks picked up their many-handed god. They folded him up. They would take him back to the temple. There was no point in this statue being here, staring at the dead. This god was for the living. The coffin would travel on its journey alone, and the smell of incense rose and spread indifferently across the grieving house. There were some who smelt it as it passed and thought it was a blessing, but mostly no one noticed.

In certain parts of the jungle, there grows an insect-eating plant not found anywhere else on the island. If disturbed, its elegant leaves close down, like eyelashes. When this happenes, the butterflies or bees, flies or mosquitoes drawn to its scent, are trapped in its vice-like grip, killed in an instant. In this remote part of the rainforest, tucked away among the curious plant life, there appeared an incongruous building surrounded by a thick high concrete wall, covered in barbed-wire circles. It had been there for many decades. No other building was within sight of it. There were no sounds except the faint rush of a waterfall some distance away cascading into a deep ravine. The jungle, in these parts, was mostly impenetrable and dense, although on close observation it was possible to see the tracks of some large vehicle, a tank or a heavy truck of some kind. Such was the density of the vegetation that the afternoon sun could only filter in a diffused way through the branches of the trees. A few birds flew harshly about. That was all.

Perhaps it was the eeriness of the silence after all the noise, or perhaps the pain on his left shoulder had finally penetrated his consciousness, for slowly, Theo found himself awake. And lying in a pool of liquid. It was still light. Although he was blindfolded, the cloth was of a flimsy material, so that he could see faint glimmers, and the movement of shadows through it. His face was wet. When he licked his lips he felt the salty stickiness of it. He knew from this, his face was covered in blood. Because his hands were tied he could not stand. He heard a sound, half groan, half gasp, which seemed as though it came from near him. Nothing happened and he drifted back into unconsciousness. When he next awoke it felt much later. The sun had vanished and it was dark. The pain in his shoulder was much worse and as he struggled to take the weight away from it he felt his face, stiff and caked over, and again he felt the wetness, although most of it had hardened like mud. The blood was congealing. The rope tied to his wrists cut into him, and his chest, his back and his lips, everything in fact, ached. He wondered how long he had lain here. It was surprising how clear his thoughts were. He was without fear, merely curious. With difficulty he began to piece together the information he had. His legs seemed fine, even though he could not stand up. His back ached but that was probably because of the way he was lying, twisted, and slightly at an angle. His shoulder was the worst and as he ran his tongue across his mouth again, he wondered if his lip was split. Where were his glasses? He desperately needed a drink.

The door opened. He could not see it open of course, but

there was a creaking and then something metal, a tray maybe, scraped the floor. Something, a boot probably, prodded him in the small of the back and he was yanked roughly to his feet. He screamed and passed out. The next time he surfaced he found himself pushed against the wall and his blindfold removed. His hands were free. Theo shielded his eyes for this sudden sight hurt them.

'Your food,' a voice said pleasantly in Singhalese.

He stared into the gloom and saw the butt of a gun as it pointed to the tray of food. Beyond the gun was the blurred outline of a face.

'Where am I?' asked Theo.

His voice sounded strained. As though he had been using it too much.

'Eat!'

Again he saw the butt of the gun.

'I want some water,' he said. 'Please, I'm thirsty.'

The man who came towards him out of the gloom was holding a chipped enamel cup and he took it with both hands and drank the cool water. It was so cold that he knew it had come from a well. The door closed and he was alone and in darkness once more. He did not have the faintest idea what he was doing here.

Suddenly, as though a light had been turned on in his head, Theo thought of the girl. It was the first time he thought of her. A single thought that, once it started, ran on through his head like an alarm bell. He could not turn it off. He felt his mind turn with slow and clumsy sickness. He was not yet afraid. Where was he? What had happened to him? Outside the door a rod of light flicked on and off. Was it night? He realised with something like relief that his hands were free. But where was the girl? He noticed there were bars up across the window and at last fear began to spread itself coldly, flatly over him. How long he had been here was unclear. In spite of the heat he began to shake. He touched his head, feeling where the skin had split open. He thought for a moment and remembered, as though from a long, hollow distance, that someone had hit him across his forehead. The memory came towards him jerkily, rushing up with the ground. When he steadied himself, he remembered a little more. He had walked out into the garden. But then, he could remember nothing else. He blacked out again.

The next time he came to he heard Sugi's voice. Sugi was telling him something. The words were slurred and indistinct. Theo frowned. But although he concentrated as hard as he could, he could not make out the words.

'What did you say?' he asked.

But there was only silence. His head was throbbing and he wondered why his trousers were wet. The thought of Sugi had calmed him a little. If he could find Sugi, he felt, things might get better. He began to edge his way around the room banging against the wall but the sounds were feeble and no one answered. Panic overtook him again and he thought of the girl once more. Who the hell has done this to me? Who the hell do they think they are? I need the police, he thought. I need a lawyer, he decided, frantic. How dare they do this?

'Let me out,' he yelled, as loudly as he could. 'Let me out. There's been some mistake. Let me out! Sugi, Sugi, where are you?'

His voice echoed hoarsely around the room. His hands beating against the concrete walls were bleeding again. But no one came.

Gerard and Vikram watched the funeral procession as it wound its way across the town.

'It's the Mendis woman,' said Gerard. 'Killed by a mosquito,' he giggled. 'One less of them!'

Vikram looked at the guests as they walked behind the coffin. He could not see the girl.

'Oh, you won't find her!' said Gerard, noticing the look. 'If the rumours are anything to be believed, *your* girl has gone off with Theo Samarajeeva. No one knows where she is. Too busy to come to her mother's funeral!'

In spite of himself, Vikram was shocked.

'It can't be true,' he said slowly, shaking his head.

He could kill Gerard, he thought, surprised at the pleasure the thought gave him. Not now, but one day, he might do it. Gerard deserved to die, he decided. Lately, for some unspecified reason, he had begun to detest him. But all he said was, 'She looked after her mother.'

'Really? How d'you know?'

Gerard was laughing at him. Vikram said nothing.

'You like her, don't you? The Mendis girl, ah? No use denying it, it's obvious!' he laughed.

Still Vikram said nothing.

'Well, in that case,' said Gerard, seeing the expression on his face, making up his mind, 'I've a job for you that you'll like. I need to find Theo Samarajeeva. Between you and me, I'm not happy with the image the Chief is getting for us Tamils. We're losing a huge amount of international sympathy these days.' He glanced at Vikram. 'Don't get me wrong, the Chief makes a good soldier, you understand, but . . .' He paused, wondering how much the boy understood. 'It's diplomats who move things along, get what's wanted. Not soldiers. And at the moment, the Tamil image is being destroyed.' He spoke with great friendliness. 'I need to change all that,' he said, more to himself now than to Vikram. 'I've been meaning to do something about it but the time's never been right. I might need your help, Vikram, in the future, huh? So what d'you say? People abroad are getting sick of this Tiger cub business. I have an alternative plan to the Chief's grand scheme that involves our writer friend. I want you to go to his house, find out where he has gone. I need to get hold of Theo Samarajeeva. As you're so friendly with the girl, I'm sure you'd like to know where she's gone! You could go now, while the whole town is at the funeral, huh?'

Vikram hesitated. His face was completely blank. What the hell is he thinking? wondered Gerard uneasily.

'OK,' he said finally, and began to walk away.

Gerard watched him go. He hadn't expected such a swift response. It was the first time Vikram had shown any interest in another person. Perhaps, he thought, perhaps the Mendis girl was the key. The boy's inscrutability got on his nerves.

'There's a manservant living there,' Gerard shouted after him. 'I think his name is Sugi. He'll know where they've gone.'

The house was empty. There was no music playing. In the past, on the few occasions Vikram had snooped around the garden, music was always playing. Now the silence of abandonment crossed the veranda to greet him. He walked around the back and forced open a window. The faintest smell of paints led him to a room full of paintings. Notebooks lay open, and images spilled out; supple limbs, eyes that creased in smiles, fragments of happiness discarded hither and thither, the careless accumulation of memories. Vikram turned, startled. What was this? He knew she drew, but this? Confused, he followed the trail. Tubes of paint, ultramarine and vermilion, fused together, for ever purple now, were discarded everywhere. In the bedroom a crumpled white sheet lay on the floor. There was a pair of shoes, straw sandals with the straps broken. And close by, a picture of the girl, eyes shaded from the sun, smiling.

Vikram was taken aback. And for a split second, with shocking unexpectedness, he thought he was looking at his sister, as he remembered her, long ago, under a banyan tree, green-glazed light, against the sun. She had been learning to knit, he remembered. Knit one, purl one, she had chanted, making a scarf for Vikram, for when he was older, she had said, teasing him; for when he went to England to study. Now, with unnerving clarity, he saw her again, as he had not seen her for years. He saw her long beautiful fingers moving deftly. Vikram picked up the photograph. He saw that it was of the Mendis girl. His head spun dazzlingly, and sitting down abruptly, he slipped the photograph out from under its frame. Then he tucked it inside his pocket in one swift movement. The smell of oil and turpentine drifted around. In the dining room, beside a gilded mirror, was a vase of flower stalks, the crimson petals fallen away. Beside the typewriter were a sea urchin and some pale pink shells. The sea moved queasily behind him while seagulls on the telegraph pole outside split their cry into two sounds. Something moved and Vikram swung round sharply, but it was only the last petal in the vase, falling. He sat at the table and touched the typewriter keys. The heat shimmered. It was so great that the trees seemed to drip with it. He felt suddenly very tired. The tension of the airport, the lack of sleep, Gopal's death, all of it had worn him out. Hastily he turned his thoughts away from Gopal. His head was throbbing badly. Vikram realised he was hungry and then, for the first time in many years, he thought of the *vadi* his mother used to make.

He shook his head trying to dislodge the thought. The girl, it was patently clear, was not here. Neither was Theo Samarajeeva. Vikram did not think they had been here for some time. He went back to the room with the paintings. One of them, a small canvas, was propped against a table leg. The paint was not quite dry. It was a perfect likeness of the manservant whose name escaped Vikram, but whom he had often seen in the town. Just then he heard the sound of the gate being closed and swiftly he crossed to the window. It was the servant woman Thercy. Hesitating, not sure he wanted to be seen by her, he looked around for escape. But Thercy was hurrying up the steps and it was too late.

'What are you doing here?' she asked, with a sharp intake of breath. 'I didn't know you were back.'

She didn't ask where he'd been. He could do as he liked. Vikram saw she was trembling a little. It dawned on him that she was frightened of him, that she must have always been frightened, but that he had never noticed before. What was she scared of? he wondered, surprised. What does she think I will do to her?

'I'm looking for the owner,' he said.

'You won't find him,' she said shortly, her breath coming out in gasps. 'He's gone, I don't know where.'

'And the girl?' asked Vikram. He felt some unaccountable bitterness, mixed with something else. 'She isn't at the funeral, is she?'

'Something must have happened to her,' said Thercy quickly. 'You mustn't think ill of her. She would have been at her mother's funeral if she could. Something must have stopped her. She was a loving child, you understand. Nothing would have kept her away. I knew the whole family. The boy was useless; the girl was the best of all, although not many people noticed.' She pulled a face. 'You should have seen how she cared for her mother at the end. I was there, I watched. She would have been here today, if she could. I am certain of it.'

The servant woman stood too close to Vikram.

'Don't listen to gossip,' she said sharply.

Her voice rose in a thin harsh sound, complaining and frightened. Vikram frowned. The woman was like an insect, her voice
got on his nerves.

'Like what?'

Thercy hesitated.

'Who knows what happens in this place?' she said instead.
'People disappear. That poor child was unprotected, uncared
for. Who knows what has happened to her? Ask her uncle. He'll
know.'

'Has she gone somewhere with the writer?'

Thercy glared at him. Then she laughed wearily, without
humour.

'Who told you that? It isn't true. Listen to me; Nulani Mendis
was a lonely child. She never got over her father's death. She
was different from her brother. Mr Samarajeeva was a widower.
He was much older than her. He became like a father to her.
Can you understand that? You know what it's like to be alone.'

She stopped. She hadn't meant to say so much and she was
uncertain of the boy. But still, she couldn't bear him joining in
with the vicious judgement on the Mendis girl that circulated
the town today. Vikram was taken aback.

'Why d'you think something has happened to her?'

'Can't you see? She would never have gone anywhere with
Mr Samarajeeva and missed her mother's funeral. And I can
tell you, even if she had wanted to, *he* would not have let her.
He was a good man.'

She stopped talking. The boy was looking at her as though
he wanted to hit her. She was suddenly very scared.

'Look . . .' she said uneasily, but Vikram moved across the
room and was barring her exit.

'Who would want to hurt her?' he asked.

His face was so close to hers that she broke out in a sweat.

Vikram smelt like an animal, she thought. He smelt of rancid sweat. He's been drinking, she thought in alarm.

'Vikram,' Thercy said quietly, even though her heart was pounding, 'who knows why anything happens in this town? There were many people who hated her father. And so they hated her too. Ask her uncle.'

Vikram moved away abruptly. He had hardly exchanged more than a few words with this woman in all his years at Sumaner House. Mostly they ignored one another. But he felt an urgent desire to find the girl. He had the strangest feeling that if he found her again anything might be possible. The servant woman, seeing his distracted look, began speaking again. There had been too many deaths on the beach lately, she said. Too many people had gone missing. Mr Samarajeeva had disappeared too.

'And someone killed my friend Sugi,' she added and, without warning, she began to cry. 'He was such a good man. He was my only friend in this town. Now I too have no one. The fishermen found his body on the beach. He was a jewel of a man. I don't know who could have wanted to harm him. He never did anything wrong. That's why I think something has happened to Nulani Mendis. Go and ask that wretched uncle of hers, will you? Please. Ask him where she is. Say you are a friend and you want to know.'

Outside on the veranda the heat had risen again and the afternoon clamoured with a cacophony of sounds as, deep within the crematorium, Mrs Mendis's coffin began, slowly, to be licked by flames.

The end when it came was quick and decisive. The girl had been totally silent during the drive. They had been quiet, for what was there left to say? Giulia sat in the back of the car with her, holding her hand, guiding her through this last journey. It had still been light when they set out, the smallest glimmer of sun fading rosily into the sky. They drove through the outskirts of the jungle. Dark branches brushed against the sides of the car. Occasionally they saw the headlights of some other vehicle but it was always in the distance, on some other dirt track that never crossed their path. Only the wind, rustling the trees, disturbed their thoughts. It was a clear night for flying, Rohan saw. But he said nothing. The visibility would be good because of the moon. She would see the island from above as she left, if she found a window seat. Giulia was thinking too. How much will she remember of this? she wondered. Sorrow spilled across the night, varnishing her thoughts. In all the endless years to come how much of it will remain to comfort her? What can her life possibly be after this? Rohan was silent. His bitterness had become a heavy thing, filling the car, impenetrable as an ancient rock. I wish we were going on this plane with her. We have to get out, he decided. There is nothing more for us here. By now they had skirted the perimeter of Katunayake Airport and darkness had fallen. The radar antennae turned slowly in the sky, a bowed dagoba. Journey's end, thought Giulia sadly, remembering the day Theo had brought Nulani to them. And how, it had been she, Giulia, who had seen, before anyone else, that he had loved her.

Then, in an unmarked space of time, in the swift way of significant events, Nulani Mendis left them, going through the barrier into the area restricted to passengers. Barely registering the last moments, or fully understanding as they took their leave of her, she was gone, her passport checked and stamped, herded along with the other travellers into the waiting area. They watched the plane through the window. The refuelling had finished. The ground staff moved away, the engines started up. The great bird was ready for flight. They watched helplessly as a fly buzzed endlessly against the window. Giulia stared at it with unfocused eyes, thinking of the long dark shadow of this moment, and all the other moments that had led up to this. And of the cost on what was about to become of Nulani Mendis's life.

The tarmac was hot with the smell of fuel, and the air filled with the drift and swell of the sea, hidden just beyond the trees. The plane began to taxi across the runway, it hurried through the darkness gathering speed, and then swiftly, too swiftly, even as they watched, it was airborne, flying briefly over the thick covering of coconut palms. She would see a few roads, some twinkling violet neon lights, thought Rohan, before the aircraft would bank gently and turn out towards the sea. And, he thought, feeling as though his heart might at any moment break, then she would see the moon stretch far across the crumpled water, and catch the last lingering sweep of coastline. Bone-white and beautiful and all that remained of her home.

10

BEFORE THE DUST COULD SETTLE ON Mrs Mendis's ashes, Gerard began making his enquiries. The town had sunk back into its usual apathy of heat and sleepy indifference. The house where the Mendis family had once lived, where children had played and the sounds of voices were heard, was no more. Empty coconut shells lay scattered everywhere, overripe mangoes still thudded to the ground, and cane chairs faded dustily in the sun. Someone had thrown a broken mirror out with the rubbish, and the two sewing machines that Mrs Mendis had made her living by had been sold. Mrs Mendis's brother had seen to all of this. He had installed himself on the veranda and in the house. He was sleeping on his dead sister's bed, eating off his dead brother-in-law's plates, enjoying himself. He told Gerard, the house was his now. Possession was everything, he said defensively, draping himself across a planter's chair. He was an odd-jobbing man, he said, in his falsetto way. Odd and jobbing, he had said, laughing at his own joke. Well, a man had to make a living. The army had offered him good money for Mr Samarajeeva, he added, helping himself to Gerard's arrack.

No, no, the man wasn't dead, at least not when he delivered him to the headquarters in Colombo.

'I say, what d'you think I am?' he asked. 'A murderer?'

And he laughed again. Gerard apologised. But he had got what he wanted, he had got his information; Theo Samarajeeva had been alive when they caught him. And the girl? Who knows, said the uncle. The army hadn't wanted her. The uncle laughed, she must have found another man by now! Anyway, she needn't think of coming back. The house was his.

'I want you to go to Colombo,' Gerard told Vikram later. 'I want you to find Theo Samarajeeva. He's our man. Someone will talk, if you hang around long enough. The uncle doesn't know any more.'

Vikram waited. He knew if he stayed silent Gerard would say more than he should.

'We need Samarajeeva,' said Gerard. 'He writes eloquently. Foreigners respect him. We need him to speak out against the government. What the Chief is doing isn't working. *I* should be in charge of the Tamil image. The Chief is just a soldier.'

He paused, absent-mindedly pouring them both another drink.

'If you are successful, Vikram, I promise you, I shan't forget,' he lied. 'If we form the kind of government I have in mind, you'll be part of it. My right-hand man, no? Understand?'

He stared at Vikram. The boy was getting on his nerves. Sluggish and constantly sullen, today he looked particularly mulish. Gerard had had enough. The boy was no longer of any use to him. After the airport bombings he had shown telltale signs of stress, wanting to save one of the team, risking his life for a lame duck. And afterwards, he had been upset. Then he had trailed Gerard back to the south in a state of exhaustion and apathy. Gerard hadn't forgotten any of this. He knew that

Vikram had come to the end of his usefulness and that his battle fatigue and his nervous exhaustion had made him a liability even to the Tigers. Added to which it would be difficult to use Vikram in any further high-profile activities. He's finished, Gerard decided.

Vikram had no idea what Gerard was thinking. Lately, he had not been sleeping well. He had begun to dream again. Those things once hidden had risen to the surface; his sister's face growing out of a plantain tree, his mother's death cry. He would go to Colombo, he decided. There was nothing for him here any more. It would take a few days for him to get ready. He was tired and in any case he needed the necessary papers. Good, thought Gerard, satisfied, watching his face. That's settled then. Of late, Vikram had become transparent about certain things.

'The Mendis girl is probably in hiding,' he said out loud. 'If you find Theo Samarajeeva for me, he will probably lead you to her,' he added cunningly.

So Vikram left, taking with him a package from Gerard to be delivered to someone in Colombo. The air was oppressive. The sea lay like a ploughed field before him. All along the coast the fishermen were back on their stilts, delicate nets fanning out like coral beneath the green water. Nothing much had changed. As the train pulled out of the station Vikram caught a glimpse of the writer's house. It sat snugly at the edge of the bay, overlooking the sea. The carriage was empty. Vikram opened his wallet and took out the photograph of the girl he had stolen. He stared at it and the girl stared back at him. The corners of her mouth were turned up with the beginnings of a smile and her eyes were dark and unfathomable. The last time he had seen her she had been standing on the brow of the hill, staring at the railway line. He had startled her, he realised, but then she had seemed glad to see him. It occurred to Vikram suddenly that she might have been planning to throw herself on the railway line. He had no idea why he had thought this. The train rattled and swung round a bend, and suddenly, without warning, Vikram saw his sister's face again. Twice in one week, calling out a warning to him. Her face stared at him like the face in the photograph, caught by a lens, cactus-sharp, rock solid and frozen for ever. Staring at the horizon, at the point where the sky met the sea, he counted the ships, idly, out of habit. His family had been dead for over a decade. In a rare moment of retrospection he supposed he had come a long way. And although he had no idea where he might be going, he was certain the Tigers no longer interested him. He saw now that they had never really interested him, they had simply been all there was on offer. Gerard too had ceased to interest him, Gerard couldn't give him anything much. Avenging his parents was not possible, he saw. Briefly, feeling strangely light-headed, Vikram remembered Gopal. And again his sister's face rose up, issuing some warning he did not understand. Or was it the face of Nulani Mendis? Had his sister really looked like the Mendis girl? he wondered, confused. He couldn't remember any more, he was too tired, everything was blurred by the heat. The train lurched its way into the central station in Colombo and Vikram took down his suitcase from the luggage rack, handling it with care. He reached for the handle of the carriage door. As he opened it there was a blinding yellow flash followed by a distant thud and the sound of breaking glass. Then, seconds before he felt the pain in his face, the handle was wrenched from his hand as the compartment buckled and collapsed to the ground, dragging him with it.

Seventeen people were killed in the bomb blast that day, including Vikram. The Tiger separatists claimed responsibility.

* * *

The river running through parts of the jungle was a wide gaping mouth. It cut deep into the interior like a gangrenous wound, neglected and rotten. Too wide to cross, to swollen to ignore, it provided a natural barrier around the low-slung concrete building that was the army headquarters. Because of the existence of the river this part of the jungle was wet and rich with vegetation. Brilliant tiger-striped orchids sprouted everywhere. Lilies grew wild, choked by the scented stephànotis, and huge creepers tangled with the trees. Birds rustled in the dense mass of leaves, their cries echoing across the valley. Everywhere, in every pocket of light, there were small clouds of tiny butterflies hovering above the flowers, slipping through the hard scalloped leaves of the *belimal* trees. For the forest was teeming and heaving with life. Close to the wall of this makeshift barracks, resting in the sun, was a lyre-headed lizard. It paused for a moment, head darting swiftly, waiting for some mysterious signal before moving on. This part of the jungle was still an area of outstanding natural beauty, but the army traffic that moved backwards and forwards throughout the day was blind to all it offered.

On the fourth day of Theo Samarajeeva's captivity and solitary confinement the guard came in. He told Theo that he had orders to move him.

'Where to?' cried Theo hoarsely. His lips were cracked and caked with dried blood. His throat was closing up, he could hardly speak. 'I want to speak to whoever is in charge.'

His voice sounded unnatural even to his own ears. The guard spoke to him in his native tongue, handcuffed him, pushing him roughly out of the cell. He told him, when they got to their destination, there would be plenty of time to speak.

'But where are we going?' demanded Theo.

He wanted to appear determined, but he heard his voice

rising in panic. The light flooded painfully into his eyes, making them water. He could not shield them. All his questions, all his pleas during the last four days had remained unanswered. Although the knock on his head had confused him at first, some of his memory was returning shakily. He remembered it had been the girl's uncle who had hit him in the garden. He remembered walking out on to the veranda, wanting to talk to the man. He had wanted to stop the man entering the house. Did the uncle know the girl was with him that night? Had he in fact come for her? The thought chilled Theo. He had wanted to question the guard but did not know the uncle's name and in any case he had not wanted to implicate the girl further. With his returning memory, his anxiety for Nulani had risen steeply. It was worse than the pain in his head. He felt weak; the wounds across his face and back ached dully. He had not eaten or drunk much. And he suspected that his whole body had been repeatedly kicked and beaten. But for what reason? thought Theo, bewildered. For loving the girl? He knew he was running a fever. As he stumbled and was pushed towards the waiting truck, the day pressed against him as though tuned to some high-pitched frequency, feverish and urgent. The light too seemed excessively bright, and although the heat was relentless he shivered violently with cold. Again, he guessed the time to be about seven o'clock in the morning but he had no idea what day it was or how long he had been in this state. Again, he tried talking to the guard.

'Look,' he said in Singhala, 'will you at least tell me where we're going?'

He tried to sound reasonable, confident, his old self. But the guard did not answer. He was too busy negotiating the rough dirt track across the jungle. They began to follow the river and Theo wondered whether it was the Mahiyangana and if they were in fact moving towards Koddiyar Bay. He saw suddenly that he might not survive what was to come. With painful clarity, he saw the girl's face, close up and very beautiful. The image was disconnected to the dull throb in his body. He knew, in some part of his brain, that capture such as this seldom led to release, and that his only hope was in finding ways to endure the minutes and hours of what was left of his life. These were his people. And now, for the first time, he felt the shock of double betrayal.

In front of them was an army jeep. Behind, following closely, were two more.

'Who brought me here?' he asked in vain. 'Tell me his name, let me speak to him.'

The guard ignored him. The jungle was full of its morning activities. It occurred to Theo with a detached, surreal irony that here, in this very spot, was the location for his film. But the film had been made in another rainforest, in another country, for there had been no possibility of entering any part of Sri Lanka at that time. He had not thought of the film since leaving England. Now, in order to stay calm, he forced himself to think about it. The premiere, his time in London, all seemed long ago, already in some other life. The critics had been appreciative; the reviews would be good. Good for the box office and good for sales of his book. But none of it had mattered. It had passed in a blur of nothingness and all his energy had been spent in getting back to the girl. He shied away from any thought of her and concentrated instead on the book. It had been written before Anna died.

Anna, he thought, with a rush of relief. He would think about Anna. Thinking about Anna would save him. He would focus on their life together, their travels around Europe, the memories they had made, the happiness. And now he recalled the hazy, halcyon days of summer when youth had been a mere careless thing, full of endless possibilities. Where had it gone? Happiness, he saw, had left silently, slipping through a crack in the door, an open window, vanishing into the night, unnoticed, going even as death arrived. Remembering how it had begun, that first night when he had missed the last train, Theo closed his eyes. The pain in his back was unbearable. The truck bounced and rattled along the dirt track road. He had stayed with Anna, that first night, and she had taken a bath with the door ajar. Provocatively, knowing he would *have* to look in. He forced himself to conjure up the moment as the truck lurched and swayed around a bend. The road appeared to be climbing upwards. Theo sat dully staring at the flickering light by his feet, his mind moving restlessly, recalling other times, other things. They had established themselves as a couple, rented their first flat, and decided to start a family. All their plans, she had laughed, wrapped around the lovemaking that followed. That night was the future, they had declared. Their future! How lovely she had looked. He could remember it still. Could he have imagined any of what followed? Some time after, the next day perhaps, they had gone for a walk and seen long-legged herons fishing gracefully on the mudflats near the lagoon, and she said she knew, she was pregnant. She had been laughing, but she meant it too. And so he tried photographing her and the heron together, but they had disturbed it and it flew away.

Remembering Anna in this way, he managed to avoid thinking of the girl, knowing instinctively that this would push him into a more urgent, immediate despair. He saw his only hope lay in staying calm. His other hope was Sugi, and this too gave him courage. Sugi would be looking for him, he was certain. And more importantly, Sugi would make sure the girl was safe. The jeep carrying him through the jungle lumbered on. Most of the windows had been blacked out and what little he could see made no real sense. Leaf-green, delicate light filtered down through the canvas roof. The moment was dreamlike and undefined, the future full of shadows and some other terrible reality he was unable to comprehend. His thoughts rushed by in this way, careering against each other in a confusion of past events. What was the past, he wondered, shivering, but only the substance of present memory? Time had lost all meaning. Staring at his bare feet he saw, from some great blurred distance, his shoes, placed neatly beside the wardrobe in the bedroom of the beach house. Already, he intuited, it had become another life. His hands were not visible to him. And he wondered at the kind of life that denied a man the use of his own hands.

Far away in the distant tangle of trees, the sound of the yellow-green iora arose, calling to its mate over and over. From this he knew they were moving deeper into the rainforest. Then this too vanished and all that was left was the steady ache of his limbs, and the throbbing sound of the engine.

Giulia listened to Rohan's breathing. Since Nulani had left he had not rested but now she hoped he was asleep. The doctor had told him it was too soon to visit the beach house.

'Wait a little,' he had said. 'I'll be able to find out more from a reliable source soon,' he had said. 'Be patient. It might be dangerous if you go now.'

Giulia was frightened. She was frightened for Rohan. She couldn't believe Theo was still alive. People didn't survive disappearances in this place. It was well known. The army came for them in the night, and then they vanished. Years later, having waited in vain, having finally given up all hope, the relatives received news. Years later the clothes of the missing were sent back. A bundle of torn and bloodied cloth, a pair of shoes with soles hardly worn, a wallet with a photograph in it was all the word they had of an unmarked death. It had happened so many times. Nobody said anything any more, no one dared. Giulia felt grief, suppressed and lead-weighted as a curtain, held back until now for Nulani's sake, beginning to break. Theo had been their closest friend. And now she had another secret worry. Supposing something were to happen to Rohan, too? It was selfish of her, she knew, but she was paralysed by fear. I want to leave this place, she thought. I hate it here. She knew Rohan was still too angry, too hopeful of finding Theo to have planned much beyond this point. When the enormity of what had happened really hit him his reactions would be unpredictable. She was frightened of this and also of her treacherous, selfish thoughts. She wanted to go back to Italy. The idea having taken hold of her ate away, unnoticed. Like acid on one of Rohan's etching plates, it corroded her days. Was it so wrong that she wanted them to survive?

Since Nulani had left, Giulia had slept badly, waking in the small hours of the morning thinking of the girl flying thirty-four thousand feet above the Italian Alps, dry-eyed, bewildered and alone. Imagining her watching Europe unfold, passing over Lake Geneva, the vastness of France, Paris, the English Channel, and then across the Thames estuary, following the tailwind to line up towards London's Heathrow. What sense could Nulani possibly make of any of it? What sense *was* there to be made, catapulted as she had been from one life to another? I can't stand any more, thought Giulia. She was reaching breaking point, she knew, despair was closing around her, walling her in. All I want is to go home.

Rohan, lying awake beside her, facing the wall, remained silent, grappling with thoughts of his own.

*   *   *

Towards late afternoon the convoy of jeeps began to slow down. The sun had moved and the light filtering through the slats was muted. As the trees thinned out, patches of sky became visible. Theo guessed it must be about four o'clock. Hunger gnawed at him and his arms ached from being tied behind his back. Finally, after another hour, they came to a standstill. The driver opened the back of the jeep and placed a black hood roughly over his head. Immediately Theo felt he was suffocating. He began to pant. As he shuffled forward he smelt the sweat of the fabric. He was still struggling with the nausea that enveloped him, when an unexpected slap sent him reeling. He felt his right eye open up. For some reason he had thought he was standing on the edge of some stairs and feared he would fall, but instead he hit a wall. He felt a warm stickiness gluing the hood against his face. In the distance he could hear the muffled sound of crying.

When he came to, he was sitting on the floor. Someone was talking to him. It was a man's voice but for a moment Theo did not understand which language it was. His thinking seemed to have completely slowed down and he asked for some water in English. The words continued, pleasantly questioning. He struggled to understand. The voice dropped to almost a whisper.

'*Tiger Lily*?' asked the Singhalese voice, pleasantly. 'A good name for a book, ah?' The man laughed easily. 'You must sign my copy when you can.'

Theo tried to speak but his lips would not move properly.

'I understand,' said the man soothingly. 'It's a great pity of course, because you write so well.'

The voice went on repeating something, over and over again, and dimly he knew the word being used was 'traitor'. But he still had no idea which language he was being addressed in. He asked in English for some water again, and again a hand slapped him across the face. Sharp pains shot across his lips. He was pulled up by his arm and handcuffed to a hook high above his head. He felt as though his arm was being pulled out of its socket and this time he knew that the screaming came from deep within him. Then he passed out again.

When he regained consciousness he was in a cell with a number of others. It was dark, apart from a sickly neon light that seeped in from the outside. The air was thick with the humidity made worse by the overcrowding; it was fetid with the smell of the overflowing hole in the ground that was the only latrine. In that moment, in the fading light, surrounded by the curious stares of his fellow prisoners, he knew with chilling certainty that he had entered a dark and terrible place where an ineluctable and malevolent fate had swallowed him whole. Survival of this nightmare depended solely on his ability to keep his mind clear. Nothing else remained except his faltering sanity. How long he would keep it depended only on his instincts. And luck. But luck, he saw with slow realisation, was in short supply.

Sleep was impossible in the cramped painful position he was in. Towards dawn the guard unlocked the door and called out the name of four prisoners. When they had left, the others reshuffled in the space, squatting or leaning against the wall or each other. The fraction of extra room brought a false atmosphere of optimism. The opening of the door had let in a small rush of fresh air and breathing was marginally easier for a brief moment. Daylight arrived unnoticed. A heavy-jawed, thickset man of about thirty stared at Theo.

'Are you Burgher?'

Theo shook his head. 'No,' he said. His voice was barely above a whisper. He no longer recognised it as his own. 'I'm Singhalese.'

'Don't say anything,' someone cried warningly from the back of the cell. 'They are all bloody spies here. Don't tell anyone *anything*.'

For the first time he became aware of the number of people packed into the small cell. A very old man in a dirty sarong and bare feet, head bowed silently, stared at the ground. Two Tamil men with broken noses were looking curiously at him. After a while they introduced themselves. They were brothers, they said. Theo stared blankly. He had no idea what they were saying.

'We were at the medical school in Colombo,' one of them said. 'But new laws forced us to leave just as we were about to be qualified, you know.'

There had been medics in their family for generations, they told Theo. Their father and their grandfather before them had been surgeons. 'Our younger sister managed to escape to England. She's training to become a doctor there,' they said.

One day, someone had approached them with a view to recruit them to the Tigers, they told Theo. They had refused but after that their house had been watched. Then the Singhalese army arrived with a warrant for their arrest.

'They said we were Tamil spies.'

Their mother had watched as her sons were taken away. They had been here for three months now. The beatings had stopped after a while and they were optimistic that their release would come soon.

Theo stared without responding. Nothing in this conversation made any sense. Nothing of what was happening seemed real. Sweat poured from his face.

'Let me look at your eye,' said one of the brothers.

'He's our own house doctor,' chuckled the old man, rousing

himself suddenly, grinning at Theo. 'Go on, let him, men. He knows what he's talking about!'

The medical students looked uncertainly at Theo, then one of them shuffled towards him and peered at his eye.

'You're in shock,' he said quietly. 'Everyone arrives like this. But don't worry about the eye. It will heal naturally. I promise you. I won't touch it,' he added, 'in case I hurt you.'

Someone, a small, bald-headed man standing in the far corner by the latrine, hooted with manic laughter. 'It'll heal so long as you don't get beaten again!'

Still Theo said nothing.

'I've seen your photo in the papers,' continued the student. His voice was gentle. 'Are you a politician?'

'I know who he is,' the man by the latrine cried. 'You're that novelist fellow, aren't you? Didn't you write a book about the war, huh?'

'Leave him,' the student said. 'He'll tell you when he's ready.'

At that the others in the cell lost interest. Only the man by the latrine kept grumbling. He had been arrested for reasons he did not understand, he said. That was nearly a year ago. He was still waiting for a trial. Each time he asked about his case, he got nowhere.

'I keep asking them when I will be released but of course they're only guards. How do they know?' But at least, he admitted, he had never been beaten.

'It is because you're a Singhalese, men. You are one of them,' said the student.

'No, no,' the man disagreed, chuckling as though the thought amused him. 'That's the last thing I am.'

11

THEO SAMARAJEEVA REMAINED IN THE SAME cell for nearly fourteen months. Apart from the overcrowding, the complete lack of privacy and the stench of the latrine, the main peril was utter boredom. Nothing changed. Day after endless day passed in interminable monotony. Time stood still. He could barely eat. The foul odours of sweat and filth, and the cramped conditions made the very act of eating repugnant. A few prisoners were removed; others arrived. Several contracted dysentery, and with the return of the mosquitoes there was a constant fear of fever. Most of the inmates soon had faces covered with bites and at night, often the worst time of all, the groaning and cursing were combined with the sound of frantic scratching. The medical students begged the guards for clean water so at least they could wash their hands, but any water they were allowed was for both drinking and washing in. Next the students tried to organise a rota, asking everyone to drink first from the bucket before washing, but inevitably this did not work either. Added to this, the tension and the inactivity caused arguments to erupt suddenly and with ferocious unpredictability, turning, occasionally, from verbal attacks to full-scale fights. When this happened a guard would simply unlock the cell door, drag out whoever was nearest and beat him relentlessly. Once or twice an innocent bystander was reduced to a bloodied pulp before being thrown into solitary confinement.

As far as they were able, the Tamil brothers, the medics, tried to prevent these incidents. But without any outlet to their frustrations this, too, was not easy. Yet in spite of this they remained optimistic, full of stories of their life before the arrest and of their younger sister in England. When she had been a little girl, they said, she had wanted to train as a Kandyan dancer. But then one day she had seen a man soaked in kerosene and left to burn in a ditch. It was the end of her dancing days. From then on she had wanted only to study medicine. She had wanted to save the lives that others tried to destroy, she had told her parents. The whole family had been amazed but she had never wavered in this decision. For the sounds of a man's screams, her brothers told their cell audience, could not be erased so easily. She had been thirteen at the time. Now she was almost twenty.

'When the war is over she will come back and marry her childhood sweetheart.'

The war could not last for ever, the brothers said. They could not be left in this place indefinitely. Soon, all of them would be released.

'We have only to be patient,' they said. 'There is talk of peace negotiations, and there *will* be the general election in the new year. However long it takes, men, things can't stay this way for ever.'

In the beginning Theo did not join in any of these conversations. His shock and sense of disorientation were so great he barely registered what was going on. All his anger had been wiped out, crushed by agonising anxiety for the girl's safety. The intensity, and the violence of his recent experiences, had sapped him of his usual optimism. His fearlessness seemed a thing of the past. He no longer recognised himself. Having become a prisoner, he began to behave as though he had been one for ever. The conditions in the cell were so appalling that survival was all he had energy for. Paralysed by his situation, terrified by what might happen next, he was unable to go beyond the one, unanswered question of why he was here. Added to this was the sense of being on a roller-coaster. He was trapped in a nightmare from which there appeared no possible escape. At night endless shadows flickered across the cell wall and the shrill cries of monkeys from some distance outside confused him further, making him shake convulsively.

After the brutality of the first hours and days following his arrival, he had lost track of how long they had beaten him. The guards ignored him, and he was too cowed, too grateful at being left alone, that he could not bring himself to ask them for any explanation. The everyday had receded to a point out of sight. In fact, he had stopped thinking in days for at any moment he expected to be hauled out and beaten again. By now, his capacity to respond had slowed down, made worse by the fact that his glasses had been broken. He could no longer focus on anything any more.

During all this time, the heat did not let up. And at night, when it cooled slightly, Theo began to experience blinding headaches. But he felt safer at night, more private, less exposed. There were fewer sounds to startle him so that in the darkness he began, fearfully and at last, to piece together his thoughts about the girl. What had his disappearance done to her? Where was she; what was she thinking now? What *could* she think, except that he was dead? Sugi would by now believe he was dead. Sugi would have heard what had happened and assumed the worst. Theo was tormented by these thoughts. The agony of not knowing what the girl would have done when she woke continued to haunt him. Had she slept at all since he left her? Was she at this very moment searching for him? Was she too in danger? And then he thought, I am to blame, this is all my fault. Nothing could take away his guilt. Questions chased around his head, refusing to be stilled. He imagined her waking, bewildered, then slowly becoming distraught. He imagined her running across the beach, staring at the sea; not knowing what she should do next. And he thought with sickness of how he had left her, sleeping, peacefully, bathed in moonlight , believing that at last she was safe. Fear twisted in him like a sand worm burrowing in the ground. Fear washed him like a wave on a shell. It broke against the brittle spine of his sanity. His only hope was that Sugi had taken her to Colombo. But what if in the panic he had forgotten the documents or the money? What then? There had been a passport. It was forged; if Sugi had been found with it on his person then he would go to prison. Briefly Theo was struck by the irony of this. The passport had only been a last resort. Oh God, he thought, what is happening to them? And then, the one terrible thought he had been avoiding all this time, unleashed at last, broke free and devoured him. Will I *ever* see her again?

Every night the questions marched towards him, relentless as an army of soldiers, drumming against his head, leaving him with no respite. During the day he managed somehow to block all thoughts of the girl, but then as darkness fell, in the stifling air, he conjured her up like a magician, and walked an imaginary beach with her. In this way he both sustained and punished himself every night. And at these moments, under cover of the unlit cell, he broke down soundlessly. He thought he was silent.

One night, as he was beginning his slow agonising discourse, he felt a hand on his shoulder.

'Why don't you talk to us?' a voice asked.

Theo froze.

'We're all the same, men, in this wretched place. Why are you so proud? Everyone understands, there's no shame in what you feel, you know.'

In the darkness Theo felt a hand, roughened and sand-papery, move across his face.

'I've read your book,' the voice continued. 'The one they say has been made into a film. You're a courageous man.'

Caught unawares, Theo shook his head. He felt himself unravel swiftly, sliding out like a thread from a piece of cloth. Silently, he shook with sobs. Something small and hard and bitter, deep within him, dissolved. The others in the cell moved uneasily.

Soon after this they began to speak to him, and for the first time Theo understood they were addressing him in Singhalese. The medical students too shuffled over and began asking him about his film. Was it like the book? Where was it shot? Who acted in it? Were they Sri Lankan actors? Would it ever be shown in this country?

They sensed he both was, and was not, one of them. So they turned, all together, standing close to him, like weary cattle waiting for a storm to break, nudging him with their hot breath, giving him comfort in the only way left to them. After a while, unasked, he began to talk a little about his life. The very act of speech ignited some hope.

'My wife,' he said, 'was Italian.'

He saw it suddenly, as though it were a thousand years ago. Anna, and the watery city. Italy was a puzzle to them, further maybe than the moon. Italy had no history to offer them, no tradition, either good or bad. But England was another matter.

England interested them. So he talked about London instead. In the darkness he talked of the greyness and the poverty of the big city. He told them that it was possible to find warmth in spite of the cold but that you had to hunt for it and some luck was always necessary.

'It is not luck,' said the old man who had first spoken to him. 'It's just a person's karma.'

He talked of his novels.

'Writing them was easy. Once I started I realised I had many things inside me that needed to be said. In fact, later on,' he added, slowly, 'when things were bad, writing was easier than living.'

Old memories stirred in him and he remembered with unforgiving clarity all that had happened. An animal, he said, he had been like an animal, howling for its dead. Then, because he had started, and also because the night made these things possible, hesitantly, he told them how Anna had died.

'There was no warning,' he said. 'She was walking home on an ordinary winter's night. It was not very dark; she had been working late. She often worked late. I had cooked a meal, nothing much. Pasta, tomato sauce, cheese. That's all. I turned the lights on and waited. But she never came.'

Even after so long he felt the power of that moment reaching down through the years. Like starlight, he thought, wistfully.

'She was mugged,' he told them, speaking quietly. 'It happened quickly. On an empty street in London, robbed for twenty pounds and a credit card. There was one witness, that's all. She died on a hospital bed, on a white sheet, as a result of a massive brain haemorrhage. They never caught the men. It was an unsolved crime.'

He had come home to Sri Lanka, he said, because he felt it was better to put his energy into his own country than waste it on foreign soil.

The cell fell silent. Somehow the telling had shocked those who listened. I can speak of all this now, he thought, detached. As though it happened to someone else, as though I had only read about it. I can say the words. And nothing in the words can convey how I felt, what I still feel. But he did not mention the girl. *Her* name was an impossibility. He had folded his thoughts of the girl into a secret petition and dropped it at the feet of a god long given up for lost.

Things changed imperceptibly after that. As the weeks lengthened into months Theo began to invent a routine for himself. There was no paper. He tried asking the jailer but in return narrowly missed a kicking. So he began to construct a story in his head. And after a while he began to tell his stories out loud. The brothers were impressed. Soon it became a daily entertainment that was looked forward to by the whole cell. He talked mostly at night, feeling as though he was following the tradition of Buddhist oral storytelling. It reminded him of his childhood and the servants who had cared for him. Softly, fearful of being overheard, fearful of being thrown into solitary confinement, he told his stories. Then as he became bolder he began to recite poetry as well. He recited long passages of *The Rime of the Ancient Mariner*. The brothers, loving it, joined in with poems they had learned in school. And so the days inched by.

One morning a boy of about ten was suddenly brought in. He had been captured during an ambush, his cyanide capsule cut off and now he waited questioning. Slumping in a corner of the cell he simply shivered, refusing to speak. There were burn marks along the lengths of his legs and across his chest. He was bleeding from his head. The brothers immediately began to look him over but moments later the door burst open again and they were both ordered out. There was no time for goodbyes.

Night descended and with it there arose sounds of screaming. The sounds came from a grating that drained the water from the latrine. At first they thought it was chanting until a shift in key, a small inflection of voice made it clear that they were screams. The noise was intermittent but clearly audible. No one spoke as it rose in a lament so pure, so full of pain, that it was obvious; sleep would be impossible. The boy continued to whimper, huddled up in a corner, snarling at anyone who came near him. Whenever there was a pause in the unearthly sounds from below, everyone breathed a sigh. But then, there would be another long cry of such agony, a cry so low and so filled with suffering that they knew it was not over yet. Pity filled the small airless cell, and silently, out of respect for what they were witness to, every man bowed his head. Towards dawn the sounds became feebler. Footsteps could be heard walking away. A light was switched off. Inside the cell the geckos continued to move haphazardly across the walls, and the boy drifted off to sleep.

In the first few days after Nulani Mendis had left, Giulia and Rohan had been hopeful. They had made enquiries; frantic now, Rohan had gone to see someone he knew vaguely in the Cabinet, but there was no help to be had there. He had tried driving over to Theo's beach house but the roadblocks made it impossible. Then he had rung an acquaintance who lived in the next bay but the phones were down and there was no response. A journalist they approached refused to run a story about Theo in the daily newspapers. It was more than his job was worth, he told Rohan apologetically, avoiding his eye. Finally, they began to believe the worst.

'We should contact his agent in London,' said Rohan. 'He'll make a fuss.'

But they had no phone number and in any case they suspected their phone was tapped.

A month after she left, a letter arrived from the girl. She had written it almost immediately on reaching London. But it had taken a month to arrive.

'Look at this,' said Rohan, bringing it in to Giulia, pointing at the envelope. It was clear the letter had been opened.

'I want to leave,' said Giulia, insistent now. 'Theo's gone, Nulani's gone, I want us to go too, before it's too late.'

Rohan did not answer. Theo Samarajeeva had been like a brother to him. He could not accept he was dead. He could not bear the thought of leaving without him. He wanted to go over to the beach house but he knew how frightened Giulia was. He had not told Giulia, but their own house was being watched. And a few days ago he was certain he had been followed home. Rohan had not mentioned any of this to Giulia. She was already overwrought, and on edge. He did not like leaving her alone in the house for too long. In his heart, he knew, it was time for them to leave.

Giulia began reading Nulani's letter out loud. The words erupted across the page, confused and desperate.

> *I don't know what I'm doing here. I feel I can't go on living. Everything is finished for me. Yesterday I was eighteen. How many more years of my life must I live? Have you no news for me? Have you nothing at all? I tried ringing you many times but the lines were down. Jim met me at the airport. He took me to the place where I'm now staying and a friend of his said he knows of a job close by. I haven't gone out much since I got here. It's so cold and I'm so tired, Giulia. I want to come home. Jim is busy, he is happy with his studies*

but what is there for me here? All I really want to do is
sleep. Waking is terrible. Will my whole life pass as
slowly as this?

The writing meandered on in this way, starting and stopping, repeating itself, full of pain. full of the absence of Theo,
understated, desperate. She talked a little about her brother.
Giulia was alarmed.

Yesterday I saw Jim again. He is pale, the same, but paler.
He's my brother but we have nothing left to say to each
other. Although he has been good to me we hardly speak.
The astrologer was right. Jim talked about Amma. Why
didn't I go to the funeral? What could I say? Jim says I'm
selfish. We met in the railway station café because he was
in a hurry. Then he went back to Sheffield. He can't see
me until next term he said. I'm staying at the address you
gave me. Using the money you gave me. I don't know
what else to say.
      Nulani.

That was all. When she had finished reading it Giulia sat
staring into space.

'Perhaps we shouldn't have sent her,' she said uneasily. 'She's
in a bad way.'

'What was the choice?' asked Rohan.

Giulia sighed. Why had they thought it would be that simple?

'I know. I thought her brother might have helped her,
somehow.'

Rohan made a sound of disgust. Then he took the letter
from Giulia. Yes, he thought, it has been opened. Tomorrow he
would make some enquiries about leaving.

'If only they had married before this happened,' Giulia said, beginning to cry. 'She would at least have had his name.'

'She would have had the royalties from his books too. Although,' Rohan stared at his hands, 'it's only money. It won't bring him back. She'd still be alone.' He stared bleakly at some point above her head.

'One day she'll make money, you'll see. That much I believe. She's a damn good painter, you know. It won't go to waste. You watch, it *will* surface. Give it time.'

He nodded, sounding more certain than he felt. Outside, the curfew had just begun. Thank God I still have a British passport, thought Rohan. And thank God Giulia was an Italian citizen. He wondered if it was possible to buy two tickets to London on the black market. Before it was too late.

After the disappearance of the Tamil brothers the atmosphere in the prison cell quickly turned to one of despair. The next day the small boy captured during the guerrilla fighting was taken out to the firing squad and shot. No one in the cell uttered a word. If they said nothing, maybe they could believe nothing had happened. On the afternoon of the following day, the metal door opened and the warden came for Theo. A simple interrogation, he said, just a few minutes. But first, a short journey. The old man shouted his goodbye first.

'May God protect you,' he said. 'You're a good man!'

Some of the others joined in.

'Maybe we'll meet in the next life.'

Before he could answer Theo was pushed outside.

He had lost track of how many months had passed. Barbed wire stood silhouetted in drums across the sky. It was late afternoon. Long shadows stretched across the ground. A fresh breeze lifted the edges of the heat as they began the drive to the army headquarters. Perhaps because of the happiness he felt from being in the open, Theo experienced a sharp stab of optimism. He did not have the blindfold on this time, the warden was driving him personally instead of some thug. Could it be his release was imminent? Here and there he caught sight of a flash of colour. Birds, he thought excitedly, he hadn't seen a bird in months. Then he saw glimpses of acid-green paddy fields and guessed they were somewhere in the eastern province. How he had got there was a mystery. He had been certain the first prison camp had been close to Colombo.

They drove on. Occasionally Theo thought he smelt the sea somewhere in the distance, but again, he could not be sure. Every now and then they passed the burnt remains of a village. They passed a truck overturned by the roadside, pockmarked and riddled with bullet holes. Once, this had been a fertile land with rice and coconut as the economy. Once, this had been a tourist paradise, lined with rest houses. The port had been an important naval base. Now there was not a single person in sight. He was hungry. They had left before the daily ration of food and uncertainty and hope were making him light-headed. After about an hour or so, he sensed rather than saw they were heading away from the coast towards the interior. Hunger gnawed at him and anxiety too began to grow. Where were they going? The warden had said it would be a short journey. Theo judged they had been driving for about two hours.

Suddenly the truck swerved and braked violently. In front of them was a roadblock. He had just enough time to register this before there was a loud explosion and a volley of gunfire. He ducked and the engine strained into reverse. There was shouting and then more gunshots. The truck swung backwards along the track they had just driven on, swerving and lurching. He tried to stand up, tried to shout to the driver, but the violence of the movement sent him flying towards the door, hitting his head against the handle. He must have passed out.

It was dark when he came to. A foul chemical smell hung in the air and he could not see clearly. His head seemed to have a tight band holding it together. Slowly as he began to focus in the half-light he saw four lengths of thick rope attached to blocks of wood screwed to the ceiling. On the opposite walls were some metal plates attached to some electric wires. Someone was shining a torch directly into his eyes and his mouth seemed full of foam. He tried to speak but his tongue was unaccountably leaden and stuck to the roof of his mouth. Still the torch continued to be directed at his left eye and he realised that, once more, his hands were tied behind his back. They were talking to him in Tamil. They asked him a question. When he didn't reply they spoke in English.

'So, you Singhala bastard, so, you dog, what d'you say to us now?'

'You thought you were in safe territory, did you? Oppressor of the Tamil people, why are you silent?'

'Where's your wonderful army to defend you now?'

'The only good Singhalese is a dead Singhalese!'

'Go on, beg. Beg!'

Again Theo tried to speak, tried in vain to say his name. He opened his mouth but no words came. In that moment it seemed that all the resistance within him, all that had kept him sane over the last months began to crumble. He could stand it no more. His mind had reached its limits. He saw a pair of hands coming towards him and a black sack was pulled over his head. The stench of foul-smelling chemicals grew stronger and was mixed with another smell, something that he vaguely recognised. Then they hit him. Soon he was suspended from the ceiling. His handcuffs were taken off and he felt something cold being stuck to the palms of his hand and to the back of his neck. He knew, with the part of his mind still functioning, that he had entered a hell like no other. That this tunnel he was being forced down was narrowing to a point where every last glimmer of hope was being extinguished. He knew that the best option for him was that he should die now, here, and instantly. Someone peeled his trousers off amid hoots of laughter, and he hung for a moment while a flash bulb went off in his face. Something wet and putrid was smeared all over his nakedness. Laughter surrounded him like baying dogs, high and inhuman. Although the heat in the room was oppressive he was shivering and although he was crying no sound came from him. They hosed him down and the metal plates began to burn steadily into his hands. He felt the heat rise through him, swiftly reaching a point where he could no longer bear it. In a flash of under-standing, moments before his body jerked into the air, he saw in the distance the stone face of a god he had once believed in, turning away. Then, mercifully, he passed out.

12

ROHAN WENT TO THE BEACH HOUSE. The doctor had found a man to drive him there. Giulia didn't want him to go but he went, promising her that if there were signs of trouble he would turn back. The driver was a patient of Dr Peris's.

'You can trust him,' the doctor said. 'He's helped other people for me. He'll take you along the side roads. It's safer than the coast road.'

The doctor spoke calmly, not wanting to alarm them. Knowing they were incapable of doing anything in their grief, he managed to make the house secure through a local contact. But he did not tell them this. Neither did he tell them that he had received a warning that the house was likely to be looted and probably vandalised. He did not tell them he had paid a man to watch over the place. He saw no point in upsetting them further. The doctor had admired Theo Samarajeeva's books and he felt it was the least he could do.

'It shouldn't take more than a couple of hours to get there. He'll come for you early. Take everything of value.'

So Rohan went. In spite of Giulia's fears he went. In the end it had taken fourteen months for the doctor to think it safe. On the morning before he left, a letter arrived from the girl. It was only her second letter, written months before, and this too, Rohan observed, had been opened. England, she wrote, suited Jim. He did not miss his home, she said. Unlike Nulani herself who thought of nothing else. The letter meandered disjointedly on.

Jim says home is a place full of foolish superstitions, best forgotten. He wants me to stop being so useless. But useless is what I am. I started to tell him a little about Theo, but I don't think he really understands.

'Well, that's a surprise,' said Rohan, grimly.
'Listen to this, Rohan,' said Giulia uneasily.

What use is anything without Theo? How can I say this to my brother? How can I tell Jim that everything I do, even eating, is a betrayal, because I live and he does not? Jim will never understand. How could he, he didn't know him. I'm glad there's no sun in this place. I'm glad it's grey. I've never seen so many shades of grey. The sky, like my heart, is full of greyness.

The worst thing of all is that already, so soon, I have started to forget things. What is happening to me? All our memories, all the things we shared, those last hours, are not clear any more. Things I should not have forgotten are evaporating. And then, at other times, everything reminds me of him. But yesterday I couldn't remember his face. However hard I thought, my mind stayed a blank. I have left all my notebooks in the beach house. All my drawings of him. My life. Everything.

'Rohan, I'm worried. D'you think she's . . .'

'Why doesn't she draw him from memory?' murmured Rohan.
He couldn't bring himself to mention Theo's name.

Some time later Rohan reached the beach house without a
hitch. Bypassing the town the driver went towards the railway
station and down a dirt track towards the beach. Nothing stirred.
Flat-webbed fronds of fishing nets dried in the sun. Rubber
tyres hung like nooses on trees waiting for men to swing for
unknown crimes. Rohan looked nervously about. There were
bullet holes everywhere.

'I'll turn the car around,' the driver said.

Rohan saw him look sharply up and down the empty road.
Something must have caught his eye.

The house, when Rohan entered it, had changed subtly. The
outside had come in. Small plants grew in cracks; fine sand had
blown in with the gales, bringing salty smells and scraps of rubbish.
The house had an air of haste and sea grass. Three large terracotta urns stood half in shadows growing tired cacti. Nothing
moved. The sea-moistened woodwork had small patches of mould.
Months of wind and monsoon rain had left telltale marks of
destruction everywhere; on the dust that fingered the pages of the
many books lying around, in the open record player. A typewriter
stood on a small table, one key, the letter 'E', stuck down as though
in mid-sentence. Rohan passed into another room full of dried-
up paint tubes. Stiffened rags, moulded into the shape of the fingers
that had once held them, were scattered everywhere. Sunlight
poured into an old glass jug. Two sea urchins and a pink conch
shell sat on a shelf. There was a photograph of Anna smiling out
at eternity. Rohan stared at it. It had been a beautiful day when it
had been taken. The house, the place, the day, all seemed insubstantial suddenly. Rohan felt his stomach churn. He felt unutterably depressed. Sitting on a stool he lit a cigarette. He should not

have come. Every part of Theo's life was public property here; stories fell open around him. The girl's notebooks, the paintings, how many had she done, Rohan wondered with a sense of paralysis. He felt unable to move, the heat seemed to immobilise him. A typewriter ribbon spooled on the table. He felt grief, suppressed for too long swell inside him like seawater. But whatever he had hoped to find was not here. Bastards, he thought, bastards! He took those things he could carry, three paintings of his friend, the photograph of Anna, the girl's notebooks. He began loading up the car. She must have what little is left of him, he thought grimly. He had not noticed the half-finished portrait of Sugi tucked away behind the mirror. They will be her memories now, he thought. And in that moment, he knew, he would leave for Europe soon.

Afterwards Theo Samarajeeva had no idea how many days or nights he spent in that place. Or how often they beat him with the hose, nor how many times he was burned. He did not recall being dragged by his feet to a cell where, semi-naked and bleeding, he was left for dead. Trauma locked his memory out. His hands were almost paralysed and there were great weals across his back. If he had had a wish it was simply to die. That he survived at all was a miracle, for in those lost hours, without pity and without witness, humanity itself was violated and what was left of his spirit was broken. Nothing in ordinary life had prepared him for this journey. Moving in a blur of constant pain to some sealed spot, silent, isolated and alone, he dreamt of the sea. It was blue and huge and the horizon rose before him, moving as one with the sky. Although he was unaware of it his body had finally given way to a fever. He shook uncontrollably, sweat poured from him and he grew weaker. But still, he remained only semiconscious. He had no idea if there were others around; he heard voices but they were indistinct. Lights flickered on and off. Sometimes he dreamt the sea was on fire and he burned alive. And he dreamt of the girl. In his dream she told him her father had burned like a tiger, running through the streets. He saw her face, very serene and certain, her eyes large and very lovely. And he heard her talk to him. Her father, she said, had been running forever. It was time he stopped. And then, she reached down and touched the great wounds on Theo's body. Screaming, he opened his eyes and found that he was lying on a bed in a white room. The sun had forced its way to the edge of the blinds. It slipped through the veiled slats in the windows and a cool breeze lifted the edges of the sheet. His body ached. Someone, some indistinct figure, stood over him offering him a glass of water. He drank it and the water tasted clean.

'It was a mistake,' the figure said. 'I am sorry to say they got the wrong man. You aren't one of them. It was a mistake. Some idiot was left in charge. So now, you must rest here and when you are better you will be released.'

The man addressed him in English. A bowl of hot rice was held out to him. Seeing it, Theo felt his stomach contract. He vomited before passing out once more.

It was several days before he was awake enough to understand that he was in a makeshift hospital in Kandy. This time when he woke, it was a different voice that talked to him.

'We're sending you to a safe house,' the voice said. 'To rest. All you need to do now is rest and eat and not worry. It's been a bit of a mix-up.'

The voice made it sound very easy. He, it was a man, Theo saw, smiled thinly, showing gold-capped teeth. He told Theo that he had pardoned two other prisoners that very morning.

'Nothing to worry about,' he said. 'It was an unfortunate mistake. You are our guest now. Just ask if there's anything special you want to eat. We have a very good cook here! Tamil cooks are the best in the world.'

The man laughed good-humouredly. Outside the sun shone tight against the khaki blinds.

'We are fighting for recognition and freedom,' the man said, his eyes glazing over. 'We're fair-minded people. But sometimes in these troubled times, we make mistakes. It is impossible not to make mistakes during a war. Don't forget,' he said as though Theo had argued with him, 'this is a war brought on by others. But you know all that!'

Two small boys holding Kalashnikovs stood guarding the doorway. They wore camouflage and around their necks were cyanide necklaces.

'See,' said the man, 'they are your personal bodyguards. If there is anything you want just ask them.'

He smiled again and ruffled the heads of the boys, who grinned. Then he left. Theo stared after him, unaware that his face was wet. Outside the Kandyan heat simmered gently. He stared at a patch of uninterrupted sunlight. It was dazzling and very clear and also, for some reason, unbearable and full of life. Then he turned his face to the wall, away from the bright luminous heat outside, folding himself against the cool parts of the bed. Slowly, like the leaves of the nidikumba plant, he closed his eyes.

In Colombo, the dark face of the army was on alert for the beginning of the election campaign. White uniforms paraded the streets. They marched purposefully among the monks, the rickshaws and the propaganda blasting out of loudhailers. Angry mobs formed and re-formed like armies of beetles. Riots were hastily staunched only to spill out in other places. Outside the parliament buildings, and in between the cool water sprays of Cinnamon Gardens, the limousines glided like stately barges.

'I simply cannot stand this any longer,' shouted Rohan.

He had not painted for months. He had not stretched a single piece of linen on its frame. His dead friend's life spilled across every empty canvas. On their return from the beach house, the driver had noticed they were being followed. Later on, someone had tossed the bones of a chicken into the garden. Luckily Rohan had been outside when this had happened and he had managed to remove them before Giulia became aware of anything amiss. Then one morning a roadside spirit offering was left outside the gate. Rice and fish and pineapples were placed in a coconut woven basket, threaded with crimson shoe-flowers. Passers-by crossed the road to avoid it. Later on, Dr Peris came to visit. Two bombs had gone off in his part of town and his days had been spent dealing with the victims. The first blast had been the result of a suicide bomber. Dr Peris had come to talk privately to Rohan.

'You should leave,' he said. 'While you still can. I can get you two tickets. One of my patients has a source . . . it isn't safe here for you both.'

He looked meaningfully at the painter. His friend the driver had been watching their house, he said. There might be trouble ahead.

'My advice is go. While you can.'

Two days later the telephone rang several times in the middle of the night. But when they answered it there was no one there. They had not heard from Nulani again. The post was no longer getting through. Rohan got the tickets. They would fly, via Singapore, to Milan. Then they would take the train to Venice. They had no place to stay in Venice yet, but it no longer mattered. Something would come up

'This place has defeated me,' Rohan said. 'Ultimately, even I have given up on my country.'

The new year had not brought peace. They were being buried alive. Someone threw a petrol bomb into a crowd and death stalked the city in a monk's saffron robe. Petrol was in short supply, except when it was needed for random burnings. How had two thousand years of Buddhism come to this? A Cabinet minister was assassinated, seventeen members of the public injured, three killed on a bus. Glass rose like sea spray, shattering everywhere. But the radio stations still played *baila* music in a pretence of normality although no one knew what was normal any more. They packed. Hastily, frightened to speak of their imminent departure, frightened to use the telephone, frightened to leave the house for long, they packed.

They were to leave at night. But because of the curfew and the unpredictability of the journey they decided to leave in early evening. They hoped there would be less likelihood of ambush if they left while there was still some light. The last of the sun was disappearing rapidly, the evening had a rosy glow, and the air was filled with the distant cry of birds. The plane would take off at midnight. Once in the airport their tension eased slightly. No one knew they were here and for the first time since Theo had gone they felt they were safe. The airport itself was subdued and empty. Security was much heavier since the bombings of eighteen months previously. There was only one flight out of the country and they had hours to wait before they could board the plane. But it was worth it, they told each other. Better than driving through the jungle in the dark, they said. The trip with Nulani had been enough, they added, remembering the last time they had come here. That too was already a lifetime away. And already, Giulia thought sadly, they had accepted Theo's death.

'I'll never return,' Rohan said with finality. 'This time I'm finished with this place for good.'

He told her he had worried they would never be able to leave. He had been afraid, he said, that something would have stopped them, that one of them might have been captured.

'The house was watched, you know,' he told her, in the safety of the airport lounge. 'Every time I went out I knew I was watched and I wondered if I would return home again. Or if you were all right on your own.'

Giulia shivered. Now he tells me, she thought.

'There was a man on the hill above the bay, watching us through binoculars. I'm not sure if he saw me take the paintings from Theo's house. Not that I cared. I wanted Nulani to have something of him. But we were followed all the way back to Colombo.'

He did not tell her he had been suspicious of their neighbours too. What was the point in letting her lose all hope in the place? But the cheapness of life in this paradise was more than he could stand any more. At eleven o'clock they were allowed to board the plane. Night had fallen unnoticed while they sat in the airport, and outside the sea moved darkly, for there was no moon tonight. Ten minutes to twelve, thought Giulia. Ten more minutes left, thought Rohan, and still I feel nothing. Theo had been dead for nearly eighteen months.

In the darkness, as the plane began to taxi, in a house that appeared occupied, in a leafy suburb in Colombo, a fire started. It was uncertain what might have caused it. Arson was commonplace enough. The fire rushed through the empty rooms, taking everything in its path. Burning canvas, melting tubes of oil paint, cracking mirrors, incinerating the furniture. It tore through the corridors in a fury of heat; it destroyed pictures and documents, and the paraphernalia of the recently departed. When it had burned itself out, when all that was left was blackened rubble, the fire brigade arrived. And the neighbours came to gaze in awe at all that remained of the house where the painter and his Italian wife once had lived.

13

HE SAW IT ALL IN COLOUR, dark green with a touch of blue. The images fragmented, like rushes from an uncut film, full of light and sharpness. But every time, before his mind could investigate them further, he drifted back into sleep. Whenever he regained consciousness he drank the water that arrived, by mysterious means, in his hand. It was cool and fresh and he drank it without thought or question, without pleasure. He drank it simply because it presented itself. And then he slept again. Something had happened to the seal on his eyelids because all the time the light seeped through to his eyes, so that while he slept he dreamt of sun, dazzling on the sea. He could not have been further from the ocean.

Other things happened while he slept. Voices flitted across his brain, like fruit bats. Words circled him like gulls; words like, 'in the beginning', and 'flailing', biblical words, words that had no end. In the background was the sound of artillery moving in and out of focus.

At night, the single light bulb, unshaded and comfortless, cast an aching, dull glow. It reflected the slow tortuous routes of the geckos and the cockroaches that crawled past him. He watched them through a curtain of pain and sweat, these routes that crossed and criss-crossed along the wall, passing through imaginary enemy lines. Although they came from the hole in the broken window they never went back that way. They would always disappear from his sight line somewhere to the left of his bed. He never turned his head to find out where they went. He never turned his head for anything. He was simply not interested. Like the beetles, he seemed to have arrived here through a broken skylight, crashing in from some other life, never knowing that this place, this spot, would be where he would land. Here in this bed, with this small pile of sodden cloth, his only possession.

Some time later, he woke once more, to walls that were bare of beetles. The sun was raking long fingers through the blinds and the voices were back.

'How long has he been this way?' Gerard asked.

The man in the doorway shrugged. Ten days, two weeks? 'There's nothing much the matter with him now. His wounds are healing well. He could walk out of here if he wanted to.'

'No,' Gerard said hastily, 'that's not what we want. He needs to stay here for a while.'

'He can't stay here. The Chief doesn't want him. You'll have to move him.'

'Yes, all right,' said Gerard. 'But you'll have to give me time. I can't work miracles.'

'Look, he's waking again. Now he'll have a drink of water and stare at the ceiling. Then he'll go back to sleep. We can't spare the bed much longer.'

'OK, OK. I'll move him.'

They watched curiously as Theo finished drinking. He was unaware of their presence. Secretly, though, Gerard was shocked. The writer had taken a severe beating, far worse than he had expected. The fingernails on both his hands were ripped and blackened and he looked smaller than Gerard remembered. He lay motionless, like a broken fishing boat.

'Can he hear us, d'you think?'

They moved closer, watching him in silence.

'Who knows? It was a mistake.'

'Yes, yes, I know, men.'

'These things happen. All the time. He's lucky someone found out before it was too late. He's lucky they didn't finish him off.'

Luck, thought Gerard, laughing inwardly. No, you fool, it wasn't luck. It was my doing. While you rush around in circles with your machine guns, shooting at shadows, I pick up the pieces. Louts in charge won't make a government. But he said nothing. He wondered if Theo would be useful in the way he had hoped. Would his mind be too damaged to write again? Well, the first thing would be to move him down the valley, into a remote part of the hills and give him some peace. Then we'll see, thought Gerard. Rome wasn't built in a day. Let them slaughter each other for a bit longer.

'OK,' he said, making up his mind, 'we'll move him in the morning.' And he went out.

The next time Theo looked at the sky it seemed more intensely blue. And the green of the leaves were dark and succulent. As always, the smell of food made him want to vomit. A man came into view.

'Hello, Theo,' said Gerard. 'I'm here to make sure you're looked after until you get better. You're in a safe house, now, OK? You've nothing to worry about. All you have to do is get better. Do you understand? You're safe now. We've got you away from that place.'

There was a pause. Outside a bird cried harshly and repeatedly.

'I'm not sure how much he understands,' said Gerard. Perhaps they went too far, he thought. Perhaps I'm wasting my time. He's become a cripple, with a cripple's mind. Broken and rubbish-can empty.

'I want to sleep,' said Theo, faintly.

'That's OK, men,' said Gerard heartily. 'You have a sleep. But you must eat something when you wake up. I shall be gone for a few days, but everyone here will take care of you. And I'll see you soon. OK?'

There was no reply. Theo had shut his eyes again. He had become a curvature of bones across the bed, bereft of words. Violence had washed away his hope, robbed him of speech.

'Make sure he eats,' was all Gerard said. And he left.

Days sifted by. Nights passed without notice. Theo moved uneasily between consciousness and sleep. At night the darkness cocooned him and he hardly stirred, moving from one dream to another. He dreamt as once he had read, sifting through images as once he had turned pages. He was neither happy nor unhappy. Mostly these dreams were nebulous things filled with people he did not know. One in particular repeated itself night after night. He saw himself sitting at a desk beside a long, high window, working. He was writing furiously. In his dream the rain fell heavily from a leaden sky and leaves drifted, like flocks of birds, towards the ground. But he had no idea what he was writing. And the dream never went any further. Then one night, without warning, he saw a face that was vaguely familiar. He was sitting with a woman on the balcony of a funny little flat. The balcony was filled with pots of bright red geraniums. Somehow he knew the flat was in London. He remembered the place being called Shepherd Market. But that was all.

'Write it down,' the woman urged him. 'Write it down, Theo. That way you won't forget.'

In the dream, the woman peeled a fruit. He could see the yellow insides of the fruit as she ate. The juice ran down her arm and on to her white dress. He thought he had seen that image somewhere else. The woman frowned and licked her arm, then, seeing him looking at her, she laughed.

'Why d'you never listen to me?' Her eyes were sharply focused and very blue. 'You're a writer, Theo. You should be writing all of this down.'

He woke feeling agitated and found the sunlight sleeping on him, heavy as a dormant cat. A little later, how much later he couldn't say, he had the same dream again. And on that same day he remembered the name of the fruit the servant brought him. It was a mango. He must have moved about a little after that, because he began to notice there were other rooms leading on from his. His whole body ached and the wound across his back bled as he walked. The servant woman came and went, nodding at him, occasionally speaking to him. The man he knew was called Gerard visited almost daily. One afternoon he handed Theo an exercise book and a pen.

'Yes,' he said, as though he was continuing some previous conversation with Theo, 'it's a good idea to try to start writing again.'

A bit later Gerard returned, bringing a doctor with him. Why are you here? Theo wanted to say. But he could not bear to hear the sound of his own voice, so he said nothing. The doctor looked him over. He felt his arms and examined the wound on his back. Theo flinched when he came near him. But the doctor was smiling. Don't smile, thought Theo. I'd rather you didn't smile. But again he remained silent. The doctor told him he was fine, his ribs and pelvis were mending, as were his collarbone and arms.

'With time, the scars will all fade,' the doctor said. He sounded pleased.

'Good,' Gerard said, heartily. 'Good. You see, Theo, you'll soon be fit and ready to start your new book.'

Theo looked at him blankly.

'You don't remember, do you?' Gerard said, laughing. 'Well, I think you should reread one of them, in that case. Your most famous one, perhaps!'

And he handed Theo a book. *Tiger Lily*, it was called. So, he *had* been a writer. Inside the book, he read, *For Anna*. He stared at the name blankly. There was a photograph on the back cover that he supposed was of him. He squinted at it.

'Of course!' Gerard said. 'You wore glasses, of course. How stupid of me! Wait, men, let me see if we can replace them.'

Maybe it was because of the new glasses that had been found for him, not quite perfect but usable, that he began to move around more. The house, he saw, was large and shabby, though not uncomfortable. There were two other people in it, the Tamil woman who cooked for him, and outside, discreetly out of sight, was an armed soldier, a boy of about fourteen.

On the second day that Theo was up and walking, the servant woman came into his room and lifted the blind. Soft light poured in. The woman gave him a mango. She spoke to him in a low voice. Theo did not speak Tamil. He asked her for the time in English.

'Up, get up,' she said, pointing at the sun. 'Morning.'

Later on that same day, she brought him a clock. He had been sleeping for hours, he realised. Maybe days. Fully conscious now, he thought he heard voices. But the gaps in his memory distressed him more than his aching body. He could not leave them alone, probing and fretting over them. Something gnawed away at him, constantly. Or was it *someone*? He had a feeling there was a missing person somewhere in all this. He decided to read *Tiger Lily*. Perhaps the answer was in the book. And the name Anna.

During the long, solitary day, he had discovered an urge to write. But what about, or who to, he couldn't say. In any case he was easily tired, easily frightened. And his fingers ached constantly. Something marked time in his head like a metronome. It moved almost on the threshold of his thoughts so that he felt himself edging towards an abyss. The sight of his face in the mirror, the man called Gerard, all these things both terrified him and left him curious. Maybe I should read the book, he thought at last, reluctantly opening it.

'*No one should be an exile,*' he read. '*For it is an indignity curiously difficult to overcome.*'

Theo shuddered. A sliver of memory uncoiled itself silently. He read on.

'*What can I tell you about the boy? He was a Tamil, brought over from the Indian subcontinent, olive-skinned and handsome. It was meant to be the perfect solution. Except it didn't work out that way.*'

He felt the stirrings of suspicion. And interest too. The sunlight on the wall beside him fell in a slanted disc. Outside the window the branches of the mango tree drooped heavy with fruit. Something has happened, thought Theo. Again his skin grew taut with fear. He began to smell colours. Crimson lake, he thought. Cobalt blue. The greens and yellows, the browns of the yard outside the window filled him with nausea and intense panic. They were army-camouflage colours, he thought, unaccountably depressed. Suddenly he had the urge to write all this down.

'*There is no such thing as freedom,*' he wrote. '*Nor do I want to have an ideology. I see no sense . . . To have an ideology means having laws; it means killing those who have different laws.*'

He looked at what he had written. He had no idea why he had written this. Something was scratching away inside his head, struggling to get out.

'*Man kills as no other animal kills,*' he wrote. '*He kills himself, as if under a compulsion, not out of hunger, not because he is threatened, but often out of indifference. We live in a jungle . . .*'

Again he paused. A thought crawled along the rim of his brain and then slipped maddeningly away. Perhaps, he thought, perhaps it's to do with the woman I keep seeing. Outside a bird pecked at the air as if it were puncturing it.

'Oh good,' said Gerard, walking in. 'You're up! And writing too!' His friendliness was terrifying.

'I've been trying to remember,' said Theo slowly. 'Perhaps you're right, perhaps I was a writer.'

Speech, the smallest utterance, was distressing. Every word quivered on the edge of a scream. But Gerard seemed perfectly friendly and one night, after his visit, Theo determined to finish reading *Tiger Lily*.

'*At last he knew the meaning of what had occurred. That the things he had been through were too terrible to utter out aloud. That one part of him had gone ahead while the rest of his mind remained frozen. And he knew too that he had been tipped into an inexplicable no-man's-land, not of his making.*'

Theo stared at the words, knowing with sudden, sharp shock how the novel resolved itself. Fragments from the past detached themselves and floated towards him. He stopped reading and saw again, with perfect ease, the high-ceilinged room, with its vases of peonies and his desk, littered with papers. There was a cup of coffee beside him; hot, rich, strong coffee. A hand lingered on his arm. And then he saw what must have been his own hand touch the silky cloth, and then the arm, and finally the face of the woman it belonged to. And in the clearest of moments of certainty, he understood that the woman's name was Anna. Memory flooded over him.

The house had been shut up for the night. The guard sat near the gate, his footsteps occasionally crunching on the gravel.

'Why am I a prisoner here?' he said out loud. 'What else have I forgotten?'

Panic rose out of nowhere, with a new urgency. He turned out his light and lay rigid in the darkness listening to his own heartbeats and to the faint sound of a waterfall in the distance, thinking of the woman in the silky dressing gown, certain now that Anna had been his wife.

Towards dawn he slept a little. When he woke it was morning. He saw again that something had been working silently within him. Like a spool of tape threaded through a machine, it replayed itself in slow motion. Anna, he thought. She had died. He had marked the place where she had fallen like a leaf to the ground. He had marked it with flowers. Bunch after bunch, wrapped in foil to stop them withering. Week after week he had gone to the spot, marking it so it no longer remained an unmarked grave. Month after month, long after they said he should have stopped going, long after they said was healthy. He had wondered what was unhealthy about loving. Should his love for her have ceased when her life did? He had gone home after they'd told him she had died. It had been an early-spring day, sharp and cold and with splashes of crocus colour. A day full of birdsong and fresh air. He had registered all that with the curiously detached other part of his brain. Then he had seen her small delicate bra, suspended like some strange beautiful flower, pegged out on the washing line. Hanging out to dry. And without thinking he had taken it down out of habit, and even though it had been washed, even though the sun had dried it, still he could smell the secret parts of her. All this he remembered now. Seeing it like a photograph, still and deceptive, and potent. Opening his notebook he began to write of Anna. Lest he forget.

I saw you for many days before I spoke to you. In those days you were always laughing. I sat at a table with my book, occasionally glancing up at the blue shirts of the vaporetto drivers. This was their café too, after all. They gathered here whenever they came off duty, shouting at the barmen for their 'cappuccini' and their 'cornetti' as they walked in through the door. You were there every morning; what you did or where you went afterwards was a mystery to me, but I was struck by the blueness of your eyes and your curly blonde hair among all the dark heads. Beyond us lay the lagoon, blue-green, grey, yellow-tinged, depending on the currents. I didn't know this then, but the currents had different colours that changed several times a day in spring.

It was March when I first saw you; still cold but with a hint of the warmth that would come. I remember your long, slim leg, and your small foot balancing precariously in its red shoe. You were Italian, so of course you had no time for sitting. You simply knocked back your macchiato and then you went away again tossing your hair in the breeze. Across the water the sunlight fell on the island of San Michele, the island of the dead. Had I been the true child of my mother, had I remembered the warnings of my country, I would have taken this to be an omen of what was yet to come. But the East, and my troubled homeland, was a thing of the past. I had shed old habits like a lizard sheds its skin. In those days in Venice, I was full of expectations, thrilled by my own discoveries, like

any romantic foreigner. Only later would I discover how
bored you were by all of it! But to start with, in those
first weeks, I knew none of this. And so I watched you,
day after day. In reality it was probably only a week
before you spoke to me, joining me at my table. You, and
Gianni, and Sara. All chatting, all laughing, talking to me
in Italian.

'Sei un studente?'

No, I said, I was writing a novel set in the
Renaissance. At this you burst out laughing. A tricky
subject, you said. After that I saw you every morning,
either by chance or deliberately. I hoped it was the latter
of course. Sometimes you were with your friends and
sometimes you were alone. When you walked in, your
eyes searched the bar, looking for me. Then, when you
caught my eye, you pretended not to see me, but I knew,
you were glad I was there.

I found out that you too were writing a book, on the
sculptures of Ulysses. I found out you had lived mostly in
Rome but that you were here for the spring. And that
Gianni was in fact not your boyfriend. Somehow, in the
days that followed, I saw a lot of you. We talked, we
walked along the Lido, we ate together and finally,
inevitably, I went back to your tiny flat, glowing with its
art-nouveau lamps, its threadbare velvets, its warmth.
And I knew then, this was serious. Afterwards, even years
afterwards, after you died and all the flowers I placed on
the pavement had been swept away by the road sweepers,
still I could remember that first night with the utmost
clarity. How could I have forgotten it now?

And so we continued, you and I. We had both loved
others; we had both been disappointed. Maybe that was

the reason we felt so complete, together. Maybe that was why our lovemaking was so candid. At the time it was a revelation to me. You were almost as tall as me and as I peeled off the layers of your clothes, revealing the pale glow of your skin, the small mole on your back, the soft downy blonde hair at the entrance to your secret chamber, I knew that for you too, this time would be different. I lost myself in you after that, in the visceral perfume of our two bodies, and the small murmurings and gasps of our limbs together. Later, we both slept but it was I who woke first to stare at you, delighting in watching the innocence of your sleep. How was I to know that many years later you would look this way as you lay dying? Sleeping, not in my arms but alone on a hospital bed. With the same curl of eyelashes, the same fit of lips against each other. This time your eyes never opened. This time I knew I would never again see that flash of piercing blue. This time there would be no tomorrow.

Theo closed his exercise book. Memory was rushing towards him as though he was parachuting to the ground. He felt his life hung on a thread which at any moment might break. He felt the tension within the house stretch tightly around him. His body seemed to be weeping from an invisible wound. What was love but a memory? How could he have forgotten so much? He was aware that something else, something he could not quite grasp, fluttered vainly within him. But what it was he could not say. What more was there to remember? he wondered fearfully.

The intrusive roar continued for a moment longer and he realised a radio had been turned on in the next room. There had been a tragedy at Mannar, the voice intoned. Hundreds were left to drown. Villages along the northern coast had been burnt down; women and children hacked to death. A British journalist, some foolish man in search of a human story, having strayed in through the security system, had his eyes plucked out. His captors had released a photograph of him. Appalled, Theo listened.

'Ah,' said Gerard, walking in, making him jump. 'You're up! Good, good. You're on the mend. Soon you'll be well enough to start working.'

'Why am I here? When can I leave?'

Perhaps it was the unfamiliar sound of a foreign voice speaking English on the radio, but he felt some assertiveness, something he might have possessed in another life, return.

'I told you, Theo,' Gerard said easily, watching him, 'you're here for your own safety. Have you begun to remember what the Singhalese did to you yet? No? Well, I'm afraid we need to keep you out here for a while. Consider it a bit of a holiday, if you like, a chance for you to do some writing, to rest, get your memory back even. Don't worry about it. And try to eat a little,' he added, with all the appearance of friendliness.

14

WHEREVER HE LOOKED, ROHAN SAW THE SEA. Every time he thought of beginning to paint again, the sight of it distracted him. But when he looked closer it was the tropical waters of his home that he saw. The perversity of the human mind never failed to amaze him. He remembered the beach, whitewashed, picked clean, pared down and smooth, a strong breeze scuffing the waves. The water had always looked benign enough, but underneath there were shark-toothed currents lurking. He knew those currents well enough to know that they could pull a man under in seconds. He tried to imagine the catamarans, hide-grey and rotten, half buried in the sand. Husks from long ago, withered and crumbling, was how he recalled them from this distance. Like his life, he thought, staring into space. If he were honest, if he allowed himself a moment's truth, away from Giulia's anxious eyes, this was what he believed. And the beach that Rohan saw was always empty. No one fished in that sea any more. No fishermen lifted their boats up and along the sands. The small, dark-limbed urchin boys who had played there no longer filled the landscape, and the sea and the sky belonged only to his dreams. I must paint it, he thought, daily. But he was too apathetic to do anything.

They had been in Venice for several months and had returned to the old routine of crossing and recrossing the bridges every day, on trips to the fish market, to the bar, to an old favourite restaurant. For hadn't they lived here together, once, long ago? At first the relief on reaching Venice had outweighed everything else. Sorrow was to come slowly. So at first Giulia was glad. She was glad to be back in an ordered world again. Putting the water on to boil for the pasta, making the *sugo* of tomatoes, delighting in the fragrant perfume of basil plants. Yes, she was glad of all these things. But then she saw, something had happened to them both.

On their arrival, desperate to meet up with the girl, they wrote several letters. They had brought her paintings and her notebooks with them and they wrote, giving their new address, telling her they longed to see her again, telling her they had talked about nothing else. At first, they hadn't worried when there was no reply. Rohan had tried phoning the doctor to find out if he had heard from her. But as usual the line was dead.

Unpacking their luggage, they reread her letters more carefully, now that they had time on their hands. The letters felt old, as though they had been written in another life. They were full of other time zones.

> *Jim has found me a room in a house. Here is the address.*
> *There are five other people living here but I never see*
> *them. It is dark and very cold. Next week, Jim's friend has*
> *promised to get me a job. The money you gave me will be*
> *enough for the moment but soon I will have to find some*
> *work. Jim's friend says there is a newsagent nearby where*
> *I can work. I am very tired all the time. But at least*

because I am so exhausted I can sleep and that helps to
numb the pain. Only sleep releases me.

Reading the letters from this distance made them uneasy.
There were things that had slipped their notice before.

'Oh God, Rohan, it's much worse than we realised,' Giulia
said urgently. 'We *must* find her.'

'Sure, sure,' he agreed. 'She'll write, don't worry. We are her
only real family now. Her brother is a useless fellow.'

'She's young. She should meet someone else,' said Giulia,
'make another life.'

And Rohan had agreed again, although he been less certain.
He too looked at the letters once more, with fresh eyes.

Yesterday, I was staring out of my window at some yellow
flowers in the garden next door. Something, the old habit
I suppose, made me want to draw them. Without
thinking, I found a pencil and some paper. I began to
draw quite fast, not taking my eyes off the flowers, but my
mind must have been somewhere else. And then to my
horror I saw that I had been drawing his face again.
From memory, as I used to. Do you remember?

Months passed and their uneasiness grew. Why had she not
responded? In all they had written six letters and all of them
remained unanswered. Giulia's distress had grown, so that, really
anxious now, Rohan booked two flights to London.

'Wait,' he calmed her, 'we'll go over and find her. We'll be
able to speak freely then. Things will become clearer, you'll see,'
he promised.

So they had packed up Nulani's paintings and put the notebooks into a small bag and left with a confidence that would

astonish them afterwards. They had no telephone number for her, just an address. Perhaps, reflected Giulia with hindsight, that was when things in their own life began to fall apart.

For London was not as they remembered. And the house where the girl had lived was full of new tenants. Bills and circulars sat together in the letter box, but their own letters were not among them. No, they were told, there's no one of that name here.

'Sorry,' said the lodger shivering at the entrance, 'I can't help you, I'm afraid. Never heard of her. Try the next house.'

They took the tube to Kensington and walked the street where the Samarajeevas had once lived. There was a new owner in the top flat. A new name on the bell, curtains at the window. The woman who opened the front door looked at them in surprise. What had they wanted? They could not for the life of them say. Giulia shook her head, confused. Rohan apologised, hurriedly. They must have got the wrong address. What had possessed them to knock on *that* door? After that, they looked in the telephone directory. But what name did they want? Samarajeeva? Mendis? Passing the place where Anna had been murdered, they saw, without comment, the unmarked, flowerless pavement. Time had passed with steady inevitability and they took what comfort they could from this fact. London traffic moved with swift indifference all around. They felt small, angry, gagged. Then, silently, for what else was there to do, they took the plane back to Venice.

Depression enveloped them, and gradually, Giulia saw that this was the price they had paid. Rohan changed. Slowly, like the tide submerging the beach, Rohan began to drown. He became morose and irritable. Giulia did not like to dwell on it, but leaving Sri Lanka had broken him in a way that she had been unprepared for. She feared the worst. She feared he would never paint again. And she noticed he was for ever cold. Even in that first high summer, when Venice overflowed with humidity, even then, she saw, he hated the climate. *She* had come home but Rohan was somewhere else. Every time she delighted in her native tongue she felt his loss keenly. He had escaped with his life but other things had been lost instead. Something had severed his spirit, broken his determination and cast him adrift. And now a strong current was taking him away from her. Helplessly, unable to follow, she watched as he stared out across the Adriatic Sea. She knew it was some other stretch of water that he longed for. Guilt cemented their relationship where once there had been love. Guilt served to make matters worse. And although the Lido filled with the sound of children's laughter, still he complained, there was not a single conch shell to be found on the beach. However beautiful it was, still this was not his home. Giulia said nothing.

One day she caught him looking through the girl's notebooks.

'Let me see,' she said eagerly, wanting to break the silence, longing to talk.

They had never mentioned their failed trip to London. It had joined all the other untouchable subjects.

'Look,' he said grudgingly. 'All she had were crude graphite sticks, but look at the line of his hand.'

'Theo was all she ever wanted to draw,' said Giulia sadly.

'She's a better painter than I could ever be.'

He would not have it otherwise. There was nothing she could do. He simply said he could no longer paint.

'Perhaps when I've settled in this place,' he said restlessly.

But how can he settle, Giulia worried, if he never paints? All around, the lagoon reflected the milky sky. They were surrounded by light, surrounded by safety. There was no curfew.

What more do I want? thought Rohan impatiently, trying to shake this sickness off.

'Maybe she lost our address?' Giulia said. 'Or maybe she's busy now and wants to forget.'

It was possible. But they both knew she was not the sort of girl to forget. And the lurking fear, the unspoken horror, that she might have ended her life finally, added to their guilt.

The year turned. Spring tides came and went and the swallows departed, leaving the city to its storms of mosquitoes.

'Just like home,' murmured Rohan, knowing it was not.

That spring they gave up hoping for news, waiting for the letter that never came. Nulani Mendis is a thing of the past, Giulia chided herself sternly. We must learn to live with only our memories. And she cooked fresh fish for Rohan in the way she used to, in Colombo, serving it with hot rice and chilli, hoping to bring some small comfort to him. Meanwhile, he began to go for long walks on the Lido. He wanted to listen to the mewing seagulls, he told Giulia. He wanted to be alone, he said, to think. And Giulia took some comfort in this, hoping his solitude might inspire him to paint again.

The weather changed and it began to rain at night. After days of silence, the rain fell in persistent folds, not like tropical rain at all, but gently, lingeringly. Theo lay awake listening to it. Once he slept all the time, but since he had begun to write things down, sleep eluded him. Often he would remain awake until dawn, thinking, or scribbling in his exercise book, and then falling into an uneasy sleep as the light appeared. He felt safer that way. His memory was returning slowly. A few nights previously he had remembered the post-mortem after Anna's death. She had been pregnant, he remembered.

His memory had come with the rain. Lying on his bed

listening to the house breathe and creak, listening to the heavy drip of water, he longed for some kind of peace. For although his wounds were healing, the tension within him was increasing. He had been here for months. Gerard continued to visit. But the visits had become less friendly. Gerard watched him with open hostility. Instead of asking after his health, instead of bringing him newspapers to read, he had only one question now.

'You did a good job for the Tamils with *Tiger Lily*. You're a local hero, you know. So when are you going to start your next book about our plight?'

Yesterday, annoyed at Theo's continuing silence, Gerard had asked to see his exercise book.

'There's nothing in it to interest you,' Theo had said. 'Just things about my wife.'

'Now, you listen to me,' Gerard had threatened, flinging the book across the room. He advanced towards Theo who'd shrunk. 'You are trying my patience a little too much. I don't care about your precious memory loss. I'm not interested in your deceased wife. If you want to leave this place alive, if you have any hope for the future, then you are going to have start working fast. D'you understand?' He had paused. And lowered his voice.

'Start with something small.' he said quietly. 'Write me an article for a British newspaper. About the things the Singhalese bastards have done to us. Something with your name attached to it. Forget about your damn memory. I'm trying to help you, Theo, but if you refuse to cooperate, I'm afraid you'll be removed. Understand? Things will be out of my control then.'

Theo had broken out in a sweat. Gerard stared at him.

'If you can write another book,' he said at last, reasonably, breathing deeply, 'if you can contact your publishers we'll be able to let you go. If not . . .' His voice trailed off.

So he knew now. But what could he write about. That night he lay awake, terrified, imagining metal hooks were screwed into the walls above his bed. Finally, Theo slept fitfully. Then towards dawn something woke him. A sentence was repeating itself in his head.

'*Now that there are no priests or philosophers left, artists are the most important people in the world. That is the only thing that interests me.*'

And then suddenly, as the dawn light filled the sky, he knew. As though he were retrieving a lost language, he saw them. Rohan and Giulia, standing grey-black in the rain. Coffin-rain, made for the dead. Astonished, he thought, But how could I have forgotten them? Unravelling their names from the tangle of forgotten things, he saw Giulia against a waterlogged sky, wintry and far away. Because there was no one to share his new discovery with, he paced the floor of his room. The Tamil woman, hearing his footsteps came in, curious to see what he was doing.

'I've remembered something else,' he shouted. But his excitement was tempered with fear. 'What else is there?' he cried, forgetting the woman did not understand.

Outside, the upcountry rain, which had held off in the night, began falling again. It brought with it the faint smell of tea bushes and blossom. Sharp bird calls stabbed the air, and dark clouds hid the trees.

Giulia had not meant to spy on him. At least that was what she told herself later. She had been on her way to the fish market when she had decided to take a boat out to the Lido instead. The foolishness of it did not strike her until afterwards, but by then it was too late and she had seen Rohan. He was not walking on the beach and he was not alone. She stared mesmerised, uncaring that he might look up and notice her. Rohan was laughing. At least, it seemed that way to Giulia from where she stood, drinking her coffee. The woman looked vaguely familiar. As her heart constricted with a sharp stab of betrayal, Giulia saw Rohan reach over and light the woman's cigarette. Then he lit one for himself. But he's given up smoking, thought Giulia, bewildered. And she flushed with pain. Moving closer, she searched Rohan's face. It appeared as that of a stranger. What is it? she thought. What is he laughing about? She could not remember the last time she had seen him laugh. And try as she might she could not see happiness in his face.

Back in their flat, she opened the suitcase with Nulani's things in it and looked at them. All the small, useless tokens they had brought for her lay untouched, along with the letters she had sent. Some bangles, a lime-green skirt, neatly folded, a bottle of cheap perfume. The sum of a life. There were a few photographs of Theo, one of Theo with Anna, and another one of Nulani's brother Jim. Giulia stared at them. Suddenly she began to weep, thick heavy sobs.

'Will he leave me?' she cried.

This, then, was how it was to end. Anna gone, Theo dead, our marriage finished. Is this how he means to forget all that we have been through together? Throwing me out with all that has hurt him? Is this my fate, now? She had been unable to foresee such an ending. How foolish of her. In the old days, she remembered, when she had first wanted to go to Sri Lanka, he had refused, saying nothing good would come out of it.

'Oh, Giulia, don't you understand?' he had said. 'My country is damaged. This war will go on and on in the minds of the people long after it is over. They will try to pretend it's forgotten but how does one forget when your father and your mother and your brother have been slaughtered before your eyes?'

The aftermath of a war was mostly scars, he had told her bitterly. Giulia was crying more quietly now, rocking gently, sitting on the floor beside the tokens from Nulani Mendis's life. Remembering his warning words. At least, she thought, neither Anna nor Nulani had been betrayed in this way. At least they were loved until the end. Picking up the last letter they had received from the girl, she unfolded it for the hundredth time and stared blindly at it.

'*Jim won't see me for a while,*' Nulani had written. '*He is busy with his final exams. Then he has to look for a job. I miss you.*'

Suddenly Giulia was galvanised into action. Nulani's brother had been at Sheffield University, she was certain of it. Someone had mentioned it, Theo maybe, or the girl herself. Why had they not thought to follow this lead? I will find her, thought Giulia. Closing the suitcase, wiping her eyes on her skirt, she picked up the phone. She would ring Sheffield University. And find Jim Mendis.

Later, after the rain had cleared, the light retained a softness, not unlike a spring day in England. And in the afternoon the sun came out. The old woman brought in a plate of fruit. She had placed it on a tarnished metal tray covered with drawings of Hindu gods. As she walked towards Theo something else seemed to come with her but then she grinned her discoloured, toothless grin and he lost the wisp of it again. All afternoon, after that, he was agitated and restless. Something was very wrong. Blood throbbed at his temples, and he started to shudder. Gerard had said he would be visiting but after the scene of the day before Theo was reluctant to see him. By mid-afternoon he had curled into a tight ball of worry, glancing at the door, expecting Gerard to walk in at any moment. But still he did not appear and terror, never far from the surface, rose in Theo.

He had begun to feel sick. His leg ached constantly and he wondered if the glasses they had found him were, in fact, the cause of his never-ending headaches. Glancing towards the door, straining for the slightest sound, he paced the floor nervously. A bit later on he vomited. Then he lay on his bed and slept, moaning and tossing feverishly. When he woke the old woman was standing over him saying something. Her voice was insistent and harsh and there was another sound that puzzled him. The woman was talking to him in Tamil. She stood too close for his liking. He felt hot and faint and wondered if a mosquito had bitten him. The woman pointed towards the roof. Theo looked at her through a wave of sickness. He had no idea what she meant. He tried asking her to fetch the radio. But either she did not want him to have it, or she could not understand him. In the end he gave up. In any case the woman was getting too friendly and he felt the need to keep a distance. As there was still no sign of Gerard, Theo picked up his notebook. Rohan, he thought, I must not forget Rohan. I mustn't lose that thought.

He was staring at his notebook thinking of the books Anna used to keep, filled with her small beautiful handwriting, crushed all together on the page. The look of things had always struck him forcefully. Rohan's paintings with their faulty horizons sitting uneasily on the canvas, rich and luminescent, had had the same effect. Making the invisible visible, Rohan had said. Had it been Rohan? Or had it been someone else? He felt as though his face was on fire. The sun had gone down completely. The walls of his room, flat and empty of objects, had the effect of cutting him off from the world on the other side. He felt not merely alone but ejected into dangerous isolation. It struck him that he was hardly human, locked up, pounding away in a twilight hell of gunshots and violence. He was *certain*, something was terribly wrong. Perhaps he was ill with malaria? He began to shake then, with an awful sense of premonition, feeling a clamouring inside him, some struggle beyond his control. And then, in the purest moments of shock, without warning or sound, without preparation, the thought came forward, crashing against him with the roar of the sea. His memory of Sugi. And of the girl.

He must have collapsed. When he came to, it was dark again and he was sitting on the floor. The girl's face appeared clear and very serene, framed in light, made sharper by his own exhaustion. And he felt at last with shattering horror, the true weight of his loss. He heard a noise approaching from a very long distance and felt it vibrate against him in slow, nauseating waves. It dissolved into the sound of a king coconut being cracked open with a machete. Held between two hands. Liquid gushed between long fingers, cloudy and plentiful. Small, rough-papered notebooks lay on a table, unwavering stories drawn in black lifted off its pages and came towards him. Hither and thither they fell, clamouring for his attention. Sunlight poured into a cracked glass jug, an arm, bare to the elbow, rested by a typewriter. And all around was the fragrance of linseed oil, of turpentine and colour. Rooted to the spot, Theo saw all this as if he watched through a mirror, rising darkly, out of the piano music that tripped down the steps into the tangle of garden light. Somewhere out of sight a gate was clicked open. A silver tray was placed on a table. It held a cup of tea and a glass of lime juice. He saw a man standing beside the table, smiling broadly. Still the noise approached. It was coming from the sky. Voices rose in confusion.

'I haven't seen you for four days,' the girl was saying, her eyes shining, her black hair a curtain against her face, and all the heat of the afternoon gathered into a moment of such sweetness that Theo gasped for air.

'Where have you been?' he mumbled, struggling to stand up. The noise was getting louder. It drummed in his head.

'Sir, you have been away too long. But not to worry, I have looked after Miss Nulani.'

'Sugi,' he said, tentatively. 'Sugi?'

'You have a scar. I can feel it as I draw you.'

'Draw, draw, draw. . .'

The voices were indistinct. They were muddled with other sounds that he could not understand. He saw the treetops being whipped up by a wind. Maybe a storm was brewing. The beach flashed past him like a mirage, scorching white, lace-edged by water. Someone had knocked the stone lions off their plinth; someone had picked a great branch of blossom and placed it in a jug of water on his table.

'Was it you, Sugi?' he asked urgently.

'Yes, it was me,' Sugi admitted. 'We were worried, you were away for so long. We thought something might have happened.'

'But you're here, now,' the girl seemed to say. Her face appeared strangely distorted, and part of the whirling noise outside. He wanted to speak, but his mouth would form no words. He could not move.

'I have been tortured, Sugi,' he wanted to say. 'What do you say to that?'

He wanted to shout, to catch his attention, but the image of Sugi had become indistinct.

'They showed me no mercy,' he tried to say, 'and once that has happened, once you have been tortured, you can never belong in this world. There is no place that can ever be your home again.'

But the words that had remained locked within him for so many months could not be voiced. And the pain that he had carried for so long, unknowingly and fearfully, seemed an impossible thing, too elusive and too raw to speak of. A slab of meat. That was what he wanted to say, that was what he had been. That was what he was.

In the darkness that had descended unnoticed, at last, he understood the sound was that of a helicopter. It whirled and chopped the air, swinging closer and closer. Unable to move, he watched as the beam of light swept across the jungle outside.

Oh Christ! he thought. Oh Christ!

And the only real thing that remained forcing itself upon him was the roaring of an engine in his ears, and the heavy sound of falling rain.

15

THE TAMIL WOMAN SCREAMED AND DARTED into the room.

'Helicopter,' she said in English. 'Singhala army.'

The noise was deafening and directly overhead. Theo froze, his heart was racing, his leg a lame weight against his body. Then with one swift movement, with catlike speed, the youth on guard duty was standing beside him. Theo drew his breath in sharply but the youth shook his head violently, putting his hand out to stop him.

'Quiet, no more noise,' he hissed. 'They look for Gerard.'

'What?'

The helicopter's rotor blades whirled closer. It was about to land. The noise was so great that it wasn't possible to hear anything else and then the boy threw himself on to the ground.

'They have guns,' he said, through clenched teeth.

Theo braced himself, shrinking into a corner of the room. But the whirling continued without attack and the searchlights moved in a circular fashion across the trees again.

'What's happening?'

'They look for Gerard,' the boy whispered from the floor. He began crawling towards the window.

'Who?' asked Theo. 'Who's looking for him? Who are these people?'

'The Chief. He wants Gerard. He told the Tigers, Gerard is traitor. He wants find him. All day they are looking for him. They kill him when they find him.'

The boy spoke in a matter-of-fact way now, as though none of this frightened him.

'But he's not here,' Theo said. He was sweating badly. 'He hasn't visited today.'

'I know. He and Chief have big fight. Big fight!' The boy seemed to be relishing this. 'Gerard wants finish from Tigers. He tells world. Now, everyone look for him. Tigers, Singhalese, everyone.'

The boy stood up. The searchlights were back, close up, by the house and the helicopter blew a hurricane of air over the trees. Then they heard a different sound and seconds later a truck drew up. The Tamil woman was whimpering quietly. She had moved closer to the boy and was plucking at his arm but he pushed her away roughly and spoke to her in Tamil. Dimly, in spite of his state of shock, Theo realised the boy must be her son. Through the haze of fear and confusion, he saw she was frightened for the boy and he saw for the first time that the boy was very young. All the time he had been guarding the house the woman must have been frightened for his life. All the time she had served Theo his meals, or grinned at Gerard, she had been worried for the boy's future. And then he thought, in however many months I have been here, I never cared to ask her name. The thought came to him simply, without the complications of grief or the fear of the past months. The boy was crouching by the window and had cocked his gun. The idea that they were about to die fixed itself firmly in Theo's mind. Again the thought was uncluttered by fear. Outside the rain increased. It fell in small dashes on to the glare of the searchlights. Someone was moving against the darkest parts of the garden. Fleetingly he remembered the girl again. She appeared in his mind un-sullied by the moment's sudden real violence and by its terror. He sensed, rather than saw, a figure inch its way along the corner of the bungalow. Somebody, screened by the creepers, was breathing hard, close by. The sound was very loud and rasping as if whoever it was had been running for a long time. As if they were very frightened. Theo understood the sound, and the feeling that went with it. Next to him, the Tamil woman and the boy stood absolutely still, waiting, listening. Suddenly there was a shout, followed by running footsteps and Gerard appeared briefly in the beam of the headlights. Two men in camouflage uniform were dragging his arms back as the helicopter rose swiftly and disappeared above the trees. Now Theo could see Gerard clearly. At some point in the scuffle he had been blindfolded and his hands tied together. His mouth was working but no sound came out of it. As he watched, Theo saw two men force Gerard to his knees and in the light from the truck he saw one of them pull out a cigarette, smoking it silently and with an air of calm. Then the man threw his half-smoked cigarette away and picked up an axe from the back of the truck. With a swift movement, a wide arc of his arm, he brought the axe down sharply on Gerard's bowed neck. Once, twice, at the third attempt, Gerard's head rolled to the ground like a coconut.

Afterwards he had no idea for how long the three of them stood there, rooted to the spot. Silent as the dead, themselves. Luck had entered the arena and saved them. Fate had given them a hand. The men dragged Gerard's body into the back of the truck. They wrapped his head in a green cloth, as if it were a trophy, and tossed it in. Then they drove off. Not a single shot had been fired. All was darkness once more as the rain continued to fall unnoticed. The old woman began to weep quietly.

'We must go,' the boy said at last. In the darkness his face looked unearthly. 'They will come back. You must leave here. Go!'

Theo stared at him. He was incapable of moving, incapable of speech. His mind and body had seized up as though in rigor mortis.

'Come,' the boy urged again, his face calm. 'I take you to the border. Then we leave. You must go. They might find you here. Just go. Back to your home.'

The old woman nodded. She wiped her eyes and Theo saw, without surprise, that her face too was devoid of expression.

'Come,' the boy said again, seeing Theo could not understand. 'Before they return.'

The old woman began to speak in Tamil.

'What's she saying?' asked Theo. He was terrified.

'She says we are not normal. We cannot speak in normal voices ever again. Even if the peace comes,' the boy said, 'there is no peace for us.'

Together they stepped out into the rain, and hurried away from the house, towards the gate, where a battered jeep was hidden in the undergrowth. The old woman was still muttering and the boy turned to Theo.

'She says, peace is a jack tree that grows on the blood that has been spilt,' he said. 'It is an old Tamil saying.'

All around was an eerie silence. Above was a splattering of stars. The jungle appeared before them in the headlights of the jeep, immense and impenetrable. And as they drove into it, Theo saw that all the time he had been standing at the window, all the time his heart had been tied up with fear, he had been clutching the exercise books in which were the salvaged remains of his life.

Rohan had begun to paint. Giulia was not sure how this happened, but he had found a small warehouse in Dorsoduro and turned it into a studio. His early-morning trips to the Lido had stopped as abruptly as they had begun. And he was working seriously again. Too much time had been lost already, he told Giulia. He didn't want any more distractions.

'People will come and go. Only art survives,' he told her, airily.

Giulia said nothing. In the end even she had been unable to trace the girl. On the day Giulia had seen Rohan laughing with the unknown woman she had rung Sheffield University in search of Jim Mendis. But there she had drawn a blank. Jim Mendis had graduated a year earlier and moved on. He had left no forwarding address. Next, Giulia had tried contacting a fellow student, a contemporary of his. But the student had only known Jim slightly, and had no idea where he could be or if he had a sister. With no other clue there was nothing else Giulia could do. Perhaps, she thought, sadly, Rohan was right, and it was time to give up on this hopeless cause. The girl had been swallowed up by an indifferent world.

'Time has passed, events have moved on,' Rohan said briskly, seeing her looking at the notebooks. 'Put them away, forget about it now.'

Giulia smiled, agreeing, but the smile did not reach her eyes. Although she did not blame him, Rohan's coldness towards her brought an unbearable loneliness in its wake. She was glad he was painting again; glad to see him so busy. But every night when he returned home exhausted and preoccupied with his work, she looked for signs of other distractions, fearful of what she might see.

Outwardly Rohan appeared happier. He was relieved to be painting at last. He had missed his work. When he stretched his first canvas he hoped he would be able to pick up exactly where he had left off, using the colour grey, painting the large, soft abstracts he once had. But he found this was impossible. Life had taken him to a different place. So instead, he began to paint in dark austere tones. He painted blocks of flats from which light seeped out and formless human presence, ghosts sitting patiently, waiting for or guarding some unseen treasure. He hardly knew what he was doing. The size of his canvases had become smaller too, partly because of the cramped nature of his studio and partly because what he wanted to say was more intimate, more secretive. He had the strangest feeling of living in a closed box, from which no light could escape. Loneliness preoccupied him, and the blank empty spaces of loss. The twilight world of the displaced interested him in a way quite different from before, the slow disquiet of the home-less. All that had been familiar and certain vanished from his work. The war was embossed on Rohan's life like a watermark, visible only under close scrutiny. His palette changed. Ignoring the soft tones of the Adriatic, the blues and the greens, he began to use crimson and pink. He refused to look at other colours. Giulia thought the surfaces of his paintings were like bruised flesh, visceral and close to death. But fearful of Rohan's sudden bursts of anger, she dared not say anything. She was aware he was drinking too much, but she could not stop this either, and whenever they were alone together he became bad-tempered and argumentative. Dimly aware of his new, unspoken dislike of her, Giulia merely hid her own unhappiness under an air of false cheerfulness, refusing to question it. Privately, she believed, the war in Sri Lanka had become her war too. Sometimes on a busy *calle*, in broad daylight, she would become lost in a daydream, caught up in some unresolved memory. She would stop walking and stand absolutely still as passers-by stepped around her irritably. I'm no use, she would think, rising from her reverie, scurrying home with pounding heart. And it was at these moments that she saw clearly how her husband's country had wormed its way under her skin, invading her life, incapacitating her. It had carved out its violence on her too, so although she still loved Rohan, showing this love was gradually becoming a complicated and reluctant thing.

When Rohan had done about a dozen paintings, he told Giulia he had decided to find a gallery to represent him. Venice was a small town filled with tourists and the contemporary art available mostly serviced this industry. It was easier to find a meaningless painting in Venice than not, Rohan complained. Then one day he introduced Giulia to a woman. He had met her in the piazza, he said, where he took his morning coffee. The woman ran a small gallery tucked away behind the Calle del Forno. She represented only Venetian artists, serious artists, but, because he lived here, because his wife was from these parts, the woman told Giulia unsmilingly, she was prepared to take Rohan's work. They were sitting in his studio sharing a bottle of wine. Giulia had a feeling she had seen the woman somewhere before.

A month later two of Rohan's paintings sold for a substantial sum of money.

'I'm so proud of you,' Giulia said, after that first sale. 'See, there's hope.'

She spoke sadly, for she now remembered where she had seen the woman before. Rohan pulled a face. He had banished hope.

Two storks nested on the roof of the beach house. There had never been storks there before. Mother, father and the nest waited patiently for the egg to hatch. Maybe they felt the house was vacant so they felt safer here, or maybe they liked the uninterrupted view with nothing as far as the eye could see. Only Antarctica lay beyond the ocean. The seagulls left them alone; they were too big to be argued with. Inside the house all was quiet but not empty. Inside the house was a life, of sorts. There were small signs, small stirrings of living, ebbing and flowing feebly. For inside the house was Theo Samarajeeva. He was home at last. It had taken almost four years but he was back. He had been back for some time, days, months. Time did not matter much, he had no train to catch, no appointment to keep. Mostly he slept on a bed, *the* bed; it had belonged to him once long ago. It was his again. And he was back now and sleeping on it, all day and all night, hardly ever getting up. There was no one to recognise him and no one to care. There wasn't a soul around, just the storks. Soon the egg hatched and the baby stork breathed fresh sea air. It breathed the same air as Theo. Neither of them cared much if the air was free. They both just breathed it.

Had Sugi been there he would have told Theo it was good luck to have storks nesting on the roof. Sugi would have seen it as an omen. He would have cleaned the house and polished the floor with coconut scrapings, and made Sir some milk tea, bringing it out to the veranda on a silver tray. He would have fixed the doors and shutters that hung limply on their broken hinges, and then he would have picked up the stone lions that had crashed to the ground. But Sugi wasn't there. And the house, neglected and vandalised, remained uncared for.

On that first day of his return, Theo waited for Sugi. He had been patient for nearly four years, another day or so made no difference. Sugi would be back soon, he was certain. The girl, he hoped, was somewhere safe, waiting for news of him. He was too nervous to try the lights on that first night; he simply waited. When Sugi did not appear the next day or the next or even the day after that, he began to stumble around the house, dragging his lame leg against what furniture remained. He opened the tins of food in the larder, which by some miracle had not been stolen, and when he could no longer stop shaking he tried to eat a little. But his throat had closed up to food. Only the bottles of whisky, hidden away with a few documents inside the covered-over garden well, held his interest. And this was how Thercy found him.

Thercy still lived in the town. She was no longer the person she once was, and the town, too, had changed. With new developments further up the coast most of those who lived here now were newcomers, indifferent to its history. Four years and two assassinated prime ministers had altered the way the war was fought. Loyalties had changed, and changed again. Blood had cooled. Four years had buried the past. Only the ghosts stayed on. Thercy was like a ghost, she had meant to leave long ago, but apathy had stopped her. She had aged, walking up the hill wasn't easy any more, but when she saw a light in the beach house something stirred within her. Something she had never thought to feel again. Thinking of her dead friend, panting, she walked slowly towards the house.

'Aiyo!' she said. 'Mr Samarajeeva!' and then she stopped, unable to go on.

She had recognised him, but only just. Theo looked back at her. He was frightened. The woman stood in the doorway, blocking his escape.

'I was Sugi's friend,' Thercy said, barely above a whisper, staring at this remnant of a man. Mr Samarajeeva looked like a ghost. 'What has happened to you?'

'Sugi? Where has he gone? Tell him, I'm home.'

'Aiyo!' said Thercy softly. 'Sugi is gone, my Sir. He's dead.'

It was the word 'Sir' that Theo heard first. And it was the first notch of his undoing.

'Nulani,' he said. 'Nulani Mendis . . .'

'I . . . don't know, Sir. Maybe she's . . .' and Thercy caught his crumpled body as he fell.

Later, she cleaned the house for him and made some mulli-gatawny chicken soup. Later, when he was less frightened, she talked some more. Soothingly, as though he was her child.

'Nulani's uncle has gone,' she said. 'The people who bought the house have divided it up. There are two families who share the garden now.'

It seemed that the lane down which Theo had driven, on that carefree distant night, was almost unrecognisable. Someone had cleared the path of all but memories. The Mendis family might as well not have existed. Other things, Thercy told him, had changed too. The convent school and the boys' school, having joined forces under new staff, had moved up the coast. Nothing remained of its former self. New schoolchildren took the bus to school now. Young girls in faded skirts and with ribbons in their hair walked chattering down the road.

'And the traffic island, Sir,' Thercy said, 'd'you remember, Miss Nulani used to say it was her father's headstone? Well, that has gone too.' Even the hospital, she told Theo, had been relocated to another place. Theo listened. He hardly responded, but he watched her as she served his broth, and swept the floor, and collected the empty arrack bottles. Then she told him she would be back tomorrow with some food.

Thercy came every day, after that. She came with rice, and with dhal and with string-hopper pancakes. She made more mulligatawny soup, and she asked Theo if there was anything else she could buy for him. She went to the bank at his request and drew out the money he wanted. She told him, no one had been in the least interested in his name. And all the while she talked to him, telling him about the changes in the town.

'Sumaner House is changed, Sir,' she told Theo one day. 'The owner had it boarded up and now it's waiting to be sold. I never liked it much, although when the orphan was there at least it was a good job. Plenty of money for me, then. But after the boy disappeared, his guardian saw no point in returning to our useless island. Why should he, when work was plentiful elsewhere? He gave me a pension and I now live in Bazaar Street, behind the railway station.'

Thercy talked determinedly on. She hid her shock, having quickly got accustomed to the frailness of this man, and did whatever she could to help him. Besides, she felt he was getting stronger daily. Every time she visited, she thought of another little snippet of information. To waken his interest in life.

'D'you remember the gem store, Sir?' she asked him one morning. 'It used to be so popular with tourists. One night, about a year ago, the police came without warning, raided it, and shut it up for good.' She raised her hands heavenwards, shrugging. 'There were stories about what had gone on in there for a while, terrible rumours about the man who owned it. But so many things have happened in this wretched town that one more story means nothing. No one is surprised for long.'

She was silent, not wanting to say more, aware of Theo's unspoken desire to know how Sugi had died.

At night, because there was no longer a curfew, when he was alone, Theo would walk for hours on the beach, listening to the sea. Then, the depression he had held in check all day descended. In his headlong flight, chasing his freedom to the coast, snatching at its tail feathers, touching but never quite catching it, he had not thought about the future. After the Tamil boy dropped him at the border, he had simply headed for the sea, the sound of it, the smell of it. His heart had yearned for the girl; his arms had ached with the need to hold her. But now all he had was a pair of broken straw sandals and a notebook lying open with all its stories gone. The wind had whisked them away; the rain had washed them out. Time had rendered them useless, making them old stories from long ago. It dawned on him that recovery would not be easy, maybe even that these stories were un-recoverable. At moments like this, despair grew like sea cacti, piercing his heart. He stared at the sea; it was a blank canvas of nothingness. It moved with the richness of silk but, he felt, underneath it was cruel. Often at night, after Thercy left, reality rocked against the walls of the beach house, and at these times, Theo discovered forbidden thoughts. They rotted like fruit beside his silent typewriter where once his manuscript had been. Then, staring at the undulating phosphorescent water, he understood at last that freedom was a double-edged thing, which, like inno-cence once lost, was unrecoverable.

Towards dawn always, after these wanderings, he would return to lie like an emaciated stain on the bed where once his love had slept. Wearing a thin sarong that had belonged to Sugi, two legs placed carefully together, the soles of his feet worn and smashed, his face turning of its own accord to the wall. So that Thercy, coming in to sweep out the night, would stare at the scar across his back and heave another little sigh of pity. And fill a vase with shoe-flowers from the garden, for time, she knew, was what he needed most.

One day Thercy found the half-finished portrait of Sugi behind the bookshelf.

'Sir,' she had said, 'Mr Samarajeeva, I . . .'

It had been too much for him, days of bottled-up emotions gushed out.

'All the other paintings she did have gone,' he said after-wards, when he could speak calmly again. 'Why would anyone want to steal them?'

'Maybe,' Thercy suggested, tentatively, 'maybe your friends in Colombo came and collected them. What d'you think? I heard that someone came to this house after Sugi was gone.' She frowned, not wanting to be impertinent, but anxious to help. 'Why don't you contact your friends? How are they to know you are still alive if you don't contact them?'

There, she thought, she had said the thing utmost in her mind. But the idea filled Theo with horror. All day it worked in him, all day he gazed at the painting. And that night, having finished off a whole bottle of arrack, he decided to go for a swim. Throwing off his clothes on the deserted beach, he waded into the water, swimming slowly, thinking he might head out towards the rocks. There had been a storm the day before and the sea was still rough. Within minutes he was out of breath but, deciding to turn back, Theo found he was further away from the shore than he realised and an undercurrent was pulling at him. The harder he swam, the further away from the beach he seemed to get. A train hooted, appearing suddenly around the bay. Theo shouted and waved, but the beach itself was empty. By now he was panting. The alcohol had made him dizzy and his legs were beginning to give out. He realised that unless he could reach the shore soon he would drown. A wave rose and hit him, pushing him further out. He was struggling so much and the roar in his ears was so loud that he did not hear the shout until the catamaran was alongside him and a hand hauled him up and over the side of it. Two pairs of eyes stared at him in the thin light of a lantern.

'There's no point in drowning,' a voice chided him sternly. 'You'll only have to come back to live another life.'

'It's a good thing we saw you,' the second fisherman added. 'Are you new here, or are you just a fool? This isn't a place for swimming. The currents are treacherous. You have to go to the next bay if you want to swim.'

They shook their head in amazement and took him back to find his clothes, joking with him that they would have better fish for sale in the morning. And then they left him, putting out to sea, vanishing into the darkness.

That night, for the first time in years, he slept uninterrupted and when he woke at last it was from a dream of the girl and their single night together. The mist was already beginning to clear on the horizon and he could hear the '*malu, malu*' cry of the fishermen in the distance. Thercy stood unsmiling beside his bed, holding out a cup of morning tea.

'I heard what happened to you last night,' she said, shaking her head.

She waited while he took a sip of tea.

'I have to say something to you, Mr Samarajeeva. I have said nothing all this time but now I won't be quiet any longer.'

She made a small gesture of anger. She was breathing deeply and her voice, when she spoke, was rough and close to tears. It surprised him into listening.

'Sir, you are a clever man,' said Thercy grimly. 'Sugi told me all about the books you wrote and your film. Sugi was full of admiration for you. And love. He was my friend, so I knew about the things that were in his heart. And I must tell you, Sir, the fishermen were right. I am sorry, Mr Samarajeeva, you *are* behaving like a fool! Go and find your friends in Colombo, find out what happened to Miss Nulani. She was a loving girl. I know how you have suffered, how you feel, but can't you *see*? She would want to know you are safe. What is wrong with you? At least go and talk to them.'

Her voice had risen and she was gesticulating wildly. Theo handed her his empty cup.

'Twice in one day,' he said faintly, with the barest movement of a smile, 'there must be some truth in it. You are right, Thercy, and thank you for saying it. I must try to overcome this fear. I must stop being a coward. I will go to Colombo. Tomorrow, I'll go tomorrow and find Rohan and Giulia. I promise. I know that only they can tell me what happened to her in the end.'

16

IN COLOMBO THE MOSQUITOES WERE BACK. Thin, fragile and deadly, they coated the walls of buildings in their thousands, filling the waterlogged coconut shells, turning the surfaces of everything they alighted on into a living carpet. They fed on the flesh of rotting fruit, sucking out what remained of the honeydew nectar. Arriving with the mosquitoes was a new breed of women from the north of the island. Like the mosquitoes, they came with the rains. But unlike the mosquitoes, the women were full of a new kind of despair and a frightening rage. Their desire for revenge was greater than their interest in life. They had been trained; a whole army of psychologists working tirelessly on them had shaped their impressionable minds. The female mosquitoes' purpose in life was the continuation of their species, but the suicide bombers cared nothing for the future. Steadily they changed the shape of the battle lines, appearing everywhere, in government buildings, at army checkpoints, beside long-abandoned sacred sites. They appeared in churches when mass was being said, at roadside shrines and during Buddhist funerals. Neither place nor time mattered much to these women. Nature had not designed their limbs to grow once broken. Killing was what interested *them*. For these women were the new trailblazers, the world epidemic slipping in unnoticed, just as the malaria season returned.

Unaware of this and eventually after much procrastination, Theo dragged himself to Colombo. Thercy watched him pocket his reluctance and go, pleased, but saying nothing. She had thought he would change his mind. Thercy understood the shame he felt, she had seen it before in others. She knew what torture did. But she knew also the desire to find the girl and his friends was greater. Speech was not necessary; all he wanted was to catch sight of her. If his karma is good, Thercy thought, then he will.

'She must have a chance to forget me,' he said out loud. 'I know my age never worried her but, well, things are different now. Now I am old in an inescapable way.'

He looked at Thercy but she didn't seem to be listening. She was cleaning the mirror.

'I have lived on the edge of an abyss for so long that the world and I are separate. I have nothing to offer her, even if she has been waiting for me. Even if she still wanted me I have no more to give.'

Thercy finished her cleaning and went outside. She knew he liked cut flowers, so she cut some of the jasmine creeper and brought it in. Then she found a vase and trailed the branch in it.

'All I want is the chance to see her from a distance,' Theo told her, watching her arthritic hands. 'Out of curiosity really, nothing more. Just to know that she's happy, that she's painting. That she has retained her hope.'

'Yes,' Thercy said.

The scent from the jasmine began to fill the room.

'After all, I must face reality. Probably she has married, by now. Who knows, she might have several children.'

The scent filled Theo with unbearable sadness. All gone, he thought. Every single one of them. Thercy looked at him. She pursed her lips and wiped the table. Then she went into the kitchen to make him some tea.

The train hugged the coastline, running parallel to the road. It was a journey he had made many times before. Wide sandy beaches unfolded before him, a few scattered villages screened by coconut palms. Staring out of the window he saw that nothing had changed; everything was as it had been yesterday. But the man who had once rested his eyes on the view had vanished. He had held this view within him during all the terrible years in prison. The girl's face and the view had been so closely linked, so connected that they had been inseparable in his mind. He had imagined her waiting for him on the brow of the hill and all of this, and Sugi, had been the sum of his hope. Somehow, he realised, he had kept the hope alive. Now at last he was free, and the beach and the sea had waited for him, but the view he had dreamt about in prison was no longer as he imagined. And he was no longer that man who had been able to dream. A sense of loss, terrible in its hopelessness, washed over him. You will not recognise me, he thought, staring at the sea. I have been to places I can no longer describe. And he thought again, no, she must not see me. Better for her to remember me as I was.

In Colombo there had been a temporary clean-up. During Theo's imprisonment most of the heaviest fighting had moved away from the capital and was now concentrated elsewhere in the north. Only the suicide bombers operated with a disregard for boundaries. Because of them, the outside world had woken up to what was taking place and had become interested in the country at last. The suicide bombers, it seemed, had started a cult following. Muslims in the Middle East were beginning to follow suit. At last, Sri Lanka was newsworthy. A few days earlier the ex-Governor from Britain had visited briefly. After meeting the Prime Minister he travelled north to shake hands with the head of the insurgents. Peace was a long way away, but it was what he had in mind. The ex-Governor left a trail of bunting behind him. They still lined the streets, while elsewhere, wilted flowers covered up the bullet holes as best they could. Whitewash brightened the bombed-out buildings. All was sunlit activity. Colombo, Theo saw, was like him, struggling with the pretence of normality. But the army was still a presence, and seeing a truck Theo panicked. He rushed into a shop to hide, his heart pounding. No one followed him and gradually he became aware that he was being stared at. Then, as the shopkeeper approached, he ran out. Like a petty thief, he thought, fleetingly, unable to stop himself. He should not have come. Outside in the glaring light, looking around for escape, he became frantic. How long would it be before someone caught up with him? Hurrying across the road he expected a roadblock, or the sound of gunshot, at any moment, but still nothing happened. Forcing himself to calm down, to breathe deeply, he lost his way. He looked at a passing bus, but such was his anxiety that he was unable to read the sign. This, then, was what it meant to be hunted.

Eventually, he found his bearings. After the near drowning Theo had begun to realise how weak his legs were, yet in spite of this, rather than take a bus and be stared at, he decided to walk. Rohan's house was fifteen minutes away. Four years and two months away. A lifetime away. Theo walked slowly now, head down against the sun, remembering. The smell of limes and frangipani filled the air. It was five o'clock. Rohan would have finished work. He would be cleaning his brushes, wiping his hands absent-mindedly on a rag, staring at his painting. And Giulia, most probably, would have brought in the tea. Theo would be the last person they would expect to see. Once again he began to wonder at the wisdom of this trip. What if he were not welcome? The idea had not occurred to him before, but time, he knew, changed things. *He* had changed. What if they had too? As he turned the corner into their road, he hesitated. His bad leg was throbbing and he was shaking all over. What if the girl was there? What if he frightened them? He was no longer as they remembered. And the enormity of what he would need to say to make them understand struck him suddenly and forcefully. He was sweating heavily, partly from the heat but mostly from fear. Maybe, he thought, they would simply not believe him. In *Tiger Lily* he had written about a man whom no one believed. The man had gone from one village elder to another, telling of atrocities done to him, but no one believed him. In the end, doubting himself, hounded from his home, followed by demons, the man had thrown himself into the river and drowned.

Feeling unutterably exhausted, Theo walked the length of the road. Rohan's house was nowhere in sight. Although he peered into gardens, walking halfway along driveways he could not, for the life of him, see the canopied terrace that Giulia had pain-stakingly made. Rohan's studio was at the front of the house. In the past, whenever Theo had arrived at their house, Rohan had always been the first to spot him, rushing out with a greeting. But today, although he retraced his steps several times, Theo could no longer see the studio. Perhaps he had mistaken the road, he thought, momentarily distracted. Some construction work was going on nearby. Puzzled, he stood watching the workmen on the scaffolding. A lorry passed through what must have once been a driveway. Theo could have sworn this was where Rohan and Giulia had lived. It dawned on him that they might have moved. Then a black VW Beetle pulled up in the driveway of the house next door.

'Are you looking for someone?' the driver asked, getting out.

Theo stared. The man half smiled at him, uncertain. 'I know you, don't I?' he asked. 'Haven't I met you before?'

'I'm looking for someone by the name of Rohan Fernando,' Theo said reluctantly. 'I thought he lived here but . . .'

'Rohan? You knew Rohan?'

'Where is he?'

'You haven't heard?'

'No,' said Theo.

'You from around here?'

'No,' said Theo.

'Ah, I see. You've been overseas,' the man said, nodding, understanding.

Theo nodded too.

'I'm sorry. In that case you wouldn't have heard. About two years ago, there was a fire in their house, one in Rohan's studio, and one on their veranda. Two years ago. It tore through their house, men. We were in bed, my wife and I, when we heard it . . . there was no chance, none whatsoever. I'm sorry to tell you this. You aren't a close friend, are you? I can't understand it really. This whole road was puzzled. They were quiet people, and Rohan's wife wasn't even Sri Lankan.' The man shrugged apologetically, his pleasant features puzzled. 'Things were very bad two years ago, very savage. Now, thank God, this new government is trying to negotiate peace talks. The first in decades. Everyone is hopeful, you know. Now that the ex-Governor has visited. It can only be a good thing. You recently returned?' he asked.

And when Theo said nothing, the man continued, pointing at the building site: 'There, that was where their house stood, over there.'

17

WITHIN A YEAR THE GALLERY IN Calle del Forno offered Rohan a solo show. The demand for his small paintings had grown. The urgency, the intensity of the colour, their size, all added to their odd charm. He had been an abstract painter for years but now slowly he found himself propelled towards empty interiors, furniture and unclothed figures. The rooms he painted were always dark. Wardrobes opened out in them like gaping holes, beds remained unmade, figures were silhouetted against barred windows. And all the time, small glimmers of light escaped through cracks in the canvas.

In the past Rohan had always talked to Giulia about his work. When they lived in Colombo she used to come into his studio at the end of each working day and they would drink tea together. And then they talked. In those days Rohan moved his vast canvases around the room and they would look at them together. He used to do all this energetically. Giulia, given half a chance, would tease him about his seriousness. Afterwards they would go back to the house for dinner. Now all this had changed. Now Rohan did not joke. These days he hardly said anything. Neither of them could say when it had happened but they had established separate rhythms to their life. Giulia had begun to teach English, making friends with several people in the neighbourhood. And she had taken up her translation work again. Often when Rohan worked late she would have supper with a neighbour. Once or twice she had tried including Rohan in these visits but it had never been successful. Both of them knew they were drifting apart; neither knew how to stop the change. Whenever Giulia attempted to talk about their past, Rohan blocked her. So now they never mentioned Theo or the girl. Their life in Sri Lanka might never have happened. Lying awake at night while he slept, Giulia wondered if this was all they had escaped for, this empty void they called freedom. Months passed. Rohan's exhibition was mentioned in an Italian newspaper. An unknown critic praised his work. The paintings, he said, reminded him of a shared grief, of dreams vaguely remembered, furniture that served as receptacles of memory. All of human life, in fact, reduced to memory. Rohan walked in to find Giulia reading the review. She was crying.

'Don't start,' he shouted. 'Don't start all that again. I paint what I paint. It's not my fault if they want to interpret it in this obvious, puerile way.'

'Rohan,' began Giulia, but then she stopped. What was the use? Grief had solidified into a wall between them; it had hardened and set in stone. There seemed little point to anything. When things were at their worst they had shared everything, every thought, every anxiety. Now all they had was bitterness to drown in. And yet, she thought wistfully, Theo was my friend too, my loss too. And then again, she thought angrily, your country is nothing to do with me. Resentment filled up the cracks. It covered everything they touched in fallout dust. *You were the one to take me there*, remember, thought Giulia, her eyes following him around the small flat. But she did not say it out loud. She was afraid of damaging what little they had. And she asked herself, has he forgotten my friend, Anna? No one mentions her any more, but I lived through that too. Yet in spite of this, still Giulia was unable to hurt Rohan further. Nor did she tell him that she was toying with the idea of going to London in the spring, to make one last attempt to look for Nulani Mendis. After Christmas, she decided, in the new year, I'll go over there. Alone.

'Next year, I'm having a show in Munich,' was all Rohan said.

Six years is a long time by any standards. Six years is like a steep mountain. Theo Samarajeeva climbed his mountain almost without noticing. He did not set out to do so but he began to write. What else could he do, he was a writer. He had been writing all his life, how could he stop now? At first it could hardly be called writing. At first it was more ramblings. Because his fingers had been broken, he could not type easily. Everything ached. His back, the soles of his feet, his leg. He never went in the water again. He no longer had any desire to swim. Nevertheless, the will to live remained in some strange and un-accountable way. And so he began to write again. Slowly, because he was uncertain, because his fingers were unsteady and the typewriter was too painful to use, he wrote by hand. It was Thercy who had encouraged him. Thercy who still came over to cook for him, walking slowly down the hill with her bunches of greens, her coconut milk and fresh fish. She had become less formal with him and he was no longer frightened of her. She was part of his landscape. Whenever his depression descended on him like a smoky cloud of mosquitoes, it was Thercy who would talk to him, cajoling and distracting him as best she could.

'You are a writer,' she would say. 'So why don't you write?'

There were things he could not write about, he told her. Thercy did not think this was a problem. She had seen too many things herself to be shocked, she told him. But she could understand, he was not ready to write about his experiences.

'Maybe,' she said, 'you will never be ready for that. So write of other things.'

She had only a vague knowledge of his books. It pleased him that she had not seen the film in Colombo. It pleased him that she knew very little about his past. Picking up his notebook he began to write. As always he started with Anna. Nothing could be counted before her. It was she who had led him to the girl. And it had been her voice he heard first.

After a while, unasked, he began to tell Thercy things.

'I was blindfolded,' he told her cautiously. 'And I was hit. Sometimes I was hit so hard that I fell forward. Then they gave me electric shocks. They put chilli inside me. They were laughing. Later, I'm not sure when, but another time I was hit with the butt of a rifle. They broke my fingers. See, three of them are broken! A writer without fingers, they laughed. They found this funny.'

Thercy was polishing the floor with old coconut scrapings. Watching her he felt his heart contract with grief. Sugi had polished the floor in this way.

'If you have a wound that you can't heal,' Thercy said very quietly, not looking at him, 'it will get bigger. You must try to heal it yourself.'

She no longer called him Sir. In fact, she seldom addressed him in any specific way. But her eyes followed him when he wasn't looking and she understood his moods. Long ago, she told him, in the early days of the war, she had had a son.

On another occasion, Theo told her, 'They played psychological games when I was blindfolded. I thought I was standing at the top of some steps and if I moved forward I might fall. But when they hit me I smashed against the wall instead.'

'Yes,' Thercy said. 'What happened then?'

But he could not say. Later, after she had gone slowly up the hill again, he went back to his notebook.

'*I have been tortured,*' he wrote.

He looked at what he had written. The ink was black. Four simple words. Changing a life for ever. He needed to write it in red ink. Who would believe me, he thought, when *I* can hardly believe it happened? But Thercy seemed to believe him, all right. Why should she not? she had asked, surprised. Violence had been done to her, why could it not happen to him?

'*Self-pity,*' he wrote, '*is all that's left. When I arrived I brought it with me. And now I'm in possession of it once again.*'

He paused, thinking. And then he wrote again.

> *Only the girl made a difference, coming back like a stray cat. At first I had no idea why this was so. I was worn out by your death, unable to believe in the future. And suddenly, there she was, appearing day after day. The war, although I didn't realise it then, was gathering momentum and all she did was draw. Everything made sense by illusion. Fabulously. Stories appearing under her fingers, stories I never knew existed, even. What took me twenty words, she achieved in an unwavering drift of a line. It was astonishing, really.*

Thercy brought him some milk rice. It was a *poya* day. She had been to the temple earlier because it was the anniversary of Sugi's death. She did not tell Theo this but Sugi was on her mind.

'He was frightened for you,' she said, chewing on a piece of jaggery. 'You and Miss Nulani, both.'

They were drinking a cup of tea together. Theo had been writing all morning and he was glad to see her. If she was ever late he became anxious. But Thercy was seldom late.

'Sugi saw where it could all lead long before I did,' he agreed. 'It was only afterwards, after she painted me, that I realised. My wife's death had left me with a set of beliefs too naive to be of use. Sugi must have known that. He must have watched me and seen what was happening. He didn't like the way I talked about this country. He wanted me to be more cautious.'

Theo glanced at her. He wasn't sure how much she understood, but Thercy nodded. He's better than he used to be, she thought.

'I had never seen anyone draw as she did,' Theo said, 'nor will I again.'

Wondering, how would she draw my life now? That evening, after Thercy went home, he continued to write.

Of course, she was so much younger. I always knew that. Who could say what might have happened had we been together? Perhaps she would have tired of me and found a younger man? After a while I would have become a millstone. You had been my whole life until that moment, Anna. Your death had robbed me of many things, I felt spent, finished, over. And then she arrived. What was I to think? Now of course I see more clearly how great the need was, to fill the gap you left. She was different from you, yet the same. You see, Anna, the truth is, the shameful admission is, that I have always defined myself by someone else. First you, and then the girl. When we met, you and I, I had the strangest feeling that I was enveloped by your identity. Then later I wanted to be supported by her. Can I be brutally honest? I went to her

*for the renewal of my courage, and for help with all I had
to bear. I was so afraid, so alone, so needing from the
outside for the assurance of my own worthiness to exist.
There, I have written the shameful truth. Have I given
you pain? Is it possible to love again, with a different
intensity, without losing what went before? Some would
say so. In prison, I was filled with guilt. Each time they
beat me, when I could breathe again it was guilt that
always rose to the surface.*

A little later on he wrote:

*In my worst moments I felt as though I had tried to wipe
you out with her. So, you see, I deserved to be punished.
And now you have both vanished. Although in the end, it
is perhaps I who has disappeared.*

Alone in the broken beach house, with its blue-faded gate,
and its endless glimpses of the sea, silence swooped down on
Theo like the seagulls. Time had passed without a sound. Time
had gathered in pockets in the landscape but he never noticed.
He walked the beach and watched the sea rise and heave
unmoved. Like memory, the sea had a life of its own. Sun and
rain came and went regardless. Further up the coast, where
once a man had been hung, a huge high-rise hotel was going
up. Daily it grew, thrusting its scaffolding into the blistering
sky. Workmen in hard hats drove on the beach where once
army jeeps had patrolled. A beach restaurant was being built,
and an oyster-shaped swimming pool with fresh water was
planned for those tourists who did not want the sea.
International cuisine was all that was needed. New glass-
bottomed boats began to appear and old ones were being

painted over. It was many years since the coral reef held such interest. Suddenly paradise was the new currency. The island began to rescue itself, hoping to whitewash its bloody past. Theo Samarajeeva watched from afar. He was writing steadily now, almost all of the time. When he had filled up three notebooks he walked the beach, thinking. He wanted to approach his old agent, he told Thercy, but he was nervous.

'Don't be silly,' Thercy said. 'Yes, yes, it's a good idea. I've told you. The only way you'll survive this life is to refuse to let them beat you down.'

Looking at Thercy, he was reminded more and more of the old ayah who had looked after him as a child.

'But I have nothing more to say about Sri Lanka. Everything has been pushed so far back inside me that I can't dislodge it. I don't want to.'

'So? That's fine,' Thercy said firmly. 'Write about the way we survive then. Tell them how we live. Miss Nulani gave you hope, didn't she? She showed you that you were still a person, capable of loving, of living. I think she gave you back yourself. What more d'you want?'

She was right. Walking along the beach that evening, he searched the sea for a sign. But the sea could not answer him and the moonlight on the empty beach unrolled silently like a bolt of silk across the sands.

Lately his eyesight was beginning to mist over. He was loath to visit an optician. It would mean another trip to Colombo and he could not face going back. Nor did he want to think of Rohan or Giulia, shying away from the thought that they too might have died because of him. But he had reckoned without Thercy. Insistently, day after day, she cajoled him until at last, reluctantly, he wrote a letter to his agent. He wrote cautiously, taking days to find the right words, hesitating, rewriting it. In the end, with a sigh, he gave it to Thercy to post. His book was growing and a certain urgency because of his eyes made him write furiously. For the first time he was attempting a book that was not politically driven. He had no more to say about injustice. Having lived it, he saw the hopelessness of defining it. This book, he saw, was about loving. This book was about something he could speak of. Every night he walked the beach, waiting for the monsoons, watching the clouds gather across the sky, seeing a new generation of children fly their box kites. Local people knew him, now. He was that writer fellow, they said, who had once been famous. Once he had been a hand-some man who came from the UK to live among his people. But then he had gone away to England and returned mad. He had gone mad for love, they told their children. He was crazy now, they said. Better if he had stayed in England and been happy. Foolish man, coming back to this place! Let this be a warning, the mothers told their children. If you are lucky enough to get to England, stay there. So the village children flew their kites and rode their bicycles, taking care to stay away from the madman in the beach house, careful always to avoid the place after dark.

A lifetime passed. Objects marked the years on Theo's table. Each was from another life, each irreversibly linked to the next. They were all his possessions. A penknife from his childhood, that was one. He had been six when he had been given it. Many words had been carved with its blade. An oil lamp, given to him by his mother, left over from the days when he used to visit the temple. He had always taken it on his travels and somehow it had never broken. A small beaded bag belonging to Anna. They had found it on the ground where she had been mugged. He had kept it all these years. Inside was the wedding ring he had taken from her finger before he buried her. A palm leaf, kept between the pages of a book. He had picked it on a trip down the Nile. A mollusc shell from the Adriatic, indigo blue and black, and pearl white. A rag, moulded and stained with vermilion, and a small hand-sewn notebook, unused and torn.

The agent was astonished to hear from him.

'For God's sake, Theo, I thought you were dead. I sent you letter after letter, but you never replied. I tried phoning you but the lines were constantly down. What sort of hole have you been living in?'

Theo laughed. It was the first time he had laughed in years.

'I've been writing,' he said.

'Theo,' said the agent, sounding hysterical, 'what do you mean? You ring me up after years and tell me you've been writing. You can't do this to me. Do you know the trouble I've gone to trying to get hold of you? I even thought of coming out to that wretched place in search of you but the Foreign Office gave out a warning against travel. Your countrymen seemed such bloody savages that I gave up. *Well*, what happened? And another thing,' the agent rushed on, 'you're a rich man now, you know. The film was a runaway success. And did you say you're writing again? Tell me all about it.'

'I'll put it all in a letter,' Theo said faintly, not wanting to talk.

So Theo wrote to him. For talking wore him out and his own voice could not be trusted. So he wrote.

'*The book is about hope,*' he wrote, '*and survival. About war, and also indifference. But you're wrong,*' he added, surprising himself by the strength of his convictions, '*they are not all savages here. There are savages everywhere, not just here.*'

Then he sent the agent the first part of his story.

18

AFTER HIS SHOW IN MUNICH ROHAN had had two more shows in Venice. In the four years since he had started painting again, he had worked with dogged determination, spending all the available hours of daylight possible in his studio. Giulia had begun collecting his reviews in a book. She was glad he was working properly again; glad he had picked up where he had left off in Colombo. It appeared they had shaken off their turbulent years in the tropics, outwardly it might have been said they had recovered. Rohan was mellower, less bad-tempered, and for her part Giulia expected less. Old age had crept up on both of them, she noticed, thinking, too, this suited them in many ways. All in all they were more content these days. Occasionally Giulia even managed to make him socialise with the few friends she had made, and they had stopped sniping at each other as they had when they first arrived in Italy. The difficult patch in their marriage appeared to have passed, but, Giulia saw with sad acceptance, the optimism had gone from it also. They lived quietly, seriously, no longer taking risks and were wary of new things. And the past with all its light and shade was never mentioned. Only in Rohan's paintings, strange, elegiac and ghostly, could it be glimpsed. Threadbare like a carpet, all his memories showed in his pictures with a transparency that Giulia found at times unbearable. He was an exile; he would remain an exile always. Once, in a rare moment of admission, he read Giulia a small notice in an English newspaper.

A spate of credit-card crimes involving a gang of Sri Lankans has erupted in London. The Home Office has confirmed that these underaged youths, currently facing trial, could also face deportation back to Sri Lanka despite the spasmodic violence still taking place in some parts of the island. Young Tamil boys, who left their homeland hoping to provide for their impoverished families, could soon be returning in disgrace often to a worse situation than the one they left behind. It is well known that Tamils who evaded the guerrilla army by escaping abroad often face execution on their return.

'So it goes on,' Rohan said. 'Once an outcast, always an outcast. Memory is all we have to rely on. Let's hope the girl is holding on to hers.'

Reviews of his paintings were appearing with marked regularity in the Italian papers. They spoke of his depiction of loss and alienation, and of warmth remembered. Giulia read them without comment. And so the years had passed. This was their life now, neither so good nor so bad. And at least, they both thought privately, they were free.

One day towards the end of summer Rohan was introduced to an Englishwoman from London. Her name was Alison Fielding, she told him, and she ran a small gallery called London Fields. Having seen his paintings in Art Basel, she contacted him, inviting him to submit slides of current work.

'London?' said Giulia, surprised. 'I thought you didn't want to show in London?'

He had not been back since that day, seven years ago, when he and Giulia trawled the city looking for Nulani. Giulia too had never returned. Somehow it had never happened. The small difficulties, the shifts and changes in their relationships, all the minutiae of the everyday, had made her reluctant to disturb the past. Too much had been lost, too much remained precarious for either of them to open old wounds. But now, as summer began to recede, before the sharp forerunners of winter winds stirred the leaves, Rohan finally had a reason to visit. Alison Fielding was enthusiastic.

'*Do come,*' she wrote. '*Bring some work. We can talk it over. I liked your paintings very much.*'

Giulia could not leave her work, so Rohan went alone to a city still basking in an Indian summer. The land was brown through lack of rain and the city glowed with an alert bustle that he had never noticed before. The gallery was smaller than he had expected, tucked away in a corner of Clerkenwell. He almost walked past it. In the window were two paintings, one black on red, thick impasto, marked and stained, and another white as marble. Small numbers were stencilled along the edges of the canvas. Something about them caught Rohan's eye. He gazed, puzzled.

'Ah,' said Alison Fielding, greeting him, smiling. 'You've noticed my other Sri Lankan artist!'

Blue flew out from a canvas. Followed by another, deeper shade, more piercing, hinting gold beneath it and something else, some unidentifiable movement of light. Rohan stared. A line, excavated, as it were, in the dark, seemed slightly muffled, bringing a mysterious sense of intimacy to the whole. Another painting hung alone on a far wall. He found himself thinking of the inner chamber of ancient, sacred tombs. Stars showed faintly through a midnight sky. The canvases glowed; there was no other way to describe them. They were both luminescent and extraordinarily still. The contradictions of this vast, aerated space within the density of the blues were magical. Darkness and light, together in the most unlikely place of entombment, appeared to sink to the depths of the earth, to the human body itself, metaphorically binding two impossible worlds. The paintings had no names, only numbers. There were more, stacked in corners. Rohan followed them around the room, mesmerised. Downstairs, the images were of carefully drawn objects, glimpsed and then rubbed out even at the moment of recognition; hinting at the ways in which the past inhabits us, shaping us at some level hovering below conscious thought. And all the time anxiety and claustrophobia remained inescapably part of the whole.

'You like them?' asked Alison Fielding. Rohan stared.

'They're wonderful,' he said. 'Did you say . . . ?'

'Yes, the artist is Sri Lankan. A woman.'

'There is only one,' said Rohan slowly, 'only one Sri Lankan artist that I can think of. Only one who . . .' He broke off, unable to go on.

'Her name is Nulani Mendis,' said Alison Fielding, smiling broadly. 'D'you know of her? Good! I was thinking of showing you both together actually. You must meet her. But first, let me see what you have brought me.'

'And that was how I met her, finally,' said Rohan.

He was back, with the promise of an exhibition with Nulani. His excitement was infectious. Since he had returned he had been unable to stop smiling. All evening they had sat drinking wine and he had talked non-stop. Giulia could not get a word in edgeways. She felt light-headed, drunk with astonishment and unanswered questions. When would Giulia see her? How was she? How did she look? What did she say when she met Rohan? Rohan laughed, delighted, remembering.

'She simply could not believe it when Alison rang her. It was comical really,' he said, pausing. 'If it wasn't so sad,' he added. 'Alison picked up the phone and just called her up. "There's a painter friend of yours from Sri Lanka," was all she said. Just like that. Can you imagine it? And half an hour later there she was, little Nulani Mendis, changed and yet not so changed, at all. Breathless with shock and beautiful as ever.' He paused, again. 'We spent the whole evening together. In the end Alison had to send us tactfully away, so she could shut the gallery.'

They had stepped out into the street. The weather had changed. He had noticed it had been raining. Fine, autumn rain, bringing a few leaves down. The air was edged with a sharp chill, but they had not cared, for home cried out to them. The smell of it, the sounds. It had been a low and haunting call, insistent and lovely, refusing to be ignored. They had gone into a pub and he had bought her a lemonade.

'She doesn't drink,' Rohan said. 'And she's very thin, and . . .' He hesitated, not knowing how to go on. How to describe the dark eyes that had looked back at him, unfathomable and softened, with a distant cast of pain.

'She's a wonderful painter,' he said instead. 'Alison's going to arrange the exhibition. She'll be in touch soon. And d'you know what her first words were? "Where's Giulia?"'

He grinned. Tears pricked the back of Giulia's eyes. Was it really true?

'So when can I see her?'

'Whenever you want,' said Rohan, laughing boyishly. 'I can't believe it either. It felt as though we had been talking together

273

only moments before, as though no time had elapsed at all. Well . . .' he hesitated, 'almost.'

They had gone on in this way all evening, saying everything and nothing. Feeling the slow ebb and flow of memory thread lightly between them, drawing them closer. How had they lost touch? At some point Rohan had sensed she had no desire to go back to her flat. He had asked her about her brother then.

'Jim?' asked Giulia. 'Theo used to call him Lucky Jim.'

Rohan nodded, his face inscrutable. Yes, they had talked about her useless brother.

'She never sees him. Hardly, anyway. Once a year perhaps.'

And then, he told Giulia, they had alluded to other things; the years that had passed. And Rohan had felt admiration rise up and astonish him and he had understood, perhaps for the first time, her terrible struggles, and the acceptance of what had happened to her life.

'You were the one who told me to accept,' she had reminded him. '"Like a coconut palm in the monsoon," you said. "You must bend in the wind." D'you remember?'

Rohan remembered. Why had he not been able to take his own advice?

'She's given me her telephone number,' he told Giulia. 'Naturally she's frightened of losing us again. I said you'd want to ring. I said, knowing you, you'd ring whatever the time was tonight!'

They both laughed and Rohan poured more wine.

'Oh, it's good to be back,' he said, meaning something else entirely.

The air was charged with unspoken things. Refreshed, reborn. They felt alive in ways only dimly remembered.

'And she's all right?' asked Giulia, eventually, as they sat in companionable silence, forgetting to turn the lights on. She did not want to probe too much, too soon, but the memory of Theo stretched in a long, sorrowful shadow between them. As it always will, reflected Giulia. Rohan sighed deeply. They continued to sit without speaking in this way. At last he stirred himself.

'Yes and no.' He was silent for a moment longer. 'She's living with some man. It doesn't sound as if it's working. She wants to leave. I think. They . . . haven't much in common except, she said, maybe a mutual loneliness at the beginning. Anyway, it's been wrong for some time. They are both aware of this.'

Once again shadows passed between them.

'But habit has kept them together. For how much longer, who can say?'

'Like us,' said Giulia softly, before she could stop herself.

Startled, Rohan glanced sharply at her. Outside the window the twilight was fading fast. Giulia's face, silhouetted against it, looked tired. She had aged, he saw, but still there was something infinitely lovely about her. Shocked, he looked at her anew and saw the light which once, many years ago, had shone faintly and transparently within her, was now very clear and very pure. As if the shaping and chiselling of all the years of her life was revealed at last, in the many fine lines of her face. Why had he not seen this before? Why had he taken her for granted? And then, with sudden insight, he knew she had very nearly given up. But how long has she looked this way, without me caring? he thought with amazement. They had embarked on a journey together. It had not been easy. Giulia had not been able to have children yet somehow they had weathered *that* storm. And he paused for a moment, head bowed, recalling again the friendship, first with Anna, and later with Theo. Anna's death, he saw, had been the foreshadow of what was to come. How happy they had been once, he thought, how young! They would never be young again. And in that moment, halfway between evening and night, with a feeling of great sweetness, he saw, at last, they had reached a different kind of peace. She was his wife. He loved her, still. After all these years, after all they had been through, he could *still* say this and mean it. In the bluish half-light reflecting the surface of the canal water, he reached out and clasped her hand. It was soft and warm and it carried within it a lifetime of touch.

'No,' he said at last, his voice firm. 'Not like us. We have come through this together. What happened to Anna and then to Theo was terrible but I no longer look for explanations. I accept, Giulia. This is life. These are the fruits of war, inescapable and terrible. I see now how important it is to end this struggle, to accept my own helplessness in all that has happened. My problem was that I always thought it was my fault and I carried the burden alone. But,' he gestured towards his paintings, 'I can't do any of this without you, you know. You have borne witness with me. We tell this tale together. You, Giulia, you are the mainstay of my life.'

She smiled at him, and he saw her eyes still shone with the grace he had always associated with her. He saw in that smile, mellow and very wonderful, that she understood. And, he thought with astonishment, she had always understood.

Later she rang the girl. Bridging the years, hearing again the voice that sounded the same, yet was not. Guessing at all the invisible changes that must have taken place. All that probably could never be spoken of now. First excitement gave way to caution.

'We brought your notebooks,' she said, hesitantly. 'We had no address to send them to.' She paused, waiting.

'And your paintings, did Rohan tell you?'

And in a rush of emotion, Giulia remembered how she had longed to find her, how the absence had served only to compound the other losses, of Anna and of Theo. Of her own marriage. So many lives unravelled by the chain of terrible events. So much destroyed by war. They talked for a while longer, laughing, interrupting each other, and slowly, imperceptibly, she began to hear the subtle changes in the girl.

'She's grown up,' she told Rohan afterwards. 'It isn't anything she says, specifically. It isn't *what* she says. More how she says it.'

'She's a serious artist, now,' said Rohan. 'People have begun to notice her. D'you remember what I told you, on that terrible night? How it would all feed into her work?'

Giulia nodded. How could she forget that night?

'I wish it could have happened in a different way, but . . .'

They had promised to meet in a few weeks, just as soon as Giulia could arrange some time off. When they had finished talking she offered Rohan something to eat. It was late but he showed no sign of tiredness.

'I could hear someone, a man's voice in the background, calling her,' Giulia said. 'But she ignored him.'

'Yes,' Rohan said, slowly. 'And, you know, the feeling I had was that all the time we were talking about other things really we were talking about him. All the time.' He wouldn't say Theo's name. Still. That hadn't changed. 'She hasn't got over him. Why should she? She was never that kind of person. They were similar in that way.'

'Yes.'

In the semi-darkness Rohan's face was gentle.

'It will never fade, Giulia. I can tell you, she will always love him. And the threads that bound them together will weave through her work for ever. Not in any physical presence, you understand. In fact, Alison Fielding was very interested when I told her of the earlier portraits. She would like to see them. I'm not sure Nulani will ever part with them, of course, but she might show them, she might be persuaded.'

'Poor Nulani,' said Giulia softly. 'How old is she now? About twenty-eight?'

'Twenty-seven.'

'All those years in London, grieving. Alone. Did she talk about them?'

Rohan shook his head.

'Not much. Her brother found her a place to live and then more or less abandoned her. She got a job in a café; she painted. She was cold.' He shrugged. 'What is there to say after all? When I asked her about that time, she just said she painted what she felt. Everywhere she looked, everything she caught sight of, she said, reminded her of how she felt. Staining the light, catching at the colours, moving her to mark it. She said she felt as though her whole body was branded by it.'

He smiled, suddenly, brilliantly.

'An abstract painter, that's what she is now. Who would have thought it!'

'And us? Did she wonder why we never wrote?'

'She didn't say. I think she assumed the letters didn't get through. She loves us, Giulia, in that trusting, straightforward way that was always hers. She knew we would get in touch if we could and the fact that we didn't could only mean one thing. You know what she was like.'

'Oh God!' said Giulia. 'Tomorrow I'll book a flight to London.'

19

THEO'S AGENT LIKED WHAT HE READ.

'At last!' he said, jokingly.

Privately, Theo astonished him. Having read his letter, having known his past, he was amazed by what he read. *Tiger Lily* had been a bleak novel, successful perhaps because of its bleakness. The film had brought a short-lived fame for its author. But *this* manuscript was different. The agent had a hunch that this new book, when finished, would be a success in a different kind of way. Yes, thought the agent, confidently, a slow burner. Slow and steady. It was an elegiac book, filled with optimism and awash with tenderness.

'The language is very beautiful,' he said, when he finally got through to Theo on the telephone. 'Your best work yet,' he enthused. 'I recognise the character of Irene, but Helena, where's she come from? Honestly, Theo, you're a marvel. I thought you'd disappeared and then up pops another book! You must never stop writing, d'you hear me? When you're ready, I'm going to sell this book at the Frankfurt fair. So will you come back to Britain, now?'

'You should go,' was all Thercy said when he told her.

But Theo had no interest in travel, to Britain or anywhere. He continued rewriting sections of the book, honing it painstakingly. It would be ready by October. Every morning, before sitting at his desk and opening the manuscript, he tried to conjure up as true a picture of the girl as possible.

I want to see you objectively. In the way you appeared to others. You see how far I have moved since that day I lost you? How time has changed me? You, the last love of my life, would understand that. If you could see me now, what would you think? Would you remember how I worried over the difference in our ages! How I agonised. You were the child I never had, the wife I had lost, but most importantly of all, you were yourself. They said we were destined to find each other. What we didn't know was that our time was wrong, the planets discordant or whatever they call it here. Karma, I suppose. Prison made me believe that. All the endless violence I witnessed has convinced me. And as I see you now, quietly sitting within the pages of what I write, distanced by words and time, detached and perfect, I know it was a gift; you were the gift.

He paused, staring out into the garden, overgrown and neglected. He wondered why, in spite of all his understanding, he was still weak with sadness? He told himself, had she returned to him both of them would have suffered. What had been taken from him was too great and because of this, he knew, he would have in turn taken too much from her. So much had changed; even his own soul had changed. He felt a stranger to himself.

'Some day,' he told Thercy, 'perhaps I might bump into her, in Colombo, on a train, somewhere by chance.'

Months passed. The new novel continued to grow with a logic and a rhythm of its own. It took its time, following a path of its own. The atmosphere of brooding darkness in a jungle of noxious violence and superstitions had developed in a manner that had nothing to do with him. And always in the midst of it was the figure of the girl, steeped in sunlight. It was, he told himself again and again, a novel about love. Anna would have been proud of him. Finally, then, it was finished. He had settled it to his satisfaction. Life in this paradise, he felt, was exactly as the beautiful mosquito that lived here, composed in equal parts of loveliness and deadliness. And he felt, too, that at the heart of all he had written, remained the puzzle of humanity. Long ago Rohan had said that only art could change evil. It was art, he had said, that changed people's perceptions. How they had disagreed in those light-hearted days, when a good argument was all there was to win. But perhaps Rohan had been right.

Later, when he had finished the last correction, replaced the last words with those he had wanted, Theo sent his manuscript reluctantly to England.

'It's over,' he told Thercy.

The agent was right. It was the best he had ever written. Anna and Nulani, he thought. A novel about them both. Why couldn't I see this before? And he thought, pouring himself a glass of arrack, I will dedicate this book to Nulani. The girl who painted the invisible.

That night, he slept dreamlessly, and without effort. And the bed where briefly love had once slept, and the room where a pair of straw sandals still remained, watched him sleep the gentle sleep of peace. The monsoons were almost over. Thercy was going to visit her sister-in-law for a while. She felt she could leave him, now. Soon it would be October and the weather would be cooler. Then I will paint the front of the veranda, thought Theo, I will make that my next task. And he remembered Rohan and Giulia. And he remembered Sugi, whom he had loved, and the girl and Anna and all the things that had made up his other life. And he thought, I have lived, I have loved, what more can a man ask for?

In London, Alison Fielding, working on a hunch that their paintings would sell, was getting excited. The exhibition was called 'Two Sri Lankan Painters'.

'They're very different,' she said. 'Similar experiences, I think. Pretty grim, actually, civil war is no joke. Things have calmed down a little, but they've suffered. Lost friends, relatives, become displaced.' She was talking to someone from an art journal.

'They're haunting,' the man from the magazine said. 'Darkly atmospheric, grainy, overcast. Every gesture is eloquent.' He thought for a moment. 'They reflect the spirit rather than the outer world,' he added, nodding, thinking of what he would write later.

'I've decided to show some of their earlier work as well, by the way,' said Alison. 'It gives the current work more context. But none of the earlier pieces by Nulani are for sale.'

'Pity,' said the reviewer, looking at them closely. 'They're beautiful. They'd be snapped up.'

He paused, looking at the three small portraits, all of the same man, still and arrested against a dazzling tropical blur of light. Caught with the sun in his eyes. Smiling.

'Who is it?' asked the journalist, curiously. 'He seems vaguely familiar.'

Alison Fielding shrugged. 'Someone she knew, I think. Her father, an old friend, she won't say, and I don't like to pry too much. She's a private person. And anyway, it doesn't matter. With some portraits, that sort of information is important, but with these, I somehow don't think it matters. There is a quality, an essence, a . . .' She tailed off.

In fact, she thought the portraits stunning. The man sat with his back to the mirror. His eyes were extraordinarily expressive and beautiful. On the table were some objects. Two sea urchins, a pink conch shell, a photograph of a blonde woman. Sunlight fell in long streaks against his arm and in the distance, shimmering like sapphires, was the sea.

'They're powerful,' agreed the journalist. 'I think we'll include an image. My editor said only one illustration, but I think we need one of the portraits as well. Have you a slide we could use?'

'Of course,' said Alison, delighted. 'Will you give me a double spread?'

Later Alison Fielding saw her intuition was right. The paintings of these two artists complemented each other. And nearly all of them sold during the private view of the show.

'They're beautiful,' Giulia said, when she saw them. 'I'm so proud of you both. Can anyone doubt the suffering that country has endured, after seeing this?'

'And *I* always knew,' said Rohan smiling at them both, 'Nulani would triumph.'

Yes, she had lost Theo, he thought, yet miraculously here he was appearing again, just as Rohan himself had once predicted. Here in her paintings. Astonished by the maturity of this work, astonished by its breath and scope, its certainty, Rohan beamed at Giulia. So young, he thought. It's only the young who can change things. And what would he say? thought Rohan. If he could see her now, how proud would *he* be? Feeling as though he was coasting along on a breeze, Rohan watched Giulia link arms with Nulani. The two of them were deep in conversation, unaware of him for the moment, talking as though they would never stop. The girl has saved us, thought Rohan, for the hundredth time. She has pulled us back from the abyss. And it wasn't over yet by any means. One day, he was certain, she would be a truly great painter.

After the private view Rohan and Giulia returned to Venice. But not before they had extracted a promise from Nulani to visit them before winter settled in. She would come, she promised. She did not want to lose them again. And so it was, as they boarded the plane bound for Italy, someone, a man who received regular invitations from the London Fields Gallery, but who had been away on holiday, opened his invitation and stared, puzzled at the portrait of Theo Samarajeeva. The man stared at the uncanny likeness; he had been reading Theo Samarajeeva's manuscript only the night before. And here was his portrait. Just as it was described in the book. The man, Theo's literary agent, went over to see Alison Fielding. To find out who had painted the writer with such power and conviction.

20

Giulia hurried across to the warehouse space in Dorsoduro where Rohan had a small studio. Normally she never disturbed him when he was working, normally she would have been working on her translations, but the arrival of the postman was too much. Excitement swelled in her like the spring tides coming in from the sea. Sunlight sparkled under the bridges, church clocks chimed, lions flew and pigeons walked, as Giulia hurried on, head bowed, carrying her letter.

'What d'you mean?' asked Rohan in a whisper, staring at her. 'What do you mean?'

'Read it, read it,' said Giulia, thrusting it into his hand.

'What are you talking about? It's a hoax. Some idiot.'

'Read it!'

Rohan continued to stare at her.

'Read it,' shouted Giulia. 'Rohan, for God's sake, read it.' She was almost crying. 'It's from his agent. Look at it. I'm telling you, Theo's *alive*. He's at the beach house. He's been there for years! Read what the agent says.'

But he had never thought of that. He had never thought of

an alternative. Even in his wildest dreams, he had not doubted what he had been told. Theo had been dead for years. Like Sugi. Hadn't they *all* thought that? The girl, he thought, the girl had been certain. Sugi had seen it happen. The same people had killed Sugi, hadn't they? So now what were they telling him? Theo alive, Theo tortured? What was the matter with Giulia?

'How long was he a prisoner?' demanded Rohan, angrily, disorientated. 'Who is this person? How do we know he really is his agent?'

It was only when I saw the invitation for the exhibition that I knew who the painter could have been. She's in his book, his latest book. I'd just finished reading the manuscript. So of course I spoke to Alison Fielding, who's an old friend. I've known her for many years. I always support her exhibitions. So now, I'm contacting you. I think he might like to hear from you. I've read the book, you see. I know the story, or at least some of it. Here's his address. Write to him. Try to persuade him to come back to Britain. Be less of a hermit! This last book is possibly his best yet.

'Write to him?!' said Rohan. '*Write to him?!*' he asked, hysterically. 'What the hell are you talking about? He must come *here*! *He must come here!*' he shouted.

Rohan threw his head back and roared, and then he threw his brushes into the jar of white spirit and whirled Giulia around in an impromptu dance. But it was Giulia who suddenly became the cautious one. Theo had been hurt. He would be changed. If Anna's death had scarred him what would torture have done? And the girl, what about his feelings for the girl? Why had he not contacted them himself? All he had to do was write to their old address and word would have got to them somehow. Perhaps he did not *want* to contact them. Had Rohan thought of that?

'No!' bellowed Rohan. He was laughing, taking in great gulps of air, as though he could not breathe. 'No, no, *no*. He is my friend! How can you *say* that! Maybe he wrote, maybe the letters went astray, maybe they were never forwarded, maybe they *were* forwarded but someone, some bastard, intercepted them. Who knows in that wretched, foul country of mine? Who knows?'

They argued all that evening and late into the night. The next day they were still discussing it endlessly.

'Wait,' said Giulia, who was frightened. 'Wait, wait, let's think of the best way to do this. And what do we say to Nulani? What will she say when she hears? She has to be told and then what might happen?'

'I know what will happen. I'll tell you. If we don't strap her down she'll be on the first plane back to Sri Lanka!'

So they talked and shouted through the night, opening another bottle of wine. For was this not a cause for a celebration? And then as they paused, as the first shock faded slightly, as they looked at each other with amazement, it was as though a terrible evil that had hung over them had begun to pass away. Theo, they cried. Theo! They had never thought to say his name again.

21

THE FOLDS OF THE ITALIAN ALPS appeared in the distance, creased like a silk handkerchief. Snow had come early and would stay late. As they flew towards it there were no clouds and the view was clear for miles. Below was the intense blue of the glacier lakes, the dark mountain rivers, the beginnings of Alpine forests. He had flown this route many times in years gone by. Now he was flying it again. The other passengers in the aircraft were restless. It had been a long flight.

'Hello again, ladies and gentleman. If you look to the right of the aircraft you will see a clear view of the Alps. In about ten minutes we will begin our descent. The weather in Venice is exceptionally warm for this time of year. The earlier thunderstorms have passed, the air has cleared and we have made up the time we lost earlier. You should be able to get a good view of the city as we land. The local time is twelve minutes past four, if you want to adjust your watches. So sit back and relax, and enjoy the rest of the flight.'

They had been flying for nearly twelve hours. He had not slept.

Ten years, thought Theo. Ten years of longing and now she was somewhere below him in the very place he had wanted to take her to. Giulia's letter was in his pocket. He unfolded it again and reread it although by now he knew every line off by heart.

'*We have found you both again. What else is worth saying?*' Rohan had written and then Giulia had continued, '*Come, Theo, please you must come. She has suffered enough. She wants to see you. If anything can bring you here it is this. That she has not once, not for one moment, forgotten you. Everything she has done, every way she has lived has been in the shadow of the loss of you. So come.*'

And here he was, flying, flying through the light, crossing oceans, leaving everything, walking out through the sea-blue gate, never looking back, unwavering as a seabird, rushing towards her, carrying in his hand luggage a tightly closed temple flower. It was as though he was a younger man. Over India he had flown, crossing the Middle East, uncaring of the meals they served, uncaring that they were flying over other war zones now. He had carried a war not of his making for so long, paid for it with the years of his life and the lives of others, that he could no longer carry anything more. Others would have to carry the burden. Again he took out the small cutting Rohan had sent him.

A REMARKABLE SRI LANKAN ARTIST BRINGING THIS FORGOTTEN WAR TO OUR NOTICE.

Nulani Mendis is a Sri Lankan artist who paints jewel-like abstract paintings. Filled with the colours of her home-land, with luminescent blues, phosphorescent greens and hints of gold, they are paintings scarred by war. In one, a vague smudge suggests a figure under an electric light.

Above are marks that appear to be stitching. Faint lines reminiscent of a hangman's noose hover overhead. The surface is slashed and broken, rivets of paint-smeared pain seem to hold another canvas together. Elsewhere, another painting, the only one with a title, *In the key of 'E'*, has a small typewriter key drawn into the paint, embedded like cattle branding. Beautifully crafted, with slow delicate glazes, this particular canvas was instantly snapped up. When invited to speak about her work, Mendis merely smiled, saying only that she was pleased they had been so well received. But about the work itself she had nothing to say. The viewer is left with the conundrum: are these hauntingly beautiful paintings directly related to the troubles that have being going on in Sri Lanka, or a feminist statement perhaps? In the end, in the words of her dealer Alison Fielding, what does it matter? These are simply very, very good paintings.

There were two colour photographs of the paintings. That was all. Here it was then, this was how she had developed, he thought, staring at the cutting, reading and rereading the words tenderly as they flew over the Alps. His typewriter had always stuck on the letter 'E'. He had forgotten how it had always infuriated him. Smiling, he stared out of the window, his heart brimming with gladness. She would have heard his annoyance. While she sat in the corner of the veranda, drawing him, she would have listened. Giulia had said she had wanted desperately to see him but that she was frightened. She had gone reluctantly to Venice, fearing, what? *She is frightened you won't come*, Giulia had written, *she is frightened it isn't true, that it is all a hoax and you are not really alive. She has believed for so long she would never see you again and now she is terrified. She has dreamt of you for so many years, so hopelessly, that she can't face a mistake. And she is afraid of all the time that has passed, afraid it has made her old! She is not old at all, Theo, she's lovelier than we remember and full of a maturity that was not evident before.*

And, he thought with astonishment, what is she *like* now? How had those years been for her, when his self-pity had got the better of him? He felt small and ashamed beside the thought of her and her courage, in the way he once remembered she had made him feel; ashamed that it was only his terrible loss that filled his thoughts; his pain. It was he who was old now, thought Theo wryly, even older than when she first knew him. And damaged, he thought fearfully. In her last letter Giulia had laughed when he said this to her. *Nulani does not care, Theo; I don't think you understand how she has longed for you. I don't think you can imagine the woman she has become. Just come. See for yourself.*

So here he was, clutching his temple flower. The plane turned towards its final descent. While he had been thinking, the sea and the lagoon had come into view. Below was the shining dome of St Mark's. The sound of the engine changed as it hurried on, swooping down towards Torcello with its Byzantine tower, its marshlands where once mosquitoes had flourished. And there beneath him, spread like a glorious painting itself, hanging like a Renaissance pendant, was the watery city. Happiness caught at his throat. This was not his home; why, then, did he feel he was coming home?

22

ROHAN WATCHED THE PLANE COMING IN, its wings tipped with the light from the sun. Graceful as a swan it descended towards the runway, growing larger as he watched. Steadily it dropped, swift as an arrow it flew, landing with a rush and thrust of tyres and airbrakes. For a moment he stood rooted to the spot, watching all the business of the gangway and luggage trolleys. He watched as the passengers began to pour out of the aircraft. Holidaymakers with their children, Italians, some coming home, others coming to visit the city, American tourists. And suddenly he saw him. The gaunt figure of a man in a light linen suit, still with the round-rimmed spectacles he remembered, only now his hair was white. He was walking slowly. As he came towards the airport building it was possible to see he had a slight limp that he was trying his best to hide. Swallowing, Rohan hurried towards the arrivals lounge.

'So, you old bugger, you've managed to stay thin, unlike me!' he said in English as they embraced and he felt the bones that jutted out from under his friend's jacket. For a moment neither of them could speak. Then Theo took off his glasses and wiped them.

'How is she, Rohan?' he asked helplessly.

'I knew there was a woman behind this visit, men,' joked Rohan, looking at the temple flower. Adding softly, 'She's fine. I left her with Giulia in the flat. I wanted to have a few minutes with you alone, knowing we'll not see you once you set eyes on her!'

He took Theo's luggage and guided him to the exit, hiding his shock.

'I thought you might be tired so we're going back in style, by water taxi,' he said, waving his arm at Theo's protest. 'Hang the expense. It's not every day you visit, men.'

And that was how they came into La Serenissima, by water, as people had done for centuries, past the small nameless islands, following the seabirds that nestled like white blossom among the reeds. Everywhere around him was the melodious sound of Italian. Theo had forgotten how he loved to listen to it, how like an opera it was here, just like a land of make-believe. And then they arrived at the Fondamenta Nuove and there was Giulia standing on the bridge and then hurrying towards them. And she was laughing and crying and wiping her eyes as she greeted him half in Italian and then in Singhalese and now in English. Just as he remembered.

'Steady on, Giulia,' said Rohan, smiling broadly. 'Wars have been fought over this kind of language mix-up!'

'She's asleep,' said Giulia, knowing what he wanted most to hear. 'It is her first proper sleep since she heard, since she arrived. *Poverina*. She is exhausted with waiting.'

'Is she all right?'

'Yes, yes, now you are here she will be. Oh Theo, oh my dear, thank God. Thank God you came. I was so afraid you would not come.'

And she took his face in both her hands and kissed him, leading him towards the house where they rented a flat on the *piano nobile*. He handed Giulia the temple flower. It had travelled well and was now fully open.

'I will put it in water,' she said. 'She'll see it when she wakes. Now go. She's in there,' she whispered, pointing towards the door.

He opened the door slowly and went in. The room was L-shaped, and a large gilded mirror stood immediately before him. The glass was old and foxed and beautiful, and the light reflected in it was thin and dusty. It gave the half-shuttered room an air of unreality. He caught a glimpse of himself before he saw her. It felt as though he was looking at one of her paintings, softened and made remote by an invisible and intractable past. Only now it was he who observed her. All that had vanished, all those small memories he had carried unnoticed within him, the longings that even he had forgotten, now surfaced and fused. Shaken, for nothing could have prepared him for this moment, he stood looking at her through the glass. Astonished too, for he saw, as no photograph could ever have shown him, the promise of youth fulfilled at last.

It had been in this way that he had left her. Sleeping. Only then it had been with the moonlight on her face and the rustle of the sea close by. Now she slept fully dressed, lying across the bed with its washes of blue light. He stood looking at her reflection, silent, rooted to the spot. She slept quietly, her body rising and falling gently as she breathed. She was wearing a soft skirt of some grey fabric. Dimly, he could see the shadows marking her breasts through the thin white shirt. Her hair was cut short and its tendrils framed all the delicate bones of her face. Her dark lashes swept down over her closed eyes. He had forgotten how small she was, how fragile, how terribly lovely. Time, he saw, had stolen clarity, blunted his memories. Time could not be trusted. What had seemed sharp and certain was in fact a pale shadow of the present.

The girl slept without moving, her brow clear and untroubled as a child, one arm raised above her head. But her wrists, he saw, were no longer the wrists of a child and peering at the glass he noticed her fingernails still had small slivers of paint under them. Seeing this, he felt his heart rise and break open with all the unspoken years between them. Softly, so as not to disturb her, he bent down and took his shoes off. His fingers trembled and as he straightened up he closed his eyes. When he opened them again he could see the reflection in the mirror had altered and the girl's face was now beside his own. Staring uncomprehendingly he watched her for a moment longer, seeing her lips move. Unable to speak he watched her frightened eyes as she said his name again. Then helplessly, hardly aware of what he did, blindly, he turned towards her, resting his face against her hair, letting her cry, holding her as he once had done. Knowing instinctively she was not crying for the horror that had passed, or the years that could never be recovered, or Sugi, or her parents, or even the home she had loved and lost. He knew she was crying for something else, something deeper and more enduring than he had thought possible. Something that had not occurred to him until now. And in that instant he saw, in spite of what had happened, and all that had been lost for ever, what mattered was the thing that somehow had remained. Unharmed and indestructible. And as he held her sleep-warmed body against his, letting her cry, knowing what she was thinking, thinking it too, he breathed again the faint fragrance of her hair, from some other time and some other place of long ago.

Outside the evening was just beginning in Venice. The orchestra in St Mark's square was playing again. Great seagulls perched jauntily on the *briccole* dotted across the lagoon, watching as the fishermen brought in their catch. And all around, between sea and sky and land, was the gentle sound of lapping water as the sun, golden and full of autumn warmth, sank softly into the reeds.

ACKNOWLEDGEMENTS

My agent Felicity Bryan, who knew my paintings long before she read my words, for her unwavering encouragement and her determination to keep me going.

Kathy van Praag, who read the manuscript and was so wholeheartedly enthusiastic.

And Clare Smith, my editor at HarperPress, who loved the book enough to make it happen.

Also at HarperPress, Annabel, Julian and Mally, all of whom made life easier for me.

To Michele Topham, at the Felicity Bryan Agency.

To my exhuberant Italian friends Rosy Colombo and Anna Anzi for their support, seminars and summer retreats during the writing of the book.

To Loretta Innocenti for her support in Venice, and Daniele Lombardi for his wonderful recording of *Preludes Fragiles*, which I listened to endlessly whilst writing.

To Vishvarani Wanigasekera, who corrected my Singhalese.

And finally to my long-suffering family, sternest and wisest of critics.

Thank you.

P.S.

Ideas,
interviews
& features ...

Slipping between Fact and Fiction

Louise Tucker talks to Roma Tearne

You fled Sri Lanka as a child: what was it like to leave your home and grow up in another very different place?

I couldn't wait to leave. For a start, the idea of spending twenty-one days on a ship was a very exciting adventure for a small child. I was only ten and enormously curious about England, having heard so much about the place. If we didn't like it in England we would simply go back, I thought. I had no idea that this was not an option. Luckily I was young enough to adapt. From the start I was desperate to fit in. When I started school, the first thing I did, to my parents' utter horror, was rapidly to lose my accent.

How did the rest of your family, particularly your parents, cope with living in exile?
My parents were devastated. It took me many, many years to see how the move had affected them. They never adapted. After my mother died I painted a picture called *Waiting for Summer*, in which a woman stands looking out towards the horizon of a wintry landscape. At this point I began to understand certain things. I saw for instance that I had spent years suppressing a whole host of painful memories and I began to see what had become of my childhood. ▶

Slipping between Fact and Fiction
(continued)

◄ **Where is home for you now and what does the concept of 'home' mean for you?**
Home now is wherever my family is. I went to school in London and I love it there. I spend a lot of time in a wonderful part of Italy that I love. But I will never forget my idyllic childhood on the coast of Sri Lanka. It will always have a special place in my heart. Whether or not I see it again. Youth, after all, is the thing we carry with us for ever.

You chose to write a book about your home country long after you left it. What was the catalyst or inspiration for writing about it at last?
After my mother's death I found a doll's house I had brought with me on the ship. I began photographing the empty, discarded rooms and a little later to paint from these photographs. Some rooms were dark and shadowy, some let in a piercing light. These were small intense images in oils, and at an exhibition in London a friend said they spoke to him of loss. Suddenly the narrative and my own lost childhood, denied for so long, spilled out in words.

Painting and writing are at the heart of all the main characters' lives and Rohan says, '"Some say art is our highest form of hope . . . Perhaps it's our only hope."' In the context of a civil war how realistic and possible is such a hope?
I have no illusions. In the context of the war 'art' itself can only be a hope at the moment. But afterwards, if and when the peace talks

begin to work, that is the time when it will be most needed. The myriad of hidden traumas, the scars from such a bitter conflict, will not heal easily. It is at that point that art can be the saviour. I have run workshops with refugees and noticed that one of the things they most want is to be heard, to be able to tell their stories in whatever way they can, be it written or visual.

Reading *Mosquito*, for those who know nothing about Sri Lanka, is as much an education about the country and its troubles as an illuminating and gentle love story. How did you balance those two key strands of narrative and to what extent do you think fiction can educate as well as entertain?

There has always been a slippage between the interface of fact and fiction both in my visual work (my films) and my writing. I didn't set out to write a book about the war in Sri Lanka. It just attached itself to the narrative. One day when I was visiting some Sri Lankan refugees I asked them about an incident I had seen as a five-year-old, of a man being set on fire. Was it possible, I asked, that I might have actually seen such a thing? They told me that yes, there had been riots at that time and many Tamils had been burnt to death. It was in this way that I excavated my memories of the politics of the place. But all the time I was interested mainly in the physiology of character. And that is why fiction is so important: without it we cannot understand ourselves. ▶

◄ **For you painting preceded writing as a career but what did you want to be when you were growing up?**
A writer, always a writer. I wrote a novel when I was nineteen and threw it away, thinking it wasn't good enough.

How does the practice of painting feed into that of writing, if at all? And does either approach to the world – visual or linguistic – precede the other for you?
When I started my second novel I had this longing to go back to painting. I began by resisting it but then I asked myself what was wrong with doing both? Surely all that was important was for me to make work? And at this point I saw that one discipline fed the other. Sometimes the visuals came first; at other times it was text-led. Always it began with a narrative. Now I've stopped

worrying and just get on with making the work.

Did writing this book change you and, if so, how?
It certainly did! All sorts of things that I didn't understand about myself made sense after the experience of writing *Mosquito*. For a start some unrecognised longings and many untold stories and memories inside me are being given room to breathe through the practice of writing. The endless notebooks I have always kept suddenly had a purpose. I also realised that I observed people and places in a particular way that was to do with writing.

What are you writing next?
Well I've just finished writing my second novel, *Bone China*. It is about a family who leave their beloved home in Sri Lanka and migrate to England and is, once again concerned with loss and memory. But, unlike *Mosquito*, it is a little comic and has a much larger cast. I am now writing a third book, which completes the picture of integration and memory. ■

Author photo © Alistair Tearne

LIFE
at a Glance

BORN

Colombo, Sri Lanka, 1954

EDUCATED

London, Oxford (MA, Ruskin)

CAREER

Painter and filmmaker. Currently holds an AHRC Fellowship in the Creative and Performing Arts, Brookes University

FAMILY

Married. Three children

LIVES

Oxford

Top Ten Favourite Artists

PAINTERS

Richard Diebenkorn, Robert Ryman, Luc Tuymans

COMPOSERS

J. S. Bach, W. A. Mozart, Richard Wagner

NOVELISTS

Thomas Hardy, Orhan Pamuk, W. G. Sebald, Virginia Woolf

A Writer's Life

When do you write?
On and off all day when I'm not teaching
or cooking!

Where do you write?
In my small study crammed with visual
sources from floor to ceiling.

Why do you write?
Because it makes me happy.

Pen or computer?
Computer, but pen in endless Moleskine
notebooks too.

Silence or music?
Non-stop music on my iPod!

How do you start a book?
With a first sentence.

And finish?
With an enormous sense of exhaustion and
relief.

**Do you have any writing rituals or
superstitions?**
I always pick four or five pieces of music
that suggest the atmosphere of the book I'm
working on first.

Which living writer do you most admire?
Orhan Pamuk.

What or who inspires you?
My husband. ▶

A Writer's Life *(continued)*

◄ If you weren't a writer what job would you do?
I guess I'd be a painter!

What's your guilty reading pleasure or favourite trashy read?
Can't read trash, it drives me demented. ■

Reflecting Memory
by Roma Tearne

THE IDEA FOR the novel *Mosquito* appeared slowly, like an apparition seen through glass. I think the story existed, out there, somewhere in the ether, complete and undiscovered. It was only my understanding of it that was slow. My habit is to think in pictures and the first thing I saw was the interior of a room cast in a bluish light. It was, although I didn't know it at the time, the beginning of the story. I kept seeing the colours in this room with a vague sense of having known the place, once, long ago, in some other life. But time had distanced and confused things, muddling them up with the paintings of Dutch interiors that I was always looking at, so that I was no longer certain which had existed and which had not.

It was in this somewhat dreamlike state that I began to write. There were good days and bad ones. On some days the images were very strong and at other times I despaired of ever fully grasping them. Slowly, as I wrote, a picture began to emerge of a house that shuttered out the piercing tropical light.

The filmmaker Chris Marker once said, 'There is nothing that identifies memory from ordinary moments. Only afterwards do they claim remembrance on account of their scars.' And so it was with me. I had begun to write *Mosquito* without realising what I was doing, with simply the idea that I needed to put something down. After I had written the first chapter, more or less in one sitting, I printed it out and read it. Only then did I ▶

11

Reflecting Memory *(continued)*

◄ identify the memory and remember an incident that took place on the eve of my departure from Sri Lanka. In the week before I left, my teacher asked me to write about the things I would be leaving behind. He wanted me to read them out in assembly. And so, on that sunlit morning long ago, with my mother rushing in to listen, even though she had so much packing still to do, I stood before the school, in my white uniform, and read my piece. Here it is again, that piece of writing, nearly forty years later in the opening lines of *Mosquito*, altered somewhat, but still with the essence of it intact.

> *The catamaran, its blue-patched sails no longer flapping, its nets full of glistening catch, came in after the night's fishing. The breeze had died down, the air had cooled, and the fishermen's sarongs slapped wet against their legs as they swung the boat above the water, to and fro, and up and along the empty beach, scoring a dark deep ridge in the sand. Often, before the monsoon broke, the sea was like a mirror. The sky appeared joined to it with barely a seam, there was a faint vibration of thunder and along the shoreline the air hung in hazy folds, suspended between land, and sea, and sky.*

I decided to make the girl, Nulani Mendis, into a painter. It was an obvious choice, given my own preoccupations. Once again hindsight revealed mysterious things I had seen only darkly until now. On rereading the manuscript I noticed there were several references to mirrors throughout the text (nearly forty, when I checked) and I saw that mirrors, both large and very old, had gilded my childhood, reflecting the iridescent light of my earliest memories.

There were endless stories existing around those mirrors, endless superstitions and fears. I once overheard a servant, after my grandfather had died, scolding my mother for looking at the moon's reflection in the mirror. Bad luck. The next day all of them were covered in black silk. For the mirror, of course, revealed the invisible, and it was this that the servant feared the most. It was this mysterious otherness buried deep in the psyche of the country and the people that live there that I now wanted to excavate.

And so for me mirrors were endowed with magical and often disturbing powers. Within and without, hiding as much as they show. Coincidentally, all my favourite paintings have mirrors in them. *The Arnolfini Portrait* with its convex mirror showing those things that one's own gaze cannot see. And *Las Meninas*, my favourite painting of all, fusing the real and the reflection together. Looking back, I think it was these barely articulated thoughts that were behind the creation of Nulani Mendis, the girl who by means of the visible discovers the invisible.

Writing the final scene of *Mosquito* ▶

Reflecting Memory *(continued)*

◄ had its own peculiar rhythm and pleasure. All the vast tracts of emotion that had been covered needed to be gathered up and laid at the feet of the, as yet, unknown reader. All the preoccupations of the last 200-odd pages defined, finally. Somehow without my knowledge a gilded mirror crept in to the ending. It was the mirror I had known best of all, in the beautiful white house by the sea that had once been my home. It filled the L-shaped interior of the final page of the book with that bluish light. Through it and beyond lies the answer to the dilemmas in the novel. I won't spoil the story for you, except to say that only by entering the mirror was it possible for the protagonist Theo to discover what lay beyond.

When I finished writing the last sentence I went out into the street, feeling lost and rather shaken by the experience, not knowing what to do with myself, unable to disengage for a moment from my past. Remembering those things that had seemed so unimportant when they had happened, yet had stayed with me over forty years. ■

Have You Read?

Roma Tearne's second novel, *Bone China*, follows the lives of the de Silva family. Faced with increasing violence as civil unrest stirs in Sri Lanka, the four children decide to leave home. But once in London, the de Silvas are all, in their different way, desperately homesick. Caught in a cultural clash between East and West, life is not as they expected.

Read an extract from the book here.

FROM THE ROAD ALL THAT COULD be seen of the house was its long red roof. Everything else was screened by the trees. Occasionally, depending on the direction of the breeze, children's voices or a piano being played could be heard, but usually, the only sound was the faint rush of water falling away further down the valley. Until this point where the road ended, the house and all its grandeur remained hidden. Then suddenly it burst into view. The car, approaching from the south side, wound slowly up the tea-covered hills. Passing one breathtaking view after another it climbed higher and higher until at last it rolled to a halt. For a moment Aloysius de Silva sat staring out. The house had been in his wife's family for more than two hundred years. Local people, those who knew of it and knew the family, called it the House of Many Balconies. All around its façade were ornate carvings punctuated by small stone balconies and deep verandas. The gardens were planted with rhododendrons and foxgloves, arum lilies and soft, rain-washed flowers. 'Serendipity,' the Governor had called it, 'somewhere deep in the Garden of Eden.' It was here, in this undisturbed paradise, viridian green and temperate, that the dark-eyed Grace had grown up. And it was here that she waited for him now.

Sighing heavily, for he was returning home after an absence of several days, Aloysius opened the door of the car, nodding to the driver. He would walk the rest of the way. It was early morning, on the first day of September 1939. Thin patches of mist drifted in the rarefied air. In his haste to return home he had caught only a glimpse of the newspaper headlines. They could no longer be ignored. The war in Europe was official, and because the island of Ceylon was still under British Crown Rule he knew it would affect them all. But this morning Aloysius de Silva had other things on his mind. He was the bearer of some rather pressing news of his own. His wife, he remembered with some reluctance, was waiting. The next few hours would not be easy. Aloysius had been playing poker. He had promised her he would not, but he had broken his promise. He had been drinking, so that, as sometimes happened on such occasions, one thing had led seamlessly to another. One minute he had had the chance to win back, at a single blow, the unravelled fortunes of his family, the horses, the estates. But the next it had vanished with an inevitability that had proved hard to anticipate. A queen, a king, an ace; he could see them clearly still. He had staked his life on a hand of cards. And he had lost. Why had he done this? He had no idea how to tell her the last of her tea estates had gone. It had been the thing he dreaded most of all.

'They're crooks,' he declared loudly, a bit later on.

No good beating about the bush, he thought. They were sitting in the turquoise drawing room, surrounded by the Dutch colonial furniture, the Italian glass and the exquisite collection of rare bone china that had belonged to Grace's mother. Family portraits lined the walls, bookcases and vitrines filled the rooms, and a huge chandelier hung its droplets above them.

'Rasanayagaim set me up,' said Aloysius. 'I could tell there was some funny business going on. You know, all the time there was some sort of message being passed between him and that puppy, Chesterton.'

His wife said nothing and Aloysius searched around for a match to light his cigar. When he found none he rang the bell and the servant boy appeared.

'Bring some tea,' he said irritably after he relit his cigar. 'I was set up,' he continued, when the servant had left the room. 'As soon as I saw that bastard Rasanayagaim, I knew there'd be trouble. You remember what happened to Harold Fonsaka? And then later on, to that fellow, Sam? I'm telling you, on every single occasion Rasanayagaim was in the room!'

Aloysius blew a ring of cigar smoke and coughed. Still Grace de Silva said nothing. Aloysius could see she had her inscrutable look. This could go on for days, he thought, eyeing her warily. It was a pity really, given how good-looking she still was. Quite my best asset most of the time. He suppressed the desire to laugh. The conversation was liable to get tricky.

'It was just bad luck, darl,' he said, trying another tack. 'Just wait, men, I'll win it all back at the next game!'

He could see it clearly. The moment he fanned out the cards there had been a constellation of possibilities. A queen, a king, an ace! But then, it hadn't been enough. Too little, too late, he thought, regretfully. All over Europe the lights were going out. As from this moment, Britain was at war with Germany. Bad luck, thought Aloysius, again. She'll be silent for days now, weeks even, he predicted gloomily. She knows how to punish me. Always has.

The servant brought in the tea on a silver tray. The china was exquisite. Blue and white and faded. It had been in the family for years, commissioned by the Queen for the Hyde Park Exhibition. Does it still belong to us? Grace thought furiously, looking at them. Or has he signed them away too? And what about me? she wanted to shout. I'm surprised he hasn't gambled me away. Aloysius watched her. He was well aware that his wife was corseted in good manners, bound up by good breeding, wrapped in the glow of a more elegant world than the one he had been brought up in. But he also knew, underneath, she had a temper. The servant poured the tea. The porcelain teacups were paper-thin. They let in a faint glow of light when she held them up.

'It isn't as bad as you think,' he said conversationally. No use encouraging her silence, he decided, briskly. What's done is done. Move forward, he thought. 'We'd have had to give up the house anyway. The Governor wants it for the war. It's been on the cards for ages, you know, darl,' he told her, not realising what he was saying.

Grace de Silva pursed her lips. The flower in her hair trembled. Her eyes were blue-black like a kingfisher's beak and she wanted to kill Aloysius.

'So you see, sooner or later we'd have to move.'

He waved aside his smoke, coughing. The servant, having handed a cup of tea to Mrs de Silva, left. Dammit, thought Aloysius, again. Why does she have to be so hard on me? It was a mistake, wasn't it? Her silence unnerved him.

'The fact is, I'm no longer necessary to the British. We were useful as sandbags, once,' he continued, sounding more confident than he felt. 'Those were the days, hah! It was people like me, you know, who kept civil unrest at bay. But now, now they have their damn war looming, they don't need *me*.'

Is she ever going to say anything? he wondered. Women were such strange creatures. He moved restlessly. Not having slept he was exhausted. The effort of wanting to give Grace a surprise windfall had tired him out.

'So, it's only the estate we've lost,' he repeated uneasily, trying to gauge her mood. 'I don't want to be a manager on a plantation that's no longer ours. What's the point in that? I've no intention of being one of their bloody slaves!'

Grace stirred her tea. Aloysius was a Tamil man who had, by some mysterious means, acquired a Sinhalese surname. He had done this long before Grace knew him, having taken a liking to the name de Silva. When he first began working as the estate manager at her father's factory he had been young and very clever in the sharp ways of an educated Tamil. And he had been eager to learn. But most of all he had been musical and full of high spirits, full of effervescent charm. Grace, the only daughter of the planter boss, had fallen in love. In all her life she had never met anyone as intelligent as Aloysius. He was *still* clever, she thought now, but his weaknesses appalled her. Soon after their marriage he had started gambling with the British officers, staying out late, drinking and losing money. Only then did Grace understand her father's warning.

'He will drink your fortune away, Grace,' her father had said. 'The British will give him special privileges because of his charm, and it will go to his head. He will not be the husband you think.'

Her father had not wanted her to marry Aloysius. He had tried to stop her, but Grace had a stubborn streak. In the end, her father, who could deny her nothing, had given in. Now, finally, she saw what she had done.

'The children have been asked to leave Greenwood,' she told him, coldly. 'Their school fees haven't been paid for a year. A *year*!'

Hearing her own voice rise she stopped talking. She blamed herself. Five children, she thought. I've borne him *five* children. And now this. Her anger was more than she could bear.

'Stanley Simpson wanted me to play,' Aloysius was saying. Stanley Simpson was his boss. 'It would have been incorrect of me to refuse.' He avoided Grace's eye. 'I have always been his equal, darl. How could I suddenly refuse to join in? These English fellows have always relied on me to make up the numbers.'

'But they know when to stop,' Grace said bitterly. 'They don't ruin themselves.'

Aloysius looked at his feet. 'When it's your hands on the wheel it's so much easier to apply the brake,' he mumbled.

They were both silent, listening to the ticking of the grandfather clock. Outside, a bird screeched and was answered by another bird.

'Don't worry about the children, darl,' Aloysius said soothingly. 'We can get Myrtle to tutor them.'

Grace started. *Myrtle?* Had Aloysius completely taken leave of his senses? Myrtle was her cousin. She hated Grace.

'We'll start again, move to Colombo. I'll get the estates back somehow, you'll see. And after the war, we'll get the house back too. I promise you. It's just a small inconvenience.'

Grace looked at him. I've been a fool, she thought, bitterly. I've no one to blame but myself. And now he wants to bring Myrtle back into our lives. She suppressed a shiver.

Outside, another day on the tea plantation continued, regardless. The early-morning mist had cleared and the coolies had brought in their baskets of leaves to be weighed. Christopher de Silva, youngest son of Grace and Aloysius, was sneaking in through the back of the house. Christopher had brought his mother a present. Well, it wasn't exactly for her, it was his really. But if he gave it to Grace he knew he'd be allowed to keep it. The older children were still at school and no one had seen his father for some time. It was as good a moment as any. He hurried across the kitchen garden and entered the house through the servants' quarters carrying a large cardboard box punctured with holes. The kitchen was full of activity. Lunch was being prepared. A pale cream tureen was being filled with a mound of hot rice. Napkins were pushed into silver rings.

'Aiyo!' said the cook, seeing him. 'You can't put your things there. Mr de Silva's back and we're late with the lunch.'

'Christopher, master,' said the servant boy who had just served tea for the lady of the house, 'your brothers are coming home this afternoon.'

'What?' asked Christopher, startled.

The box he was holding wobbled and he put it down hastily. He stared at the servant boy in dismay. Why were his brothers coming home? Just when he had thought he was rid of them too. Disappointment leapt on his back; he felt bowed down by it. He was only ten years old, too young as yet to attend Greenwood College with Jacob and Thornton. And although he longed for the day when, at the age of eleven, he could join them there, life at home without Thornton was very good. Thornton monopolised his mother and Christopher preferred his absence.

'Is Thornton coming too?' he asked in dismay.

'Yes,' said the servant boy. 'They're *all* coming home. Alicia and Frieda too.'

His eyes were shining with excitement. He was the same age as Christopher. They were good friends.

'You're all going to live in Colombo now,' he announced. 'I'm going to come too!' He waggled his head from side to side.

'Namil, will you never learn to keep your mouth shut?' cried his mother the cook, pulling the boy by the ear. 'Here, you nuisance, take these coconuts outside to be scraped. And Christopher, master, please go and wash your hands, lunch is almost ready.'

'What's going on?' muttered Christopher. 'I'm going to find out.'

Then he remembered the cardboard box in the middle of the floor. A muffled miaowing came from within.

'Namil,' he said, 'can you put this in my room, carefully? Don't let anyone see. It's a present for my mother.'

'What is it?' asked the servant boy, but Christopher had gone, unaware of the horrified expression on the cook's face as she watched the cardboard box rocking on her kitchen floor.

Further down the valley Christopher's older brothers waited on the steps of Greenwood College for the buggy to collect them. Jacob de Silva was worried. They had been told to leave their books before returning home. Although the real significance of the message had not fully dawned on him, the vague sense of unease and suspicion that was his constant companion grew stronger with each passing minute.

'Why d'you think we have to go home?' he asked Thornton.

'I thought you said they hadn't paid our school fees,' Thornton replied. He was not really interested.

'But why d'you think that is?' insisted Jacob. 'Why didn't they pay them?' Thornton did not care. He was only thirteen, the apple of his mother's eyes, a dreamer, a chaser of the cream butterflies that invaded the valley at this time of year. Today merely signalled freedom for him.

'Oh, who knows with grown-ups,' he said. 'Just think, tomorrow we'll wake up in our own bedroom. We can go out onto the balcony and look at the garden and no one will mind. And we can have egg hoppers and mangoes for breakfast instead of toast and marmalade. So who cares!' He laughed. 'I'm glad we're leaving. It's so boring here. We can do what we want at home.' A thought struck him. 'I wonder if the girls have been sent back too?'

On their last holiday they had climbed down from the bedroom balcony very early one morning and crept through the mist, to the square where the nuns and the monkeys gathered beside the white Portuguese church. They had had breakfast with Father Jeremy who wheezed and coughed and offered them whisky, which they had drunk in one swift gulp. And afterwards they had staggered back home to bed. Thornton giggled at the memory.

Jacob watched him solemnly. He watched him run down the steps of Greenwood College, this privileged seat of learning for the sons of British government officials and the island's elite, his laughter floating on the sunlight.

'I want to stay here,' he said softly, stubbornly, under his breath. 'We can go home any time. But we can only learn things here.'

He frowned. He could see all the plans for his future beginning to fade. The headmaster had told him he could have gone to university had he stayed on at school and finished his studies. His Latin teacher had told him he might have done classics. Then his science teacher had told him that in *his* opinion Jacob could have gone to medical school. Jacob had kept these conversations to himself.

'Oh, I can learn things anywhere,' Thornton was saying airily. 'I'm a poet, remember.' He laughed again. 'I'm so lucky,' he said. And then, in the fleeting manner of sudden childhood insights, he thought, I'm glad I'm not the eldest.

'Come on,' he added kindly, sensing some invisible struggle, some unspoken battle going on between them. 'Race you to the gate.'

But Jacob did not move. He stared morosely ahead of him, not speaking. Both boys wore the same ridiculous English public-school uniform, but whereas Thornton wore his with ease, already in possession of the looks that would mark him out for the rest of his life, Jacob simply looked hot and awkward. Again, he was aware of some difficulty, some comparison in his own mind, between himself and his brother. But what this was he could not say. Thornton's voice drifted faintly towards him, but still Jacob did not move.

'I can't.' His voice sounded strained. 'You don't understand. Someone must stay here to wait for the buggy.'

He was fifteen years old. He had been brought up to believe he was the inheritor of the tea plantations that rose steeply in tiers around him. The responsibilities of being the eldest child rested heavily on his small shoulders. As he stood watching his brother chasing the butterflies that slipped through the trees, he was suddenly aware of wanting to cry. Something inexplicable and infinitely precious seemed to be breaking inside him. Something he loved. And he could do nothing to stop it.

The buggy never arrived. After a while an older boy came out with a message.

'Your parents have rung,' the boy said. 'Looks like you're going to have to walk. They don't have a buggy any more. Perhaps it's been sold off to pay your father's debtors,' he grinned.

'We have no debtors,' muttered Jacob, but the boy had gone.

Eventually the brothers began to walk. Jacob walked slowly. The long fingers of sun shone pink and low in the sky as they left the driveway of Greenwood for the very last time. Rain had fallen earlier, dampening the ground on this ordinary afternoon, one so like the others, in their gentle upcountry childhood. The air across the valley was filled with the pungent scent of tea, rising steeply as far as the eye could see. In the distance the sound of the factory chute rattled on, endlessly processing, mixing and moving in time to the roar of the waterfall. The two boys wandered on, past the lake brimming with an abundance of water lilies, past clouds of cream butterflies, and through the height of the afternoon, their voices echoed far into the distance. Returning to their home nestling in the hills of Little England.

To his dismay, Christopher discovered the servant boy had been right. Jacob and Thornton were coming home. Alicia and Frieda, still stranded at the Carmelite Convent School, were waiting fruitlessly for another buggy to pick them up. In the end the priest, taking pity on them, drove them home and it was teatime before Grace was able to break the news to them all. The servant brought a butter cake and some Bora into the drawing room. She brought in small triangles of bread spread with butter and jaggery. And she brought in king coconut juice for the children and tea for Grace. The servant, knowing how upset Grace was, served it all on Grace's favourite green Hartley china tea service. Alicia opened the beautiful old Bechstein piano and began to play Schubert. The others ate quietly. For a moment Grace was distracted. The mellow tone of this sonata was one she loved and Alicia's light touch never failed to surprise her. She waited until the andante was over.

'That was lovely,' she said, putting her hand gently on her daughter's shoulder. 'It's come along a lot since I last heard it.'

'That's because we've got a new piano teacher. She's wonderful, Mummy!' Alicia said. 'She said I must be careful about the phrasing of this last section. Listen,' and she played a few bars over again.

'Yes, I see,' Grace said. 'Good! Now, I want to talk to all of you about something else. So could you leave the piano for a moment, darling?'

Five pairs of eyes watched her solemnly as she spoke.

'We're moving to Colombo,' she told them slowly. 'We're going to live in our other house by the sea.' She took a deep breath. 'Because there's going to be a war the British military needs this house, you see.' There was a surprised pause.

Alicia was the first to speak. 'What about the piano?' she asked anxiously.

'Oh, the piano will come with us, of course. Don't worry, Alicia, nothing like that will change. I promise you.'

She smiled shakily. Jacob was watching her in stony silence. He had guessed correctly. The Greenwood days were over.

'Myrtle will live with us,' said Grace, carefully. 'She'll give you piano lessons, Alicia. And she'll help in the house generally.'

No one spoke. Thornton helped himself to another piece of cake.

'There's a war on,' Grace reminded them gently. 'Everyone has to economise. Even us.' She looked pale.

'Good,' nodded Thornton, having decided. 'I think Colombo will be great. And we'll have the sea, think of that!'

Grace smiled at him with relief. Christopher, noticing this, scowled. But all he said was: 'Can I give you your present now?'

The servant boy, who had been hovering in the background, grinned and brought in the cardboard box. The family crowded around and the miaowing inside the box increased.

'What on earth's in there, Christopher?' asked Alicia, astonished.

'It's a cat,' guessed Thornton.

'But we've already got one,' said Frieda, puzzled. 'We can't have another. They'll fight.'

'Have you been stealing kittens again?' asked Jacob, frowning.

'Well, well, what's going on now?' asked Aloysius, coming in.

Having left his wife to break the news to his children he was now in the best of humours. A nap had been all he had needed. Glancing at Grace he assessed her mood correctly. There was still some way for them to go. The miaowing inside the box had turned to a growl. Everyone looked mystified and Christopher grinned.

'What is it?' asked Grace faintly, wondering how many more shocks there were in store for her.

Aloysius's news had not come as a surprise. Grace had always known that one day they would have to leave the valley where she had been born. There had been too many rumours, too many hints dropped by the British planters during the past few months. It had all pointed to this. So much of their own land had gradually been sold off. British taxes, unrest among the workers and general mismanagement of the estates had all played a part. Her drunken husband had merely speeded things up. And with the onset of war they would lose the house anyway. She felt unutterably tired. The effort of waiting for something to happen had worn her out. Now, knowing just how bad things were, she could at least try to deal with them. In Colombo, she would take charge of her life; manage things herself. It should have happened years ago. In Colombo, things would be different, she told herself firmly. And when the war was over they would come back. To the house at any rate. Of that she was certain. Christopher was holding a box out to her. But what on earth had he brought home this time? she wondered, frowning.

'It's for you,' Christopher said. 'To take to Colombo.'

Slowly she opened the box.

'Yes,' said a hollow voice from within. 'Hello, men.'

Then with a sharp rustle a small, bright-eyed mynah bird flew out and around the room, coming to rest on the grandfather clock, from where it surveyed them with interest. There was a shocked silence.

'It's a mynah bird,' said Christopher unnecessarily. 'And it can talk. We can teach it all kinds of things. It can say lazy boy, and –'

'Lazy bugger,' said the mynah bird, gazing at them solemnly.

'Good God, Christopher!' cried Aloysius, recovering first. He burst out laughing. 'What a present to give your mother!'

They were all laughing now. The servant boy was grinning, and even Jacob was smiling.

'But he's wonderful,' said Grace, laughing the most. 'He's a wonderful present!'

Later on she said, to Christopher's intense joy: 'I shall call him Jasper! And we'll take him to our new life in Colombo.'

It was in this way that Grace de Silva dealt with their reduced family circumstance. Easily, without fuss, without a single word in public of reproach to her husband and with all the serene good manners that were the hallmark of her character. Aloysius breathed a sigh of relief. Whatever she felt, she would now keep to herself he knew. Outwardly, she would appear no different. And so, as the rumours of impending war on the island grew stronger, the house beside the lake with all its balconies and splendid rooms was emptied. Its furniture and chandeliers, its delicate bone china were packed away, and even as they watched, their beloved home was closed forever and given up to the British for their military efforts. In this way the de Silva family, cast out from the cradle where they had lived for so long, moved south to Colombo. To a white house with a sweeping veranda, close by the railway line where the humidity was very often oppressive, but where the sweet, soft sound of the Indian Ocean was never far away.

If You Loved This, You Might Like . . .

About Grace
Anthony Doerr
David has a crippling gift: dreams that come true. When he foresees the death of his daughter Grace he flees his family to try to change the future. But it is his own destiny that is changed and, after decades away from those he loves, he decides to return to seek forgiveness and to find out if Grace is still alive.

Love in the Time of Cholera
Gabriel García Márquez
Can unrequited love survive fifty years? That is what Florentino must find out when he discovers that his one true love is free again, after her husband's death. Lyrical and lush, this is a wonderful introduction to Márquez and a book that gives hope to all hopeless romantics.

Like Water for Chocolate
Laura Esquivel
Tita is the youngest daughter in the De La Garza family and therefore she is forbidden from marrying Pedro, her true love, because according to tradition the youngest daughter must look after her mother until she dies. Desperate to be near her, Pedro marries her older sister and thus begins over twenty years of frustration and unconsummated love. Tita, however, is a wonderful cook and, until ▶

If You Loved This . . . *(continued)*

◄ they are reunited against all odds, she shows her love for Pedro in the only way allowed: through the magnificent meals she cooks.

Balzac and the Little Chinese Seamstress
Dai Sijie

During the Cultural Revolution, two boys are sent to the remote Chinese countryside for 're-education'. Banned from any kind of reading or intellectual pursuit, they are astonished and delighted to come across a stash of hidden Western classics translated into Chinese. The arrival of Balzac in their lives, along with their friendship with the Little Seamstress, turns their 're-education' into a wholly unexpected experience.

Silk
Alessandro Baricco

This is a novel as memorable for its extraordinary concision as for its story. When an epidemic threatens to wipe out the silk trade, Hervé Joncour must travel to Japan to find new disease-free silkworms. On his first trip he falls instantly in love with a mysterious woman, even though he has no means of communicating with her. Despite the fact that he is married, and travel to Japan is illegal, he returns over and over again to try and glimpse his love, but eventually his obsession threatens to undermine everything he once held dear.

Captain Corelli's Mandolin
Louis de Bernières

A fantastically rich, uplifting (and sometimes frustrating) love story set against the backdrop of the Second World War and the island of Cephalonia. Now made into a relatively poor film adaptation starring Nicolas Cage, the book is a classic tale of the difficult allegiances and enduring loves established under the duress of war and occupation.

Bel Canto
Ann Patchett

In a small, unnamed Latin American country, a houseful of foreigners is held hostage by terrorists determined to make their cause known to a wider audience. Amongst the captives are a famous American opera singer and her most ardent fan, the CEO of a Japanese company. Despite their circumstances, and differences, relationships form between the kidnapped and the kidnappers and love blossoms. Slowly, being trapped becomes more of a pleasure than a pain.

Suite Française
Irène Némirovsky

France 1940, and with Germany already occupying the country the war already seems lost. Against this backdrop, the tales of those fleeing the occupiers and those trying to live alongside them are told in ▶

If You Loved This . . . *(continued)*

◄ one of the best, and most illuminating, novels ever written about the Second World War. For once the hype is to be believed: a humane, engaging and unforgettable story about surviving conflict.

....

A Golden Age
Tahmima Anam

Another first novel, about a family's life and losses during the Bangladesh War of Independence. Rehana, a widow, is planning a party for her nearly adult children. Recent elections have left the city buzzing but the country is changing and no one at the party can predict the changes that are to come. ■

Find Out More

www.romatearne.com
The author's own website, where you can find information about both her writing and her painting.

http://en.wikipedia.org/wiki/Sri_Lankan_Civil_War
If you're interested in finding out more about the Sri Lankan Civil War, Wikipedia is, as ever, a relatively good place to start. The pages are very comprehensive and it's well sourced with lots of links to further reading and other sites.